THE INNOCENT PIRATE

Barry Reed

Order this book online at www.trafford.com
or email orders@trafford.com

Most Trafford titles are also available at major online book retailers.

Printed in the United States of America.

ISBN: 978-1-4269-1563-5 (sc)
ISBN: 978-1-4269-1564-2 (hc)
ISBN: 978-1-4269-8494-5 (e)

Library of Congress Control Number: 2009935505

Trafford rev. 05/21/2014

 www.trafford.com

North America & international
toll-free: 1 888 232 4444 (USA & Canada)
fax: 812 355 4082

To Linda G. Smith

For her patience and support throughout the writing of this book.
She has unselfishly given me help at every step.

Acknowledgments

Bonnie L. Reed

My wife who supported me in my quest to write a
book with the love and dedication only someone
as wonderful as she could provide.

Alton L. Hewin

My father-in-law who died while I wrote this book.

Introduction

THIS book is set in rural Heard County, Georgia, during the late 1960's. The fictional characters are a kaleidoscope of the people and personalities I have observed throughout my life. The language used by the characters, when they speak, is written in the local social color of the period and place where the story unfolds. I felt it was important that the text reflect, as closely as possible, the way people speak in this part of rural Georgia. The country was in civil turmoil during that time; the Vietnam War raged and the very social fabric of our country's moral makeup began to change.

Society was calling for the emptying of mental institutions, no matter what the consequences for families and society as a whole. The very social fabric of our country was falling apart as children were increasingly being born outside of marriage or becoming the victims of broken marriages. New social experiments and ideologies led to problems that were largely unforeseen and can be measured in terms of good and bad to this day.

The main character is a boy named Dewey. He is a character that you no doubt will fall in love with as he shows you that all children are special. Dewey, being mentally challenged, became a victim of social engineering called eugenics, whereupon he was denied any hope of having children. This was a government sanctioned program created by some states in order to lessen the financial burden of supporting offspring born to indigent persons. After spending most of his life in an institution for mentally disturbed patients, at the age of fifteen he was thrust into the care of his widowed grandfather, Al, who was elderly and lived on a farm.

Eventually, Dewey befriended a group of children that lived in the nearby Robin's Nest Trailer Park. Together, they experience many adventures as Dewey spends his first summer on the farm with his grandfather. This is where he becomes an unlikely hero, witness to horrible acts of human destruction, and innocently becomes a provider of justice.

I am confident you will enjoy learning about Dewey and his many friends, acquaintances, and family. I hope you will remember many of the characters in this book for the rest of your life. Some readers have told me that they remember characters in their past that mirror some of the characters in this book. It is my hope that you will remember this tale of love, hope, and cherished memories.

Thank you again for your interest in my first book. This is a period classic that I hope will endure with the passage of time.

Table of Contents

Chapter 1 – The Pirate Sets Sail

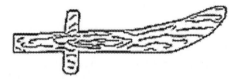

IMMEDIATELY after Al arrived at the hospital, he was told by the matronly woman at the receptionist's window to have a seat in the waiting area, as someone would be with him shortly. He stood hesitantly at the large window for just a few more moments and watched the receptionist return to her task of sorting papers. Her two fellow co-workers were also busying themselves with paperwork or answering the phones. Al realized that being in this strange place was routine for them, but it was anything but normal for him. The comforting coolness of this autumn's morning was being replaced by the dry heat in the lobby and he began to feel sweat building beneath his dress coat. His tie felt like it was beginning to constrict, so he reached up to re-adjust it as he closed his eyes and slowly took a couple of deep breaths.

Al's mind was no longer focused on the scene beyond the receptionist's window as he tried to settle the feelings of frustration and subtle panic that were rising up from the pit of his stomach. There were long hallways on both his right and left hand. At the end of each was a set of double doors with wire mesh coverings over the window panes. He could only imagine the morbid scenes and tragic events of shattered lives he knew lay beyond the large doors on either side of him.

Al stood a little straighter as he turned to face the two rows of empty chairs that lined both walls of the atrium. When he'd entered the old stately building, he couldn't help but think the chairs along the walls looked like a detail of soldiers that stood at attention facing one another to honor the hospital's guests. Like so many before him, instinctively, he chose the first chair closest to his right hand. The chairs were all alike, in that they were generic government wooden chairs, but unlike most, these had decorative carving on the upper part where one's back would rest. Al wondered, since they looked so old, if they were government surplus or they'd just been acquired by the institution a long time ago. The one Al had chosen had most of the dark stain worn away from the seat and armrests.

Once seated, Al tried in vain to find a comfortable position, only to concede to himself that there was none to be had. Al sat up straight, not only out of habit, but because there was no other position the mostly straight backed chair would allow. After a while, his lower back began to stiffen. He knew this was mostly due to the long drive he'd endured yesterday and also from sleeping in an unfamiliar bed at the hotel last night.

It wasn't long before a familiar pain began to creep down the right side of his lower back. Within minutes his right hip and his right leg began to throb. He knew his sciatica was beginning to flare up on him, as the pinched nerve in his lower back caused his hip and leg to pulsate like a painful tooth. Determined to block out the pain, he leaned slightly towards his left and sat waiting as patiently as he could under the circumstances. Occasionally, he mumbled unkind and unflattering things about the persons who'd designed the chairs, as well as out of frustration at having to wait for so long. He contemplated walking around, but figured there wasn't any point. Once his nerve was inflamed, Al knew standing or walking didn't make matters any better.

Al mulled over the notice he'd received in the mail several days earlier. Apprehension and dread were mounting ever greater as he thought about the reason for his visit so far from his home. After a few more minutes, he temporarily shoved aside these thoughts as he took in the musty smells of the old wooden structure. He was able to isolate familiar odors of cleaning fluids that wafted up from the floor and off the fixtures. Al had always enjoyed the smell of turpentine and lemons. Occasionally, he repositioned his right foot in an effort to relieve the dull throbbing pain. The slightly loose plank of wood upon which his right foot rested creaked loudly proclaiming his discomfort to the world. For just a few moments he made it creak repeatedly as he kept time with a song he reminisced about in his head. It wasn't until the receptionist loudly cleared her throat out of disapproval that he stopped. He appreciated how annoying it must have been for her as he suppressed a mischievous grin. He pondered about how many times others must have aggravated the poor lady at the window just this way over the years.

Bored, Al sat and surveyed the wooden floor, whitewashed walls, and poorly plastered ceiling with cheap light fixtures hanging from its majestic height. No doubt the light fixtures were an attempt at replicating ornate chandeliers. To the right of the receptionist's window was a board full of old policy notices that had become tattered, as well as newer notices that proclaimed office hours, a visiting schedule, fliers for upcoming events, and other various notes of interest. To the left of the receptionist window was a large portrait of a man trying to look regal in his suit as one hand was slipped halfway into his vest pocket. This pose was a replica of the ones pompous men had copied for centuries in the western world. Al silently sneered at the sight of such a thing. He spotted two holes at the bottom of the frame where screws had once held the missing name plate of this so-called magnificent creature whose regal pose greeted all who visited this place.

Al's thoughts were interrupted when, down one of the long corridors, a disheveled looking creature captured his attention as it made mild grunting noises. Al's seat allowed him to have a straight line of sight down the wide dimly lit hallway that was perpendicular to the atrium. He sat mesmerized as he watched and listened intently.

As the aberration came closer, he could see what appeared to be a woman in a loose fitting hospital gown carrying a large doll in one arm. She seemed oblivious to anything but her immediate surroundings as she concentrated on where and how she would take her next step. Hunched over, she ever so slowly shuffled her feet and dragged one of her shoulders against the wall for support as she continued her slow gait forward.

Upon reaching the waiting area, the woman thrust her body into the chair opposite Al's. Her free arm and both her legs splayed out as if they were so heavy that she didn't possess the strength to maintain any semblance of an upright and normal posture. She looked abysmally unhealthy, in that her torso was extremely large for her limbs. She didn't look pregnant, but the trunk of her body was unusually fat for her atrophied arms and legs. Al knew this was a sign of malnutrition on top of a sedentary lifestyle; he suspected she was kept sedated and deprived of exercise and fresh air.

Her smallish face and head hung down and cocked to one side as she rested her chin on her fat neck and chest. He suspected she was too exhausted from her efforts to even hold it upright. She was so near that he was able to fully take in her haggard appearance. While she attempted to focus her gaze upon Al, he looked back at her with an involuntary expression that betrayed his revulsion. He felt put off by her abhorrent condition. After she appeared to have fully focused on Al, her expression changed and she began to tightly squeeze the large stained and tattered cloth doll with both arms.

Uncomfortable with this bizarre encounter, Al tensed. He'd automatically gripped the arms of his chair so he could move quickly in the event it became necessary. Due to human nature and being unaccustomed to the surroundings, he couldn't help but become alarmed at the site before him. He could see she was utterly and disgustingly filthy. Her course red hair was unkempt as it drooped down in oily strands covering most of her face. Urine and sour body odors assaulted his nostrils with every breath. He couldn't help but see she had on yellowish stained panties underneath the loose fitting rags that were comprised of two filthy hospital gowns tied together in an effort to cover her enormous girth. Because she apparently hadn't worn shoes for a long time, her feet were thickly callused, dried, and cracked just above the brownish black soles of her feet. Many of her toe nails were long, thick, and irregularly shaped. The ones not cracked and jagged from being broken off, were growing in odd directions like horns. This made him all the more curious to look closer at her fingernails. They'd been chewed down to the quick.

Strangely, a recollection of a scene from long ago came storming back into Al's consciousness as he looked upon this unfortunate creature. She had brought back memories of so many families that had lined the docks of the war torn countries where his ship docked during the wars decades earlier. They'd been refugees looking for food and help to escape the awful circumstances the war had brought upon them. Unlike her, they were usually underweight from starvation. He pondered a moment to reflect on why they should come to mind.

Al's concentration was broken as he heard a commotion coming from the receptionist's window. "Lola Mae, git ya'self outa here. Ya know ya not suppose ta be here." When Lola Mae didn't acknowledge the stern words of the matronly woman, Al could hear the receptionist mumble to herself as she picked up a phone to call for help.

Lola Mae's head was still drooping to one side as she looked up at Al, but now she wore the smallest wisp of a smile. Her dull, almost lifeless, blue eyes seemed to be focused somewhere far off as if she didn't really have the ability to focus on any particular object. Al thought it looked as if she'd just gotten some satisfaction from something and maybe a possible victory of sorts. Al reveled in the moment with her as he suddenly felt a twinge of empathy.

Lola Mae struggled to lean forward a bit as she focused on Al. With a full-toothed grin she half whispered, "I'm rich, but nobody knows it. I met a woman with a glass eye that tells the future back home. She told me not ta tell any man I marry 'bout it, cause he'll take it from me." With that she slumped back heavily into her chair once more. Soon afterwards, a large man in a white uniform, no doubt an orderly, came storming down the hall and stood between Al and Lola Mae.

"Sorry Sir, but sometimes they's gits away from us. She says that there doll is her baby boy. She's always tryin' ta run off. Claims she has ta, soes she can protect her baby boy. Leastways that all she keeps sayin'."

With hands on his hips, the orderly turned and hovered directly over Lola Mae. Using an authoritative tone, he said, "Lola Mae, gits up from there now. We's gots ta git ya back where ya belong. Ya boy is jus' fine."

Lola Mae made no attempt to move other than to grip her doll tighter in an act of defiance. Frustrated, the orderly leaned in close and said in a contemptuous voice, "Nobody wants ta see ya nasty butt roamin' 'round da halls. 'N how the hell'd ya gits out here again anyways? **Come on now, move! Nobody wants ya here!**" To drive the point home, the orderly extended his arm and pointed back down the hallway where he and Lola Mae had both emerged.

Indignant at what he was witnessing, Al decided he'd had enough. He could see that the orderly was trying to persuade Lola Mae to comply without actually having to touch her because she was so repulsive. Al, with a stern voice filled with conviction, said sourly, "Why don't ya help her? She barely made it under her own steam. And once ya git 'er back ta wherever ya takin' 'er, how about ya give 'er bath 'n some clean clothes."

The orderly turned and gave Al an indignant look before he grabbed Lola Mae and pulled her up out of the chair. Lola Mae, being very weak, tried to stand and walk, but the orderly quickly realized he didn't have any choice but to help her steady herself. When the two arrived at a point halfway down the hall, Al heard the orderly scornfully proclaim, "Ya jus' wait. We're goin' ta scrub ya down so good ya bones are gonna shine pearly white. I don't care how bad ya scream 'n holler this time." It took some effort, but eventually the orderly helped Lola Mae slowly lumber back down the hallway from which she had appeared.

"It's about time somebody told one of those lazy bunch ta do their job 'n clean that girl up. Thanks, Mister." Al was amused by the receptionist's comment. She'd stuck her head out of the receptionist's window and watched the duo clumsily retreat down the hall and through the double doors.

Time slowly ticked away once again as the episode with Lola Mae and the orderly subsided. No longer distracted, Al once again was reminded of the tortuous pain in his lower right side. About the time he'd decided he'd had enough, a middle-aged nurse dressed in white, whose demeanor was all business, spoke quickly in hushed tones with the receptionist. Once finished, she turned to Al and curtly said, "Mr. Hewin, come with me."

Relieved the wait was over, Al began to stand as the nurse hesitated a moment to see if her order was being complied with before turning to walk down the hallway opposite the one Lola Mae had come from. Al, using the armrest for support, stood as quickly as he was able before he followed her. Because of his pain, Al was relieved that they walked pass the stairwell. Quickly they reached their destination, an office bearing the words "Superintendent Dr. Douglas Perley" boldly printed in gold.

Al couldn't help but notice a fat lump of a human being wearing a red cape and a blank expression sitting in a chair just outside of Dr. Perley's office. The boy was blankly staring at a children's book that had bold colorful pictures on the front and back covers. Al hesitated before he went into the office because something the boy was wearing captured his attention. On the knot that was tied in the front and holding a makeshift red cape, was a large old brooch. It was a cross made of silver that had a large fake pearl in its center. The cross was badly tarnished and the pearl was chipped. A momentary thought began to surface, but it was interrupted before it had time to fully form as the nurse cleared her throat in order to get Al's attention. The fleeting thought that the cross seemed somewhat familiar vanished. Al quickly dismissed it as he followed behind the nurse into the office.

Upon entering, Al was greeted by a man younger than himself, but still well past his prime. "Thank you, Mr. Hewin, for driving all the way out here. I realize it's a long way from home, but I assure you it was necessary."

Al couldn't help but look at the man's lips as he spoke his greetings because they were the same color of purple as someone suffering from a lack of oxygen or poor circulation. While in the Navy, Al had occasionally witnessed divers coming out of the cold ocean whose lips were the same shade of purple as this man's were presently. Dr. Perley came from behind his desk and extended his hand. That's when Al recognized the man in the portrait in the lobby.

Al shook the superintendent's outstretched hand, which resulted in a momentary cringe on the doctor's face. Dr. Perley quickly withdrew his grip with Al. The crown of his large gold ring had shifted before he'd shaken hands and the result of Al's powerful grip had sunk the head of Dr. Perley's own ring into an adjoining finger. The sudden harsh pain would take some time to abate.

"May I offer you a cold refreshment or coffee perhaps?" asked Dr. Perley, as he looked up from his hands after twisting the offending ring back into its proper position. He wore a benevolent smile while he waited for Al's reply.

Al shook his head to show he wasn't interested. Al was still distracted by the pain in his right lower back, hip and leg, not to mention being anxious about the reason for him being summoned. This caused him to be in no state of mind or condition for prolonged cordialities or pleasantries. Al's patience had already been pushed to its limit from such a prolonged wait past his appointment time of 8:30 a.m.

The Superintendent had yet to overtly acknowledge the nurse's presence, but seeing Al wasn't interested in any refreshments, Dr. Perley, without looking at her, said in a dismissive tone, "That will be all, Nurse." The nurse didn't immediately respond, as she was busy giving Al a thorough evaluation. Initially, Al hadn't noticed because he was too busy doing the same with the Superintendent.

Without being conspicuous, Al took in the whole of the man before him as he started "measuring" the man. He could tell he was a blue nosed northerner by his proper English, demeanor, and the way he was condescending in his tone. He wore an expensive gold watch on his right wrist, not his left like most folks from Georgia, and had engraved gold cufflinks on his shirt-sleeves that protruded from his white clinical jacket. There was no doubt in Al's mind that his wallet would be in the left rear pocket of his slacks unlike people in the south, who carried theirs in the right rear pocket.

Al had met and served under many a naval officer from the north that grew up in well-to-do families, who were, more or less, carbon copies of the man now standing before him. Once finished, he gazed at the office's decor and realized it was just as he had imagined it. Like most government offices, this one seemed to have been designed to be as bland and practical as most other government offices. There was a door that connected to an adjacent office. Al could hear a muffled woman's voice on the other side.

The superintendent's office was large and lined with bookshelves. All of the shelves were overflowing and haphazardly stacked with books, boxes, and odd sized folders. The older shelves matched the desk, leaving another whole wall filled with mismatched shelves standing out in stark contrast. The once white walls had yellowed over the years. Paint was flaking off the wall near the steam grate; this indicated that a small leak of steam had escaped during winters past. Only the dark stained oak desk seemed somewhat organized, having multiple stacks of folders and charts piled high in trays marked "In" and "Out."

On one corner of the desk was a bowl of unshelled peanuts. Just below it was a wastebasket with pieces of broken peanut shells littered all about it. The superintendent must have just eaten some when Al and the nurse arrived, because he'd spotted the man briskly brushing off the front of his white coat with the back of his hands.

The superintendent stood briefly in front of his desk while he indicated a chair where Al was to sit. The nurse, satisfied that she was no longer needed, gave a quick courtesy smile and departed, closing the office door behind her ever so quietly. Al couldn't be sure, but he thought perhaps he saw a hint of disapproval in the nurse's expression just before she'd turn to leave.

Al couldn't help but notice the little white cap the nurse wore. Unlike the hat he wore while working, he pondered about how her hat was too small to be practical for shade in sunlight and offered no kind of shelter from foul weather. He'd seen them his whole life and always thought they were more or less a decoration, or even possibly a declaration of authority. He had rarely come across anyone over thirty wearing one them that ever had a pleasant demeanor. They seemed to indicate the only difference between the nurses and all the other women working in hospitals or doctor's offices.

The superintendent walked behind his desk, took a deep breath, and stood looking at Al with an air of authority before he said, "My name is Dr. Douglas Perley. I'm the superintendent here at the Milledgeville State Hospital, and we're the primary provider of care for mentally disturbed patients in this part of the state . . . ."

Al wasn't interested in looking at Dr. Perley when the doctor began to ramble through his formal introduction. Al remained silent while busily taking in his surroundings. In the corner, he spied a very large bag of peanuts. It was one of those big ones that could be found in any local farmers market this time of year. Al mused for a moment over what he could clearly see was this man's self-indulgence before he once again turned to look at the doctor. He also had to check himself when an unseemly joke he was told in the Navy came to mind about the making of peanut butter.

"That the boy sittin' outside?" Al interrupted, gesturing with his thumb towards the door. His voice intoned more of accusation than a question.

Dr. Perley took a moment before answering. "Yes." He noted Al's piercing gray-blue eyes, hands the size of baseball gloves, and a grip as strong as a vice; the doctor's hand was still smarting from Al's almost crippling handshake.

He wasn't sure if Al's directness indicated hostility, directness, or just a lack of manners. He realized the man was strong and in surprisingly good shape for a man of his advanced years. Al's leathery skin was darkened and weatherworn from many years of working outdoors. His almost white thinning hair was flattened by hair cream, possibly to help tame the cowlick that stood up in stark contrast on the left side of Al's head. Dr. Perley could see that Al had worn a hat earlier. It had left a circular indention in Al's hair.

The doctor observed a guarded expression on the face of a man that reflected an extremely harsh life and showed little, if any, hint whatsoever of emotion. Al held an air about him that spoke to someone's innermost instinct to "not dare piss him off." His suit, though not dressy or fashionable for some time, was meticulously pressed and well-kept. The suit also had the faintest hint of mothball odor.

Before retreating behind his desk, the doctor had noticed that Al's shoes, shined to perfection, were worn from years of use and new stitches along the outline of the shoes indicated the soles had been replaced recently.

Many of the relatives of the institute's patients were just plain folks one would encounter throughout any of the southern states. Most had grown up on farms or worked in textile mills in small towns somewhere in the rural parts of the south. There was a certain code of civility expected from people in the south; to try and be cordial, even in unpleasant circumstances. Al Hewin's demeanor, although understandable, came across as somewhat overly abrasive for even this situation.

Dr. Perley well understood why some of those who came to see him about this business of discharging their loved ones arrived with confused emotions bordering on hostility. Most felt helpless and angry at not having the ability or means to care for their mentally disturbed family members. The newly enacted law forced upon Georgia's institutions required that as many patients as possible be discharged. How would, or could, the families possibly take care of them since many of the newly released patients needed "around-the-clock" attention. The hardships could become, and most likely would be, overwhelming for many as it disrupted their lives.

The doctor remained standing while again indicating for Al to sit in a big green chair in front of his desk. Al finally took the seat offered and his hip pain flared at the effort. When he again looked at the doctor, Al said, "What'd ya feed that boy? Looks like a damn cow."

Dr. Perley, on the verge of annoyance at the impertinence of such a statement, replied "Mr. Hewin, I assure you, Dewey has been well fed.

We provide quite nourishing meals to all of our residents here at the sanatorium."

"I can see that ya fed 'em, Doc. After looking at some of ya patients, I'm not sure yer in the right business. Maybe ya need ta go into the cow or hog business."

Dr. Perley let out a small sigh as he sat down and laid his pudgy forearm and pale hand on the desk. "Mr. Hewin, like I told you in my letter, we believe Dewey is your grandson."

For just a moment, Dr. Perley looked at his bowl of peanuts and then nudged it further towards one end of his desk. "Dewey was left in our care some nine years ago by a young woman who was only referred to as Jenny. In Dr. Howell's notes, he was in charge at that time, she admitted to being from Roosterville, Georgia. The long and the short of it is, Mr. Hewin, according to the Department of Family and Children's Service's representative in your area, he is more than likely your grandson." The doctor took a moment to give Al a chance to take in what he'd just been told. Al sat silently looking right through Dr. Perley as if looking at something far away.

With no immediate response forthcoming, Dr. Perley cleared his throat, looked back at the folder and continued, "Ah . . . , Mrs. Louise Jackson is the local representative in your neck of the woods. Perhaps you've met her?"

Al showed no indication one way or the other as his mind tried in vain to sort through the revelations of the letter, and now what he was being told face to face. It seemed utterly impossible that such a thing could be, and Al could not fathom how this so-called grandson came to be in such a place.

"Anyway, records indicate that a Jenny was born to you and Mary Hewin around the time that she, this young woman, would have been born. She admitted to being seventeen years old when she gave birth to Dewey. She told Dr. Howell, according to his notes here, that 'she didn't have any living relatives and was unable to care for a retarded child.' He was five years old at the time." Dr. Perley looked up from his notes and waited for some sort of an acknowledgement or response.

Al just sat there with a blank expression. After a long, uncomfortable silence, Al finally answered in halting sentences, "I have a daughter–Jenny Anne Hewin. I haven't seen or heard from her since shortly after her mother, Mary, died about sixteen or seventeen years ago." His jaw muscles protruded as he momentarily clenched his teeth and drew his lips so tight his lips all but disappeared. This caused the veins on his temples to become more pronounced. His voice possibly held just a hint of pain as he spoke, but Dr. Perley couldn't be certain.

Al gazed back at the doctor with an expression that showed he really didn't want to talk about that time, much less think about it. He couldn't remember exactly what had happened or understand why his daughter had left so soon after his dear wife's death. It just seemed to happen without warning.

Mary had always taken care of their daughter while he worked from sun up until sun down. He barely spoke to Jenny once she became a teenager. As she became older, he saw less of her due to their schedules. She was always busy with school, church, piano lessons, or being with her many friends. She had her own car and had become more independent. He rarely asked her for any help around the farm because he believed it was man's work. He gladly gave her money when she asked for it, which was seldom. He had always considered her to be a good child, beautiful and well mannered. She seemed content and always had a smile on her face.

After Mary died, Al had a hard time accepting his wife's death. He stayed busy working and kept to himself; he'd shut out everyone and everything except his work. Since little was said on the subject between them, he figured that, like him, Jenny needed a little space to sort it all out. One day she told him she was going to stay at a friend's house for a while.

Later Al heard that Jenny had quit school and had taken up with a young man who worked in Atlanta. When he went looking for her, she was nowhere to be found and her friends denied knowing where she was or what she was doing. For months he searched to no avail. The Sheriff's Department didn't have any luck either. He suspected they'ed half-heartedly investigated. Eventually, Al stopped looking and hoped she would come back once she sorted out whatever was causing her to stay away.

Initially upon Jenny leaving, Al had taken some solace at having the house quiet. He never imagined, as it turned out, that it would be so many years of living alone. Sometimes, when the nighttime came and he was tired from working hard all day, the loneliness weighed heavy on him. To pass the time, he would focus his energy towards his hobby of building replicas of ships. Many a night he pined for the time when he was in the Navy, something he rarely thought about while his dear wife, Mary, was alive. He missed the camaraderie of fellow crew members, the steady sounds of the ship's engines, and most of all the routine.

"May I inquire as to what happened to your wife?" asked Dr. Perley.

"Huh?" This question brought Al back to the present. He began speaking in a low tone. "Durin' the day, before Mary died that evenin', Jenny was drivin' 'er mother home from church. While she was drivin' through the church parkin' lot, some other car backed outa their parkin' spot 'n she hit it. There wasn't any damage ta our car 'n barely any ta the other. We had a '53' Ford that didn't have seat belts like taday's cars. Dashboards were made of steel back then 'n Mary hit her head on it. Jenny told me it knocked 'er mother out for a minute or so. Mary claimed ta be alright once she come to, so they drove on home."

Al took a moment before continuing as if he needed to contemplate something; the brooch. Slowly it finally came to him. That was a brooch just like Mary used to wear on her dress when she went to church! The reason he remembered it was because one day Mary had him fix the clasp on the back. She'd said it made her feel like God was watching over her when she wore it.

"You were saying, Mr. Hewin, that they went on home after the accident."

Al's concentration returned so he continued on, "Oh yes, Mary cooked lunch 'n supper like usual that day. Later that evenin' she complained of a headache 'n went ta bed early. The next mornin' she was dead. The coroner, who's also one of our local hair dressers, said somethin' about an internal bleed in the brain, mos' likely from the wreck." When Al finished, he shifted in his chair ever so slightly.

"I'm sorry, Mr. Hewin. That must have been a difficult time . . . . Did Jenny blame herself?" inquired, Dr. Perley.

"Never told me as much, but more'n likely that's what happened, I 'spose."

"Ah, well." The doctor picked up the folder he had previously laid down. "Mr. Hewin, as you recall from the letter, because of the State's new policy of discharging as many patients as possible, I'm mandated to ask you if you are willing and able to care for your fourteen year old grandson."

"If he's mine, why ya jus' now lettin' me know about 'im? 'N why ya jus' now tryin' ta git shed of 'im?"

Dr. Perley, ignoring the first question, clasped his hands and squirmed in his chair like he always did before answering the second; a question that he had been required to answer too many times for his liking of late. "Due to the news media's recent accusations of the state's mental health facilities warehousing people unnecessarily and how inhumane they claim we are, the government has issued a new policy. The newly enacted policy forced upon the Georgia's institutions requires that as many patients as possible be discharged."

The doctor cleared his throat and added, "The unintended consequence of this policy will become evident in the future as the streets fill with socially and mentally disturbed people going hungry, committing crimes, becoming a nuisance, and begging in the streets. But, there you have it. However, I feel confident that with enough support and training, Dewey will do fine on the outside." Dr. Perley shrugged, opening his hands palms up as he finished his explanation.

Al's eyes squinted slightly in suspicion. "What's the catch?"

"As you can imagine, it's a difficult job to care for the ones who can't take care of themselves. Dewey is one such person who needs a lot of extra supervision and patience. Are you willing and able to take him home?" Dr. Perley sat back in his chair and waited for a response, but no reaction was forthcoming so he continued, "Mr. Hewin, we believe Dewey will benefit from a loving and caring home environment, so we are asking if you are capable and willing to take him home with you?"

Al gripped the arms of the chair and leaned forward, "Damn it ta hell, what's wrong with the boy? Why is he here instead of a children's home or such?"

"Of course we tried both, but it didn't work out." Dr. Perley lifted his hands in a gesture of helplessness. He then continued in an even tone, "We conducted the usual battery of tests for retardation. The standard is set at a certain number for normal intelligence. Dewey fell short of that number, indicating he is mildly retarded. Reluctantly, I have to admit that's why he has remained living here with us at the institution."

Al sat back as he continued to look at Dr. Perley. Al's eyes didn't portray the harshness with which he now judged the good doctor and his so called justification for the boy's incarceration at such a horrid place. Al's stare made the self-assured doctor feel uncomfortable.

Dr. Perley squirmed around in his chair while fiddling with the folder and a pencil in front of him, hoping for some break in the tension. He was hopeful Al would be relieved, or at least accepting like most others, with what he was going to say next. With this man, he couldn't be sure of the reaction. Speaking to the folder, Dr. Perley said, "Due to a program called Eugenics, Dewey was sterilized per the states guidelines for people in his situation." In an attempt to soften the blow, the good doctor tried to bring to light "the benefits" of this procedure. "So you will not have to worry about his being able to produce offspring." With this said he raised his head and straightened to an authoritative posture. His ploy of theatrical confidence and elevated stature had worked on so many others over the years, but he was becoming more distraught from Al's unwavering direct glare.

According to the state, feeble-minded people needed to be "fixed" so they couldn't have children. It was considered a matter of good economics and stewardship of the populace. The state was tired of whole families of feeble-minded people reproducing feeble-minded imbeciles and having to support them throughout their lives with expensive burdensome government programs.

Dr. Perley didn't have the courage to admit that the procedure had gone badly and Dewey's testicles had become so infected they had to be completely removed, which caused Dewey to be literally castrated. Dr. Perley hoped that Al, like most, would accept this procedure as necessary once they heard about it, and even be grateful. Some family members even asked for the procedure to be performed on their sick relatives to ensure there wouldn't be any unwanted pregnancies.

Al saw nothing humane in this "so called" beneficial procedure. He looked at what he felt was surely a poor excuse for a human being, much less a doctor, and now his face fully betrayed his disgust. Everything in his being told him to throttle this man right then, but his many years in the military taught him discipline and how to control his actions, if not his thoughts.

"You butcherin' degenerate bastards did what?!" Al asked hoarsely, his tone vibrating with disgust. He stood up, pushing the chair back with his legs a little as he became erect. He couldn't believe or understand such a concept. The fact that someone would do this type of thing to another human being without their consent was beyond him. He'd always been uncomfortable helping castrate young bulls as a teenager on the farm. Even then he felt it was cruel, but hesitantly accepted it once he was told why it was necessary by his father. His father and neighbors did it to fatten up the bulls not used for stud so as to increase the size and profits come selling time at the slaughter house.

"Mr. Hewin, I understand . . ."

"The hell ya do!" Al was furious and wanted to be rid of the entire matter, so he turned to leave. He stopped short and turned back to face the doctor, "What proof ya have the boy's my grandson?"

The doctor pulled out an old photograph the mother had given to Dr. Howell those many years ago. Al stepped up quickly to the desk, grabbed the extended hand holding the photo, and using his other hand abruptly snatched it from Dr. Perley's fingers. Only as an afterthought did Al released the man's wrist while he looked upon his daughter's face. It was an old black and white photo that didn't show the beautiful blue eyes and the tiny faint specks of freckles on her nose and cheeks.

Once released, Dr. Perley fell back into his chair, striking the book shelves behind him. His heart pounded so hard he could not only hear it drumming in his ears, but he felt each beat as well. The doctor knew, because of his training, he needed to stand up in order to help equalize the dominating position that Al now held over him. Too afraid to budge, he stayed where he was and felt helpless.

Al's fists were clinched and trembled. Dr. Perley wasn't certain what the man's next action might be. To his relief, Al turned to leave the office. His fatigue and pain forgotten, Al took a deep breath to moderate the sickening feeling in his stomach and calm his rage before entering the hallway. He didn't want to meet his grandson for the first time full of rage.

The nurse who'd escorted Al was patiently waiting with the boy outside the door when Al emerged from Dr. Perley's office. She flinched when she saw the expression on Al's face, but she'd seen it before and quickly recovered. She escorted Al and the boy to the administration office to help with the discharge paperwork and procedures.

Al, without much success, tried to be patient while listening to the nurse explain what she knew about Dewey's likes and dislikes. She wrote down some instructions quickly and handed him a paper as she told him how to contact Mrs. Jackson, the local state representative, once he was settled back home. The nurse was cold and professional as she had Al sign paperwork for Dewey's release. It was her way of fending off any inquiries about the questionable activities at the sanatorium. She knew that a lot more things had been done behind closed doors than Al would ever come to learn. Her duty done, she handed Al the discharge paperwork, patted Dewey on the back goodbye, and swiftly disappeared down the hallway.

It had always amazed Al how efficient the government could be when it wanted to be. He called it "selective and convenient professionalism." He assumed it was only by chance that the state found out he was Dewey's grandfather in the first place. Only a couple of deputy's still worked at the Sheriff's department from when Jenny disappeared those many years ago. When Mrs. Jackson was conducting her inquiry, they were able to lead her in Al's direction by pulling out old files and explaining the circumstances of Jenny's disappearance.

Al wondered if Jenny had taken Dewey to the institution because she couldn't, or wouldn't take care of him. That question would gnaw at him for many nights to come.

He was sure the boy was only looked after minimally because of the staffing shortages which plagued all state run institutions. The episode with Lola Mae was a prime example.

Driving home, Al pondered the fact that he would no longer have the same quiet life anymore. Raising children is a lot of hard work and this time he wouldn't have his wife, Mary, to help. The fact that Dewey was slow would make it even more difficult. He worried about being pulled off his daily chores, which required his constant attention, to tend to this needy child. Because he was his grandson, it was his obligation. There wasn't anything else to be done about it, but try.

Once they were well away from Milledgeville, Al started to take stock of the boy and his features. He was as tall as the average man, just shy of six foot like himself, and fatter than anyone had a right to become. When he'd watched Dewey walk in the hospital, he noticed Dewey shuffled more than walked and was slightly pigeon toed. His slumped shoulders told Al the boy probably hadn't lifted anything much heavier than a plate of food for some time now.

Dewey's innocent facial features were very similar to Jenny's, only chubbier. His teeth were acceptably straight, but his blue eyes seemed small for his face. Dewey didn't look retarded. For a moment it occurred to Al that maybe they were wrong about him. For most of the trip, Dewey sat and seemed oblivious to Al as he stared down at his favorite book or looked out of the window. The book was well worn from being continuously handled over the years. Al could see it was a child's book about pirates.

Finally, Al said, "Dewey, I'm ya granddaddy." Al looked at him while he spoke the words. Judging by his non-reaction, he couldn't be sure if Dewey even heard him. He wasn't even sure if he knew what "granddaddy" meant. With no reaction forthcoming, Al decided to let it go for the time being.

During the long drive back to Heard County, much to Al's relief, the boy did everything he was told, from "use the bathroom" at the rest stops to "eat ya food" when they stopped for lunch. Maybe it was a sign that the boy was just quiet. At the very least, Al pondered, that would be something.

Driving down the two-lane road on this cool autumn day in his new 1968 Ford pickup, Al sat back hard in his seat with both hands tightly gripping the steering wheel. His frustration grew at the not knowing what was to come. The Bible scripture that came to mind was the prayer Jesus prayed on the Mount of Olives before he was taken to be crucified. It was from the book of St. Luke, chapter 22, verse 42, "*Father, if thou be willing, remove this cup from me: nevertheless not my will, but thine, be done.*" After a long while he let out a long sigh and thought, "*Lord, help me!*"

Chapter 2 – Life on the Farm

IT was already uncomfortably warm on this new summer day and the morning sun's rays were just beginning to peek through the kitchen window. Since all the days on the farm usually began and ended the same way, it made little difference to Al and Dewey that it was Saturday. Dewey was busily eating his breakfast of eggs, grits, bacon and biscuits when Snipe, the family dog, nuzzled his elbow and gave a little whining noise. "No Snipe!"

His efforts rebuffed, Snipe sat back on his haunches and waited anxiously for whatever morsels of food might fall to the floor. Snipe was always given the leftovers after every meal, but of course, like most dogs, was eager for any scraps given ahead of time. Clear strings of drool hung down like stalactites in a cave from his jaws in anticipation of food. Only when they became too large and long would they succumb to gravity and drop to the floor where they created small puddles. Never to be discouraged, Snipe was finally rewarded when a morsel of crispy bacon broke free while being bitten. Snipe caught it effortlessly just before it hit the floor. Once Dewey realized he'd lost the tasty morsel to Snipe, he signaled dismissal with the wave of his hand and returned his attention back to his plate.

Snipe was the official family pet. Long before Dewey came to the farm, Snipe's arrival had been announced by the furious loud clucks and squawks of frightened chickens. At the time, Al was peeved that his tranquil morning routine had been interrupted. Al's morning routine was a marvel of orchestrated actions and movements made up of rituals practiced for well over a decade. He believed that although he couldn't control what the day might bring, he'd at least control how it started.

Upon stepping outside, Al observed the chickens going wild with excitement and scattering in all directions. To his annoyance, Al found a half-starved mangy mutt in the yard. It refused to leave even after Al threatened it with a stick and threw several rocks. Al knew the dog was set on eating something no matter what the cost. He easily evaded Al's attempts to hit him. Al knew he had three options: feed him, shoot him, or let him get away with killing one or more of his chickens.

Snipe was a mutt in every sense of the word. He had a gray and brown coat that was as ugly and filthy as anything Al had ever seen. He didn't look like any particular breed that Al could identify. At the time, it had struck Al that the dog reminded him of himself and his fellow crew members after a particularly nasty job in the boiler room of a ship when they became covered from head to toe in grease and soot.

After many hard lessons, lots of time, and periods of frustration, Snipe was clean, well fed, and followed every command immediately. He seldom left Al's side and was rarely ever out of sight.

Al, as usual, had already eaten and was busy cleaning up the kitchen while he listened to the radio for the weather and news. He still couldn't stomach watching Dewey eat most of the time. No matter how much he tried, he couldn't get Dewey to slow down and chew with his mouth closed. Al mused over the temptation to make Dewey a miniature pig trough. This recurring thought usually gave way to a smile as Al gave in to the futility of it all and accepted Dewey's limitations at social graces. Al wouldn't eat directly across from Dewey, but sat to the side at their small kitchen table. At times, when Dewey gave a particularly gross grunt or smack while eating, Al would cringe or bust out laughing, depending on his mood at the time.

Slowly and methodically over the months since Dewey arrived, Al cut down on Dewey's portions of food to help the boy lose weight. Dewey was still obese, but was slowly getting smaller. Al had learned to scramble the eggs instead of frying them whole. He did this so Dewey couldn't count the yolks. He even went so far as to make the biscuits smaller. This and Al serving the food on smaller plates, gave Dewey the illusion of being fed the same amount. Sometimes Dewey insisted on more food, but Al stood his ground and refused to give in with the exception of giving him an apple, carrot, or some other healthy alternative.

"Finish ya chow, Boy. I need ta finish my chores so I can git ta work. The field's not goin' ta take care of itself. I seen the beginnin' of silk comin' outa the ears of corn yesterday. Time ta plow another section for late crops before I have ta hire some folks ta help pull the corn in a few weeks."

Al had practically rebuilt the tractor during the long winter months, as well as repaired, sharpened, oiled and adjusted everything in sight on the farm. It was a part of his training in the Navy that prompted him to prevent as many problems as possible due to equipment failure. The Navy called it Preventive Maintenance System (PMS). Al had readied the tractor and attached the plow the night before so he could get to work first thing this morning. It was time for the final tilling of the soil for late planting. There was no threat of rain in the forecast for the week, which would make the soil easier to work.

Al was never able to just sit and relax once he'd finished his first pot of coffee. He'd acquired this routine during his years aboard the many ships on which he'd served in the Navy. He'd get up at 0500 hours, put on a pot of strong black coffee, and then sit at his desk in the Division Office and think about the duties of the day while sucking down his coffee and half a pack of cigarettes.

Keeping the ship's engines working took a lot of planning and an enormous amount of work. Al had to have everything lined up for whoever was the latest Division Officer assigned over him and his crew at the time. The Division Officer, usually a newly appointed officer fresh out of school, would go to the Department Head meetings and act as if he was responsible for everything being in good working order. Of course the Department Head always knew that Chief Hewin was really the one who ran the division and kept everything running smoothly. Chiefs ran the Navy and every officer learned it sooner or later after joining the fleet. The only ones who didn't know it were the newly commissioned officers fresh out of the academy.

A newly commissioned officer in the Navy, called an Ensign, would go on to do well, or at any rate have the least amount of trouble, if he knew what to say when first meeting with the senior enlisted crew members. His first words should or would be, "Chief, I don't know a damn thing about anything and I'd appreciate you covering my butt till I do. Don't make me look bad if I screw up and teach me as much as you can."

As part of the hazing process of the newly enlisted crewmembers fresh out of training, the other crew members in the division would send them to tell Chief Hewin, Al, about some exaggerated problem with the engines or boiler during his morning ritual of coffee and cigarettes. When this occurred, without fail, Chief Hewin would stick his overly large German nose in the sailor's face and verbally go off on him so hard that the poor fellow felt thoroughly humiliated.

"Sailor, I ought'a empty ya head by kickin' the crap out of it. If ya had a stripe on ya sleeve I'd take it 'n put it in my desk till ya enlistment was over! Now git ya sorry butt below 'n clean the deck so clean that I can eat off it!" Chief Hewin knew his part and played it well. He'd been hazed when he was a recruit, and as a junior non-commissioned officer, he'd done it to others as well. And of course, Al knew his crew was outside listening.

Chief Hewin rarely needed anyone to tell him about any problems, because he could almost always tell if something was wrong with an engine or boiler. With his keen hearing and sensitivity to the ship's vibrations though the hull, he knew when there was a problem. Even asleep in his bunk, he would wake up at the slightest hint of trouble. Some even went so far as to claim that Al could hear ball-bearings growing rust.

The Navy had changed over the years, and most of his friends had long since retired. He and his shipmates would brag that in the old days the "ships were made of wood and the men made of steel, but now the ships were made of steel and the men made of wood."

One day Al realized it was time to move on and take whatever retirement check he had coming. He'd make a go at raising his daughter and farm crops at the only place he felt was truly home; Heard County. Besides, the Navy didn't provide a decent place for his wife and daughter to live in because he was just an enlisted man. His duties prevented him from spending as much time with them as he felt he needed to and would have liked. As a boiler technician, he was doomed to spend his life at sea or working in a shipyard getting the ship ready to go back to sea. This meant not seeing his wife and daughter most of the year and sometimes not for an entire year, especially during World War II.

Retired from the Navy, he now lived on the farm in Georgia where he grew up. It was during the trip to his last surviving parent's funeral that he and his late wife, Mary, had decided to settle on the old farmstead. They had talked about it for a long time and he missed working the land with the yearning that only comes from growing up on a farm.

These days, his routine on the farm involved getting out of bed, not a bunk, at 5:00 a.m. and putting on a pot of coffee. While the coffee brewed, he'd shave, comb his hair, put on his overalls and prepare breakfast. Al enjoyed his coffee and breakfast in peace before waking Dewey; this was his quiet time. He had long since given up smoking, but not his beloved pot of strong black coffee.

Every morning at 0600 hours, breakfast was already cooked and on the table when Dewey was given the call to reveille; the signal to get out of bed for sailors and soldiers. Dewey would always lumber in without so much as a word and eat as if it was the first meal he'd had in a week. Routines like this had taken many months to cultivate after Dewey's arrival on the farm, while others were still works in progress.

Dewey finished his breakfast without a word, if you don't count grunts, smacks, and the occasional "ummm." His plate now empty, Dewey got up with his usual clumsiness due to his overly large body for a boy newly fifteen years old. As the crumbs fell to the floor, Snipe quickly cleaned the chair and floor of every tiny morsel. With that job accomplished, Snipe went over and eagerly awaited his bowl to be filled with any leftovers and dog food. He was quickly rewarded as Al leaned down with a full bowl and said, "Thank ya, Boy. At leas' I don't have ta sweep up after 'im with you around. Well at least most of the time."

Finished with breakfast, Dewey announced, "Ship shape." He went in search of his cape and sword. Al refused to let him wear them during chow. He'd explained to Dewey that it was "against regulations aboard a ship" to wear a cape and sword at chow; meal time.

Dewey would accept just about anything as long as Al explained that it was a Navy rule or regulation. Daily, Dewey still wore the red cape one of the nurses at the sanatorium had made for him. Al had made Dewey a wooden sword in response to his always trying to get the real one hanging on the wall in the den. Al's sword hung along side his many items of memorabilia, such as his shadow box which displayed his medals and ribbons from his long career in the Navy.

Just like clockwork every morning, Dewey brushed his teeth, performed his daily constitution, and came out immediately afterwards to the sound of a loud flushing of the commode. "Granddaddy, Dewey ship shape." Al could see his hands were as dry as bone.

"Go wash ya hands, Boy," Al growled back at him, like he had to every morning.

Moments later Dewey came into the kitchen wiping his hands on the front of his overalls. Out the door Dewey went as metal screeched from the strain on the door's spring. This was followed by a loud thud when the door slammed back into place on the screened-in back porch.

Almost stepping on a dozen or so chickens as he ran through the yard, Dewey stirred up a panicked clucking as the chickens scurried away. In his most commanding voice he cried, "Step aside, me crew. The ship sets sail soon."

The chicken coop, where some of the chickens fled to, was nothing more than a small shack attached to the storage shed that was originally built to house a horse or ox drawn wagon. Just about everything that was too heavy for the shed's old wood planked floor went into the dirt floored shack.

Before Al had cleaned it out, the shed had been used mostly to store old tools and whatnots by the past generations of the Hewin family. It had contained nearly every newspaper and magazine over the past thirty years. They were either stacked haphazardly or with string bindings. Old glass canning jars were heaped into large rusted-out buckets that had been used to wash clothes or anything else that called for a large basin. Al mused over rediscovering the copper tubing and other equipment his father and uncle had used in the making of moonshine during the days of Prohibition in order to supplement their families income. Many other items lay in every corner and on shelves that were comprised of the horizontal framework of the structure. It had taken a long time, but Al had cleaned out the shed and rearranged it to house a variety of tools used around the house.

Like most people who lived through The Depression, his parents rarely threw anything away. Folks figured it could be used at some later time. That generation became the ultimate recyclers. Many a time they would find a use for things, such as old tires, tools, and whatnots. The majority of the time, however, sheds just ended up becoming depositories of clutter. Sheds and barns dotted the landscape throughout the country side.

A couple of old rusting cars were parked near the shed. They had weeds and small trees growing all around them and even through the bumpers and running boards. Nesting sites for wasps, dirt daubers, and other critters that had gathered over the years seemed to be the only things holding the old cars together. One was an old powder blue Oldsmobile and the other was the '53' Ford. A 1930's model pickup truck's final resting place was in the middle of the shack that was now used as the chicken coop. The chickens had claimed the old truck as their own. They'd built nests in the cab because the windows were left open when it had been parked for the last time. Where the wood hadn't completely rotted away in the bed of the truck, they'd built even more nests in the wooden boxes Al had placed in it for them.

Dewey greeted the early summer morning with gusto. He had the body of a full-grown man, but he had the mind of a small child. Other than his large size, Dewey still hadn't shown any signs of puberty except for a couple of short, thin armpit hairs. Dewey had light brown hair that was cropped short. In Al's usual military way of thinking, he believed that hair should be short and easy to maintain.

Dewey was ever so slowly adjusting to life on the farm. With the help of chores and a proper diet, he was losing weight at a slow but steady pace. Al accepted the fact that it was going to be a long time before Dewey would be of any real help on the farm, if ever. He gave him only the simplest of tasks while he tried to train him in the vocation of farming.

Dewey tried to run to the barn, but his movements were more like a fast lumbered walk than a run because of his size and the years of a sedentary lifestyle while in the institution. His undersized overalls could barely be buttoned up all the way on both sides due to his weight.

Al knew the boy would be losing more weight, so for his fifteenth birthday he'd bought Dewey four pairs of overalls slightly smaller than his present waist size. Eating and sitting around wouldn't be tolerated and was no longer the routine of the day for Dewey.

At the institute there hadn't been much for Dewey to do, and rarely anyone else his own age to play with. When there were others, most of the time they weren't capable of much more than drooling. Seemingly lost in their own world, they often sat in a corner near the nurse's station or in their rooms. The orderlies would always tell Dewey, "Leave them be soes theys won't start actin' out." Dewey only had someone to play with when the other patients' families visited and brought their children.

Dewey's goal this morning, as usual, was to go play in the barn that was about thirty yards beyond the shed and the old rusted out cars. Upon arriving at the barn, Dewey went straight up into the loft that faced the fields. Hay was no longer stored there because Al didn't feel the need for horses or mules, now that his tractor could do a more efficient job and with a lot less trouble. He only kept chickens because they were of little trouble and he enjoyed fresh eggs with just about any meal.

For the first time in his life, Dewey had a place he could claim as his own. Here, in the loft, he could live in his own little world which he'd cultivated during the many years of neglect at the institution. He fantasized for hours about being on a pirate ship, with himself as the captain in charge of the ship and crew while at sea. He spoke aloud to his imaginary crew and gave orders just like in his favorite and only book. Dewey had pestered staff and patients alike at the institute to read it to him over and over again. He never tired of his book and corrected anyone who tried to add or leave out a single word. He would pretend to read it to others or just to entertain himself as he turned the pages and repeated aloud the memorized text.

Al had made imaginary cannons out of some old pipes and mounted them so they would look real enough for play battles. The plank for bad people to walk, for their punishment, was a large beam with a pulley system attached to its end. It protruded eight feet into the center of the open space that was the main part of the barn and was parallel to the dirt floor. Al had set up an old telescope that he'd been given when he was a boy. Dewey had set it up to point outward through the loft's doors facing the fields. He would spend hours looking through it at all the wonders of nature. He especially liked it when he would catch sight of deer or turkey, but most of the time he only saw crows, mice, rabbits and various other farm animals.

While gazing out of the loft doors on this Saturday morning, Dewey spied some children about his age on the far side of the field. His heart started beating fast as he watched them through his telescope.

He'd been taken out of school only a couple of months after he had been enrolled last fall. He missed being with other children, even if some had been mean and made fun of him. He watched the children rummage through a pile of old stuff. He observed them pulling out old wooden timbers, jars and various odds and ends from the junk at the edge of the field. They were going through all the old stuff that had accumulated over the years where the Hewin family had created a makeshift junk yard. His grandfather explained that no one in the old days worried about dumps, so they had a pile like this one where old cars, tractors, timbers, and worn out or obsolete appliances and tools ended up. Most farmers had one somewhere out of the way on their land.

Full of excitement, Dewey lumbered down the loft's ladder as quickly as he could. Off across the fields he went as fast as his legs would carry him. He desperately wanted to catch up with these interlopers on the farm in the hope of meeting them. He lost sight of the children and the junk pile beyond the low rolling hills and the fields that still needed to be harvested or plowed. It was nearly a half a mile from the barn, but finally with sweat pouring down his face, he came upon the old junk pile only to be disappointed, as he was too late. The children were already gone.

With head bowed, he began to kick around a piece of junk here and there. He was saddened that he hadn't been able to meet the group of children, but when he heard laughter coming from somewhere not too far away in the woods, his hope was renewed so he quickly started following the sounds. A big smile came to his face as he listened to the children shouting and laughing as they walked back through the woods.

Al had worked as a boiler technician for the county school system during the fall and winter seasons. This was more a matter to keep himself busy than for the money. His Navy pension and farming proceeds were more than enough to pay the bills and have money left over, but it was something he knew well and enjoyed doing.

During the time Al was getting the school boilers ready for winter, he noticed the other children making fun of Dewey during recess, as well as before and after school. Also, the steps that lead up to the ground level from the boiler room came out in front of the row of windows of Dewey's classroom. It was there, during his breaks, that Al was able to look in on Dewey.

He noticed that Dewey just sat at the same small table all the time with a piece of paper and a box of crayons. He figured this was probably what his life had been like at the institution. The other children in the class weren't doing much else either, with the exception of picking their noses or trying to shove a crayon into someone else's ear.

The teacher could almost always be found at her desk in the front of the classroom reading a book to herself. Occasionally, she would get up and tend to one of the four children in the classroom on some minor matter or other, then promptly sit back down and return to her reading.

Al had seen enough, so one afternoon at the end of that week he went to the teacher and asked what Dewey was learning and how he was doing. Not realizing Al as one of the maintenance men, she assured him that Dewey was being taught all the subjects of math, reading and whatever skills his level of comprehension would allow. Al knew all too well she was lying, but decided to let it ride until after the job was completed on the old boilers. The following week, with his job complete, he took Dewey into the principal's office.

Al announced, "Dewey will no longer be attending class." He went on to explain that he'd observed the teacher and students activities and he didn't see any signs of learning. He considered the class a total waste of time.

The principal, Mr. Epps, replied, "Mr. Hewin, I assure you Ms. Rospigliosy fills her days helping each and every student with their class-work. She takes a keen interest in each and every one of them. Besides, the law mandates that every child is required to attend school until they're sixteen years old."

"For two weeks now I've been watchin' and seein' her sittin' all day long on her fat butt readin' books," Al snapped, cutting him short. "So don't go givin' me any of ya bureaucratic crap about the law!"

While listening to the other children laughing and having fun, Dewey nearly caught up with the gang of children after more than a mile. That's when he came upon a large creek. After finding a crossing with a worn path as his guide over an earthen damn, he once again rushed to catch up to them. He came upon them just as they were dumping their plunder upon the ground beside what appeared to be a small shack set among several others. He was amazed at the site of a bunch of rickety structures suddenly appearing in the woods.

The huts were positioned in a semicircle. Half of them looked like they were in the process of falling apart. They had all been piecemealed out of every conceivable kind of material that could be nailed or tied together.

The center of the hut village had an extremely large oak tree with swings hanging from its largest limb which was horizontal to the ground. To the left of it was a large hut with curtains in the windows. To the right was another large hut he would soon learn was the boy's hut. It had tools leaning against it along with piles of old material from aluminum siding to old wood planks. This is where the gang had dumped their plunder from scavenging through the junk pile at Al's farm. There were a couple of other smaller huts by the boy's hut. Trees served as anchors in the framing of the walls. Dewey would find out this little hut village was built over many years by the children from the Robins Nest Trailer Park located just over the hill.

Suddenly, Dewey heard growling and a loud bark. A medium-sized whitish tan dog with floppy ears came out of nowhere and confronted him. The startled crowd of kids stopped and stared as Dewey pulled out his wooden sword. Dewey didn't try to hit the dog with it, but instead used it as a sort of warning device. He was as scared as he had ever been. He kept the dog at bay, all the while repeating "BAD DOG! BAD DOG!"

Chapter 3 – Dewey Makes Friends

"HEY LOOK; IT'S THE RETARD FROM SCHOOL!" Bane Taggart shouted. Because of his age, he was the undisputed leader of the boys, and although not the biggest, he was by far the meanest. Needless to say, nearly everybody usually went along with him, albeit reluctantly, a lot of the time.

Bane had crystal blue eyes and unmanageable coarse blonde hair which needed cutting. At fourteen years old, he was only in the seventh grade because of his poor grades and unruly behavior. Bane and his older brother, Ricky, who was soon to become eighteen, were notorious for being bullies, making bad grades and cutting school. Bane was accustomed to doing what he wanted and, with the exception of Billy Davis, bossing around the younger and smaller children. He picked up a stick and started for Dewey with cruelty and mischief written all over his face. An entourage of youngsters quickly formed and followed alongside and behind him. All the while, Libby continued barking warnings at Dewey.

The girls, who had been in their hut, became curious about the ruckus and went to investigate. Immediately upon recognizing the large boy wearing the red cape from school, Crystal White shouted, "LIBBY, STOP THAT!" She quickly ran over and grabbed Libby's collar and pulled her back away from the nervous newcomer.

No sooner than Crystal got Libby under control, she witnessed Bane move forward with a stick and heard him ask sarcastically, "What's the matter? Afraid of a little ole dog? Go away! We don't want the likes of you 'round here no ways."

"Leave 'im be. He ain't hurtin' nothin'," demanded Crystal as she moved closer to Dewey to show defiance, as well as determination to protect this stranger to their hut village.

Crystal didn't fear being harmed by Bane because it was considered wrong for boys to hit girls, even in this unruly clan. It was considered an act of cowardice that even Bane understood would have consequences. Crystal, fourteen years old, was not only taller, but more fully developed than the other girls. She had large green eyes and long strawberry blonde hair. She was the prettiest and most popular of all the girls, not only at the trailer park, but at the school they all attended. Crystal was the oldest, so the other girls looked up to her. Because of Bane's propensity for unrelenting meanness, she, like the others, took careful measure in choosing when to stand up to him. She knew not to push him too far.

Crystal had witnessed Bane's and his friend's cruelty towards Dewey and his unfortunate classmates many times in the past at school. She rarely stood up to him at school for fear of retribution, not only from him, but the gang of go-a-long lackeys with which he surrounded himself. In the trailer park, Crystal knew she could be more assertive while surrounded by their group of friends without much concern. For certain, she could never take part in something as mean as teasing Dewey or his fellow classmates. Like most southern girls, she was taught to be polite and courteous to everyone; this included those who were less fortunate or weaker.

Crystal was the newest member of the group. She and her parents had moved into the trailer park the previous summer, just before the beginning of the present school year that was soon coming to an end. The previous summer had been a bad year for much of the country's industrial corporations. They'd moved to Roosterville when her stepfather was laid off from his job at the Lockheed Corporation, where he'd made airplane parts. Her stepfather now worked as a mechanic in a garage in the nearby city of Carrollton. Heard County, where they now lived in the unincorporated area of Roosterville, was made up of farms. Heard County was mostly known for its cows, chicken houses, and pulpwood trucks.

"What's yer name?" asked Crystal.

Dewey shyly replied, "Dewey."

"Well, Dewey, its okay if ya wanta hang out with us. Nobody's goin' ta hurt ya." Still holding onto the collar, she looked down and said, "This is Libby, she won't hurt ya. She jus' don't know ya is all."

"She always messes up the fun," Bane said with a sneer. Discouraged, he threw down his stick as he stepped back to join the other boys. The younger of the boys, Todd and Jason, half-heartedly agreed with him, but Billy Davis and Gabby stood silently by observing the interaction.

Billy, soon to be fourteen, was by far the tallest of the group of boys and was in the eighth grade. Billy was gentle at heart and rarely spoke a harsh word. He tolerated Bane's tendency for such cruel antics so as to tamp down unnecessary hostilities, but didn't feel intimidated by him since he had gotten much bigger and stronger over the last couple of years.

Gabby, thirteen years old, was in the same grade and class with Bane because he had failed the year before due to bad grades.

Billy's younger sister, Gail, who was in the raiding party to the junk pile at Al's, now joined the other girls who stuck together like peas in a pod when in opposition of "the boys." She went on the raiding party with the boys because she liked being included in their many adventures.

Gail was solidly built and as strong as any boy her age. She was a tomboy at heart and enjoyed getting as dirty as much as anyone else, as her dirty knees and hands could attest. She kept her black hair short, above the shoulders, so it wouldn't be such a bother. Her father said it made her big brown eyes even prettier. Her mother had to force Gail to wear a dress to church and sometimes needed to threaten her with a switch to put on shoes for church or school.

Dewey, still nervous, didn't move. He waited for the onslaught of teasing that always came when Bane was around. Because it was at least some kind of interaction with others close to his age, he'd learned to tolerate it and accept it for what is was. He relaxed slightly now that Libby was no longer growling at him or appeared to be a threat.

Confident that Libby was calmed down, Crystal let go of her collar, patted her and said, "Good, Girl." Feeling proud of herself and relishing the praise, Libby happily began going from one person to another in an effort to gain approval from everyone in the group.

"What ya doin' here, Retard?" demanded Bane. The others watched and waited in anticipation of Dewey's reply.

Dewey finally spoke, "Dewey saw y'all gittin' stuff from Granddaddy's."

"What ya gonna do about it, Retard?" defiantly retorted Bane.

Dewey looked down, shuffled his feet and quietly said, "Dewey wants ta play."

"Git outa here! We don't want no retard hangin' 'round here." Bane looked around for approval from the others. Only the two youngest boys, Jason and Todd, chimed in agreement and waved their hands as if shooing Dewey away.

Crystal interrupted, "You can stay if ya wanta. It's a free country. I know ya already know Bane, but let me introduce ya ta everybody else." She stepped over towards the girls and went on, "This is Pattie, Jill, Bonnie Lou, and Gail." She moved over to the boys and pointed, "This is Billy, Gabby, Jason and Todd."

Bane let out a hiss and waved his hand in dismissal of Crystal before he again spoke to Dewey. "Why ya won't ta bother us, Retard? We don't got no crayons ta color with."

Dewey just stood there forlornly without responding.

Finally, seeing it was a stalemate of Bane's inability to have his way and Dewey's quiet determination to stay, Crystal smiled at Dewey and joined in conversation with the other girls.

Losing interest, the group turned away from the somewhat demoralized and silent Dewey. They'd turned their attention back to matters at hand and began to take stock of the inventory they had just brought back. Everyone had ideas on what to do with all the pieces in the pile. As usual, the oldest got first pick and the ultimate say about the best pieces.

Dewey took the discontinuation of Bane's bullying as an unspoken sign that he was allowed to hang around. Keeping his distance, Dewey watched with interest while everyone went about their activities.

Eventually, Billy walked over to Dewey and said, "You can help if ya wanta. We gotta fix that hut over there." He pointed to a small shack that had two crushed walls. A really large limb had fallen on it during a recent storm. As much as everyone tried, they couldn't budge the heavy limb.

Dewey hesitated, so Billy motioned for him to follow saying, "Come 'n help, Dewey. We need ya." As Billy and the others struggled to pull the limb off the structure, Dewey stood and watched as he tried to ascertain the situation.

Gabby walked over to Dewey and pulled on his sleeve while saying, "We need ya help movin' it. Looky here, I ain't as big as you. So, help me."

With that, Dewey grabbed hold of the thick end and started lifting. As soon as he did, the large limb started moving. Dewey was taking the brunt of the weight himself. He and a few helpers eventually moved it to where Billy directed. Gail had jumped in to help as the other girls looked on in astonishment. This turn of events didn't go unnoticed by Bane, who was now leering at Dewey while the others commented to one another about Dewey's obvious strength.

"Ship shape," Dewey exclaimed as he wiped his hands on his overalls.

"Good job, Dewey," said Billy as he patted him on the shoulder.

Not long after Dewey began helping, Gabby, who's real name was Norman Grizzle, asked, "Dewey, why ya wearin' that red cape with a cross on it 'n got that there wooden sword?" Curious, everyone else nearby gathered closer to hear his answer.

"Dewey is a Pirate. Dewey is the Captain." In a display of pride, Dewey lifted his chin to the air and puffed out his chest as he rested his hand on the handle of the wooden sword.

Bane bellowed a fake laugh, "Ha! Ha! Ain't no ships 'round here ya retard! Captain, ha!" The others just kept quiet and waited to see what else Dewey would say. Bane, feeling his oats, walked over and tried to grab Dewey's wooden sword from his overall's loop. Dewey just pushed him away with ease.

"What's the matter?" Bane snorted. "You afraid I'll cut myself with that big ole piece of wood? More 'n likely I'll only git a splinter. Ya couldn't cut hot butter with it I bet ya."

Dewey just stood there, not sure what to do as Bane came in close again in an attempt to show he wasn't intimidated by Dewey's size or strength.

Billy, seeing this could get out of hand, chided Bane, "Why don't ya jus' leave 'im be. He ain't hurtin' nothin'."

Soon after he arrived at the barn, Al realized the loft was empty and wondered where Dewey had gotten off to so early in the day. He felt certain Dewey was going about his chores. Al continued to hum to himself as he gave a quick look at the fuel level of the tractor. He did this by dipping a stick into the gas tank that sat atop and back from the engine. It was located just in front of the instrument panel and steering wheel.

Al's tractor was parked just inside the barn with the harrow already hooked up. After another quick look around, and figuring the boy was somewhere close by as usual, he put it out of his mind and went about his work.

At lunchtime, Al went into the kitchen expecting Dewey to be sitting at the table like clockwork waiting for his lunch. Surprisingly, Dewey was still nowhere to be found. Al started to get a little concerned.

"Snipe, where'd that boy git to?" Snipe just lay on the kitchen floor resting his head on his paws as he diverted his eyes to look in Al's direction. "Reckon he'll show when that belly of his gits the bes' of 'im, which probably won't be long now, huh." Al ate his usual light lunch of one sausage biscuit and a cup of coffee. He made a couple of sandwiches and poured a glass of milk for Dewey. He placed them on the table and went back to work.

All day long Dewey helped the others as much as he was capable of helping. They went about repairing the huts that had been neglected during the cold winter months and torn apart by storms. Of course, he had never done anything like this before, so he needed to be shown and told what to do in detail. He looked to Billy, who'd taken him under his wing, for guidance. This was all so new and exciting to him. He felt joy at being accepted by the others and not being constantly teased.

Around noon some of the children disappeared and returned within a short while from home. When Gabby returned from eating lunch, he had a jar of grape jelly preserves and half a sleeve of crackers. He shared this treat with Dewey at the swings. "Here ya go, Dewey. I figured ya needed a snack. Would ya like some jam crackers?" Dewey licked his lips at the sight of the treat Gabby offered.

"Dewey likes jelly," was all Dewey replied.

"All right then, I'll fix us some," said Gabby.

"Ya momma make that jelly?" inquired Bane. Bane, although he could've gone home to try and scrounge what little food was there, was put off when Gabby neglected to share any of the jam and crackers with him.

Gabby only glanced at Bane and nodded in acknowledgement as he handed Dewey yet another cracker that was heaped with grape preserves to overflowing. He then made another for himself. Bane commented, "Yeah, my Grandmamma makes that kind of stuff. Wonder if it tastes the same?"

Gabby didn't acknowledge Bane this time as he was busy trying not to spill any of the preserves on his clothes while he ate his cracker. Bane didn't want to seem needy or come straight out and ask for any of Gabby's food. Instead, with envy, he sat stewing over the fact that Gabby didn't take the hint or appear as if he wanted to share any with him. It wasn't long before all the crackers where gone.

Gabby left the near empty jar of preserves on the ground by the tree's trunk close to the swings. Gabby and Dewey got up and went to be with the others who were coming back from having lunch at the trailer park.

Bane hopped off the swing he was on and retrieved the jar of preserves. "Shoo, flies," he demanded as he picked up the jar. Gabby had licked the spoon clean he'd been using to scoop out the preserves and had taken it with him. So Bane carried the jar across the way and picked up a stick which he used to get out some of the remaining grape preserves. Satisfied he'd gotten what was easily retrieved from the jar, Bane observed how the stick attracted pest. He watched as flies buzzed all about the jar as well.

Dewey was so thrilled to be with the others that he had forgotten all about missing lunch and the passing of time. Gabby's crackers had been a welcomed treat. When thirsty, all the children went down to the creek and drank the cool, crystal clear water as it fell down a naturally occurring five foot waterfall. All day long, they haggled and bartered for this and that and worked like busy bees. The hours seemed to fly by as they joked and teased one another.

Bane seemed especially interested in hanging around Dewey soon after the rest of the gang got back from lunch. He was making it a point to praise Dewey and pat him on the back, shoulder and arms. "Dewey, ya shor' are one strong fella." Sometimes he said, "Glad ya come ta see us." These comments were always followed by a congratulatory pat of his hand.

Amazed at this turnabout by Bane, some of the others began to become confused at Bane's demeanor towards Dewey and watched with some suspicion during these odd exchanges of friendship.

During one of these so-called friendly exchanges, Gabby noticed that Bane had a small stick in his hand. Once Bane pulled back his hand Gabby noticed a small purple streak on Dewey's shirt at the place where Bane had patted him with the stick in his hand.

"Yeah, Dewey, we sure are mighty glad ya come ta play with us. Hey, why ya got so many critters flyin' around ya," Bane asked in a genuinely concerned tone.

Then Bane gave a chuckle as he went on to say, "Look everybody, the flies' sure do like ole Dewey here." Once this was over, Gabby observed Bane immediately afterwards go retrieve the jar of grape preserves and watched as Bane swizzled the small stick inside the nearly empty jar.

Gabby once again turned his attention back to Dewey and watched him being constantly bombarded by flies and the occasional yellow jacket over the next few moments. Once he understood what was going on, Gabby quickly said in a loud voice, "Dewey lets go down to the creek 'n see if there's any fish. Ya know where that empty jar got off to we were eatin' out of a while ago? Oh yeah, there it is."

Gabby then went and retrieved the empty preserves jar where he'd just watched Bane place it on the ground. Together, he and Dewey walked down towards the creek. Bane, unaware his scheme had been discovered, became slightly annoyed when he realized that his entertainment had been stolen for the time being.

Once out of earshot from Bane, Gabby said, "Now Dewey, you don't go lettin' Bane keep pattin' ya on the back, cause when he acts friendly, you can bet he's up ta no good."

"I like it when he nice to me."

Gabby didn't know how much Dewey understood or if he should even tell him what Bane was up to, so he just said, "Well, I guess it's alright then, but looks like ya got somethin' all over ya shirt. I'll wash it off when we git to the creek. Ya know we keep a tin box with soap in it down there."

Bane smirked as he watched the two come back from the creek a little while later. He assumed his little trick hadn't been revealed as of yet, so he asked in a loud voice for everyone else to hear, "Hey, Dewey, ya didn't catch any flies while ya was down there did ya?" Bane smiled in anticipation of drawing everyone's attention while he disparaged Dewey. He wanted to make Dewey seem disgusting and nasty.

Gabby jumped in, "We didn't see no flies, but there was lots 'a mosquitoes. Thought they was goin' ta suck us dry." Gabby then grabbed Dewey by the sleeve and stopped him as he forced Dewey to lean down so he could whisper something in his ear. "Now, Dewey, if anybody ask ya about flies . . . ."

It wasn't long before Bane noticed that the flies that had previously harassed Dewey were absent. He couldn't make it out. As he was mulling it over, his initial thought was that the preserves had played out and there wasn't anything for the flies to eat anymore. While lost in thought, he heard Dewey say, "Dewey likes Bane. Ya wanta play pirates? You can git a stick or somethin' for a sword and I can be the captain."

Dewey reached out his hand and placed it on Bane's shoulder. "Git the hell away from me ya, RETARD!" shouted Bane as he contorted and jerked his shoulder away from Dewey's touch.

"You said ya liked Dewey."

"The only thing that likes you is flies. Where'd all ya little fly friends go anyway, Fly-Boy?" shouted Bane with revulsion and hostility, as he thrust his face forward for emphasis.

"Dewey, don't got no flies no more. I eat 'em all up. Ummm." He put his face real close to Bane's. Oooh's and ahhh's erupted from the others watching.

Bane stepped back in astonishment and disgust with his lips agape and eyes wide open. His back was arched and his hands were up in a defensive stand. He recovered just as quickly and walked towards the boy's hut muttering to himself. When he passed Gabby and Crystal, he couldn't be sure, but he detected a peculiar look passed between them before Crystal stifled a snicker.

Late in the afternoon, the ringing of a bell echoed from over the hill in the direction of the trailer park.

Billy turned to Gail, and with a sigh said, "We bes' git goin' or mom 'll git mad if we don't come home quick. I sure don't want ta cause her ta throw one of her hissy fits like she did yesterday." With that, they and most of the others started for home.

"I don't feel like goin' home yet," pouted Gail.

As he started for home, Billy just retorted, "Fine. I guess ya don't feel like eatin' tanight." Crossing her arms in defiance, Gail let out a small huff and followed Billy and the others as they one by one peeled off the group and started for home.

"Wait for me," said Bonnie Lou as she rushed to be in the middle of the pack with Jill and Pattie. Bonnie Lou was the smallest of all the girls and the quietest. She was twelve years old and the only child in her family. She was the spitting image of her mother, with long brown hair and light brown eyes. Sometimes the others called her "Little Bit" due to her being so petite.

Crystal walked over to Dewey and spoke in a gentle voice, "Dewey, ya need ta go home now. It's time for us ta go home for supper." After Dewey looked towards the woods, he turned back looking perplexed. Out of concern Crystal asked, "Ya know how ta git there don't ya?"

The look on Dewey's face warned her he was beginning to panic as his eyes darted around. Crystal became concerned when she realized she didn't know where his home was and how he was going to get there. With a shaky voice Dewey replied, "Dewey don't know. Granddaddy goin' ta be mad if I don't go home." Dewey became agitated and looked all around.

Gabby, who had been watching and listening to the two talking, announced, "I'll show 'im how ta git back home."

Crystal studied Gabby for a moment and then made up her mind. "Jus' wait right there." She disappeared into the hut where she had spent most of the day and came back with a ball of orange yarn. She handed it to Gabby. "Ever so often, ya tie a piece of this here string ta a tree limb or bush or somethin' so Dewey can find his way back if he wants to."

Dewey and Gabby took off through the woods. Along the way, Gabby told Dewey more about everyone and why he should steer clear of Bane. "My daddy says that boy is high strung like his daddy and his big brother. So make tracks when ya see that 'up ta no good' look in his eye. Course, he's up ta no good most the time, specially when his daddy's had 'n all-nighter. His daddy 'n brother are as mean as snakes 'n whoop on 'im regular. Guess that's what makes 'im so mean."

Of course Dewey didn't have the slightest idea what Gabby was talking about most of the time, but he enjoyed the attention.

Every so often Gabby, with his pocket knife at the ready, would cut off a piece of yarn and tie it to a small tree or a low-hanging limb. Gabby pointed out landmarks as they walked though the woods and recounted past adventures. Because of the stops and starts to hang string, it took them close to forty minutes before they came to a clearing on Al's farm. The sun was blocked by the large trees in the forest, so it was a stark contrast to suddenly step out into the bright sunlight on the edge of the open fields.

With joy, Dewey recognized where he was. He was standing close to the pile of junk the others had raided earlier that morning on the farm.

Gabby hung a string on the tree close by. After tying the knot, he said, "See ya 'round, Dewey." Off he went before Dewey replied. Gabby added a few more strings to the trees as he made his way back to the hut village.

Watching Gabby disappear into the woods, Dewey initially stood and shuffled his feet as he thought about the day's adventure. Although he was glad to be home, he didn't want it to end. Reluctantly, Dewey started across freshly plowed fields once he saw Al coming across to greet him. When Snipe, who had been close on Al's heels, caught sight of Dewey, he sprinted ahead to greet him.

More relieved than angry, Al gently demanded, "Where ya been, Boy?"

With excitement in his voice and with short clumsy sentences, Dewey began to tell Al all about his exciting day as best he could. Before they arrived at the house, Al's anxiety began to dissipate somewhat. He firmly gripped Dewey's shoulders and turned him so he was facing him. Al wanted to be sure he had Dewey's undivided attention before he spoke.

"Boy, ya gotta tell me 'fore ya take off like that. You could git inta trouble or lost or somethin'."

Al was glad to see that Dewey was okay. He felt a special sense of pride after the surprise of hearing what Dewey had been up to with the other children. He couldn't help but think that maybe there was hope for Dewey yet, despite the boy's slowness. Al was pleased at the thought of him being accepted by other children.

Al knew about the trailer park and figured the folks there were just hardworking poor souls who didn't have much in life because they were down on their luck or just couldn't do better for themselves. Unlike some of the dirty ragamuffins in the county who he considered to be lazy sluggards, he appreciated how some folks worked hard but just didn't ever seem to make much headway in this world. He knew you could be poor as dirt, but that was okay as long as you're clean and respectable. His mother and father always said, "Ya don't have ta have fine things, but ya can keep what ya have clean. That's the pride ya show for what God's given ya."

When Al would drive past the trailer park, he'd noticed it was always well kept. The trailers were mostly old, but presentable enough. He'd grown up knowing John Grizzle, the owner of the park, and thought him a decent man. He occasioned to cross paths with John now and then at the local store where he picked up supplies. Like most small rural stores, it sold just about everything. They had tractor parts, electrical and plumbing fixtures, hardware, clothes, some groceries and almost anything a person could need to get by on until they could get to the city.

Immediately after supper, Al made Dewey finish his chores of cleaning out the chicken coop. Another of Dewey's Saturday tasks was scrubbing his own underwear of all the stains from poor hygiene. This was accomplished with a bucket of soapy water and a brush while holding them against the rounded end of the silver propane gas tank in the yard. After Al supervised this task, he would then load them in the washing machine to finish the job.

"Looks like you tried to pave a road in them shorts of yers, Boy. They've been soakin' since this mornin'. Now git at it." Al liked everything to be kept on schedule, but due to Dewey's adventure he was late loading the old noisy washing machine. They didn't have a dryer, and because of the late hour the clothes wouldn't have the warm sun to dry them. He knew he would have to dry some of the clothes in the house tonight, which meant they wouldn't smell as fresh or be as soft as they would have been had been dried in the sun and wind.

The house was built long before indoor plumbing, so once they were able to get an electric pump and a second well, a room had been added to accommodate a bathroom with space enough for a washing machine. An electric pump supplied the bathroom and kitchen with water from the second well. The original well was nothing more than a hole in the ground with a stone and mortar circle wall built around the top and down the sides. The old well had a hand cranked spindle on top to lower and raise a bucket to retrieve water just like people have been doing for thousands of years.

Al's late wife, Mary, had demanded he tear down the outhouse and fill in the hole. She said they had indoor plumbing and she didn't want to look at or smell that nasty thing ever again. Al's mother, when she was alive, had insisted on keeping the outhouse and used it regularly. She said it was just her way.

One of the drawbacks of having well water was the constant battle of fighting red stains left in the sinks, commode, and bathtub. This was the result of the high iron content in the red clay that makes up most of Georgia's soil. Being a recent addition, the bathroom was the only room in the house that was decently insulated. The rest of the house was cold in the winter and hot in the summer. The shade from several large oak trees, which towered over the house were the only things that made the summers bearable, along with the help of electric fans and the high ceilings.

It was well after dark by the time Al handed Dewey a towel and wash cloth. He said, "Go git ya bath, Boy. We don't wont ta show up ta church tamorrow lookin' like ragamuffins. And don't forget ta scrub that head of yers this time. Ya head smells like chicken poop."

Off Dewey went with a fresh towel and his pajamas.

Out of concern for Gabby, Crystal waited for him to get back from showing Dewey how to get home. Gabby was younger than her, but she adored him for the kind of person he was; he was kind hearted, friendly and helpful to everyone. He was always the first to jump in and help someone else, even when it wasn't expected.

She sat silently by herself in the girl's hut sewing on cloth to make new curtains. All the other girls had gone home when Billy and Gail heard the bell for supper. Other than the sounds she made, there was no other sound made by another human being coming from outside. She was certain everyone else was gone. She sat in the only rocking chair in the girl's hut. She didn't dare rock back and forth while sewing because some of the nails were loose and she was afraid she might make matters worse and end up on the ground. The regular chairs, discovered last year, were comfortable enough, but some of the nails needed to be hammered back into place on them as well, and maybe a few more added.

Due to the sun going down, it had become slightly chilly and was getting difficult to see how to sew in the dim light of the hut. She felt a little weird being by herself in the woods so late in the day, so she began to feel not only the chill from the temperature dropping, but the chill of fear creeping in on her. Underneath her clothes and on her arms, goose bumps began to rise. She was determined to wait for Gabby, despite everything. She didn't know exactly how long it would be until Gabby got back because she wasn't with the group that morning when they went on the raiding party. To pass the time, she decided to try and fix the loose chairs. She thought it might warm her up a little and take her mind off her feelings of apprehension. Knowing that the only hammer and nails in camp were kept in the boy's main hut, she went outside.

She couldn't help but notice how eerie and deserted the place looked and felt. Even Libby had followed the others home. Libby didn't exactly belong to anyone in particular. She just ended up at one trailer or another getting food wherever she could. There was no shortage of food or kindness for her at most of the trailers. She more or less offered herself up for adoption to everyone and they more or less all adopted her.

Crystal walked past the tire and wood swings that hung from the large oak tree branch that was located in the center of the hut village.

A strong breeze was now blowing through the woods, so she wrapped her arms around herself in a hugging maneuver in an attempt to shield herself from the chill. Once across the opening, she approached the boy's main hut.

Pulling back the curtain that was used as the door she suddenly found that someone was in the corner of the hut with their back to her. She thought it was Gabby. She wondered how long he'd been back. A bit agitated at herself for not paying better attention and hearing him arrive back at the hut village, she stepped inside while still holding the curtain aside to allow more light inside so she could see better before entering.

Pleased to see him, and without saying anything, she let go of the curtain and made a bee line around the sparse furnishings to face him. Once inside her eyes began to adjust. It was then she realized it was Bane! He was so occupied that he hadn't noticed her intrusion. His pants were down around his ankles. In one hand he held a magazine up to a sliver of light coming inside from a window and with the other he was making repeated motions near his groin.

Standing there, Crystal still hadn't realized what she was witnessing while her eyes continued to adjust to the dimness. Then in a flash, she understood and gasped in horror! A strangled horrified squealing sound came out of her throat as she stood paralyzed by the spectacle before her.

With wide startled eyes, Bane turned his head to face hers. The magazine fell to the dirt floor of the hut. Momentarily paralyzed with shock, he stood there looking into the terrified face of the one person he would least like to have been caught by. "**What the hell ya doin' here!**" he shrilled with a high pitched squeak and cracked voice.

Bane's yelling broke through Crystal's petrified shock. Before he could finish shouting the last word, she'd turned, flung open the curtain door, and was running home as fast as she could go. Bane quickly leaned over and fumbled as he pulled up his pants. He was mortified and confused at what had just happened.

Chapter 4 – Complacency

ROBINS NEST TRAILER PARK

PANIC stricken, Bane paced back and forth in the boys' hut while tearing up the Playboy magazine Crystal caught him looking at. Every second seemed like a minute. Every minute seemed like an hour. Then, feeling as if he would suffocate within the dimly lit walls of the hut, he flung open the cloth doorway and rushed outside looking anxiously around. Butterflies filled his stomach as his panicked mind raced. His emotions reeled from complete embarrassment to all-out rage as he kicked at the nearby hut's wall in the hopes of releasing his pent up anger and frustration, all the while letting out a stream of cuss words.

In his mind, he could hear and see the others pointing their fingers in his direction as they laughed and teased him. He was convinced Crystal was telling the whole world what she had witnessed, making him the laughing stock of school and the trailer park. The thought, "*If only I'd stopped her before she got away,*" kept running through his mind as he paced back and forth.

All he could think about was how he'd missed the opportunity to run Crystal down and threaten her into keeping her mouth shut because he hadn't reacted fast enough. Anger, frustration and anxiety were swirling through his head and eating at his stomach with a vengeance. He was certain he would be stigmatized from now on with names he'd called others or teased to the point of utter humiliation. One thing was for certain, he couldn't and wouldn't face anyone just yet, and he sure wasn't about to go home until he was certain he wouldn't get caught by anyone while entering the trailer park on the way to his trailer.

Bane was still stewing when Gabby happened by on his way home through the huts after returning from walking Dewey home. Once Gabby entered the center of the hut village, Bane came storming out of the shadows and confronted him. Caught off guard, Gabby initially recoiled in fright and stood frozen near the swings.

"**What ya doin' here?!**" Bane shouted. Then he roughly slammed his palm against Gabby's shoulder, indicating he wanted to fight.

Gabby halted his natural instinct to strike back because he could see in the fading light that Bane was in one of his more outlandish moods. He stood still, with his hands frozen by his sides. He knew now was not the time to make jokes, talk back, or do anything that might further aggravate the situation. Whenever Bane got that look on his face, Gabby had learned to keep still and say as little as possible out of fright for his welfare.

"Well?!" Bane demanded. This time he hit Gabby on the chest, knocking Gabby backwards two steps.

"I'm come back from showin' Dewey home is all!" Gabby exclaimed with a slight tremble in his voice.

Bane leaned forward, almost touching his nose to Gabby's. Fury was etched on his face and one fist was knotted, ready to strike. "Damn ya sorry ass, don't ya come 'round here no more ya little runt. Understand?!" He poked Gabby's chest hard with a forefinger for effect.

"Uh?" was all Gabby could utter.

"Get los', 'n I bes' not hear ya talkin' behind my back!"

With trepidation, Gabby slowly moved around Bane, ready to jump or duck if needed. Although he was stocky for his age, Gabby still didn't want to test his ability at this time by taking on Bane. Gabby's pupils were dilated so wide with fright you couldn't see how green his eyes were anymore. With one more look over his shoulder to make certain Bane wasn't following, he took off running at full speed up the hill. He didn't slow until he was certain he wasn't being chased.

Crystal came home to an eerily empty trailer. She knew her mother had driven to Carrollton earlier to pick up her stepfather from work. She made sure all the windows and doors were locked. Then she curled up in a sitting position on her bed and tried to calm herself while tightly hugging her favorite stuffed blue and white teddy bear, all the while trying to draw comfort and security that never seemed to come.

Suddenly, aware of the darkness that filled the trailer, she jumped up in a frenzy and rushed to turn on all the lights and recheck the locks on both doors once more. Sitting alone in the dark was the last thing she wanted to do right then. She was scared and worried her parents might be gone for a long time. She knew they sometimes stayed in town to eat supper before going grocery shopping. They did that because her stepfather got paid at the end of the day on Saturdays. She also knew she could never tell her parents what she'd witnessed because it was too embarrassing. To her relief, she soon heard their car pull up outside.

After Al hung the remaining clothes on the various lines throughout the house, he settled into his favorite chair in the den where he spent most evenings. He placed his cup of coffee on the stand beside his chair and looked around at his collection of memorabilia until his eyes fixed on a large brass bell. It had hung on the Quarterdeck of a ship he'd once served aboard that had been decommissioned by the Navy.

An old friend of his, Chief Petty Officer Charlie Ardinger, sort of "relieved" the ship of this burden before the Navy scuttled the ship into the deep blue sea. The obsolete vessel was one of many used for target practice off the Carolina coast during naval exercises. Sometimes the Navy used old ships for target practice to test various types and designs of ammunition. Once sunken, the ship would become a coral reef on the continental shelf that marine life would inhabit. This was done to help the local fishing industry grow in the future.

Before Dewey went to bed, he'd join Al in the den and sat in his assigned chair. It was beside his chair that Al had already placed Dewey's usual glass of milk and a small snack of gingerbread cookies. This had become their evening ritual.

Al rarely turned on the television, unless he wanted to listen to the news or weather report. He didn't want Dewey sitting in front of it and becoming a zombie like the way he had when he first came to live on the farm. He figured it was just another bad habit from Dewey's institutionalized days. To keep him entertained, Al would read him a book, usually the Bible, or tell stories of his times in the Navy. Al sensed that Dewey enjoyed this time spent together and he was glad he had the opportunity to give the boy much needed attention.

Once Dewey learned which picture sitting on the piano was his mother, he would occasionally push Al to tell him something about her. Most of the time, Al just said, "Ya mother was a sweet-n-beautiful young lady. One day she felt she had ta leave home. Someday she'll come on back ta be with us. Things'll be better then." He'd then change the subject and tell him about the Navy or the farm, and sometimes about how life was when he was young. Al always tried to instill some sage advice about life and how to be a good man in every story he told. It always seemed to be enough until Dewey was sent to bed at 2100 hours.

"Who's that holdin' a rifle?" Dewey asked, while he stood and pointed to a picture of a solider in an Army uniform.

Al, after a quick inspection, popped his false teeth back into his mouth and looked at the pictures on the wall where Dewey was pointing. Beside a picture of his parents was his only sibling, his older brother, Taylor.

"That's my brother, Taylor. He died of consumption soon after he arrived back from Germany at the end of World War II."

"What's 'con sopin'?"

"That's what they called it when ya died from tuberculosis. It made it hard for 'im ta breath. One day he couldn't git enough air ta keep livin' 'n so he up 'n died." Al sighed and then took another sip of coffee. "Taylor was in the Army during the war over there in Europe when we put a stop ta some crazy fella named Hitler. This fella, Hitler, was as mean a person as they come. He killed folks jus' for bein' who they was. He even thought he could take over the whole world. Image that."

"Well, Teller–that's what we called 'im at home–he died within a year of comin' back from the last World War. He fought in two big wars, and in all that time with not so much as a scratch, jus' ta come home 'n die from bein' exposed ta some tiny little ole bug. He caught it while he was over there tryin' ta help put a stop ta all that foolishness. Teller was much older than me. My mamma, ya great-grandmamma, said that when I was little, I started callin' him Teller instead of his real name Taylor, 'cause I couldn't, or didn't know any better. Well, the name Teller kinda suited 'im 'cause he had a tendency ta always start everythin' he said with 'let me tell ya somethin'. I still have his medals and stuff from the war somewheres." Al paused and chuckled as he took another sip of coffee. "Everyone sort of let the nickname stick, 'n folks around here all called 'im Teller from then on too."

"Teller never married so when the first war broke out in Europe, he up 'n joined the Army 'cause he felt it was his duty. I turned seventeen jus' before that war was over, so I got permission from my folks ta enlist in the Navy. Mamma figured if I was goin' ta join, I might as well go in somethin' a little safer than the Army. At first I tried ta go in the Army, but she wouldn't have none of that. Since I had ta have her 'n daddy's permission, I went in the Navy instead."

"See that card with the two blue stars just above Teller's picture? That's what mamma put in the window ta show both her sons was fightin' in the las' big war."

By this time, Dewey was back in his chair and eager for more. Al went on to tell Dewey some of the stories of his childhood and how he and Teller use to help on the farm and take care of the livestock and plow the fields using mules. He explained how most folks were struggling to make a living before the second war, during The Depression, and how people who lived on farms had it much better. "Ya see Dewey, if ya know how ta grow ya own food, then ya know where ya next meal is comin' from." Then he came back around to talking about the war and how it put a stop to life as they knew it.

"Jus' remember, Boy, apathy is as much a sin as breakin' one of them Ten Commandments ya learned in church."

"What ya mean, Granddaddy?" Dewey was gazing at him, plainly trying to understand what his granddaddy's new word meant.

Al sat there a few moments in thought before he spoke, trying to figure out how to explain this important concept about life. "Books don't exactly explain what it truly means. It actually resides deep down inside yer soul. If you listen ta it, it's kinda like an uneasy feeling ya git down in yer stomach. It's tryin' ta warn ya that what yer seein' is wrong. And if ya don't do somethin' about it, like maybe yer jus' standin' there watchin' somethin' bad happen, yer still partly guilty of what's goin' on if ya don't try 'n stop it. The sin ain't failin' ta stop the wrongdoin', it's the not tryin' ta stop it if somebody's in trouble."

Al looked at Dewey's expression of utter bewilderment. Al knew that many of his soapbox speeches were lost on Dewey, but he really didn't have any other outlet for his thoughts that manifested during the long periods of mundane hours in the fields while doing repetitive mind numbing work. Sometimes, like now, he had to try and repeat it in simpler words so Dewey could understand what he meant. "It means ta not be indifferent and jus' think about ya'self. It means ta think about others 'n how you'd feel if no one tried ta help ya."

"Jus' remember Dewey, if ya was ta see that cripple on the side of the road who was tryin' ta go 'n see Jesus, like that man the preacher talked about on Sunday, wouldn't it be good for ya ta help 'im? Same goes for somebody bein' hurt by someone else or seein' somebody take somethin' that don't belong ta 'em. Ya know, like don't stand around twiddlin' ya thumbs while someone is hurtin' one of ya friends or stealin' from 'em cause yer afraid ya might git hurt." Dewey seemed to grasp Al's more basic rendition this time and started nodding his head.

"That's what the World Wars was about, folks helpin' friends and other folks when bad people were hurtin' 'em. Sometimes, like in Korea, they weren't really our friends or somebody we even knew, but we knew if we didn't help 'em, the bad people might git foolish enough to come for us next. Course we didn't really win the Korean War, but we put a hurtin' on the bad people enough that they stopped." Al let out a long sigh before he continued. "Some folks think that's what we're doin' in Vietnam. All I can tell ya is that we shor' do lose a lot 'a fine young men every time we try 'n help others."

Dewey always listened to the best of his abilities during these lengthy lectures because he liked his granddaddy's attention. Most of the time Al just gave him orders to do stuff, but during this time together at night it was different, in that Al spent time actually talking to him instead of just talking at him. It made Dewey feel important.

Bane finally came out of the hut when he was certain it was late enough to avoid others on his way home. Although he had forgotten about his hunger for hours in his shame of the earlier event of Crystal catching him engaging in self-satisfaction, he was now so hungry that he felt like his stomach was literally gnawing at his back bone. Once Bane came to the top of the hill overlooking the trailer park, he sat and waited until he was absolutely sure he could sneak into his trailer park without being spotted.

It looked as if most of the residents were already in bed for the night. Most of the trailers had all of their lights turned off. His trailer was in the center on the other side of the two long rows of homes. Bane was sure he could go between two trailers that had all their lights off to get across the street without anyone being the wiser.

While sneaking between the two trailers, a small dog barked inside one of them, which alerted Bane's presence outside, so he quickly ran across the lane to the other side and down to his trailer's front door. It was locked! He knew his father wasn't home yet because his truck was absent from its parking spot. Bane knew his father would most certainly be out late drinking and running around the county most of, if not all night. He was grateful for that much at least.

Bane could hear his older brother, Ricky, inside with his friend, JoJo, laughing and carrying on in loud conversation. Bane's anxiety continued to build and his stomach began to churn. He gently knocked repeatedly without any response, so he knocked louder and louder until he was sure of getting his brother's attention.

His brother finally came to the door and cranked opened the glazed glass louvers that made up the window on the upper part of the door. "Hey, Jerk Off! Ya look kinda lonely out there all by ya'self in the dark."

"Let me in, Jackass!" demanded Bane.

Ricky shrugged and walked away, rejoining JoJo. Bane could see the two of them sitting in the trailer making gestures towards the door and laughing. Bane didn't want to get loud enough to draw attention from the neighbors, so he worked his way down one side of the trailer, testing the windows and then the back door. When he went around to the other side, he found one window that was always unlocked. It was to his father's bedroom. When he started to push it open, he was suddenly drenched in cold water.

"What the hell ya doin', Boy?" came his brother Ricky's mocking voice from inside the trailer.

Bane tried to control himself, but the anger and frustration he'd felt earlier reignited as he shouted with fury, "**I'm gonna ta kick yer sorry butt ya son of a whore!**"

Now this was a "no go" area because Ricky's mother wasn't the same as Bane's. Ricky stopped laughing as he instantly darted away from the window. His footsteps could be heard thumping, as well as his muffled rantings, as he ran down the hallway of the trailer. Bane listened to the front door being slammed open on the other side of the trailer. Bane knew he had said the one thing that would get Ricky furious and spoiling for a fight. Ricky was three years older than Bane. When their father got drunk, he would talk bad about Ricky's mother by calling her a whore. Ricky didn't have a choice and had put up with it from his father, but he would never tolerate someone else saying such things to his face, especially Bane.

Ricky came around the corner of the trailer, so Bane turned and ran the other way. Ricky's friend JoJo, having circled around the opposite way, grabbed Bane as he rounded the back corner at the other end of the trailer. Unable to break free of JoJo's grip, Bane shouted, "Let go, ya fat son-of-a-bitch!" Try as he might, he couldn't wiggle free. Suddenly he felt a fist slam into his right kidney. Only then did JoJo let him fall to the ground, where he landed hard in excruciating pain.

Ricky kicked Bane several times in the stomach, back and legs. After a moment of hesitation, he took careful measure and kicked Bane directly in the mouth. Satisfied with his handiwork, Ricky bent down and sarcastically asked, "Ya got somethin' ta say now, Loudmouth? What's the matter ya little puke? I thought ya was goin' ta do somethin'. Well, I guess ya must'a changed ya mind, huh? We'll leave ya be so ya can think on it awhile."

JoJo helped Ricky stand erect as he softly, but with urgency, said, "Hey man, ya really hurt 'im bad. Why don't we take 'im inside?"

Ricky didn't answer as he jerked his arm free of JoJo's grip. Together they watched Bane writhe in pain on the ground. Finally Ricky piped up, "Don't he look cute all curled up like a little kitten?" Then Ricky leaned over Bane as he went on to say, "Well, if nothing else, ya learned nobody wants ta hear ya mouth while their kickin' the crap outa ya."

With one last look, Ricky shrugged his shoulders and said, "Let's go finish our beers. Guess the poor thing run outa stuff ta talk about." JoJo chuckled softly as he followed Ricky back into the trailer.

Bane lay on the ground for several minutes in his wet clothes. He was in so much pain that he began to cry. He cried as much out of humiliation as for the pain that consumed his body. He buried his face to muffle the sobs so he wouldn't give Ricky the satisfaction of hearing him. Curled up on the ground, he stayed long enough to pull himself together and give his body time to get over the initial shock and pain. He knew the man next door wouldn't bother to come out and check on him because this was an all too familiar occurrence for which the Taggarts were notorious. Once Bane was able to struggle to his feet, he went back to the front door and found it unlocked this time. Reluctantly he turned the knob and stepped inside to hear his two tormenters jeering. "Hey, glad ta see ya decided ta join us . . . ."

"What the hell happen ta ya, Twerp?!" teased Ricky. JoJo found this particularly amusing and began to snicker, choking on his mouthful of beer.

Bane didn't look directly at them as he struggled to walk normally past the two. He could smell and see they'd been smoking and drinking while country music blared on the radio. "Screw you," he muttered to himself once he passed them and entered the hallway.

"What ya say?" He heard them getting up as they slammed down their beers on the coffee table. He knew he needed to get away fast, so he sprinted the rest of the way to his room and slammed and locked his door quickly. A loud bang came from the other side of the door as Ricky pounded his fist against it. Bane heard JoJo say, "Good thing ya didn't catch 'im that time. Ya might'a killed 'im for sure." After a few moments, Bane heard their footsteps receding down the hall. Bane actually took some comfort in the fact that Ricky and JoJo hadn't said anything about his being caught earlier by Crystal. If they had heard about it, they'd never let up about it all night long, probably forever for that matter.

Bane slumped on the bed and rubbed his back. Although he was hurting and upset over what'd happened at the hut, he was still famished. He was never sure whether his dad would come home later that night or on Sunday morning. Joe, his father, always went drinking with his buddies on Saturday night after payday. His dad worked for an outfit that dug wells, post holes, graves, or anything else that required making holes in the ground or just moving dirt. His father, Joe Taggart, was known to run off every woman he ever had a relationship with because he was a mean drunk who liked to cuss and beat women. He took pleasure in knocking Bane and Ricky around on a regular basis. Bane had heard him brag to his friends about the pride he felt over how well his sons could take a "good butt kickin'."

Bane figured this was going to be just another night he would go to bed without supper. He knew there was very little, if any, food still in the kitchen. Also, there was no getting past Ricky and JoJo for the rest of the evening. His dad always went shopping on Mondays after work because the Blue Laws in Georgia prohibited grocery stores from being open on Sundays. At least he would take Ricky and Bane out to eat lunch at the BBQ House tomorrow. He claimed this was their family time and made it a tradition.

Bane was accustomed to hiding in his room for safety, so he always kept a stash of junk food in a box underneath his bed. He pulled out a bottle of Coke and one of his two remaining candy bars. He opened his Coke with the bottle opener attachment on his pocket knife, peeled the candy wrapper off and ate hungrily.

With his immediate need for food satisfied, he began to think about what he would say if confronted about being caught in the hut by Crystal. He was grateful there was only one week left until school was out for the summer. He just needed to avoid Crystal, and if possible lay low until then.

After eating, Bane felt better and wanted desperately to get revenge on his big brother for beating him. That was when he remembered his uncle Elam telling them about a prank he'd pulled on his little brother, Joe, Bane's father, when they were growing up.

Bane tiptoed into Ricky's bedroom with his knife and cut several inches of the seams on Ricky's feather pillow. This would allow the feather stuffing to come out during the night as Ricky slept. That way Ricky would think he'd busted the seam and not suspect Bane when he woke up with feathers everywhere. Satisfied, Bane tiptoed back to his room and smiled as he lay down for the night.

Despite the pain from the beating, Bane soon fell into a fitful sleep as he worried about Crystal telling on him to the others.

During the middle of the night Bane was awakened by the sound of Ricky shouting cuss words between sputtering and spitting loudly. Once he realized Ricky hadn't suspected him and come banging on his door, he smiled as he fell back asleep.

Chapter 5 – Dewey Becomes a Hero

AFTER Al and Dewey arrived home from church, Al began to cook fried chicken, mashed potatoes and gravy, turnip greens, and a pan of cornbread. Al had already killed, de-feathered, and dressed a chicken before going to church with the speed and efficiency taught to him by his father. Al always preferred the taste of freshly killed chickens to the ones he had to eat while in the Navy, which had been raised in warehouse-type coops and then frozen for long periods of time. Since his wife Mary died, it was out of necessity that he'd learned to cook, but it was out of pride in his workmanship and his desire for good food that he became an efficient and good cook. On occasions when he went out for his meals, he always tried to get his favorite foods: fried catfish, hush puppies, potato salad, and sweet iced tea.

Dewey came and sat at the kitchen table after he finished changing out of his Sunday clothes and into his overalls. It wasn't long before he said, "I'm hungry."

"If ya hungry, wash ya hands 'n git ya'self a carrot. Lunch 'll be ready in a bit."

Reluctantly Dewey got up from the table and started for the sink. Snipe, ever vigilant, jumped up in anticipation. Once Dewey retrieved a carrot from the refrigerator, Snipe let out a sigh as he slumped back to the floor.

Al glanced over to see if Dewey was eating the carrot. He just shook his head and smiled to himself once he saw Dewey reluctantly chewing it with a sourpuss expression.

Al rarely went to church after joining the Navy, but felt, upon Dewey's arrival, that it was his responsibility to take Dewey to church so his grandson could have a proper upbringing. What had been his wife's ordained job while she was alive, now fell to him.

When Al and Dewey started attending church, everyone was surprised to see them. It took a while, but they soon became regulars for Sunday worship. Most people gladly accepted them as a part of the congregation, especially the members who still remembered Mary. It took a couple of months of coaxing, but Al eventually took Dewey to church earlier for Sunday School classes. Although Al thought the sermons were not very well thought out and the preparation lacking, he still enjoyed the music and joined in whenever possible.

During Al's and Dewey's second trip to church, Al placed cash into the offering plate. Immediately, nearby parishioners suddenly began whispering to one another after seeing the large wad of bills. Al hadn't been to church for a long time and therefore decided he owed the Lord a lot of back pay. He'd forgotten to take into account the absurd way people reacted to large amounts of money. The loud whispering continued to grow as the plate was passed among the others behind him.

Because there is one in every church, someone a couple of benches back shouted, **"Hallelujah! Praise the Lord! God done blessed us taday! Look Preacher Rakestraw!"** Because the man who shouted was close by and within Al's peripheral vision to his left, Al, as well as many others turned to look at the man waving the wad of cash in the air. When Al turned his attention back to the podium, he witnessed the preacher's eyes go wide and begin licking his lips, all the while rubbing his hands and shuffling his feet as if he couldn't stand still. Al dropped his head slightly and shook his head at the obscene outburst and gestures of such people, who no doubt put a lot of stock in money.

After the sermon, which seemed much too short, the preacher, Timothy Rakestraw, didn't let go of Al's hand for far too long as he thanked Al and Dewey for coming back to visit their church. After finally gaining his freedom from the preacher, many others from the congregation swarmed around him and Dewey. Most thanked him for his "gift to the Lord" before they began asking him what kind of business he was in and offered up their own life stories, some hinting about their needs and how money would sure be welcomed.

Once Al was finally in his truck, he rolled up his window, despite the heat, so he could fend off someone trying to gain his attention. He suspected they just wanted to chit-chat, but he was never one for such things. While he drove away, Al resolved to get a few tithing envelopes before he put any money into the offering plate ever again.

As is typical in small communities, Roosterville being no exception, it didn't take more than a couple of Sundays before most of the community had gotten word that this boy was Al's long lost grandson, but not much else. Al was the "mind yer own business" kind of person, so he deflected or outright ignored most questions concerning Dewey or the absent parents. He told them Dewey was his grandson and little else. This just made folks all the more curious and some to the point of being downright belligerent in their nosiness.

Al had received the same grilling by one of his distant cousins at the courthouse when he'd first gotten Dewey. When Al had gone to the courthouse to file paperwork for Dewey's adoption, he'd been assaulted by busybodies, most of which had gone so far as to leave their prospective offices just to come in and meet Dewey. The chatty clerk in the Probation Judge's Office had gone on and on about everyone's business while she helped Al with the paperwork. After Al's multiple trips to the courthouse, he knew what'd happened to many of his old classmates, long ago friends, and just about anybody he might or should have known in the county. Many of the things he heard were so personal that they shouldn't have been repeated in private, much less in such a public place. Upon first attending the church that first Sunday, he'd recognized a couple of the same people he'd met at the courthouse.

Preacher Rakestraw and his wife always made it a point to freeload a meal from one of the church families every Sunday, as well as any time the opportunity presented itself. It was on such occasions that the Rackestraws collected gossip on the congregation and many other people in the county. They used this gleaned information like currency in order to acquire even more invitations from willing partakers of their kind of busybody antics and gossip. Both were known as hearty eaters, to which their pot bellies could attest. Not that the preacher hadn't tried, but Al never took the bait and invited them to his home for a meal, even when the pestering preacher persisted. Al would just ignore Pastor Rakestraw and his wife's overt attempts by pretending not to have heard them or outright deflect and change the subject altogether.

Upon Al and Dewey sitting down to enjoy their Sunday dinner, Snipe's ears perked up and he bolted for the back door. Snipe stood on his hind legs and pawed at the screened back door while barking and whining at the same time in his excitement. Perturbed at having his lunch interrupted, Al opened the back door for him and said, "Git."

Snipe, hell-bent after something, rushed outside and disappeared around the corner of the house. Al figured that Snipe'd heard, seen or smelled something or other that was intruding in his domain. No sooner than he sat back down to eat, Al and Dewey heard loud angry barks. At first Al didn't give it much thought, certain Snipe was just taking on after some critter or other, until he was surprised by the sound of someone's voice yelling from outside.

Al rushed to investigate and found none other than Pastor Rakestraw sitting on top of his own car hood with his feet pulled up. Al had to suppress his smile at this comical site. Mrs. Rakestraw was still sitting in the front passenger seat of their car with a horrified look on her face. It was made all the more exaggerated by the enormous amount of makeup she was wearing. Al had, on more than one occasion, thought she might have been a clown before she became a preacher's wife. She held up her purse from behind the car's rolled up window. Her large beehive hairdo bobbed up and down and side to side as she attempted to keep up with where Snipe scurried to in his attempt to keep the preacher trapped on the hood.

Snipe was not a large dog, but he was plenty big enough that any grown man would most certainly want to avoid a confrontation with him. Al pretended not to notice as he strolled over to the car. "Afternoon, Preacher. What can I do for ya?"

Still shaken, and with a nervous tremble in his voice, the preacher answered, "Jus' thought I'd come 'n see how y'all be gittin' along since we was passin' by is all, Brother Al."

"Oh, we been doin' jus' fine, Brother Tim. I was jus' sittin' down ta a fine meal of fried yard bird 'n some greens."

"And Dewey?" inquired the preacher.

"Oh, he be doin' jus' fine. Thanks for askin'."

While these pleasantries were being exchanged Snipe kept his vigil, all the while baring his teeth and continuing a low growl of warning. The preacher kept darting his eyes back and forth between Al and Snipe. Every time he started to unfold his legs in an attempt to get down, Snipe would repeat his earlier warnings and pose to pounce until the preacher resumed the position on the hood. All the while, Al took no notice.

"Don't ya wanta call off yer dog?!" Preacher Rakestraw asked reproachfully.

Al just ignored him. "Ya know it looks like summer is here ta stay for a while. Corn's 'bout ready for harvestin', 'n soon it'll be time to ready the late crops. Yeah, it looks like it's gonna be a good crop this year too. Yeah, Gods goin' ta be good to us for sure." At this point Preacher Rakestraw wasn't really interested in small talk anymore as he stared at Al with indignation. His social demeanor had changed to frustration and anger. Al waited for a response, but none was forthcoming.

"Well Preacher, I reckon Dewey 'n I bes' git back ta our lunch before it gits cold. Y'all have a good day now." Al turned to Dewey, who had come outside to watch, and took him by the shoulder and gently turned him around before guiding him back to the house.

"Snipe, come on, Boy!" With that Snipe forgot about the preacher and eagerly followed Al and Dewey. It wasn't long before they heard the preacher slam his door shut, which was followed by shouting between the two as they drove away.

"Did ya see how he treated me!" hollered the preacher.

"I don't care if ya have ta climb a tree every time ya see 'im as long as he keeps given us lots'a money!" his wife shouted back.

That was the last time Preacher Rakestraw ever made it a point to speak to Al, other than a socially expected form of politeness such as "mornin', afternoon'," or some other cursory greeting in passing.

After lunch, Al found Dewey in the bathroom with the door open. "Ya done brushin' ya teeth 'n washin' ya hands yet, Boy?"

"Ship shape," was Dewey's jubilant response.

"Boy, follow me. Got somethin' ta show ya."

Dewey, having already donned his cape and sword, followed Al to the barn with Snipe close on their heels. Al carried the large brass bell from the den in his arms. Because it weighed close to sixty pounds, he was about out of breath by the time they arrived at the barn. He set it on the ground beside the outside corner of the barn that faced the plowed fields. He went inside the barn and retrieved an old fashioned hand-crank drill with a bit already attached. With practiced efficiency, Al soon drilled a hole in the side of the barn where the corner post was located.

While Al drilled, Dewey enquired, "What ya doin', Granddaddy?"

Al appreciated it when Dewey spoke directly to him instead of referring to himself in the third person like he did when he first came to live with him. He noticed when Dewey became uncomfortable or upset he still reverted back to that old habit. Al couldn't help but ponder and appreciate how far Dewey had come in so many ways. He was grateful that the retardation wasn't as bad as it could have been. The boy seemed forever lost in innocence and he thought, just maybe, that wasn't so bad after all. At least there was hope of a somewhat normal life for the boy.

Al grinned and said, "I'm puttin' up a brass bell ta let ya know when it's time ta come home ta supper, Boy. That triangle bell I've been usin' on the back porch won't quite do it for the distance you got off to yesterday." Dewey's confused look told Al he didn't understand. "Don't ya worry none, I'll show ya in just a minute."

Al pulled a large brass screw out of one pocket and a large flathead screwdriver out of another. "Now hold that bell against the wall while I fasten it." He helped Dewey put it in place and soon it was mounted with three additional holes and brass screws.

"Now, Dewey, repeat after me." He took Dewey by the shoulders and forced him to look directly at him by holding his chin when his head started to wander. Dewey never liked looking directly into someone's eyes. "When I hear the bell, it's time ta come home ta supper." Al repeated it until Dewey could say the entire sentence. Then he let Dewey repeat it several times more to his satisfaction.

"Now pull on that there rope," Al said as he pointed at the bell.

Dewey halfheartedly pulled the rope with a knot on the end. The bell made a small rich ringing sound.

"Let me show ya how it's done, Boy." With that, Al yanked hard on the rope and it rang so loud it startled Dewey and sent Snipe running at full speed towards the house with his tail tucked between his legs. From then on, Snipe would run for cover every time Al reached for the bell's rope. Dewey took a couple of steps back and gaped at the bell in astonishment. He could never have imagined that a sound so loud and crisp could have been produced by this yellowish metal object.

"That's how ya bring the bell ta life, Boy. It was made for hearin' many a mile away."

Dewey looked at the bell with sheer delight and astonishment. Then he looked towards the trees that hugged the fields. Al grinned big with pride at his grandson's excitement and the familiar sound of the bell that stirred up good memories of his past life onboard ships.

"Now Dewey, ya hear me good. When ya hear that bell, come straight home. Do ya hear me, Boy?"

Dewey stood there looking at Al and the bell, then after a few moments he started nodding his head. Al was always amazed at how slowly Dewey absorbed new ideas.

"Now what'd I say?" He stood there while Dewey concentrated a moment.

"I come home soon as I hear the bell."

"Good. Now go play with ya friends. I'll ring it when ya need ta come home for supper."

Dewey excitedly took off across the fields, his cape flapping behind him. He was just about to enter the woods when Al rang the bell hard while he waved goodbye to Dewey. Dewey stopped, looked and started back towards Al from across the fields.

"What in the world is that boy doin'?" Al asked to himself when he realized Dewey was walking back towards him. The he realized it was because he had rung the bell. He waived his arms to let Dewey know to go on.

Dewey stopped and stared in bewilderment, then finally turned around and disappeared into the woods with his sword raised and cape flapping.

Al couldn't help but worry over what might happen to Dewey if something prevented him from being able to take care of the boy. He mumbled to himself, "The poor child is slower than cold syrup and has the attention span of a gnat." Al hoped he hadn't confused Dewey and that he still understood what he had just been taught. He worried over the subject as he ambled back towards the house to clean up the kitchen and put away the leftovers. Snipe, upon seeing Al coming back towards the house, ran across the yard to greet him.

Dewey followed the trail of orange strings left by Gabby to the hut village. He was too excited to notice much else along the path as he wound his way through trees, pass several gullies and over the big creek.

When he arrived at the hut village, he saw only a few of the gang standing around the swings. He was relieved to not see Bane's blonde head among them. This time the dog, Libby, came running up to him and acted friendly, indicating she wanted to be petted. When he was slow to pet her, she whined and whimpered a little as she pawed at his leg. He gave her a few scratches on the head as he shuffled past her to be with the others.

"Hey, Dewey the Pirate!" shouted Gabby, who pointed and waved for the benefit of the others at the swing. Gabby now considered Dewey to be a friend. Jason and Todd halfheartedly moaned a greeting while they hesitated a moment from fighting over who would get the wooden swing. They, as well as the others, all wanted the swing with the wood seat and not the tire swing.

Pattie interrupted, "Todd, I think you should get the wood swing."

"Who ask ya?" demanded Jason.

Pattie bit her upper lip on one side as she thought about her reply. Then she said, "You're probably right. I shouldn't have said that. Ya know, Jason, you deserve ta always git the bes' swing."

Todd shoved past Jason and demanded, "Why should Jason always get the bes' swing. I deserve it as much as him."

Jason tried to push Todd aside as he declared, "She's right! I deserve it more'n you, cause she says so."

Todd was about to speak, when Pattie interrupted him. "Whoever is the bravest should always git this seat." She gently took the rope connected to the wood swing from them and sat down. The two boys looked at one another and then again at her and began to protest. After listening to them a while she went on. "Well, to prove which one of ya is the bravest." She hesitated when she saw who was coming. "When ya see Bane next time ya have ta kiss 'im on the lips for long enough ta count one Mississippi or ya have ta kiss Gail for five Mississippi's." With that she indicated with her head for them to look at Billy and Gail coming down the hill.

Jason and Todd went back and forth as to who they'd rather kiss, because they knew they'd get beat up by either one. Jason and Todd wouldn't admit to liking girls openly. They were always kidding each other over which girl they thought the other one liked just to get a rise out of one another. They heckled each other constantly on the bus to and from school over which one liked girls.

Gabby pulled them aside and talked to them in hushed tones until they began to nod in agreement.

Suddenly, Todd and Jason rushed the swing, grabbed Pattie, and took turns kissing her over and over until they decided she'd had enough. They stood back with arms crossed and looked at her smugly, only to discover she was smiling and looking as if she enjoyed their showering her with kisses. She giggled at their surprised reaction. The two looked at Gabby while he shrugged and shook his head, smiling.

Embarrassed, the two put up their hands to show they conceded. They didn't know what else to do.

"Ouch! Slow down, Billy!" cried Gail as she stepped on a sharp rock while following her brother down the hill into the hut village.

Billy turned to see what'd happened, "Put on some shoes or quit ya belly achin'."

Libby took off running to greet the new arrivals, all the while barking loudly. Jason and Todd huddled together and began to nudge one another and grin, cupping their hands as they snickered and admitted to each another that they kind of liked what they did to Pattie. Even that soon turned into a hushed argument as to whose kiss she liked best.

Upon reaching Billy and Gail, Libby's whole body seemed to rock as her tail swung from side to side with excitement. Billy always greeted her with equal enthusiasm and spoke to her in an excited baby's voice. This seemed to make Libby even more excited as she relished being scratched behind her ears and firmly rubbed on her neck and head.

Billy approached the group and asked, "Anyone seen Bane? We could hear some kinda ruckus over at his place las' night. Sounded like all hell must'a broke loose."

The others just shrugged and said, "I duh know."

Gabby spoke up, "He shor' was in some kinda tizzy las' night." He shook his head. "Thought he was gonna beat me good when I come back from takin' Dewey home. Hope he went 'n got hisself killed. It ain't like he don't deserve it neither." Some of the others just nodded or half moaned their agreements.

Jason injected, "Ain't seen Crystal neither. When I walked by her place, her momma said she ain't feelin' so good taday. Hope she ain't sick like my baby sister. Boy howdy, did she keep us up mos' of the night with 'er barkin' like a dog with a whistle in 'er throat. The only way momma got 'er settled down was ta put 'er head in the freezer. Momma says sometimes babies' git sick like that after they done had a cold or somethin'. She called it croup."

Gail looked at Jason like he had grown horns while some of the others jeered at him for making up such a tale. Only Pattie, who also had a baby brother, defended him, saying, "Sometimes babies' throats swell up so tight that the only way ta help 'em is ta git some cold on 'em soes they won't suffocate. I seen my momma do it before." This seemed to satisfy everyone's doubts.

Gabby got a funny look on his face and then a grin just before he spoke. "When I git home, I'm gonna git one of them dog biscuits we keep for Libby when she shows up at the house 'n take it ta Crystal. I never seen Libby sick after eatin' one, so just maybe it'll help her feel better." Pattie and Gail became indignant at such a silly suggestion and chased Gabby around while slapping at him as the others enjoyed the show.

"Guess we gonna have a quiet day of it then," replied Billy after he stopped laughing. While the others were busy with Gabby, Jill took over the wood swing.

Billy joined in on the fun of tussling over a turn at one of the swings and even made Jason and Todd let Gail have a turn. Dewey was still not sure if he wanted to get on one of the contraptions, so he declined when offered a chance to swing on the tire. He didn't like the idea of trying to lug himself inside of it because it looked too small.

"Jus' as well, ya might a busted it anyhow. Looks like the rope is givin' out soon," observed Jason as he jumped in the tire swing with ease.

"Hey y'all, how 'bout we git back ta' fixin' the hut?" suggested Billy as he pointed to the hut they had removed the tree limb from the previous day. Everybody agreed.

Gail, always looking for a reason to go into the boy's main hut said, "I'll git the hammer-n-nails." With that, she took off at a trot towards the boys' large hut. Todd and Jason were still fussing over temporary ownership of one of the swings while the rest of the group voiced their ideas for the best course of action to take concerning the roof. They bickered over their supplies and wanted to make sure what they had was put to the best use.

When Gail arrived at the hut's entrance, she shoved aside the cloth door and slipped inside. Her eyes, unaccustomed to the darkness due to the window being closed, ran her fingers along the inside wall as she moved to where she knew the hammer and nails were always kept. They were stored inside a box just underneath the only window that was presently shuttered from the outside. After a few steps, she stumbled over something and fell to the ground.

Whatever it was, **it moved!** Then she heard a low moan coming from underneath her legs. Startled, she muttered, "What the . . . ?"

Someone or something grabbed her hair! Surprise turned into terror as she looked into the dimly lit face of an old man with whiskers who smelled of filth, cigarettes, and alcohol. **She screamed!** That only made her captor all the more agitated from being awakened from his stupor. He tugged at her hair and shook her head as he rose and yanked her to her feet.

"YA LITTLE RUNT! SHUT UP 'FORE I BEAT THE HELL OUTA YA!" he ordered gruffly between coughs. Then he flung back the curtain door and pulled her out of the hut, still holding her by the hair.

The gang came running at full speed upon hearing Gail's scream. Confused by the others reactions, Dewey soon followed. In his attempt to be patient, Al would comment 'Boy, ya got only two speeds: slow 'n easy and then jus' plain slow'. Because Dewey had sat on the ground by the tree, it took an effort for him to get up and pursue the others.

Upon reaching the front of the hut, the children came face to face with none other than Little Jay. He was just emerging from the hut with a tight grip on Gail's hair. He was the old drunk who stayed with his sister in one of the trailers at the trailer park. Still holding Gail by the hair, he stood scowling at the others while his scrawny frame struggled to stay erect. He had to use his other hand to grip the framework of the hut's doorway.

Little Jay's sister, Ms. Nutt, was a part time cook and server in the cafeteria at their school. She'd never married or had children, but babysat all the time. At some time or another, she had been a babysitter to most of them. Her disgusting drunkard of a brother was in jail almost as much as he wasn't because of his drinking and stealing. No one had seen him for months.

"LET GO 'A MY SISTER!" demanded Billy.

"What ya gonna do about it, Scamp?" replied Little Jay as he slung Gail to the ground. Libby was barking up a fury and trying to intimidate Little Jay as she made lunges at his legs, only to be kicked away. Libby had no love for Little Jay due to his always being mean to her. "Git the hell away, ya Mangy Mutt!"

Little Jay was in a state of ready and looking for an excuse to mix it up with anyone or anything. He was still drunk. He tried to make out the group through his large pair of horn rimmed glasses that were held together by gem clips at the temples. The lenses were thick and scratched from many years of abuse. He was able to see well enough to know Billy was just a medium size boy. The rest of the group was much smaller and already starting to back up.

"Leave me be, 'fore I tan all yer sorry worthless hides. I ought'a knock the snot outa the lot of ya. Now git outa here 'fore I take a notion ta beat ya. GIT NOW!"

Billy started to go around Little Jay to help his sister, who still lay mortified on the ground, but he was knocked to the ground by Little Jay before he could reach her. When Billy started to get up, Little Jay grabbed him by the arm. "Ya messin' with me, Boy. I'd jus' a soon . . . ," he stopped suddenly in mid-sentence as he was caught short by something slamming into his chest.

Dewey, having caught up to the others, came around the corner in time to see Libby trying to defend the children. He'd watched Billy get hit while he was trying to help Gail. Upon seeing the man knock Billy down, Dewey quickly brandished his wooden sword and lifted it over his head, running forward and knocking the others aside. He jabbed the dull pointed end hard into the chest of Little Jay while shouting, **"BAD MAN!"**

Little Jay tumbled hard to the ground. When he attempted to get back to his feet, he almost fell again while clutching his chest. Little Jay had no idea who or what had just hit him or where it came from. His confusion soon gave way to rage as he strained to peer through his glasses. He had to readjust and hold them just so on his nose while he looked for answers.

Little Jay was awe struck once he understood he was being confronted by a boy who was much bigger than himself. Being just a little over one hundred and twenty pounds, Little Jay began to have misgivings about trying to combat his large armed assailant. Little Jay was both amazed and confused by the fact that Dewey had on a red cape and was wielding a stick at him ready to strike him once more. Bewildered, Little Jay backed up, all the while attempting to curse between coughs and grasp for air. He could only manage a few high pitched noises as he tried to breath through the intense pain in his chest.

Dewey's arm was extended full-length with the sword pointing towards Little Jay as he slowly stepped towards him, all the while shouting, "BAD MAN. WALK THE PLANK!"

Little Jay, still in a stupor and in considerable pain, was confounded by all that had just happened. He couldn't wrap his head around what was going on, but he knew he wanted to get away before he was struck again. Everything was coming at him too quickly to grasp through the alcohol induced fogginess in his head.

Little Jay looked around desperately for a way to retreat as he slowly continued to back away from Dewey's menacing presence. He realized that behind him was a gully that had been carved out of the ground by many years of runoff coming down the hill. It was only five feet deep, but there were rocks and large roots at the bottom that had been unearthed by years of rain and erosion. He backed up to the edge of the gully with Dewey still standing vigilant guard over him and slowly advancing with his imposing size. Little Jay was teetering near the edge and looking for an escape when he spotted an old tree near him that lay across the span to the other side. The group of children had begun to make a semicircle around him; all the while Libby barked and continued her lunges at his ankles.

Disgusted and overwhelmed, Little Jay decided he had little choice, so he started across the gully on the downed tree trunk. Halfway across, he stumbled and fell into the gully. He landed with a thud on one of the larger rocks, making him feel like he'd fallen a hundred feet for all the increased pain it caused him. He lay there until he caught his breath once more. He rubbed his right forearm across his mouth and nose as he sat up, renewed fire smoldering in his eyes as hatred glowed on his ever reddening face. "Jus' you wait. I'll kick the crap outa all ya little PUNKS!" He spit out the last word with venom.

With some trouble, he tried to get to his feet. His right foot was partially stuck in a soft part of the hill, so he kicked and wiggled his foot until it came free. Satisfied with his progress, he looked back up at the children and started to rant again, "**I'm gonna whoop the livin' . . . !**"

His tirade stopped as abruptly as it had begun, because individual pangs of fire erupted all over his exposed arms, face and neck, as well as up his right leg underneath his pants. Unbeknownst to him, Little Jay had dislodged his foot from the opening of a large yellow jackets nest. He was soon swatting at his face and neck in a flurry.

Yellow jackets continued to swarm and sting him all over with the fury that only yellow jackets were famous for when provoked. Because they weren't limited to just one sting like so many other bees, they repeatedly stung him as many times and as fast and furiously as they could.

Little Jay started screaming as he scrambled up the other side of the gully, flailing his arms and swatting at the unrelenting onslaught of little yellow and black striped winged devils. Once out, he fled as fast as he could away from the relentless swarming insects. While he ran up the hill towards the trailer park, Little Jay fell and stumbled. Upon arriving at the crest of the hill, he tore at his belt and flung off his pants.

Gail, her injuries forgotten, had joined the others in time to watch Little Jay getting stung by the yellow jackets. She was no longer crying as she hung onto Billy's arm for comfort and security. Upon realizing the danger of them getting stung, she'd gently tugged at Billy and Dewey, urging them to back up with the others because she saw more yellow jackets coming out of the nest.

Even after Little Jay had cleared the crest of the hill they could still hear him shouting. When the initial shock and awe wore off, they all, with the exception of Dewey, began to laugh nervously.

Jason came up behind Todd and with urgency in his voice said, "Todd, don't move. Ya got a yellow jacket on ya." Then he slapped Todd on the back of his leg below Todd's shorts. Todd jumped and swatted furiously away at the back of his right leg where Jason had slapped him. Everyone was bewildered when Jason pointed and burst out laughing.

Indignant, Todd shouted, "WHAT'S SO FUNNY ABOUT ME GITTIN' STUNG!"

Jason held up his palm to reveal he had a little twig stuck between his fingers. "Ya big baby, you didn't get stung. I just barely touched ya with this tiny stick, ya Cry Baby."

"Well, jus' for that I hope ya really git stung then," replied Todd as he jutted out his chin.

No sooner had Todd spoken, when Jason started slapping at the back of his neck and making squealing noises as he ran over towards the swings. "WHAT'D YA DO TA ME, TODD?!"

Gabby was the first to look and see what Jason was yelling about. Sure enough he saw where Jason had been stung. "Dang Todd, how'd ya do that?"

"What?"

"How'd ya manage ta git Jason stung for real?" asked Gabby.

"I don't know, but he deserves it for what he done ta me though!" Everyone looked at each other with bewilderment as they gathered around Jason to see the where he'd been stung. Sure enough everyone could see the welt growing on the back of his neck where a yellow jack had actually stung him. Through his pain, Jason watched with satisfaction as others admonished Todd.

Dewey looked at Jason's sting before turning to Todd and saying, "That's not nice ta sting Jason." Soon everyone was laughing at what Dewey had said. Even Jason joined in despite the pain.

When they finally stopped laughing, they gathered around Dewey and patted him on the back, all the while congratulating him for what he had done. Dewey stood beaming with pride at the adulation being shown him. He'd never had such an honor before. His acceptance among the group was assured for all time by the present members.

Collectively, they forgot about working on the huts as they went into the boys' hut to investigate. They soon discovered it in a state of disrepair. It didn't take long before they discovered Little Jays bottle of liquor. They tried to figure out why Little Jay tore up one of the magazines in the boys' hut. The boys knew what kind of magazine it was and kept it to themselves.

As they gathered around the swings, once again they laughed again and again about Little Jay's comeuppance and kept congratulating Dewey while they played. Through their elation, they all vowed allegiance to one another and promised to try and stay away from Little Jay. They knew they would have to warn the others to watch out for him as well, because he would probably be set on vengeance.

Once they were convinced the yellow jackets had calmed down, Billy took some of the kerosene they had for starting fires and poured it into the hole of the nest. Gabby then threw in a match which caused the nest in the hole to burn. While they watched, the yellow jackets flew franticly around the nest causing most to die in the flames.

Bonnie Lou, who hadn't been at the huts during all the commotion, came rushing down the hill with a perplexed look on her face and a little out of breath. "What's happened here? A ambulance come 'n took that old man from Ms. Nutt's place. The Sheriff is askin' everybody what happened ta 'im. He claims a bunch of kids attacked 'im 'n threw him in a beehive."

They all stood around looking at one another and snickering now and then while Billy explained what'd happened. Hearing what Little Jay had done to Gail, her brown eyes grew bigger with each detail.

"Oh! You bes' go 'n let the sheriff know then, 'cause all ya folks is in a tizzy 'n makin' a fuss. They told me to tell all of ya ta git home right now," exclaimed Bonnie Lou.

"Yeah, I reckon so. Our mommas is gonna be peeved over this 'n," said Billy with some of the others agreeing.

"Don't fret none, Dewey, 'cause we'll tell what he done. Sides, ain't nobody got no use for 'im anyway. My daddy always says ya don't carry nails in ya back pocket les ya wanta git stuck in yer butt," said Gabby.

"Ya bes' go on home now, Dewey," said Billy. Pattie looked at Dewey with her beautiful light brown eyes and shrugged when he looked down at her. She reluctantly lagged behind the others, because she didn't believe there was any good reason to let anything spoil their fun. With only slight trepidation they went as a group up the hill, all the while excitedly mulling over the facts and feeling mostly confident that they hadn't done anything wrong.

"Ship shape," Dewey said as he gave a salute and then started for home. Along the way, he took his time to looking at the sights. He didn't want the day to end. Because of the others, he felt good about himself. He still didn't really grasp the full extent of what'd happened, but according to his granddaddy he supposed nobody had a right to be hitting his friends.

While playing in a creek closest to his home, Dewey took notice of all the different bugs. The ones that fascinated him the most were the ones that floated and scooted on top of the water. He took off his boots and just let his feet soak in the coolness while he watched dragonflies dart all about him. When he spotted a shiny blackish brown rock at the bottom of the calm waters of the creek, he pulled it out of the water and examined it carefully. It was flat, pointed at one end, and looked kinda like a triangle. He didn't realize it was an old arrowhead and one of the few items made by Indians to be found in this part of the country that nature hadn't already reclaimed. He thought it was neat looking and decided to keep it, so he put it in his pocket. He sat around for a long time daydreaming and admiring all of nature's treasures.

He eventually pulled his boots on and set out for home using the orange strings once again as his guide. Just before Dewey came to the fields, he heard the brass bell ringing loudly. Since all he'd had all afternoon was some creek water to quench his thirst, he was very hungry. Looking forward to supper, he hurried across the field.

Al was standing alone by the bell, since Snipe had already run for cover, when he saw Dewey emerge from the tree line. He waited for Dewey while he digested what the Sheriff had just explained to him.

"Boy, the Sheriff come by a little while ago. He told me a story about a fella named Little Jay. Do ya know what happened ta 'im?" Dewey just stood and looked down at the ground.

"I hear ya come ta the rescue of a little girl 'n boy taday. I reckon ya listened ta me good when I told ya not ta ever tolerate someone hurtin' others. Ya bes' be careful with that thing though," as he pointed at the wooden sword hanging from Dewey's overalls. "That stick of wood wasn't made ta hurt nobody. It was made for playin' with."

Of course Dewey didn't fully understand that concept, seeing it was a sword. Until today, he had used it only to kill imaginary pirates. He felt it was his duty to defend what he though as his crew members.

"Yes Granddaddy, Dewey wanted ta help." Dewey was feeling uneasy as he was being admonished more by Al's tone than by his words of reproach. The good feelings about himself he'd felt all afternoon was dissipating under the sternness with which Al spoke to him. He worried his grandfather would take away his sword.

Dewey told Al everything as best he could recall and answered every question. Since it all seemed to match with what he'd already been told, Al was satisfied.

The Sheriff thoroughly investigated the whole matter with each of the witnesses at the trailer park, and was convinced it was time Little Jay spent a long time in jail again. If nothing else, the Sheriff knew Little Jay was good with a broom and mop, and he would be cleaning the jail for a very long time. According to the emergency room doctor, Little Jay would be fine, but needed to spend the night for observation. Once discharged from the hospital, Little Jay would go straight to jail for disorderly conduct and assault and battery on the children.

Al contemplated the matter and worried that maybe he should take Dewey's sword, but eventually decided he would let the boy keep it for the time being. He was sort of proud of him. "Don't git ya nose outa joint, Boy. I won't take ya sword away jus' yet. But, ya gotta promise me you'll be careful with it from now on." He decided that after supper he would dull the tip a little more on the belt sander just to be on the safe side. He was also glad to know that his talks with the boy didn't fall totally on deaf ears.

Seeing Dewey standing there crestfallen, Al placed a comforting hand on his grandson's shoulder. During his walk with Dewey to the house for supper, he said, "Well Dewey, sometimes when somebody acts like a mean junkyard dog ya have ta treat 'em that way. Accordin' the Sheriff, that fella ya went after is as worthless as tits on a boar hog."

That seemed to comfort Dewey some, even if he didn't understand all of what Al had just said. Al didn't want to discourage Dewey, just tone down his possible tendency to resort to violence as a way of dealing with situations he didn't quite comprehend. He just wanted to get through to Dewey how to respond appropriately when situations arose.

Later that night after Dewey finished getting ready for bed, he joined his grandfather in the den for his cookies and milk. Al was already seated in his chair, reading *The Farmer's Almanac* while he drank his last cup of coffee of the day. Once Dewey was settled and munching away at his nighttime snack, Al dropped the almanac on the nearby coffee table. He took his hands and interlocked his fingers before resting them on his stomach while he decided how to approach Dewey regarding the things he wanted to discuss tonight.

After he sat with his eyes closed for a while, he began to speak, "Dewey, do ya know the difference between a man 'n a so called grownup?"

No reply.

"Well, I'll try 'n explain it ta ya, then."

"The difference is, a man gits up every mornin' 'n goes ta work, doin' his level bes' ta make the world a better place for not only his family, but the world, by tryin' ta live up ta Godly standards. The key word is he *tries*."

He paused to give what he'd said a chance to soak in before continuing. "A sorry grownup is someone who gits up late 'n the day 'n don't really care about himself or anyone else, for that matter. Never mind work. They jus' live on the foolishness of others who will tolerate 'em, like givin' 'em money 'n such. That's what Welfare has become now-a-days. It use ta be for folks who really needed it on a temporary basis ta git themselves back on their feet. But, ya can bet there's always them who wanta handout soes as they don't have ta take responsibility for things they ought'a. They're jus self-centered, intolerable jackasses who float through life never really takin' hold of their actions. They never consider, or give a toot about the consequences of their foolish choices, like makin' babies 'n such for no other reason but ta git more free money from the government. The first words that usually come outa their mouth when somebody calls 'em on anything, is 'it ain't my fault', or they go on ta tell ya how wronged they've been done 'n now everybody owes 'em somethin'."

Finished with his cookies, Dewey continued to drink the glass of milk as he watched Snipe scratch his ear with his rear paw. Al glanced at Dewey and then Snipe to see what was so captivating. Then he let out a sigh. He'd learned to accept Dewey's limited attention span, but he was determined to get through to him, especially after today's event.

"Dewey."

"Yes, Granddaddy?"

"Ya show me a grownup that don't wanta work for his keep 'n goes around drinkin', stealin' 'n askin' for handouts, 'n I show ya somebody not worth havin' around or toleratin'. Try 'n become the bes' man ya can. Ya understand me, Boy?"

"Yes Granddaddy."

"The bible says in Proverbs, chapter 10, '*He who has a slack hand becomes poor, but the hand of the diligent makes rich*'."

"That fella ya caused ta git stung all over probably got what was coming ta 'im, but ya gotta be careful that ya don't git ya'self inta trouble. Ya gotta learn when ta use force, ya know, like hittin' someone, 'n when not to. I'm not exactly saying ya done wrong, but ya have ta be careful 'n not hurt folks anytime they do somethin' foolish. Chances are ya got lucky this time. But yer a big fellow, so be careful. Specially with that sword of yers. Don't let no one goad ya into doin' stuff that might git ya inta trouble. If somethin' inside ya says it's wrong, then don't do it. Think on that while ya put away them dishes 'n git ta bed. We have a lot 'a work ahead of us in the mornin'."

After Dewey left the room, Al remembered how the Sheriff described Little Jay. At the time he didn't quite put together what they called him and his last name, Nutt. It was only then that he realized he knew the man the Sheriff called Little Jay. He had gone to school with him and was five years older than Jay Nutt.

He knew him as Jay Winger Nutt. Back then the other kids, and sometimes the adults, called him Wing Nutt because he was so screwed up and he was wound so tight. He'd go crazy at the slightest provocation. Some of the other children use to play horse shoes or some other games with him just so they could tell him he'd lost. It didn't matter if he won or lost, just so long you told him he'd lost, that would send him into a frenzy. He'd run around screaming and shouting, throwing rocks at the school windows, or just plain run around the place acting all weird for a few minutes.

Back then, people thought the poor soul would end up dead in a fight before he ever reached adulthood. He remembered hearing that Jay joined the military, but was sent back home within the week. Al had seen a man the Sheriff described on and off over the years, but he didn't know that he was his fellow childhood classmate.

"Ain't that somethin'," Al muttered to himself as he turned out the light in the den.

The next day, Al found the arrowhead in Dewey's overall pocket. He couldn't bear to throw away Dewey's "little treasures." He was glad he found this rock arrowhead before he did the wash. Al thought *Lord knows what this woulda done to the washer*. He'd learned the hard way to check every one of Dewey's pockets before putting his clothes on the washing pile. Sometimes, Dewey's 'prizes' chipped off the enamel in the washing tub. This would cause the exposed metal underneath to rust if he didn't catch it in time and paint the chipped area. Too many times a shirt or something would show up with rust stains caused by such oversights. Al kept a small container of enamel paint right next to a can where he put all of Dewey's trinkets, once he found them.

Chapter 6 – Dewey Loses His Secret

"DON'T YA SQUIRT ME NOT ONE MORE TIME, TODD JACKSON! I ain't afraid ta miss school on account of hittin' ya with these books!" threatened Jill as she raised her school books in an ominous manner. Just as Todd raised his water pistol and took aim at her again, Gail, who was standing behind him, knocked him in the head really hard with her school books.

"Dang it Gail, what'd I do ta you? That hurt," demanded Todd once he turned to see it was Gail who'd hit him. Gail just shrugged.

While Todd was confronting Gail and rubbing his head, Jill quickly snatched the green plastic water pistol from his hand and threw it into the bushes on the other side of the road. When he turned back to Jill, he stopped short of saying anything because Gail hit him on the head once more.

"Damn it ta hell! Quit hittin' me," demanded Todd as he quickly moved out of the reach of the two girls. He was mad, but he knew he wasn't going to be able to do anything about it.

"What's the matter? You afraid of a couple of girls?" chided Jason as he followed Todd. No sooner had Jason made fun of Todd, than Jill and Gail rushed him as well and began to hit him with their books. This was followed by heckling and laughs from everyone watching how Jason had also became the victim of the two girls' playful scorn.

"Dang Todd, what'd ya do ta start that? Those two done went 'n gone crazy," complained Jason as he rubbed his shoulder where Gail had hit him.

"I didn't do nothin'. I don't know what made 'em start hittin' me like that," claimed Todd. "I guess we better leave 'em alone before they up 'n kill us though. Guess I'll have ta wait till we get home from school ta git my water gun. My daddy was right. All girls *are* crazy." Jason nodded in agreement with him as they rubbed their particular wounds and waited with the others for the bus to arrive.

Although it was Monday morning, the children of the Robins Nest Trailer Park embraced it without their usual dread because it was the last week of the school year. The only exceptions were Crystal, who was unusually quiet as she stood among the other girls, and Bane, who waited well away from the others. Bane's bruised and swollen lip didn't go unnoticed.

Once the bus arrived and they began to board, everyone but Crystal and Bain began shoving and rousting about with wild abandonment while piling into the school bus. With little success, the bus driver repeatedly shouted for everyone to settle down.

After they were down the road a mile or so, the bus driver pulled over on the side of the road and walked down the aisle to push and prod many of the rowdy offenders into their seats. Satisfied that she'd gotten everyone settled, she then proceeded to drive them to school.

As usual, Gabby was sharing a bus seat with Bonnie Lou. This had become their normal practice over the past two years. Suddenly their seat was rocked violently by a kick from behind.

After Gabby and Bonnie Lou recovered from the jolt, they heard a familiar mocking laugh that belonged to none other than Gabby's arch rival, Stephen Marrow. Gabby immediately jumped to his knees and turned to face the seat behind them. "What's the big idea, Booger-Breath? Ya momma make ya blow ya nose this mornin' causin' ya ta not have nothin' ta eat for breakfast?"

Stephen's smirky grin quickly disappeared and his brows sunk down as he squinted. "I don't do that no more!"

Gabby knew this was a sore subject with Stephen and the quickest way to humiliate him when the occasion called for it. This was used to get him to back down. When Stephen was younger, he had an uncontrollable propensity to pick his nose and eat it. No matter how much the others made fun of him, he'd continued to do it openly through the fourth grade. No one knew it, but the ultimate reason he stopped doing it in public, if not in private, is because his mother had taken a wooden spoon to his knuckles every time she caught him doing it during the summer before he began fifth grade. This was only after her brother publicly told her to keep her son, Stephen, away from his four year old son because Stephen was teaching his son disgusting nasty habits. When she protested, others in their family jumped in and said the same thing, humiliating her and her husband.

"Ya kick this seat again 'n yer gonna have some blood ketchup ta go with them boogers for lunch, ya hear!" Gabby snapped. In everyone's opinion, Stephen was one of the most obnoxious people ever to be born. He had a face that reminded people of a rat. His long slender hooked nose was far too large for his skinny face. He had dark eyes and large jutting ears which completed the picture. Even the teachers at school despised having him in their classroom. Every year, they'd go so far as to lobby for him not be placed into their class. He was only tolerated because of his family's political connections throughout the county, and especially at school.

With matters seemingly settled, Gabby twisted back into his seat while Bonnie Lou sat quietly like she always did in these situations. No sooner had Gabby and Bonnie Lou calmed down and rejoined the others in gleeful talk about the up coming summer break, when Stephen's head suddenly hovered close above them.

Acting as if she hadn't noticed, Bonnie Lou shyly said, "Don't worry about 'im, he's so little-a-nothin' that I'm surprised he don't just evaporate." This made the others listening and watching for Stephen's reaction snicker.

"Hey trailer trash, bet ya don't pass school this year," Stephen proclaimed for the benefit of everyone within earshot. Stephen knew that Gabby not only got furious when someone teased him and his friends about living in a trailer park, even though Gabby's family lived in a house, but he knew Gabby was having trouble in school. The teacher had on several occasions left her green grade book open on her desk. It was there for anyone to see one another's grades. Gabby wasn't really sure if he would pass this year after receiving so many bad grades on his previous report cards, so he just sat with arms folded and worried about the real possibility of failing.

Bonnie Lou knew that Stephen had struck a raw nerve with Gabby and whispered softly so no one else could hear, "I bet ya pass."

Stephen didn't get the response he was after, so he decided to push another button. "Hey, Bonnie Lou, why don't ya sit with somebody smart for once?"

Bonnie Lou continued to stare straight ahead as she replied, "You're so dumb that you'd smother ta death if ya closed ya mouth, cause yer too stupid ta know that ya nose is made for breathin', not jus' for pickin'."

This made Gabby smile and take his mind off his troubles, if only for a moment. Some of the other kids within earshot began to laugh and heckle Stephen. Stephen blushed as the others pointed and began making gestures of picking and eating their "boogers" while they relentlessly mocked him.

Humiliated, Stephen sat back in his seat. Because he didn't have any friends, he usually had the seat all to himself. After a few minutes he shouted, "Hey toothpick! Yer so skinny you'll always be itty-bitty and as flat as pancakes."

Bonnie Lou lowered her head in shame as tears of hurt filled the corners of her eyes. She tried not to let anyone see that Stephen's remark had hurt her. She, as well as everyone else, knew her mother had never really developed breast, and she always deeply feared that was probably her fate as well. Bonnie Lou had watched as the other girls her age began to blossom, so her fear was becoming all too real. Gabby sensed her feelings were hurt once she turned away from him to avoid what she thought was pity. He wasn't really sure why she was so self-conscious about her breasts, but this was one time he wasn't about to let Stephen get away with his hateful smart-aleck remarks.

Gabby jumped out of his seat and came around to confront Stephen. Stephen sat there looking smug; feeling satisfied that he'd achieved his goal of upsetting Gabby. Standing there for a moment in frustration at knowing the consequences, Gabby was torn between his choices. He glared at Stephen, believing Stephen would back down once he was so close to being hurt.

Undeterred, Stephen began to mock Gabby. "Yeah, yeah, gonna flunk, cause ya grew up in a trailer dump. Gotta honey with no money, flat as . . . ."

Overcome with rage, Gabby struck Stephen in the face with his fist as hard as he could before Stephen could finish his mocking chant. Stephen howled and slunk down in his seat, putting up his arms and hands to cover his face. Gabby tried in vain to pull away Stephen's protection so he could get another clear shot at his face. Stephen's skinny body balled up even tighter as he tried to protect himself from the onslaught of blows.

Gabby was about to finish the job when the bus driver slammed on the brakes. This sent him tumbling to the floor in the center aisle with a thump. Gabby quickly recovered and was attacking once more. The fat woman bus driver began shouting and stormed up the aisle towards him. Her wide hips brushed hard against each seat as she rushed to intercede. The other children chanted, "Fight! Fight! Fight! Fight! . . ." Gail and many others close by continued to egg Gabby on and to keep hitting Stephen. The flustered bus driver pulled Gabby away and marched him to the front of the bus before shoving him into a seat where the goody-goody children sat.

For the remainder of the trip Gabby was forced to sit up front, directly behind the bus driver, where he could be watched and kept under control. Meanwhile, Stephen kept his face buried in his knees, feeling humiliated as his nose and head throbbed with pain. Drops of blood dripped onto the front of his shirt while he used it to help hide his humiliation.

Upon arriving at the school, the driver gripped each of the offenders by the arm as they disembarked and practically dragged them to the principal's office. Once she deposited her charges into chairs in front of the main office, she shouted, "You'd better stay put! I don't wanta see ya so much as twitch a muscle!"

After charging into the Principal's office, with hands on hips, she angrily said, "Those two are at it again. Ya gotta do somethin' about it or go pick 'em up ya'self." Mr. Epps was familiar with the rivalry between the boys and sat patiently while the driver vented her frustrations and concerns.

Once the bus driver stormed out of the office and disappeared down the hall, Mr. Epps calmly guided the two offenders into his office and had them sit in front of his desk. He looked at his nephew and asked, "Now, Stephen, what's this all about?" He pulled out a folder from a file drawer with Gabby's name on it so he could make notes.

Gabby jumped up, trying to explain, "Stephen started it and was . . . !"

Mr. Epps snapped, "You'll have your turn, Norman Grizzle. Now sit down and keep your yap shut until I get to you!"

Gabby, red faced and frustrated, sat back down and crossed his arms as he glared with defiance at the Principal. He knew all too well what was going to happen.

"Uncle Ralph, he started it! I was jus' sittin', mindin' my own business 'n he up 'n hit me square in the face for no reason," squealed Stephen in a high pitched voice as tears started to stream down his face. He continued his story while occasionally lifting up the front of his shirt to wipe away blood from his nose that had stopped bleeding long before they'd arrived at school. He did this to dramatize and make a show of how badly he'd been hurt. Principal Epps could see that Stephen would most likely have black eyes soon enough.

"I'm fixin' ta do it again if ya say another thing about Bonnie Lou, Crybaby," protested Gabby as he came halfway out of his seat with his fist ready to deliver more blows.

Principal Epps felt he had the information he needed from his nephew. He then called for one of the office assistants listening in the outer office to take Stephen to the Nurse's Office to have his nose and eyes looked after.

Turning to Gabby, the principal said in a tone of controlled contempt, "Norman, perhaps you can go ahead and tell me your side of it now."

Gabby knew Stephen was once again going to get away with his lies like he always did, but he was going to have his say on the matter. "Well, he kicked our seat 'n started makin' fun of Bonnie Lou on account of her being in the seat with me. He made fun of her 'n called her itty-bitty." It never occurred to Gabby to tell what Stephen had said about him.

Mr. Epps looked at him and "made a show" of trying to figure out why that would have caused a fight, knowing all too well what was meant by the remark. "Norman, kids make fun of each other all the time about their weight, hair, and other things. That's no excuse to go around punching them in the face. You could have hurt him very badly."

"No one has a right ta call a girl itty-bitty 'n hurt their feelin's! I don't care if he is yer kin!" he exclaimed as he jutted out his chin defiantly. Gabby knew anything he said was futile, but he was going to try and have his say anyway.

"You'd better git your mind right this instant, Young Man. Your attitude is beyond me. And wipe that scowl off your face." To accentuate his meaning, Principal Epps slammed both hands on the desk top and shouted, "**NOW!**"

Mr. Epps waited for Gabby to settle down and show some respect, but it never came. He wanted Gabby to understand that what he did was improper and would not be condoned, but he wasn't making any headway at backing down Gabby. Finally, he decided corporal punishment was the only way to settle this, which was generally his conclusion, as well as expelling them for three days, where boys were concerned. He knew it was too late in the school year to expel Gabby, so he decided to dole out double the only punishment at his disposal.

"You've earned ten licks with the paddle, Young Man. Now get over here and put your hands on the desk!" That got a quick look of surprise from Gabby, expecting only the usual five.

Gabby slowly complied, facing the desk. Gabby, all too familiar with getting into position for the normal five licks, placed his hands on the desk and jutted out his buttocks. He stood perfectly still and didn't make a sound as the wooden paddle landed loudly with searing heat for ten tormenting strikes.

Everyone in the front office and hallway heard the paddle land with loud audible pops as they stood silently looking at one another. Most whispered how sorry they felt for poor Gabby, while others made their own painful faces from first-hand knowledge of how it felt. Because the door was open, they watched and listened as Principal Epps demanded, "Do you think you can conduct yourself like a civilized young man now?" No reply. While raising the paddle as if to strike again, he angrily asked, "WELL, have you learned your lesson yet?!"

Unflinching, Gabby stayed right where he was, holding his position, and shouted, "**I reckon not, cause ya missed a spot right here!**" while he took one of his hands off the desk and pointed to his left buttock cheek. Three more pops ensued, much louder than before, with the last strike making a crackling sound. They could clearly be heard in the hallway over the snickering, nudging, and flat-out laughing by some grownups and students alike.

The office staff that had initially grinned at the comeback began to exchange looks of dismay as they heard the loud sounds of the last strikes. They knew all too well that the paddle was a very thick piece of wood and could seriously harm Gabby.

"GET OUT! And no more fighting! You hear me, Young Man?!"

Gabby rushed out of the office with a red face full of fight while tears of anger and pain streamed down his face. Suddenly he spun around and kicked the principal's door, which caused it to finish swinging all the way open and bounce back to shut with a loud bang. Everyone stopped laughing and snickering as Gabby stormed passed them. They knew Gabby was one person without fear and it wasn't over yet. By the first recess everyone knew all too well about what'd happened.

To the amazement of everyone, the principal didn't come out and follow Gabby to pursue the matter of Gabby's open defiance.

Mr. Epps didn't come out of his office for a very long time. After a while, the secretary reluctantly went in to give him some paperwork on tardy and sick call-out students. She was taken aback when she discovered him sitting at his desk with a broken paddle, one piece in each hand. His feet were on the desk and he was recovering from what must have been a good laugh. He looked at her with a smile, "I would've killed to have had a platoon of young men just like him in the unit I commanded during the Korean War." He couldn't wait to tell the boys at the VFW what'd happened. He figured it was as good a war story as any.

Gabby disappeared the rest of the day and no one knew where he'd disappeared to. After school when the gang was getting off the bus, they saw him emerging from the woods. They were all laughing as they gathered around him.

With a questioning look, Gabby asked, "What's so funny?" That led to even more laugher as they looked from Gabby to Bonnie Lou and back again.

Finally Jason and Todd, almost in unison, said, "Bonnie Lou slapped Stephen in the nose before she got off the bus." Then they burst out in uncontrollable laughter.

Bonnie Lou, who was the only one not laughing, looked down in embarrassment at all the attention she was receiving. Gabby looked at her with surprise and admiration as the others talked about how they'd heard about the beating he'd taken, the door incident, and how Bonnie Lou slapped Stephen. They all agreed Stephen had it coming since he was bragging how he would have beat Gabby's butt if he had been on the bus ride home.

Gabby grinned as he quoted something his father said sometimes. "A fool's lips enter into contention, and his mouth calls for blows. My Momma says that's from the Bible. She showed it ta me once."

Everyone was curious where Gabby had been all day, since he wasn't anywhere to be found at school. Acting as if nothing had happened, he said, "Aww, I was jus' hangin' around the woods celebrating Christmas." This was received with strange looks from the gang. They quickly dismissed it as they always did when he said strange things.

On the bus ride to school the next day, and for the remainder of the week, Stephen was especially subdued and didn't make fun of Gabby, or anyone else for that matter. The children figured his parents had gotten after him and that was the end of it. Gabby, as well as the others, just left well enough alone and didn't give Stephen the time of day.

Bane continued to keep an especially low profile in school all week as well and didn't stay long the few times he did show up at the hut village after school. Unbeknownst to the others, it was because he was still apprehensive about what Crystal had seen, or what she might say or do. He gave a wide berth to her and the other girls in the group. Of course they all rode the same bus to and from school, so he would just look straight ahead and scoot past them to avoid seeing the ridicule he was sure would eventually come.

The last day of school finally arrived and everyone was full of excitement. It didn't go unnoticed by the others that Bane and Crystal had kept their distance from one another all week. It didn't matter how persistent the other girls became, they couldn't pry anything out of Crystal as to why she was suddenly so quiet where Bane was concerned.

Still aching from his brother's pounding over the weekend, Bane didn't even roughhouse with the boys and bully the other students during this last week of school. Everyone just presumed he was in one of his moods and was keeping to himself. They all knew, through word of mouth, about the beating his brother had given him and they could see some of the nasty bruises as they transformed from dark blue to yellowish as they healed over time. They still hadn't heard if he passed the sixth grade yet and no one was brave or stupid enough to ask. Only Crystal knew why Bane was really keeping to himself, but was too ashamed and embarrassed to say anything.

Friday afternoon, to everyone's relief and amazement, they'd finally gotten the news that everyone had graduated from their respective grades. The group was elated and relieved by the wonderful news. Combining this with the jubilance over the start of summer break, everyone seemed to be full of joy and excitement as they gathered at the hut village to congratulate one another. Even Crystal's and Bane's spirits were up and everyone was glad to see the two had come out of their doldrums.

Even though Bane was still leery of Crystal and shied away from her, now that his confidence had been restored by passing the sixth grade, he became his normally obnoxious self towards the others.

Dewey hadn't been seen all week at the hut village because Al knew that the other children were in school that week and had kept him home.

The weekend began with a refreshing rain shower just as the sun came up. Within hours the air was heavy with humidity from the vapors caused by the sun's rays upon the warm wet earth. Trailers became smoldering hot houses by ten o'clock in the morning. For the residents who could afford one, air conditioners hummed to life and mixed with the sounds of trailers whose window box fans where at full speed in an attempt to cool their occupants. Clear blue skies with small puffy clouds guaranteed a Saturday afternoon of beautiful weather for the children of the Robins Nest Trailer Park to play in. Winged insects enthusiastically greeted the warm humid temperatures as they buzzed about in search of a place upon which to light.

By mid-morning, the gang began arriving one-by-one at the hut village as their parents had released them from their morning chores so they could go play. Everyone had only one thing on their mind, having made it through yet another grade, have fun.

Some admitted passing onto the next grade was done only by the seat of their pants. Only Crystal, Jill, and Bonnie Lou modestly bragged about how easy it was to make good grades and pass without worry, while Billy, Pattie and Gail admitted they did well, but had to work hard for the grades they'd received. Bane, Gabby, Jason and Todd complained about how difficult school was as they compared their bad grades with one another, all the while jockeying for bragging rights as to who had fared the best in what subjects.

Together they all basked in the glory of their accomplishments, rarely straying from the swings and the base of the old oak tree in the center of their little hut village as they regaled one another with stories of their past experiences in school.

Bane gave Gabby a friendly punch in the shoulder and said, "Tell 'em how ya caused that retard teacher ta git sick. That was the funniest thing I ever seen."

Gabby searched the others' expressions to see if they really wanted to hear it once again. Seeing their expressions of interest, he sat back against the oak tree's trunk and looked off into the distance. Only Crystal and Pattie hadn't heard it before because they were the newcomers to the group. "Well, one day our regular teacher had to leave at lunchtime. Mind ya, this happened a couple of years ago. Anyway, that's when Ms. Rospigliosy was sent in ta watch over us for the rest of the day. She had ta bring her class with her though."

"Retards ya mean," interjected Bane.

"Yeah," agreed Gabby. "Anyway, one of 'em sittin' near me pooped in his pants. Man it smelled something awful. So anyway, she takes 'im to the bathroom. When she gits back this girl sittin' in front of me named Cathy raised her hand ta ask permission ta go to the bathroom. Guess she didn't feel so good after that slow kid had done it on hisself." Snickers erupted. "Anyway, I didn't like 'er cause she was mean ta Bonnie Lou. 'Sides, she made fun of me for makin' bad grades. I know 'er momma is mean, so I reckon that's what caused 'er ta be the way she was."

"Well, anyway she raised 'er hand 'n asked to be excused as soon as the teacher got back with that other kid, I made a little . . . ." Gabby put his hand to his lips and made a fart sound. "The teacher thought it was her 'n told 'er ta go on ahead. Well, after Ms. Snooty left the room, me 'n some others started pointin' 'n sayin' 'gross' 'n stuff like that. That's when Ms. Rospigliosy come over 'n see what we was pointin' at. She could see there was a few pieces of somethin' dark 'n moist layin' on good ole Cathy Williams' seat. I guess the teacher was use ta that sort of thing 'cause she told us ta stop actin' so silly. When she went ta get some tissues off her desk and was comin' back ta clean 'em up . . . ."

"She heard me dare 'em ta eat one of 'em," Bane proclaimed to the disgust of Crystal and Pattie. The others jeered and poked at Gabby.

"Anyway, I reached over my desk 'n popped one of them things on her seat right in my mouth 'n chewed it up with my mouth wide open soses everyone could see. Well, at first Ms. Rospigliosy thought we was jus' tryin' ta be funny till she got up the other two little pieces off the seat and smelled 'em. That's when she knew those *were* real. Well, then 'n there she started screamin' 'n turned funny lookin' jus' before she vomited over 'n over all on that girl's desk."

The others in the group started jeering while saying "gross", "disgusting" and other things as Gabby smiled big looking at Crystal's and Pattie's shocked expressions. "She couldn't git outa there fast enough after that 'n 'bout knocked Ms. Snooty down goin' out the door."

"When Ms. Snooty saw what happened ta 'er desk, she put 'er hand over 'er mouth and ran outa the room quick. That's when some of the others started ta vomit'. 'Fore ya knew it, more'n half of the dang room was filled with folks either sick or about ta be sick."

"Yeah, even Henry Jacobs lost it," injected Bane as he laughed triumphantly. Henry Jacobs was one of Bane's friends. When the mood struck him, out of cruelty, Bane would mock and make fun of Henry by bringing it up.

Crystal grabbed Gabby by the arm and yanked him hard. "Why on earth would ya eat somebody else's poop? That's disgusting even for you." By this time Pattie was looking confused as the others tried to suppress their snickers.

Gabby acted as if nothing was wrong as he smiled innocently and gently pulled his arm free of her grip before he continued. "I'm gittin' ta that. Calm down. It wasn't that girl's poop, geesh. It was that retarded kids poop. I'd took a piece of paper 'n scooped up a couple of little turds that rolled out of his pants and put it there is all. It ain't like it was hers."

"That's jus' as bad, Norman Grizzle! You ought'a be ashamed of ya'self!" shouted Crystal. The others watched Crystal's reaction with amusement.

"Can I finish the story?" asked Gabby as he raised his hands in submission while the others were completely enraptured with Crystal's reaction.

"Go ahead." Crystal said as she jumped up and crossed her arms.

"At any rate, that was the first time I was called to the principal's office. That Principal Epps looked at me like I was some kind of a nut case. He called my momma and daddy 'n told 'em what I'd done. When my daddy got to the school he was so mad he picked me up by my belt with one hand and carried me to the truck. He didn't say a word to me till we got home. Before we left the school though, my daddy told that principal he was an idiot for believin' I ate somebody else's crap."

"When I come through the door my momma grabbed me 'n started actin' like I'd los' my mind. So daddy hollered at 'er ta shut up 'er yappin' 'n threw a bag of chocolate caramels on the table. You ought'a heard her take on after she finally figured out what I'd done 'n remembered givin' me some for desert that day with my lunch."

Crystal looked at Gabby funny as she cocked her head to one side. Realizing she'd been fooled, she put her hands on her hips and huffed, "That wasn't funny."

"Guess ya had ta be there," was Gabby's reply as he leaned to one side and passed gas. The others in the group slapped at him as they roared with laughter at his antics. Even Crystal popped Gabby on top of the head while he was busy laughing at himself for being able to deliver such a well timed fart.

After lunch Dewey came strolling into the hut village. His arrival was announced by Libby's loud barks. Once she got within smelling distance of Dewey, Libby stopped and began wagging her tail as she coaxed a flurry of petting from him. Today he produced a treat he'd gotten out of Snipes box of dog biscuits. From then on Libby would come to expect a treat every time he arrived. This brought a few seconds of sheer bliss as she devoured the crunchy delicacy.

Gabby, always friendly, excitedly greeted Dewey. "Hey, Dewey! How ya doin'?"

"Ship shape," Dewey replied.

Before being allowed to go play at the hut village, Dewey had to sweep out the chicken coop and do other simple chores Al could find for him. Al was set on getting at least a half day's work out of Dewey before setting him loose to play. Since Al was getting "long in the tooth" as he put it, he was determined to teach Dewey something about the benefits of work and life before it was too late.

"What's that on Libby?" Dewey asked, while quizzically inspecting Libby's ears.

"What ya talkin' about?" asked Gabby as he leaned over to see what Dewey was touching around Libby's ears. "Oh, them are ticks, I reckon. Look at the size of 'em!"

Dewey just stared at the brown, bloated-looking blobs a bit closer before he asked, "Why they on Libby?"

"Oh, their suckin' 'er blood. That's how they feed themselves. Guess we'll have ta do somethin' about those, won't we, Girl?" Gabby said, and he scratched Libby's ears. "Hold 'er while I heat up a stick with my handy dandy lighter."

With that, he pulled out a lighter and lit one end of a small stick. Once the fire was burning good, he blew out the flame. He then placed the hot tip on the backside of the tick until it began to move its tiny legs and unbury its head. With the release of the tick's grip from Libby's skin, he pulled it off, dropped it on the ground, and smashed it with the other end of the stick. A group of onlookers gathered around to watch while he repeated this action over and over until all the ticks were gone. This took some time, and attracted quite a crowd of captivated onlookers.

Jill Jackson was especially captivated. She repeatedly had to adjust her headband until she was finally able to get all of her hair to stay put as she watched with fascination. "Why'd those ticks grow on Libby?" she asked. This was the first year Jill was old enough to hang out with the gang. She felt at home with Pattie and Bonnie Lou, who were only a little older than her.

"They don't grow on 'er exactly. They jus' crawl up her legs till they git ta 'er ears 'n start sucking blood till they're full. You know the ole sayin' 'full as a tick'. That's where it comes from. Then they jus' fall off 'er 'n start makin' lots of babies that'll do the same thing. That's jus' what they do is all," replied Gabby.

Bane, although still keeping to himself some of the time, still participated in most activities, but without his usual ordering and bullying. The others were grateful his mood had changed for the better, hoping it would stay that way. Still apprehensive, they kept their opinions amongst themselves and went along with Bane to appease him. They noticed he was still especially quiet around the girls and avoided Crystal most of all.

Todd Jackson came back from relieving himself in the bushes and said, "Hey, I jus' found a giant ant bed." He pointed to where he had just come from.

"What kinda ants are they?" asked Jason.

"Don't know what they were before, but now they're piss ants." Everyone started heckling and telling him what a bad joke that was. "You gotta see 'em. They're as big as those giant black ones that live in that big old hollowed-out oak tree we're always goofin' around with. They're reddish brown 'n mean as hell. One of 'em even bit me." He turned and motioned persistently for them to follow as he headed back to where he'd just come from. Everybody eagerly followed.

Once they arrived at the spot, he pointed to a large mound and everyone could see that they weren't the biggest red ants they had ever seen. It was obvious where Todd had peed because the smooth mound had a wet carved out spot where the ants were concentrated and trying to repair the breech to their nest. They weren't as big as the black ants, but their nest was almost as big as a washbasin turned upside down. A couple of the boys took sticks and poked at the mound. When they did, the ants took off in all directions while some climbed on the sticks and bowed their backs as they attempted to sting and bite it. "Ouch!" shouted Jason once one got pass the stick and bit him on the hand.

"I ain't afraid of 'em," claimed Bane. He reached down and let some climb on his hand and arm until the stinging got the best of him.

"Ouch! You damn Piss Ants!" He slung his arm wildly around while he used his other hand to finish knocking them off. He stomped a few just to show them who was boss. He looked at the others with a satisfied grin, "I bet ya a quarter none of the rest of ya could do that."

"I'll do better 'n that. Show me the money," piped Gabby. Bane pulled out a quarter and showed it to him. A quarter was about the normal allowance for most of them. "Alright, give it to Billy ta keep then."

"What's the matter? Don't ya trust me?"

Gabby, as well as everyone else, knew Bane couldn't be trusted, but he knew better than to come out and say it plainly to his face, so he just stood quietly waiting with his arms crossed.

"Fine then!" Bane handed Billy the quarter with indignation. With a sneer, he said, "Who's goin' ta decide if ya beat me, Twerp?" Everyone agreed Billy was the one to decide.

Bane turned to Gabby, "Well, let's see what ya got."

"Good 'nough." Gabby, who like several others wasn't wearing shoes, stood right in the middle of the ants and let them crawl onto his dirty feet, up his legs, and bite him as they went. He stood almost in a trance-like state while they swarmed and bit him. Suddenly his eyes became wide and he said, "Good 'nough?" Everybody quickly agreed he had won.

Suddenly, as fast as he could, Gabby took off running for the creek while he yelled. On his way, he pulled off his shirt and jumped into a large pool of water. Once in, he took off his shorts and underwear, tossing them onto the bank of the creek.

Gabby had jumped into a pond that beavers had created when they dammed up the creek. The beavers, having long since gone, left the small pond as a reminder of their incredible engineering abilities. Of course, it wasn't as big as it once was, but it was still big and deep enough for the gang to enjoy on hot summer days.

The gang ran after Gabby laughing, while others were 'oohing and aahing'. After a minute or so Billy said "You're nuts, Gabby. How long ya goin' stay in there?"

"Long as it takes for 'em ta stop bitin' my butt. And that's not all they're bitin' neither!" All the girls started giggling while the boys groaned with puckered lips while holding their hands over their private parts.

Because it was late in the afternoon and he figured the cool clear water looked inviting, Billy turned to the group and asked, "Anybody else up for a skinny dip?" He started shedding his shirt and most of the other boys quickly followed suit. As the boys got naked and started for the large pool of water, Gail, Pattie, and Jill giggled as they followed suit. Confused by what he was witnessing, Dewey stood silently watching as Todd began to coax him into doing the same by saying, "Ah, Dewey, it ain't nothin' but swimmin' without clothes is all."

"Don't ya know how ta swim?" No answer.

"It don't matter, the water ain't really deep enough ta swim in any ole way," replied Billy. Their swimming hole was only four feet deep towards the center, but near the five foot water fall that fed the pool, the water was six feet deep.

Jason waved at Dewey and shouted, "Come on Dewey, it ain't deep. Sides it feels good." Dewey took a moment and decided it looked fun and he was hot anyway. He shed his clothes and soon joined the others in the water. He wanted to be one of the gang and not feel left out. He was slow to get in the water because it felt cold, but soon realized the feeling of cold gave way to a sense of pleasure that only water can give on a hot summer afternoon.

Crystal and Bonnie Lou, being the only ones still to join in, stood on the bank of the creek with apprehension as they looked to one another in excited embarrassment as everyone else urged them to "come on in 'n join the fun!"

After consulting with Bonnie Lou, Crystal called out, "We'll join ya if y'all look the other way." Everybody but the girls turned their backs to Crystal and Bonnie Lou.

With trembling hands from the excitement of doing something that felt exhilaratingly naughty, Crystal pulled off her top, revealing her already well developing breasts. She immediately grabbed the shirt off the ground where it had fallen and covered herself by putting the ends of the shirt under both armpits like a bra. With her hands free, she took off her shorts, leaving on her panties.

Bonnie Lou was younger than Crystal and was just starting to bud. She found herself even more self-conscious than she'd been the previous year, so she mimicked Crystal's actions. The two turned away from the group, dropped their tops on the ground and covered their breasts with their hands.

When Crystal began entering the pool, she glanced around at everyone. Bonnie Lou just looked down as she slipped into the water up to her neck. Crystal realized that Bane had turned to watch. He was looking at her with rapt attention and hunger in his eyes, so she quickened her entry and veered towards the side where the girls were now beginning to gather into a group. For a long time, Crystal, Pattie, Jill, Bonnie Lou, and Gail huddled together at one end of the pond, whispering and giggling amongst themselves. Out of modesty, most of the girls had lowered their bodies until the water covered them up to their shoulders.

Skinny dipping happened in one way or another every year in this same spot and usually soon after school let out for the summer. Most of the gang were veterans of skinny dipping, yet it always seemed awkward as to how it started for the first time each year. After a while, everyone started loosening up and splashing each other. With inhibitions relaxing, they all began to enjoy the cool water and relief from the sweltering heat. Bonnie Lou, being shy, still stayed towards the edge of the group allowing only one boy, Gabby, to come close.

Gabby went over to where Jason was and asked, "Hey, Jason, does the water seem like it's gittin' warmer ta ya? It sure feels that way ta me."

"Yeah, it does. Wonder what's causin' it."

"Mus' be cause I'm peein' on ya, Dummy." Gabby laughed when Jason gave him a quick jab to the chest and swam away quickly. Everyone else jeered and laughed at his antics and cajoled him for being so gross.

Not to be outdone, Todd said, "Watch this." He came out of the water to just below his waist and turned his back to the others as he shouted, "Butt bubbles!" Different size noisy bubbles came spewing out of the water at the surface just as he jutted his buttocks towards everyone. Most began howling with laughter, while others berated him for farting. Jill was the closest, so she kicked him as she lunged backwards in the water to get away. Todd went head first into the water and landed against the bank from the kick. Everyone laughed with delight at the justice of it.

The water was usually crystal clear, but the movement of the children's feet caused clouds of sediment to rise up from the bottom and make the water temporarily cloudy, only to be swept away slowly by the lazy, almost undetectable current. It was common enough and acceptable to dive under the water to satisfy any curiosities, so long as no comments were made and no inappropriate touching occurred. Some of the boys did just that. Not to be outdone, Gail, Jill, and Pattie took a few peeks and giggled amongst themselves after whispering and comparing notes among one another.

Dewey was between Bane and Crystal in the pool, which was intentional on Crystal's part as often as possible. Bane went underwater for another of many looks, only to see Dewey while once more trying to get a good look at Crystal. When he came up, he loudly pronounced, "Dewey ain't got no balls!" He repeated it to make sure everyone in the group heard him. They all stopped and turned their attention to Bane.

"They're probably jus' hidin' from the cold water, like the rest of us," laughed Billy.

"Yeah, it's so cold in here I think mine are up inside my stomach," shouted Todd.

"Mine got ate off by the ants," proclaimed Gabby.

"No, they're really missin'. I figured he'd have a set like a bull as big as he is, but he ain't got none at all," replied Bane. "Where's yer nuts Dewey?"

Dewey got a confused look on his face and shrugged.

It took some doing, but finally the boys were able to get Dewey to understand what they were talking about. He looked at the other boys' parts and then at himself and knew he was different. He then told them, "The doctor said I don't need 'em, 'cause they was hurtin' me real bad, so he took 'em off."

After the shock of their discovery and Dewey's explanation, the magic of the moment dissipated, so everyone decided it was time to call it a day on the swimming. They all got dressed and whispered among themselves over the revelation of Dewey's deformity.

Bane's callousness and drive to heckle someone for mean sport had overcome his fascination with Crystal, so of course he couldn't let it rest and started making up nicknames for Dewey that referred to his lack of testicles. "Hey, Nut-Less!" "What's up, Dewey No-Balls?"

The others tried to get him to let up, but Bane just kept on inventing names. Finally, Crystal stood between Bane and Dewey and gave Bane a glare that turned him ice cold. He knew she could blab about what she'd seen and probably would if he didn't stop, so he ceased his cruel teasing of Dewey, for the time being.

For the rest of the day, Dewey helped work on the huts and collected old pieces of wood from the forest. Billy explained to him how they held a bonfire to celebrate the end of the school year every summer. "Now, Dewey, tamorrow we're goin' ta have a cookout, so ya need ta git ya folks ta let ya have somethin' you can cook on a stick, like hotdogs or somethin'. Do ya know what I'm talkin' about?" Dewey understood, because sometimes at the institution they held special cookout days for all the families to come and participate.

A distant bell rang out from the direction of Al's farm. Dewey perked up and said, "I'll bring somethin' tamorrow, promise." Off he went at a fast steady pace towards home.

The gang gathered around the swings before heading for home. Bane asked, "Gabby, why didn't ya kick that Stephen's butt for causin' ya ta take such a dang lickin'? I'd put a bad hurtin' on 'im for that. I guarantee he'd had more 'n a black eye 'n busted nose if he'd got me beat that bad."

Gabby took Bonnie Lou's hand and motioned for the others to follow, "Follow me 'n I'll show ya how come." He led them down a path that went deeper into the woods. After walking for a short while, Gabby abruptly stopped. The shadows of the trees and the overhead foliage made the area dim. He looked at Bonnie Lou and said, "That's what happens ta anyone who makes fun of ya."

Bonnie Lou, as well as everyone else, looked at Gabby in confusion. Gabby just stood there grinning as he looked upon their baffled expressions. "What ya talkin' about Gabby?" asked Pattie. The others looked to Gabby for an answer, only to see him smiling as if he was the cat that swallowed the canary.

When Gabby was satisfied that everyone had become completely engrossed and the moment felt right, he slowly pointed his finger upwards.

They all stared up in amazement at all of the stuff they saw hanging in the tree limbs above them. There was a bike in different pieces, clothes, toys and all manner of stuff that looked like it belonged to a young teenage boy. Some things were hung over limbs, while others were secured with string or rope. It seemed like they were looking at a Christmas tree from the bottom. The large massive oak tree seemed magical to everyone, as it held the various items.

"Whew! All this stuff belong to who I think it does?" asked Billy in amazement.

"Damn!" was all Bane could say as he took in the wonder of it all.

"Yep, it's all his stuff. Didn't ya notice him wearin' new clothes durin' the last week?" With that, Bonne Lou's arms flew around Gabby's neck, almost choking him in a fit of joyous unbridled excitement.

Chapter 7 – Dewey Learns to Tie Knots

THE GANG, most of which had just came back from church with their families, began gathering at the hut village to celebrate the end of the school year. Nearly everyone had their arms filled with food, drink, and the occasional flyswatter for winged party-poopers. With each new arrival for the celebration, the crowd grew louder and more excited. Although the earlier rain showers had worried some that there might not be a celebration, the mood was lifted to that of joy as the sun now beamed brightly upon the grateful crowd.

The sun was occasionally hidden by small puffy clouds that drifted by in the now blue sky. Their passing above was made known by the shadows they produced upon the ground. This visual break between the sun's rays and shadows gave one the occasional chance to run and chase the darkened spots as they glided along the earth. They would occasionally travel briskly down the center lane of the trailer park. Due to the wind speed aloft, only the fastest runners who attempted this feat could keep pace with the shadows.

In the Deep South during warm weather, and especially after a fleeting downpour, hordes of flies and mosquitoes become especially aggressive in their pursuit of flesh upon which to feast. Traveling through these southern roads, one would find people sitting on porches or under shade trees seeking comfort from the hot sun. The price to be paid for this comfort is facing determined insects whose only goal is to make life miserable. Usually the folks had their trusty swatters in hand. If the swatters aren't visibly in their hands, you can bet there was one close by for quick retrieval. Of course the only truly acceptable replacement for flyswatters in one's free hand is a fan to give relief from gnats and lack of a cool breeze. The hand fans usually displayed one's church association printed upon it, as well as touting scriptures of wisdom or praise.

The rain may have dampened the firewood, but not the enthusiasm of all in attendance. Many of the parents came with small children in tow or a reluctant spouse. Pattie's mother was easy to spot, as she was the only one toting a baby.

Someone started the fire with butane from a tin can they used for refilling their cigarette lighter. The fire quickly roared to life with the help of some old newspapers. Everyone agreed it was a good thing that the nearby trees were damp from the previous rain because the flames shot up high enough to nearly touch the lower limbs.

Dewey came along shortly thereafter and met up with Gabby, who was hanging out down by the creek. He carried a bag filled with his favorite root beer sodas, a pack of hot dogs with buns, and a large bag of potato chips. Al had made sure that Dewey had enough to share.

When Dewey got home last night, he told Al all about the celebration plans for tamorrow, so Al made a special trip to the store right after supper. He didn't want Dewey to feel left out during the festivities.

Upon his and Gabby's arrival at the hut village, Dewey felt overwhelmed from seeing so many people there that he didn't know. As soon as Libby spotted Dewey, she ran to him for her usual petting and dog treat and then excitedly scurried away. The gang was surrounded by adults and younger children alike. It reminded him of his days at the institution on Family Day.

Gabby and the others introduced Dewey around to their respective families. Because the adults made it a point to recall all the good things they'd heard about him, Dewey soon became more relaxed. Most were taken aback by his large size initially, but their shock over his size soon gave way to their fascination at his childlike innocence.

After Billy and Gail introduced Dewey to their father, Mr. Davis said, "Boy, I shor do appreciate what ya done for my sweet Gail 'n 'er brother. Yer welcome anytime 'round here."

Crystal's mother, as predicted, declined to attend. Crystal's step-father, Jimmy John White, JJ to everyone, gladly accompanied her to the celebration. Her mother, as usual, offered a vague reason for not wanting to go be with the others. Crystal and JJ had reluctantly become accustomed to Jenny's unexplained melancholy since moving to Heard County. Her mother's behavior of shying away from the other residents in the trailer park had caused many to accuse her of being uppity. They went so far as to make it a point to avoid even having to be cordial towards her. JJ on the other hand, was liked and admired for his personality and willingness to help others, especially with their car troubles. It was because of Crystal and JJ that most overlooked Jenny's ridiculous claim of just being shy.

Bane showed up with his older brother, Ricky, just as the festivities were in full swing. Although they hadn't brought anything, together they swaggered in and among the throng of people expecting to be offered food and drink. They'd just come from the BBQ House where they'd eaten lunch with their father. They made it understood that as a matter of good manners, they would gladly accept and help the others eat *their* food. The pickings were easy, so the Taggarts, believing shyness was a sin, boldly helped themselves to the abundance of readily available food.

Gabby's father, John Grizzle, was much older than everyone else's parents and had even gone to school with Pattie's and Jason's grandparents. He was stout and built much like a football linebacker. He had a broad chest with arms as big around as most peoples' legs. When he pumped Dewey's hand, he shook Dewey all the way down to the bones.

"Dewey, I shor am glad ta meet ya, Boy. I reckon Little Jay forgot he ain't nothin' but a little tadpole; all mouth with a scrawny little tail." John let out a thunderous laugh at his own wit as Dewey looked on in bewilderment. Others close by heard what was said and joined in agreement.

This made Dewey feel a little uneasy until Gabby patted him on the back and said, "Yeah, Dewey shor showed 'im. Didn't ya, Dewey?"

John was always friendly and quick with a smile, as long as he didn't feel somebody was after his money. Everyone knew he was the biggest penny pincher in the county. The joke around the county was that John "was as tight as the bark on a tree when it came ta money." Folks would tell how he was so busy trying to make money that he just plain forgot to find a wife and have children until he was old and fell off a truck.

The story of how he came to finally getting married and having Gabby, was one day while trying to unload a large cabinet off a truck by himself, he hurt his back when it fell on him. He was so cheap he refused to stay in the hospital after the accident. Rumor has it he married the nurse who took care of him at his home so he wouldn't have to pay her. Even John admitted one day while he was being kidded, that he never holds money with both hands anymore because every time he did, he'd either tear the bill in half or bend the coins.

Once the flames receded and the wood pile glowed red hot, people gathered around the bonfire holding long sticks with small steaks, hot dogs, or sausages hanging off the ends. While they stood over the fire cooking their meats, they went on and on about this and that as they constantly shifted around the fire whenever the wind changed directions and smoke blew in their faces. They bragged about how well the hut village was looking and how nothing ever seemed to change much from one year to the other.

Jason's father, Eddie, was prone to be a cutup and a prankster. He was on the other side of the pit holding his hot dogs over the embers when he spoke loud enough that everyone could hear. "Hey, John, ya wife's new car shor looks mighty good."

Everyone quickly glanced at Eddie and then to John for his reaction. Some snickered for a moment and went back to staring straight ahead to avoid looking directly at John because they knew this was a sore subject with him. Everybody knew that John's wife had come home one day from working at the hospital driving a new Ford LTD. This infuriated John and sent him into a rage. They also knew he didn't speak to his wife for almost a full month afterwards. Berta, Gabby's mother, had told everybody she was tired of going to work in a piece of junk that broke down all the time and didn't have air conditioning.

John's face immediately turned red as a beet. Seeing that everyone was having fun at his expense, he thundered back, "I'm glad y'all like it so much! You'll be payin' for it when I raise the rent at the end of the year!" This was met with weary faces and low groans.

Berta, who was standing beside John, gave him a warning stare and proclaimed, "John Grizzle, I paid cash for that car with my own money 'n ya bes' not put nothin' on me ya old cheapskate, or I'll leave ya for sure 'n take half of everything ya got. 'N don't ya take on false hopes neither, 'cause I know how ta find most of that money the government don't know about. Ya bes' die before ya git old 'n feeble or ya jus' might see me buy a lot more nice things." John turned and looked at her with a scowl on his face, then snarled before he walked away with his hot dogs not fully cooked.

This lightened the mood, and everyone got a chuckle over John's reaction. Berta winked at Eddie and the others to let them know she enjoyed what just happened.

It didn't take long until everyone was sitting or standing around scarfing down their tasty meals as bag after bag of chips circulated amongst the crowd. Empty bottles of sodas began to pile up, as well as dirty paper napkins. Flyswatters were in full use as everyone swatted flies and yellow jackets alike. As a result of a lifetime of practice, it was apparent that nearly everyone was an expert at killing the little critters.

To most Southerners, swatting winged critters came as easy as breathing and with just as much thought. Only one small yelp erupted from the crowd when a yellow jacket bit them. It was Ricky. He'd reached around Bane in order to take Bane's root beer soda that was on the ground. He got stung on the palm because he grabbed the top of the bottle where a yellow jacket was perched.

"You do that on purpose ya Little Puke?"

"Wish I had. That's what ya git for stealin' my stuff!"

The festivities seemed all too quickly to come to an end as parents and young children alike picked up after themselves. They threw anything that would burn into the still burning embers of the bonfire and boxed or bagged everything else for the trip back to their homes. With full bellies and glad hearts, the parents and younger children made a human wave as they ascended the hill with the leftovers from the gathering.

The gang stayed and continued to stuff themselves under the old oak tree that held the swings. Together they contently basked in the shade, letting their bellies absorb all the junk food that weighed them down and caused most to become lethargic. Some sucked down Kool-Aid while others worked at drinking the remaining sodas.

Gabby and Billy had promised their parents they would douse the fire, so after a long rest, they grudgingly got up and took turns carrying buckets of water from the creek.

"Hey Dewey, come over here 'n take a turn," encouraged Gabby. They had to explain what they were doing and why. With delight, Dewey was soon helping and having fun as the water made hissing sounds when it hit the glowing red hot embers.

Dewey made many trips until he was satisfied he had drowned every smoldering ember in the pile. "Ship shape," he said, as he sat down to join the others.

"Good job, Captain Dewey," said Billy.

Gabby reached over and patted him on the back. Gail bumped Bane's hand aside and snatched one of the two remaining sodas from a box while Bane was reaching for the other. She handed it to Dewey as a reward for his hard work.

"Hey, save one of those for me," snorted Bane. He quickly grabbed the last one. The others exchanged looks at one another as if to say "What reason does he think he deserves anything?" Bane noticed, but kept quiet and acted like he hadn't. Depending on his mood or the circumstances at any given time, he may or may not care what they thought. This time he didn't.

Ricky, Bane's older brother, was the only outsider still left hanging about. "Hey Crystal, why don't ya come hang out with me? I have the keys to my ole man's pickup. We could go somewheres else 'n maybe take in a movie or somethin'." Ricky was usually allowed to take the truck on Sunday afternoons because most of the time his father took a nap to sleep off the beers from the night before. Ricky's words sent a shock wave through the whole group. Bane became angry at the gall of his brother's bold invitation to Crystal.

Bane decided he had to put an immediate halt to Ricky's advancements, so he started mouthing off at Ricky. "Why don't ya hang out with ya own friends? We have plans 'n don't need no help findin' somethin' ta do. What's the matter? Ain't JoJo comin' over?" He knew he went just far enough to rile Ricky, but not so far as to cause a fight. Ricky gave him a warning glare.

"No thank you, I'm gonna hang out with my friends," replied Crystal. All the while she scooted closer to the others sitting nearby and wrapped her arms around Bonnie Lou's shoulders.

Ricky watched her reaction to his offer with disappointment. He wasn't exactly sure why, but her rejection of him felt more like an insult. Bane smiled big as he turned to look at Ricky after watching Crystal's rejection. At this point, Ricky was in no humor to have a confrontation, so he acted like it was no big deal. He sensed he had stepped over an unseen line and wasn't really wanted by the group as a whole. "Guess I'll go have some fun 'n let ya little kids do whatever it is ya do then. 'Sides, I got better things ta do any ole way. Bet my friends is waitin' on me right now."

Just as Ricky turned to walk away, he kicked Bane hard in the leg and then made out as if he'd done it unintentionally. Bane, as well as the others knew better, but remained silent. So as not to provoke Bane's wrath, everyone diverted their eyes and made out as if they hadn't noticed.

Bane and Gabby had become consumed with constantly rubbing or scratching at their respective limbs where the ants had bitten them the day before. Their limbs were covered with small red pustules that had tiny heads filled with yellowish fluid.

Jason was the first to comment, "Phew-wee, those critters nearly eat y'all alive."

"Do they hurt bad?" asked Dewey, in wide eyed fascination.

"They don't hurt none, Dewey. They itch somethin' awful though," replied Gabby as he reached down and popped a couple of pustules. He squeezed them until all the clear fluid was released and tiny drops of blood appeared. Dewey watched with rapped attention.

"That's gross!" exclaimed Pattie as she slapped at Gabby's leg closest to her. Crystal and some of the others chanted in agreement. Most of the girls' faces showed expressions of disgust.

"I'm fixin' ta go crawfish huntin'," Gabby announced with delight while he stood up. "Anybody else up for it?"

Dewey didn't know what crawfish were, and looked to the others for an explanation. Billy, noticing Dewey's dilemma said, "Dewey, we call 'em crawfish, but they're actually crayfish according to the school books. They're little lobster-lookin' critters that live in fresh water creeks 'round here. Critters like raccoons eat 'em. Some folks actually cook 'n eat 'em if they git enough ta make it worth their while. My daddy says that folks down there in New Orleans make a fuss over who could cook 'em the bes'. He says those folks down there'll eat jus' about anythin', as long as ya throw hot sauce on it."

Billy gazed in thought before he continued. "He told me those was some of the drinkin'est laziest people God ever put on this earth. They live like the folks in the Bible that lived in Sodom 'n Gomorrah, before God destroyed it for bein' so sorry 'n actin' like heathens. He said it wouldn't surprise 'im if one day God don't up 'n wash it away."

With that, soon everyone was on their feet and speculating about the best place to find the crayfish in the nearby creek. The group immediately gravitated into their usual teams. Gabby, Bonnie Lou, Crystal, Jason and Jill decided on one spot, while Billy, Gail, Todd, Pattie and Bane agreed on another. Because Dewey was so new to the gang he didn't have a team to belong to, so he stood watching the others, hoping to be included.

Bane looking for an angle to humiliate Gabby, announced, "Gabby, let's make a bet. The one who comes back with the mos' gits ta make the others eat 'em."

Bane felt somewhat cheated because he'd already planned to bring up the idea for a crayfish hunt. Although disappointed, he readily went along with the idea, believing it was going to be easy pickings. He was eager to make up for yesterday's loss to Gabby over the ant biting business. He was certain his team would win because he'd scoped out his team's usual spot yesterday when he was sure no one was watching.

Gabby looked at Bane and started to agree when he felt a nudge. He then glanced at Bonnie Lou for a moment before he replied, "I can't speak for nobody else, but if ya wont to, you can have mine."

"All right then, how 'bout I win back my quarter if we win 'n *you* have ta . . . ." Bane stopped in mid-sentence as everyone's attention was drawn to Libby.

Libby was retching up some of the food she'd been fed earlier by the crowd of picnickers. A somewhat large pile of hotdog chunks was visible amongst the vomit.

Gabby walked over and, as delicately as possible, picked out half a piece of hotdog between two fingers and examined it carefully. "If we win, ya have ta eat this piece a hot dog." Many "eews" followed.

Bane, now over the initial disgust, could see the others were looking to him to see if he would take the bait. "That's not fair!"

"Alright then, how 'bout if y'all win, I'll not only give ya back ya quarter, but I'll eat this as well." Gabby held up the piece of hot dog higher to make sure Bane could see it clearly.

"Deal!" Bane was absolutely sure that the quarter was as good as his, and he was going to relish seeing Gabby eat that nasty thing. "Ya have to take that retard with ya, though. I don't want 'No-Nuts' scaring away our crawfish."

"Fine with me," replied Gabby. Again, everyone's attention was drawn to Libby as she began sniffing and then eating some of her own vomit to nearly everyone's surprise and disgust. Gabby just shrugged and stuck the recovered piece of hot dog on a high tree limb and covered it with a paper napkin. Everybody went about finding a glass jar, bucket, or a can in which to collect their crayfish.

"I'll have Jason blow his whistle after a while to signal times up," explained Crystal. That seemed acceptable to everyone and off they went. Jason always wore a whistle around his neck on a string. His mother had given it to him when he was younger so he could use it just in case he got lost. Of course he never told anyone how he came to have it, because he didn't want them to make fun of him. His mother stopped making him wear it, but he'd got use to it and so he kept wearing it because he wanted to. It always seemed to come in handy at times like this.

When Gabby's group arrived at the creek, he showed Dewey how to slowly lift rocks so the silt wouldn't cloud up the creek's clear water much and scare away the crayfish and salamanders. Then he showed him how to coax the crayfish into the jar to catch them when they swam backwards to get away. Because Dewey was a novice at this sort of thing, he put Dewey downstream to allow for possible excess clouding of the water.

The others in Gabby's group were starting to make good progress when all of a sudden they started moaning about how the creek was getting cloudy. They knew someone upstream was stomping on the creek bed, sending clouds of silt down to aggravate and hinder their search for crayfish.

As loud as he could, Jason screamed, "Knock it off, Cheaters!" After a few minutes the creek cleared up enough to begin their task of looking for more of the critters. Everyone went back to slowly turning over rocks and collecting more crayfish.

After about half an hour had passed, Crystal told Jason to blow his whistle and they all headed back to the hut village. Both groups arrived at the same time with their jars and cans filled with water and their catches.

They huddled together in their respective groups and tallied their catch. Bane spoke first, "We got twenty-three. That dog vomit ought'a be mighty tasty."

Gabby laughed as he said, "We caught thirty-four." Gabby's group started heckling the other group and jeering Bane to eat the hotdog.

Bane, disappointed and angry, got all huffy and claimed, "Ya had one more ta help, so it ain't fair."

"You're the one who made up the rules, not us. Anyway, he never did catch any," exclaimed Crystal, with Billy and all the others in agreement.

Bane just stood there getting more flustered and making wild claims about how unfair it was. After awhile he said, "Fine, I'll eat the damn thing then."

Everyone watched closely as Bane went over to where the hotdog was perched on a limb in the tree. Slowly he cleaned it off with the napkin after rinsing it in one of the jars of creek water. After a few moments he took a few steps and purposely dropped it on the ground. "Oops!" Bane made sure it landed right in front of Libby's snout, where she immediately snatched it off the ground and swallowed it. Everybody jeered and called him a cheat.

Bane placed his fists on his hips, grinning with pride at his own accomplishment of cheating fate, and blurted out, "I can't help it if it fell 'n Libby ate it before I could git it. I was fixin' ta eat it." More half-hearted name-calling labeling him a cheater ensued.

Dewey, in his innocence and gullibility, agreed with Bane's explanation and couldn't understand why everyone was so down on him. "I saw Libby eat it, so it ain't his fault."

The others tried in vane to explain to Dewey that Bane did it "accidentally on purpose." Dewey couldn't grasp the concept, so he just shrugged and sat down.

Billy spoke up, "Well, the least ya can do is take all these crawfish back to the creek 'n let 'em go then. That sounds fair enough, don't it guys?" Half-heartedly, they agreed.

With a sheepish smile on his face, Bane said, "Fine with me." He took two jars full of crayfish and started for the creek. Since there were more jars with crayfish in them, Billy and Gail helped. They figured it was only fair, since they were on the losing team anyway. Dewey followed along with some containers as well because he was still fascinated over the whole thing. He wanted to help let the crayfish go and watch them swim away.

After Bane and the others departed, Crystal took Gabby by the arm and whispered in his ear, "How'd we come up with that many crawfish? I know we didn't have near that many."

"Well, it's like this, I seen Bane scoutin' for crawfish yesterday 'n knew what he'd pull, so I kinda went down to the creek earlier 'n gathered some of the crawfish from their spot. I reckon he didn't notice I had a different jar when I come back." Bonnie Lou moved in close enough to hear what Gabby told Crystal and gave him an unconvincing look of admonishment.

Crystal just shook her head and smiled. "You're a mess for shor, but I'm glad ya done it. He's about the sorriest thing I ever met."

Now that school was out for the summer, every day seemed more or less the same as the day before as they gathered at the hut village when it wasn't raining. The next month went by fast for Dewey because he was so elated to have someone to play with everyday. The hot lazy afternoons were interrupted by the call to come home for supper when the bells rang out at either the trailer park or at Al's farm. Dewey was the only one who would not return after supper. On any given week, one or more of the gang would disappear on vacation trips with their parents or go by themselves to stay with other relatives. This sometimes prevented having the whole gang together in the hut village all at one time.

While Crystal was gone for a week on vacation, everyone noticed Bane had become his usual obnoxious bullying self, but now with a new twist. He began terrorizing the girls and younger boys alike. He seemed more aggressive towards the boys, in that he wanted to fight with one or more of them much more often. With the girls, he seemed more aggressive in other ways, like trying to find ways to glance at some body part or another, while making lewd comments.

Everyone noticed that Bane was always the last to leave the hut village. Also, the boys could see that the dirty magazine pile had become larger. Of late, the peach fuzz on Bane's upper lip began to thicken and darken, along with nasty looking whiskers in patches on his face mixed in with his growing collection of pimples.

Like the others, Bane was growing and getting taller and fuller. Even Billy must have grown over two inches or so since school let out for summer. Gabby seemed to have exploded as he began to grow thicker arms, broader shoulders, and a muscular chest. He was continuously doing pushups, pull-ups, and many other forms of exercise when he became bored. It was becoming obvious that he was going to be built like his father, large and muscular. Puberty was spreading through the group like a wildfire.

One day, Bane was so beside himself that he even went so far as to shove Dewey in the chest with all his might because he felt he hadn't gotten in his way. Dewey, not quite sure what this meant, stood his ground. Dewey didn't stand up to Bane out of any macho inclinations, but he felt Bane was being mean. Bane took this as an assault on his pride and began hitting Dewey with his fist. After a quick furry of strikes, Dewey retaliated with a backhand blow that knocked Bane to the ground. When Bane got up and came back at him, Dewey took out his sword and nailed Bane in the stomach hard. "Bad Bane!"

Bane was knocked to the ground gasping for breath. He sat bent over until the initial pain passed and he could breathe once more. After he finally recovered and got up, he made sure to avoid Dewey's reach with the sword. He didn't say a word as Dewey stood ready to deliver another blow if the need arose.

Billy tried to smooth things over. "Bane, he don't know no better than ta use his sword. I don't even know if he understood you were jus' spoilin' for a good ole fight." He turned to Dewey, "Now Dewey, yer not ta use that sword 'less ya protectin' somebody like ya done against Little Jay, ya hear? When ya use ya sword, ya cheatin'."

Dewey became confused, but felt sorry for what he'd done after Billy admonished him, so he apologized. "Dewey sorry for hurtin' ya," Dewey explained to Bane who was still holding his stomach.

Bane didn't take it very well, but he accepted it grudgingly by not making anymore of it. He at least felt everyone acknowledged Dewey cheated with his sword. It wasn't much of a consolation to his pride, but it was something anyway.

Todd and Jason were talking between themselves about going down to the creek and soaking their feet in it for awhile. They also wanted to prove to one another that they could catch a minnow with their bare hands. Pattie turned to them and said, "I'll come with ya. It's so hot, it's hard ta believe all the lakes 'n such don't jus' dry up 'n turn the whole place into a desert."

Gabby suggested they all go skinny dipping, but noticed all the girls looked at Bane quickly and whispered among themselves.

Gail spoke up, "We decided we don't want no part of that no more."

"Why not?" asked Jason.

The girls indicated with their eyes and heads in Bane's direction, which told the boys their reason. Bane got their meaning and returned their judgmental stares with a manufactured look of innocence. With a little "hum" he continued to tear at the loose bark on a twig he was holding.

"I'm still gonna join Todd 'n Jason cause I want'a soak my feet 'n play in the water," said Pattie. The others agreed it was a good idea and soon they were all vying for the best shady spot on the edge of the creek. Most had a flat rock to sit on while others sat on soft grass. Together they basked in the goodness with the cool water on their legs and feet. Occasionally someone would splash water on someone else.

Dewey, the only one with long pants, rolled up his overalls so he could join them. He immediately walked to the other side while looking at all the different rocks and looked for crayfish.

After a while Dewey turned and said, "Look there!" He pointed to a rock on the side of the creek at the water line. "I see a frog with blue eyes!" He leaned over in order to lift up the rock on the edge of the creek to get a better look at the frog when suddenly a chorus of shouts stopped him. Some in the gang were screaming "**NO, DEWEY!**" He stood looking at them in bewilderment.

Billy, Gabby, and Gail came splashing across the creek as some of the others stared in wonderment at this turn of events. Gabby grabbed Dewey's overall strap and started to pull him away from the rock while saying, "Dewey, that ain't no frog underneath that rock. It's probably a snake. Frogs ain't got no blue eyes around here."

Dewey followed him away from the blue-eyed creature with its head still protruding just under the edge of the rock. Billy and Gail went around the rock and found a big stick. When they were satisfied everyone was out of the way and Bonnie Lou was holding Libby real tight, they jammed the stick underneath the rock. A large water moccasin came out from underneath it and began swimming out into the middle of the creek. Everyone scattered to give it all the room it wanted.

After it disappeared further down the creek and everyone was sure it was well away from them, they settled back down in their places. Gabby spoke first, "Dewey, the reason that there snake has blue eyes, is 'cause it's 'bout ta shed its skin. So, don't ya never go pickin' up no blue-eyed frogs, okay, Dewey?"

"Dewey promise ta not pick up no critters with blue eyes."

Just as Dewey finished speaking, Bonnie Lou squealed, "It's comin' back!" All the boys found large rocks and limbs and once it got close enough they pounded it until there was no way it could possibly be alive. Then Gabby, using his long stick, picked it up and slung it far into the woods.

Gabby said, "Tanight I'll bring my .22 gage rifle 'n kill any snakes that show themselves." Like many in the south, he'd gotten a rifle for his twelfth birthday.

Pattie asked, "Why would ya hunt snakes at night with a gun?"

Gabby replied, "Well, what ya do is put a candle or a lantern on the side of the creek jus' as it gits dark. The water moccasins will come up ta it 'n stick their head out of the water beside the light, cause it attracts 'em. That's when ya shoot 'em." Some of the other boys agreed to come with him if their parents would let them.

Just then, bells began to ring, which could be heard from the trailer park and from Dewey's place, so the children disbursed.

Just after dark that night, about a dozen shots could be heard near the trailer park.

Dewey took his seat in the den after his bath so he could eat his snack before being sent to bed. Tonight, instead of cookies, there was a piece of pie left over from supper. It was apple pie, which was his favorite. Al pulled out his *Bluejacket's Manual* from the Navy and was reviewing his knot tying skills, as well as replacing his urge to smoke. He had cut several pieces of rope many years ago for such practices like this in the evenings. It was things like this that made him feel still connected to his past and sparked his memories of long-ago friends and ships.

As he sat tying various knots, like the Cat's paw, Blackwall hitch, and many others, he realized that Dewey was staring in fascination. He continued to manipulate the rope into more and more complicated variations of knots until he decided to take thinner cords and make fancy work on an old broom handle. He was something of a celebrity in the Navy for his skill of creating fancywork on the quarterdecks of some of the ships on which he served. A few times he had been invited to go on temporary duty to other ships as a guest to help with their fancywork, decorating the quarterdecks and other parts of the ship. He learned this skill when he started out as boatswain's mate upon entering the Navy. Even after becoming a boiler technician, he made it a point to keep his skills up out of enjoyment and for bragging rights.

"Dewey, while I was at the store pickin' up some oil for the tractor taday, some carpetbagger fella from up north sold me some new kind of oil he was peddlin'. The store manager got sore at the fella 'n started tellin' 'im ta git his Yankee butt outa there. I was . . ."

"What's a Yankee?"

"Huh?" Al looked at Dewey, who had interrupted his story for the moment and decided he'd have to explain what a Yankee was or forget telling him the story since Dewey was probably going to get stuck on it. "Well Dewey, a Yankee is someone from up north. Ya know like New York, Chicago, or some place like that. Well, at any rate, we call 'em Yankees if they come down for a visit here in the south. But if they up 'n decide ta stay, we call 'em Damn Yankees."

"The reason we don't care for 'em much, is cause they come down here 'n like what they see, but the first thing they do after they git here is try 'n change everything, mostly ta the way things was up there where they come from, which is stupid. Why leave some place cause ya don' like it, jus' ta turn around 'n try ta make it like the place ya left."

"I know the Bible says 'if a stranger dwells within your land, you shall not mistreat 'im 'n treat 'em like they was born among ya', but most folks never fully take ta 'em, even if they live here the rest of their lives. Bless their hearts, they seem ta always mix up culture for intelligence or vice versa. But mostly, everybody thinks that the Yanks think they're better 'n us. At any rate, the Yanks' children usually git accepted since they grow up here 'n go ta school 'n make friends 'n so forth."

"Anyhow, ya ought'a seen the store owner's face when I bought a case of that new oil. I knew what the oil fella was talkin' about, 'n I figured I'd give it a whirl, 'specially if it'd keep my engines from wearin' out so fast. Regular oil breaks down too fast 'n messes up the piston rings, cause of friction 'n heat."

The matter settled, Al went about tying a few more knots. Seeing that Dewey's attention still remained, he decided to let him give a knot or two a try. To his amazement, Dewey did exceptionally well at duplicating each knot with only one or two demonstrations. He showed him more and more knots with increased difficulty, with the same results.

From then on, Al made his mind up to pursue this new found talent to its fullest. He would help Dewey learn new knots and teach him how to make fancywork every night during his talks. He couldn't imagine just how this talent could possibly help Dewey make a living, but at least he found a talent in which Dewey could excel. It gave him and Dewey a common hobby that'd never existed before.

During the middle of the night Dewey was awakened by the sounds of howling and yapping coming from outside. This kept up for a long time. After a while the sounds got closer to the house. He could hear clucking from the chickens out back. Curious, Dewey got out of bed and looked out the window.

Not seeing anything, he wandered into the kitchen and turned on the light so he could see his way to the back door. The light from the kitchen's overhead light radiated out of the window and illuminated part of the back yard just enough so that Dewey could see the ground close to the house. Although he could no longer hear the howls or yapping, the noise from the chickens began to build into a crescendo.

Dewey's curiosity increased from the sounds made by the chickens outside. He slowly stepped outside to see what was making the chickens carry on so. The light from the kitchen shining out through the window and doorway was enough that he was able to see his way down the steps and into the yard comfortably.

Squawks from the chickens' coop turned to shrills of fright and dull flapping sounds. The air seemed to fill with unexplained heaviness as Dewey became frightened. He instinctively reached for a sword that wasn't there. Paralyzed, he stood in the yard dressed in his pajamas as the hair on the nap of his neck stood up in response to this unseen thing of horror. Suddenly many sets of glowing eyes appeared out of the darkness.

"BAM, BAM!" came a loud thunderous sound and a flash of light with each roaring noise from just behind and to the left of him. Dewey didn't have time to react to this new sound and it was over before he realized what had happened. Al had quietly come out of the back door with his double-barreled shotgun and unloaded on the peering eyes in the darkness. No sooner had the shotgun fired than the night became filled with howls of pain and yaps as the injured offenders fled. Snipe growled and barked as he pursued something into the darkness.

Still in shock, Dewey stood frozen in the same position he'd held when the ominous glowing eyes first appeared. There was a shadow that moved and grew on the ground beside and in front of him. Dewey didn't understand what it was and that it was created by the light from the kitchen behind his Grandfather as he was approaching him. It was only when Al placed a comforting hand on his shoulder and said in a gentle voice, "They was coyotes," that he was able to move. Dewey turned and looked at the partially lighted face of his grandfather.

"Let's go inside, Boy; we can see what damage was done in the mornin'." When Al noticed that Dewey was hesitating, he added, "It's alright, Boy. Come on inside." Al placed his hand on Dewey's back and guided him to the house. As they reached the top of the steps, Snipe suddenly appeared and darted through the doorway immediately before them.

Snipe fidgeted about the kitchen, all excited at having achieved what he believed was a great accomplishment. Al guided Dewey to the kitchen to sit and laid the shotgun down on the table. He went and retrieved a dog biscuit while Snipe bumped into his leg, full of excitement, and took the treat greedily. "Good, Boy," Al said as he watched Snipe crunch the tasty treat and swallow it in a hurry.

Seeing Dewey was still frightened, Al joined Dewey at the table. "Dewey, those critters ya saw in the yard was coyotes. They was after the chickens. I'm sure they killed more'n they took. I probably wounded or killed more'n two or three of 'em." Seeing that Dewey didn't understand, Al added, "They're kinda like small ta medium sized wild dogs. There as clever as they come, but they like ta brag about bein' around with their howls and such. They howl ta declare their territory or ta jus' let others know where they are. Anyway, they was jus' lookin' for an easy meal."

Dewey replied, "Dewey don't like 'em. They have lights in their eyes."

"Yeah, they don't really have lights in their eyes. That was jus' the light reflectin' in their eyes is all. Jus' like it does Snipe's eyes when he's outside in the night facin' the light." Dewey relaxed even more as Al went on, "Ya see, Dewey, all creatures on earth are in the business of eatin', but I'm in the business of stoppin' their business so we have food. Ya can't hold it against 'em though."

"Why did they come ta git our chickens?"

"Well I guess it was easier than lookin' for mice, rabbits, 'n such. Leastways they thought so, but I bet they'll steer clear of here for a long time ta come. Well, lets git some shuteye 'n worry about it tamorrow."

Al made sure Dewey was asleep before he hid the shotgun once more. He knew Dewey wasn't mature enough to have access to guns and he didn't want him to get hurt.

Chapter 8 – The Blue Blanket

"DON'T ya no-never-mind. We'll fix it up again, Crystal," promised Pattie before she placed a comforting hand on Crystal's shoulder. Crystal and the others had only just arrived a few minutes before.

Crystal now sat in one of the chairs in the girls hut hunched over with her face buried in her hands crying. She eventually looked up at the others while wiping away tears. No one said anything for a long pause as they watched and waited for Crystal to say or do something. Crystal slowly drew a deep breath and nodded her head as she tried to put on a brave face and attempted a smile.

Jill, Bonnie Lou, and Pattie felt awkward as they stood in a semicircle beside her. Crystal was devastated to find the girls' hut in complete disarray; the new curtains were shredded and other things such as seat cushions destroyed and spilling out their stuffing.

Crystal had been out of town staying with her adoptive grandparents in Marietta, Georgia for the past two weeks and had only just arrived home the night before. After Bonnie Lou, Pattie and Jill came over to welcome her home, she'd readily confided in them about someone she had met while she was away. His name was Grant. She told how they'd met while she was staying at her grandparents' home. She admitted, in so many words, to falling head over heels in love with Grant. Crystal's emotions were still raw from having to say goodbye to Grant less than twenty-four hours ago.

She and the other girls had worked diligently for a long time making the curtains and repairing the fixtures. It hurt her deeply to see what some wild creature or group of creatures had done. She, as well as the other girls, had to plead for the materials from their parents. What had been so beautiful the day before was now in shambles.

Crystal began to cry again. Within moments, Dewey pushed aside the tattered curtain that acted as the hut's door to peek inside to find out what was wrong. Dewey could see Crystal was sad as he watched the other girls try again to console her. "Crystal hurt?"

Crystal looked up at Dewey momentarily and pointed all around as she tried to stop crying. The other girls explained, "Dewey, Crystal's cryin' cause some critters got 'n our hut 'n tore up most everythin'. We ain't got no more stuff ta fix it back up with."

Dewey felt bad for them. For a while he stood in the doorway with a blank look, then suddenly his face beamed. He started tugging on his large red cape. After some wrangling, he removed the large brooch, the cross with the pearl, stepped inside and draped the cape over Crystal's lap.

"You can have this. Dewey don't need it no more." With a sense of pride, he stuck out his chest. "Ship shape?" Awestruck, Crystal held his cape in her lap. She knew how much he adored his cape and how much a part of him it was.

"Dewey, I can't take something so precious ta ya." She stood up to hand it back to him. Dewey put up his hands as he took a step backward.

"Dewey don't need it no more." It was then she realized her crying was making him sad and he wanted to make her feel better. Her tears stopped as she looked at him in wonderment.

"Oh, Dewey yer so sweet. Are ya really sure?"

He nodded his head, then smiled real big. She reached up and kissed him on the cheek, which made him feel funny inside. He didn't remember anyone ever kissing him before. This new experience flooded over him and made him feel good all the way down to his toes. He felt joy knowing he had made her feel better. He could tell the others were pleased as well from the big smiles on their faces.

"Ship shape?"

"Yeah, ship shape, Dewey." Crystal almost started to cry once more, but this time from the joy of the love she felt for Dewey. She forced herself to hold back the tears of joy for Dewey's sake and just tenderly put her hand on his arm. Although she had always been kind and looked after him since his arrival, she would, from this moment on, feel a special sense of closeness and affection for him. She reached for his brooch and fastened it to his overall strap, the one closest to his heart.

Just then Gail stuck her head in and was about to say something when she noticed the mess inside. She didn't say anything as she stepped inside and whispered, "Wow. What happened here?" No one said anything because it was so obvious.

Feeling satisfied, Dewey smiled and pushed his way past Gail to go see what the other boys were doing.

"Hey, Dewey, Todd got a bow 'n arrow set from his granddaddy while he was on vacation. We're fixin' ta go huntin'. Come on," shouted Jason, motioning for Dewey to follow. Dewey quickly caught up to the other boys as they slipped down a well-worn path through the woods. They soon passed over the beaver dam that made the pool they used as their swimming hole.

Billy and Bane carried spears they'd made one afternoon earlier in the summer when they'd gotten bored. They used young hickory tree trunks that were nice and straight for the shafts. They'd cleaned off all the limbs to make the shafts smooth and jammed rusty old steel kitchen knives between the slits that they made into the thickest end of the sticks. Because the old knives' handles were missing, holes were now exposed that could be used to securely fasten the blades with baling wire to the shafts. This made for a very strong and secure spearhead. They prided themselves on creating spears similar to the way Indians had once done in the past, but with arrowheads and twine.

It wasn't long before the boys came to a small natural meadow. Bane and Billy assumed the lead and kept everyone quiet. Of course Gabby wanted to talk about this and that as they made their way through the fairly dense forest, which made Dewey happy, but the others agitated. Upon the boys' approach the squirrels, seeking safety, chattered as they scrambled up the trees to higher ground. In their rush to find safety, their claws made tearing sounds on the tree bark. Birds could be heard making noises in the distance as they also took notice of the boys' approach.

You could usually spy deer, rabbits, squirrels, and occasionally a small fox or opossum in these woods much of the time. Sometimes they would even come right up to the huts if you kept very quiet. Once last year, a bobcat was seen prowling around the edge of the huts. Libby would bark and chase away just about anything that came snooping once she glimpsed or smelled it. On this trip, the boys made sure she stayed behind with the girls.

Bane, who was leading, stopped and gestured for everyone else to stop and be quiet. They'd spied a young deer with white spots about thirty yards ahead of them. The doe was playfully jumping in a patch of tall grass near some large trees at the edge of the clearing.

Jason readied his bow and inched to the head of the group for a shot while Bane and Billy readied their spears. With the release of the arrow, Bane and Billy threw their spears in unison. They didn't realize it yet, but they had come upon several deer bedding down in the grassy areas beneath the large hardwoods.

In a flash, several deer sprang to their feet. Their white tails flagged their retreat as they sprinted deep into the woods at incredible speeds. Within mere seconds they were gone, quickly blending in with the colors and shadows of the trees and underbrush. It wasn't long before they could no longer be heard moving through the woods.

In their excitement, the boys felt their pulses racing as they surveyed the scene before them. They stumbled into one another as they ran to where the fawn had been standing. There they found Jason's arrow stuck into a nearby tree. "Good shot, Jason. That tree's goin' ta taste mighty good once ya skin it," teased Gabby.

Jason sighed in silent frustration and yanked the arrow from the tree trunk. "I ain't had much practice, but I'll git the next one." He made a show of firing an imaginary arrow with his bow.

"I got a piece of it," Bane proclaimed as he lifted up his spear head to show a tiny bit of tuft that was stuck to it. All the boys gathered around and admired the fur that was stuck to a chipped part of the blade. Bane turned and asked Billy, "How'd you do? Bet ya didn't git no piece of 'em like I did."

Billy joked, "Oh, I only missed him by a mile. I'll have ta git closer next time, I 'spose." He then started jerking and making funny gestures as he aimed and threw the spear at a nearby tree, missing it completely.

He, as well as the others, laughed while he walked past the intended tree and went around a large stump to retrieve his spear. Just then he halted and hunched over the ground.

"Hey y'all, come 'n take a look." He waved for the others to come quickly as he stared down at a hole in the ground. The hole was dug under one of the stump's larger roots. He'd seen something go into it upon his approach. The others figured it was nothing and were slow to respond.

"Hey, I think I seen a rabbit skedaddle down this here hole. C'mon!" he called again and pointed down at the hole.

No sooner had they gathered around the hole, when out leaped a large gray rabbit that sprinted between their feet and ran for the nearby underbrush. Bane tried to turn and throw his spear, only to be blocked by Dewey.

"Get outa the way, Retard!" His opportunity now gone, he turned to Dewey and pointed the spear at him in frustration and said, "I could a got 'im. But no thanks ta you, he got away, ya Big Dumb Klutz."

"Dewey sorry. I didn't mean to."

The others knew that Bane never really had a chance anyway, but kept it to themselves. Dewey stepped away from Bane a little and went back to looking into the hole along with the others.

"Ya think there's baby rabbits in there?" inquired Jason.

Bane pushed everyone out of his way and began poking his spear down into the dark opening. A baby rabbit's head bobbed up then disappeared back down again just as quickly. This encouraged Bane, so he went about thrusting his spear more vigorously. He moved it from side to side and all around. He was determined not to miss one square inch of the bottom of the den.

"Don't kill the bunnies," pleaded Dewey after he saw the rabbit pop up and retreat back into the hole.

"Mind ya own business, No-Nuts." Bane retorted as he continued to jab this way, then that.

"Hey Bane, leave the poor things alone. Ya probably killed some of 'em already," protested Billy in utter disgust.

Bane stopped and looked over his shoulder with a satisfied grin as he pulled out the lifeless and bloodied body of a baby rabbit. "Looks like rabbit stew tanight boys."

Dewey felt sick as he stared at the lifeless creature. The others didn't seem too thrilled either. They knew it was a senseless killing because it was so tiny.

"Why'd he kill it? Ain't nothin' but a baby rabbit! It weren't hurtin' nothin," whined Dewey to no one in particular.

"What's the matter, No-Nuts? Don't ya eat meat? I killed it cause I wanted to, 'n ya ain't got nothin' ta say 'bout it," declared Bane as he waved the impaled rabbit in front of Dewey's face. Dewey gasped in horror when it was thrust within mere inches of his nose.

"I don't want ta hunt no more." Dewey turned and walked back the way they had come. Gabby immediately joined him. Everyone but Bane soon fell in line and started back to the huts. Bane stood there for a few more moments feeling incensed over their reaction, but then reluctantly followed.

"Y'all are a bunch of wimps," shouted Bane as he stopped momentarily to admire his prey with pride before grudgingly pursuing the rest of the group.

When Libby began to bark and the girls heard the boys approaching, they came out of their hut to greet the hunting party. With prideful zeal Bane showed them his "prey," still impaled on the spear head. The girls recoiled at the sight of the baby rabbit's bloodied carcass, which Bane found especially amusing.

"What kinda monster kills a little baby rabbit? Git that thing outa my face," growled Crystal. Except for Gail, the other girls nodded and muttered their feelings of agreement.

The boys told how Bane came to kill the poor creature, which added credence to the girls' accusations of Bane being unjustly mean and vile. At first Bane took the criticisms in his usual stride and acted like it didn't bother him, but soon he became annoyed. His pride wounded, he started to feel a hint of embarrassment. Angrily he blurted out, "You're jus' a bunch of babies 'n wimps. Git outa my face!" With that said, he swung his spear hard, which dislodged the lifeless body and sent it sailing through the air into a patch of briars in the distance.

"Satisfied?" Bain stormed away from the group towards the boys' hut as everyone watched in silence.

Gail noticed Libby heading towards the briar patch so she shouted, "Libby, leave it! Come girl!" Quickly, Libby obeyed and trotted back to the group.

"Poor baby rabbit," Dewey kept repeating over and over.

"Don't ya mind now, Dewey. It'll be alright," Crystal said while patting him on the shoulder. "Let's think about better things, like how ya helped us with our hut. Alright?"

That soon brought a little smile to Dewey's face. "There now, that's better. Come take a look at how nice we cleaned up our place." Dewey followed her back to the girl's hut. Gail, Jill, Bonnie Lou, and Pattie stayed to hear all about what happened during the hunt.

While Billy and the other boys went over all the gory details, a sudden ringing of bells echoed from over the hill, mingled with shouts from the mothers who'd rang them. The faint sound of a siren could be heard in the far distance.

"Come on!" shouted Billy, while he and the others turned and started running up the hill towards the trailer park. Bane soon caught up with them as they reached the summit of the hill. Since they could survey the whole trailer park from this high vantage point, they all stopped to see what was happening.

"Look!" shouted Gabby and Jason in unison, pointing towards the last trailer where Ms. Nutt lived. They could see thick black smoke coming from the kitchen's exhaust vent. Because most everyone's trailer was similar in design, they all deduced the possible origin of the fire was the stove. The kitchen was just off center towards the front where the hitch was located in most of the trailers. It being a week day, only the mothers and wives were at home with children during this time of day.

"Come on!" shouted Billy. With that, everyone began charging down towards the trailer park as fast as they could on the steep decline. Dewey and Crystal topped the hill just in time to see everyone else running down towards the fire. They quickly followed after them. Crystal stayed with Dewey because he was having a hard time traversing the unusually arduous trail. He'd never been to the trailer park, so he was unfamiliar with the footings of the trail leading down.

"Hurry, Dewey!" Crystal kept urgently repeating as they descended the hill. The others were already entering the trailer park.

In the stagnant air, smoke was starting to form a small dark cloud above the trailer. Upon getting near the burning trailer, Billy and the other boys heard people shouting for everyone to go get as many hoses as they could find and hook them up closer to the burning trailer. When they saw their mothers and others struggling to find, unhook and drag the hoses, they jumped in and assisted wherever they could. The nearest trailer's spigots served as the source for water. Some of the other residences served as guardians of the smaller children. Small streams of water began to appear once hoses were hooked up to the nearby spigots and charged. Due to some hoses not having a nozzle on them, some were having to place their thumbs over the ends to create a stream. The water pressure also dropped with each new hose charged and added to the cause. All in all, the streams of water were not very effective in their efforts.

Ricky had been late getting to the fire because he'd had the radio blaring full blast and hadn't heard all the initial commotion. He and the other boys started hosing down the area of the trailer where they saw flames just beginning to show on the roof above the kitchen's open window.

"Where is Ms. Nutt?!" shouted Ricky.

"Oh my, Lord! I'm sure she's home cause I seen 'er jus' this mornin'. She's always home this time a day," said someone in the crowd.

"Bane, git over here!" demanded Ricky. He gripped Bane's shoulder and they ran up the small wooden porch built in front of the trailer's main entrance. Smoke was bellowing from the upper edge of the door where time had dry rotted the door's weather stripping and allowed gaps for air flow. Ricky grabbed the handle. Although it was too hot to hold for long, he managed to quickly twist it open. Just inside the door, Ms. Nutt was lying on a couch. They dropped down to their knees and hurriedly crawled to the couch and pulled her by her arms down to the floor as the door slammed shut behind them.

Ms. Nutt was totally limp. Her rotund body made it hard to get a good grip. Finally, they dragged her over to the door that had closed behind them. After a couple of failed attempts to get the door open, Ricky grabbed a nearby piece of cloth to grip the handle because it was too hot to touch with his naked hand. He soon got the door open.

Staying crouched down low, Bane lifted Ms. Nutt by the ankles and Ricky by her arm pits as they crawled through the doorway. No sooner did they drag Ms. Nutt through the doorway and onto the porch, than the trailer exploded into a ball of fire.

Towards the front of the trailer, all of the windows blew out in unison as flames billowed outward in an angry show of orange and yellowish colors that produced plumes of dark black smoke. Without stopping, they carried Ms. Nutt down the steps and across the drive towards the adjacent trailer lot. The main crowd watched as the Taggart boys hauled Ms. Nutt's lifeless body towards them. Some of the onlookers, trying to stay away from the dangerous fire and smoke, now broke ranks and rushed to assist the two boys. With the help of others, Ricky and Bane laid Ms. Nutt on the ground among the crowd. Soon others gathered to offer help.

Ms. Nutt lay on the ground unconscious. She began to cough when someone patted her face roughly in the hope of reviving her. Her face and clothes were blackened from the heavy smoke. Ricky and Bane were coughing hard and wiping away blackened snot streaming from their nostrils.

The heavy smoke was beginning to fill the air all about them. The aroma from the burning trailer was almost sickening as the fire continued to fully engulf most of the trailer. The smell of plastic, paint, and chemicals of which the trailer was made was becoming overwhelming. Instinctively, the people joined in to pick up Ms. Nutt once more and move her farther away from danger.

"Is she alright?" was repeated as folks approached to get a closer look. "Yeah, but barely," was mixed in with "She's coughin' but still breathin'."

While this was going on, someone shouted, "Hey Dewey, what ya doin'? GIT OUTA THERE!"

Dewey and Crystal had been the last of the gang to arrive at the trailer. Dewey, not realizing the danger, had wandered towards the back of the burning trailer where the fire hadn't yet reached. Crystal, on the other hand, had run to her mother's side. She and the others stood vigilance over Ms. Nutt.

Dewey appeared oblivious to anything happening around him as he began to strike the rear door of the burning trailer with all of his might. He was using an old car wheel without a tire. There were no stairs leading up to this particular door, so he had to lift the wheel high and swing at head level.

With a sudden crash, it finally burst inwards. He jumped into the trailer with speed and agility no one would have imagined he possessed. When he entered, his wooden sword was knocked loose from his overalls' loop and dropped to the ground as he scraped his belly along the floor of the trailer.

"DON'T, DEWEY," Gabby shouted as he tried to get to him before he disappeared. Gabby was pulled back by a deputy who'd just arrived.

The deputy hollered, "Who was that idiot?!" He didn't wait for an answer.

The deputy rushed to the broken door and shouted, "GIT YER ASS OUTA THERE. Are you crazy! You tryin' ta git ya'self killed? Git outa there NOW, YA DAMN FOOL!"

While all the hoses from the other trailers streamed water on the trailer and inside the now cracked windows, a fire engine finally arrived. More county deputies arrived as well. They and the fire engine had trouble avoiding onlookers as they hurried to the fire.

When the first fire engine arrived at the trailer park entrance, the lone firefighter had to stop the fire truck so he could hook up a hose to the fire hydrant at the road. The attached hose, anchored by the hydrant, caused the rest of the hose on the back of the fire engine to unravel as it traveled down the narrow lane. Once he'd gotten the hose ready with the help of others, he ran back up the lane to open the hydrant. The feeder line charged, he ran back down the hill and engaged the pumps to charge the hoses. By this time, another fire truck and other volunteer firemen arrived. The crews were made up totally of Volunteer Firefighters.

Through an ever thickening cloud of smoke, Dewey suddenly appeared in the doorway cradling a small bundle in his arms. He jumped down to the ground and was met by an angry deputy and firefighter. The fireman began shouting, "Ya dumb kid, git the hell away from here!" "What ya doin', Boy? Keep ya butt outa the way."

"Dewey wanted ta help," Dewey said softly as he looked down at the bundle.

Not hearing him, the fireman turned back to the job of putting out the fire. The deputy almost dragged Dewey clear of the scene to the group of onlookers. Crystal and her mother, as well as a couple of other women, saw the blue blanket move and investigated. It was then they realized Dewey was holding a baby. One of the mothers took the baby from Dewey and uncovered it to further investigate and see if it was okay.

"Dewey, how'd ya know there was a baby in there?" inquired Crystal's mother.

"I don't know. Dewey wanted ta help." He stood looking confused and feeling uneasy.

"Dewey, yer so brave." Crystal hugged him around the neck.

By this time, Bane had gotten close enough to see and hear what'd happened and understood what Dewey had just accomplished. His initial pride of helping pull Ms. Nutt out of the burning trailer, in his mind, was diminished and upstaged by Dewey's heroic act. *Saving a baby*, Bane thought to himself, *meant more ta everyone than what he'd done.* Several adults still acknowledged and congratulated Bane on being brave and saving Ms. Nutt, but jealousy had already stolen most of his attention. No longer could any of the praise being heaped upon him penetrate his emotional isolation. He no longer responded to their kind words of gratitude as he menacingly stared at Crystal and Dewey. His jealousy had taken over.

Despite the efforts of everyone, the trailer became completely engulfed with flames shooting out of every opening as the roof collapsed inwards. Only the back end of the trailer, where Dewey had been, was still intact. The outside of the trailer bubbled as the paint became hot and pealed right before their eyes as the fire moved through the trailer. Most of the crowd stayed and watched while the firemen soaked the trailer that used to be Ms. Nutt's home.

Eventually the fire reduced the trailer to a skeletal smoldering heap. The remaining onlookers disbursed to their homes, hugging one another and thanking God and Jesus it wasn't theirs.

Later, the Fire Chief explained that the earlier fireball that erupted was called a flashover. He went on to tell how Ricky and Bane were lucky that the door had closed immediately after them as they entered the trailer or the air would have ignited it sooner. He said that Dewey was lucky the door to the last bedroom had been closed. It gave Dewey just enough time to get the baby out alive before the fire broke through. The Chief congratulated Ricky, Bane, and Dewey for their heroics in saving Ms. Nutt and the baby. He made sure to take down their complete names for his report.

Before the crowd disappeared, the Sheriff questioned as many of them as possible to find out how the fire could have started and to make sure everyone else was okay. The local reporter for the county paper took photos of the heroes, the crowd, and the trailer while he noted all the particulars. Gabby handed Dewey his wet sword just before the reporter took Dewey's picture for the paper.

Just then, Dewey heard a distant bell ringing. "Dewey got ta go home now." As he started for the hill leading towards the huts and home, the Sheriff stopped him and said, "Hold on there, Partner. We'll take ya home. Where do ya live?" Gabby told him where to take Dewey. That's when he remembered going to see Al about the episode with Little Jay. The Sheriff placed his hand on Dewey's shoulder as he instructed his deputy to take Dewey home in a patrol car.

"We can't have such a brave young man walking home taday now can we? By the way, I take it you are the kid that put the hurtin' on Little Jay?" Dewey looked down and nodded ever so slightly because he though perhaps he might be in trouble.

"I'll be glad ta give 'im your regards. He won't be out for quite a spell. When he does git out, I'll make sure he don't bother you 'n ya friends no more, okay?"

Dewey was elated to have been given a ride home in a police car. The Deputy assigned to drive him, once he realized Dewey wasn't normal, let him play with the siren as he drove him down the road.

When they arrived at the farm, the deputy explained to Al all about how Dewey had saved a baby from the fire. Al thanked the deputy and took Dewey by the shoulder and said, "Boy, ya can have anythin' ya want and as much as ya want for supper tonight. I can put the leftovers back in the frig, so jus' name it." Dewey smiled from ear to ear and gleefully shouted, "Pizza! Pizza! I want pizza!"

It hadn't been lost on Al that Dewey wasn't wearing his red cape and now was wearing the brooch on one of his overall straps. He immediately made up his mind that he wasn't about to mention it, because he hoped Dewey had made up his mind to give it up. He was tired of washing it separately to prevent its red dye from leaking all over the rest of the clothes. He also felt it was a sign that maybe Dewey was maturing. He thought, *'let sleeping dogs lie.'*

Chapter 9 – The Hero's Reward

DURING the following Sunday service, Preacher Rakestraw praised Dewey for his act of bravery. Then with a raised voice, he proclaimed that God had a purpose for everybody and had used Dewey to make the world a better place. He went on to demand that everyone in the congregation follow Dewey's example and do something good for his fellow man. Standing on the pulpit, he pounded on the lectern and shouted, "God has sent this innocent child to lead us. We will follow!"

Then he invited everyone to stand and sing the hymnal "*Onward, Christian Soldier.*" While everyone sang, Preacher Rakestraw lifted his knees high as he marched in place in unison to the music. Dewey tried to sing along with everyone as he stepped out of the confinement of the pews and mimicked the preacher's actions. He kept marching even after the song finished until Al placed a hand on his shoulder to get him to stop.

After the sermon was over and the last song finished, Dewey, while standing next to the preacher at the entrance of the chapel, was congratulated by everyone in the congregation with a hand shake or a pat on the back as they departed. He thrived on the adoration from the other parishioners and swelled with pride. His self-confidence had grown over the summertime and he'd even begun to look more and more directly into others faces when they spoke to him.

The week following the fire, Dewey, Ricky, and Bane were scheduled to be given an official "thank you" at the county courthouse in downtown Franklin. Their pictures were in the newspaper, along with photos of the burned out trailer and descriptions of their acts of valor. It told how Ms. Nutt and the baby were fine because of the actions of the three boys and all the neighbors pitching in until the fire department arrived.

To get ready for the momentous occasion, Al decided to take Dewey into Carrollton and buy him a nice new suit and a pair of shoes. Al was proud of how much weight Dewey had lost since arriving home with him nearly ten months earlier, "Boy, ya goin' ta look as shiny as a new penny when we go ta the court house tamorrow. Now, let's go git ya hair cut."

Dewey liked visiting the barber shop because Alfred, the barber, spoke to him like he was an adult. When he finished cutting Dewey's hair, Alfred always gave him a special treat. "Dewey, I hear talk of ya savin' a little baby caught in a fire the other day. Ya looked mighty good in the paper. We're all proud of ya for being so brave."

"Yes sir. I helped the firemans. It was a boy baby." He held up his hands to show how little it was and how he'd carried it. "I weren't scared neither."

After Alfred finished cutting Dewey's hair, he spun the chair around to face the mirror which took up almost the whole upper part of the wall above the counter. Alfred smiled as he opened a large drawer at the bottom of the counter. He pulled out a large red plastic fireman's helmet and a silver metal whistle.

"Dewey, I'm a Volunteer Fireman and I was busy visitin' outa town when the fire happened. I knew you'd be comin' by, so I got ya this here fireman's helmet 'n whistle for ya ta keep. Since I couldn't be there, I figured ya took my place so, here ya go." He handed Dewey the whistle and put the helmet on his head. Dewey beamed with pride as he looked in the mirror at his reflection.

Dewey gave a short blow on his new whistle. "Put that thing away till we git home. You can blow it when ya outside in the yard," demanded Al.

"Now here's ya candy." Alfred handed Dewey a red sucker. To be sure not to disappoint Dewey, he always kept a red sucker tucked away just for him once he'd learned it was the only color Dewey ever asked for.

Upon arriving home from the barber shop, Dewey changed clothes and received permission to go play with his friends. He set off down through the woods, his upcoming award ceremony all but forgotten for the moment.

Upon his arrival Dewey told all the kids about how his barber had given him a fireman's helmet, which he still had on, along with his whistle. He blew it long and hard for the gang as they gathered around the swings. He continued to blow his whistle every so often when someone else in the gang arrived or he hadn't shown it to them yet.

This caused Bane to become irritated. Dewey's whistle-blowing was interfering with Bane's bragging about how he'd saved Ms. Nutt, much to the amusement of Bane's reluctant audience. As much as they tried, no one could escape Bane's endless yammering about the fire and his heroics. To the dismay of the others in the group, with each passing day, Bane's heroics became more and more dangerous and incredulous.

Bane's growing confidence caused him to become more emboldened towards Crystal as well. He even went so far as to imply to the others that he was her boyfriend. When the occasion presented itself, he would sit next to her by forcing others to shift around to accommodate his blatant intrusions. After this occurred a couple times, Crystal became uncomfortable and asked the others if they knew what was going on with Bane. Her uneasiness around him grew even more so after the others explained to her that Bane though she was his "girl."

"Like I was sayin', me 'n Ricky was just . . ." Again Dewey blew his whistle during mid-sentence. Bane stormed up to Dewey and demanded, "What right ya got ta have that whistle, Retard? You didn't do nothin' but carry a baby. I carried somebody a whole lot bigger through a ragin' fire. Any sissy can carry a baby." With that, Bane snatched the whistle from Dewey's neck. Dewey, not sure what he should do, just stood there staring at the broken string dangling from the whistle in Bane's hand.

"Gimme my whistle!" Dewey demanded just before he tried to grab it out of Bane's hand. He missed. Bane then began to jump and prance just outside of Dewey's reach while mocking him. "Dewey wonts it back! Bad, Bane!" Dewey reached for his wooden sword.

Billy jumped between them and faced Bane. "Bane, give it back ta 'im. Ya can see how much it means ta 'im."

"Mind ya own business, Billy!" Bane shouted as he pushed Billy aside.

"That don't belong ta you, Bane Taggart," Crystal chimed in as she moved closer and stood next to Billy in a show of unity.

"I deserve it more'n he does. What y'all care for anyways?"

Gabby came up close to Bane and attempted to grab the whistle only to have Bane spin and shove him to the ground. Feeling crowded, Bane moved a few steps away from the ever tightening group. Everyone watched in anticipation to see if he'd give it back. Instead, Bane picked up a rock and used it to smash the silver whistle against the base of the nearby tree trunk. Bane smirked as he took in everyone's shocked expressions. Bane, hoping to make a show of it, began rubbing and slapping his hands together as if he were washing his hands of the whole matter, all the while the others groaned or mumbled unflattering descriptions of him.

Crystal placed both hands on her hips. "You're a mean jackass! Nobody likes ya anyhow! How does *that feel*, Bane Taggart?" She got no reaction from him. "And by the way, we saw what ya done for Ms. Nutt, so don't go makin' it sound like ya done more 'n ya did." With a scowl on her face, she stared hard at Bane. This made Bane's smirk of satisfaction quickly dissipate and was replaced with a scowl and a look of warning.

Dewey began whining about how mean Bane was for breaking his whistle. For Bane, this took some of the sting out of the way Crystal had just spoken to him. He reveled in Dewey's misery while he listened to Billy and the others try to console him.

Bane stood around and mocked Dewey's whining. "Poor baby, ya don't got no whistle no more. Boo-hoo, I'm so sad."

"Leave 'im be, Bane!" Gail screeched.

Bane acted out an over-dramatization of being sorry for what he'd done. "I'm sorry, Retard. I won't do it no more." With self-gratification, he continued to smile as the others tried to convince Dewey into forgetting about the whistle.

Crystal even put a comforting arm around Dewey. "Dewey, don't forget, tamorrow they're goin' ta give ya a reward for savin' that there baby. Cause of you, Mrs. Carolyn's baby's alright now. Now don't ya worry no more about Bane. He can't help bein' mean." After a moment she added, "Maybe tamorrow they'll give ya a new whistle." This seemed to make Dewey feel better, and he began to smile as the others backed up her assumption.

"I git ta' wear my new suit. 'N Granddaddy says I can have pizza again."

"Good! Don't ya feel better now? Ship shape?!" Crystal asked cheerfully.

With subdued enthusiasm, while looking down at the ground, Dewey replied, "Yeah, ship shape." Then he looked at Bane and blurted out, "You should not do mean stuff!"

The next day at noon, it appeared as if half the county had shown up in front of the newly built county courthouse. It was designed and built to look as bland as possible and not last very long. It wasn't placed in the center of the square like the old one, but just off the square down a busy main street.

The old courthouse, built in 1894, was a beautifully designed majestic building that would be a source of pride for many more generations to come, but instead it was torn down by simple-minded and shortsighted people who thought it was old fashioned. The politics that surrounded its demise is still a contentious topic among many in the county.

The Fire Chief, Sheriff, and many of the county personnel gathered in front of the court house. The large crowd assembled in the street, on the sidewalk, and on the narrow strip of grass in front. The same reporter who'd covered the fire was busily taking photographs with his camera. The street was closed to accommodate the large crowd. Police cars and fire trucks, with their blue and red lights flashing, were stationed to cut off the flow of traffic for the event.

Al, Dewey, Bane and Ricky had been taken inside to meet the County Commissioner. Ms. Nutt, now recovered from the fire, and Mrs. Carolyn, holding her baby, were there as well. The County Commissioner explained what was going to happen during the ceremony. Ms. Nutt thanked Bane and Ricky, her unlikely heroes, for saving her life. Mrs. Carolyn did the same for Dewey and Al.

When they emerged from the courthouse door, everyone cheered and shouted while a fire truck's siren blared.

Al walked to the front of the crowd and stood next to a beautiful young girl with strawberry blonde hair who was cheering for Dewey the loudest. Looking down at her, Al asked, "Ya one of Dewey's friends?"

Still applauding, she glanced up with a big smile and said, "Yes, Sir. I'm Crystal." Al smiled back and turned his attention to the proceedings that were beginning. Everyone hushed when the fire truck's siren stopped wailing.

The County Commissioner cleared his throat and began to introduce all the officials on hand. He introduced Ms. Nutt and then Mrs. Carolyn, who was holding her baby. Both women proclaimed their gratitude for what had been done for them. Someone shuffled Dewey, Bane, and Ricky closer to the Fire Chief and Commissioner.

As the Commissioner told the story of what each one had done to save a life, he handed them a plaque with their name on it while the reporter took pictures for the News & Banner. Dewey started to fidget and looked very serious. Al knew this meant Dewey was nervous.

The Commissioner held up his hands to quiet the crowd. "I have two announcements to make that I'm sure all of you will be pleased to hear." He pulled two envelopes out of his coat pocket and held them up, one in each hand for all to see.

"This first announcement concerns Ms. Nutt. A lot of generous people who know and love Ms. Nutt have unselfishly given money to help her with her losses. I have a check for four thousand dollars to help her get back on her feet again. I know it's not enough to replace all that she's lost, but we sincerely hope it will help."

To her amazement and joy, he handed Ms. Nutt the check from the envelope to a thunderous applause. With tears in her eyes she took it in both hands and held it tightly to her bosom.

"The next envelope holds an opportunity for Ricky Taggart to once again show his courage and make us proud. I am pleased to give you, Ricky Taggart, your draft notice to report for duty at the United States Army Induction Center in Atlanta . . . ." He went on to extol on him the pride he and his country felt for him and those who'd served our country with dignity and honor.

Ricky turned pale as soon as he heard he'd been drafted. He didn't hear the Commissioner's words after that. His eyes quickly darted around while panic began to consume every fiber of his being. He felt trapped and wanted nothing more than to flee. The Commissioner then turned to him with the envelope. When Ricky didn't respond, the Commissioner grabbed Ricky's wrist and shoved the draft notice into his hand. Upon getting the envelope, Ricky almost dropped it on the ground due to his hand trembling so badly. The crowd broke into cheers and enthusiastic applause.

With one last round of applause the crowd disbursed. Al hurried to be with Dewey who was looking confused and anxious as people milled all around him. In his enthusiasm, Dewey almost hit Al in the face with his plaque when he tried to show it to him.

"Dewey wants a whistle. Bane broke mine."

With a grin on his face, Al took Dewey by the shoulder and led him towards the fire trucks. The firemen were giving away black plastic whistles and red plastic firemen's hats to all the children who came to the ceremony.

Dewey grinned big when he received his new plastic whistle, although it wasn't a shiny silver metal one like he'd had before.

"Now that you have ya whistle, are ya hungry for pizza?" inquired Al.

"Yes Sir! Pizza, pizza!" Suddenly Dewey was confronted by Gabby, Crystal and all of the others in the gang. "Congratulations Dewey. Ship shape," they said, as they each gave him a pat on the arm or back. They all disappeared just as suddenly because Gabby told them his father was waiting for them in his truck and wanted to leave.

"I see ya gotta lot of friends now, Boy." Dewey was all grins and smiles as he nodded his head and tested his new whistle.

Joe, Ricky, and Bane walked in silence back to their pickup truck. Ricky was still pale and shaken, while Bane was excited and in his own world as he stared at his plaque with pride.

Joe was the first to speak, "Sorry, Boy. Tough luck gittin' ya number called." He looked sideways at Ricky while shaking his head. He couldn't seem to find any more words. They had all seen the carnage shown on the evening news with the body counts updated daily. Joe realized that most Army recruits were sent directly to Vietnam after training. They also had the highest casualty rates. Ricky had heard stories from friends and their families of how horrible things were over there. Even Heard County, as small as it was, had suffered boys being injured or killed.

They piled into the cab of the truck with Bane in the middle. Bane asked, "What's it like bein' an Army man, Hero?" The sarcasm was thick in his voice.

"Shut up, ya little dog turd!" Ricky gave Bane a quick elbow jab to the ribs along with a hard stare when Bane looked up and started to protest. Bane turned to his father who was driving and could see he pretended not to have noticed, so he just muttered inaudible words under his breath.

That afternoon, Joe went to work and returned that evening with a case of beer. Coming through the door Joe proclaimed, "If my son's old 'nough ta go off 'n fight for his country, he'd be old 'nough ta git drunk with his ole man." Before getting one for himself, Joe reached into the case of cold beer and threw one to Ricky and one to Ricky's best friend, JoJo.

Because they always had to hide their drinking from him, Ricky and JoJo sat looking at him in amazement. "Well, drink up, Boys! It's not like ya half-witted jackasses haven't had 'em before. I know ya been stealin' 'em from me for years now. How damn stupid do ya think I am anyhow?"

Ricky said, "Dad, the law says ya got ta be twenty-one ta drink." JoJo, not wanting to wait, popped his bottle top and began slurping it down in a big show of machismo. Joe only grunted and waved his free hand, backhanding the air as if to indicate "the hell with it."

"Where's that brother of yers?"

"Still playing with his little friends, I s'pose. Claims one of 'em's his girlfriend—ya know the cute redheaded one that moved in last year. Ya know, Crystal," answered Ricky.

"Like his ole man, I reckon. Knows how ta git the women," Joe retorted.

With his beer finished, Joe got up from his easy chair. "Best put on some vittles. That's *chow* ta ya Army boys," he said with a big wink. He went into the kitchen and started cussing when he discovered the pan he wanted to use was still dirty. He was so busy preparing the kitchen for cooking he didn't noticed his chow comment had sent a chill through Ricky. JoJo noticed the change on Ricky's face, so he sat quietly for a while.

Trying to lighten the mood, JoJo commented, "Man, I'm sorry ya number come up. Don't worry though, cause I know you'll kick some butt 'n come home with tattoos all over ya."

"Why don't ya come with me 'n find out for ya'self, ya yellow bellied jackass? Ya chicken or somethin'?!" retorted Ricky with contempt. JoJo, Ricky's best friend since the fifth grade, had dropped out of school with Ricky the previous year. They were both eighteen, so Ricky felt that if he should have to go to war, so should JoJo.

"I ain't about ta volunteer for no crazy crap like that. Hell no! Hey, I feel for ya, but there ain't no way in hell I'm goin' 'less they make me. Besides, I've been savin' up for one of those new Pontiac GTO's. My ole man is helpin'. I done put in my order for one with the hood scoop and the spoiler on the back." JoJo sat silently, as there didn't seem to be anything else to say. Ricky had crawled into his own thoughts, so JoJo did the same.

Joe came back into the living room to retrieve another beer. When he saw them both just sitting there looking all solemn, for just a moment he thought about trying to console them, then he realized what he had to do. "What the hells ya problem, Boy?! I didn't raise no coward! Wipe that crybaby pout off ya face!" This brought the boys to full attention. They hadn't seen that coming.

"Now ya listen ta me real good. You'll kill as many Gooks as ya have ta so ya come home in one piece. Ain't no Taggart ever won no metal for bravery, but they always come home. Don't ya forget that! Now drink some beers 'n let 'er go. There's more 'n 'nough time ta worry if 'n when ya git through boot camp."

Later that night, Joe was awakened by a strange sound. He decided he needed to use the bathroom anyway so he got up. When he passed by Ricky's door he realized the sound was coming from inside. He stopped and listened. At first he wasn't sure what the sound was, but it got just loud enough momentarily so that he understood. Ricky was crying. Joe didn't know what to do so he just lingered there for a few moments longer. Although he didn't mind embarrassing Ricky and

Bane for his own entertainment, he knew that Ricky would be utterly humiliated if he went in to check on him. He walked away.

After Joe climbed back into bed, a tear rolled down his own cheek upon the stark realization that he didn't want, nor could he do anything about the possibility of his son going off to war. He'd seen what war had done to his older brother Elam. He didn't want it to happen to Ricky. He knew there was just acceptance of life as it came at you.

So he could get some relief from the heat, he rolled over to let his room fan blow directly into his face. Then he quietly uttered, "Damn it ta hell." Between the beers and working hard all day in the hot sun, he was exhausted, so he quietly slipped back to sleep.

That night while Al and Dewey practiced tying knots, Al started telling Dewey how proud he was of him. "I hung yer plaque for ya on the wall so everyone can see how brave ya was." He pointed to a spot beside his own shadow box. Dewey was amazed at this and got up from his chair to get a closer look. Just above the plaque was a framed newspaper article that described Dewey's actions along with a picture of him proudly holding his wooden sword.

"Dewey, I don't reckon ya ever heard of the 'general orders' before, but they're real important in the military. Every sailor has to learn 'em when he joins the Navy. They're kinda like rules for standing watch on board a ship. Ya have ta know 'em ta be a sailor in the Navy. I learned 'em from The *Bluejacket's Manual*; it's kinda like the Navy's Bible. Ya sorta obeyed 'em when ya helped that baby. I can still remember every one of 'em. Wanta hear 'em?"

Dewey leaned forward and listened intently as Al, with a far away look in his eyes, straightened up in his chair and began. "I will take charge of this post and all government property in view. I will walk my post in a military manner, keepin' always on the alert and observin' everything that takes place within sight or hearing. That's the one ya obeyed, Boy."

After Dewey smiled, he went on. "I will report all violations of orders I'm instructed ta enforce. Ta repeat all calls from posts more distant from the guard house than my own. Ta quit my post only when properly relieved. Ta receive, obey and pass on ta the sentry who relieves me all orders from the Commanding Officer, Command Duty Officer, Officer of the Deck . . . ."

After finishing, Al relaxed and slumped back into his chair with a sense of pride at remembering the general orders so well. "What ya think about that, Boy?"

Dewey just kept looking while he absorbed what he'd heard as best as he could. His lips moved as he tried to repeat some of it to himself.

"Don't worry, Dewey, Ya don't have ta memorize all of it ta be a good sailor. But ya do have ta follow my orders 'n try 'n be the bes' person ya can."

With that, Dewey sat back in his chair and let out a long sigh of relief.

Suddenly Snipe sat up and gave two quick soft barks and a short quiet growl while he looked around the room as if looking for something to appear. After a silent moment, he laid back down, relaxed and signed as if the danger was gone.

Dewey had witnessed this many times before, but this time he asked, "Why'd Snipe do that?"

Al gave a knowing grin as he replied, "Oh, that's called chasing the devil." Dewey cocked his head to one side as he looked confused. "All that really means is he heard something we didn't. Some folks claim dogs do that when the Devil tries to sneak up on a body. They claim dogs know when a bad spirit is around, so they chase 'em away." This seemed to satisfy Dewey.

"Now finish ya knot 'n git ya'self ta bed. Even brave men like ya'self need ya sleep. I'll be in direc'ly ta turn out the light."

Chapter 10 – The Challenge

WITHIN minutes of stepping outside to do his chores, Dewey began to sweat profusely. He went about collecting the chicken eggs, feeding the chickens, and cutting the grass closest to the house with a manual push mower. It cut grass by the motion of gears on the wheels turning the blades as he propelled the heavy steel contraption with brute force. Al had refused to let Dewey use the motorized lawnmower in the hopes of helping him to lose weight and build more stamina.

Dewey longed to go play with his friends as he went about his morning chores. Well over a month had passed since he'd made friends with the gang at the hut village. The joy of spending time with his friends had become as much a part of the fabric of his life as eating and sleeping.

The dog days of summer dragged on as the stifling temperatures and humidity felt at times almost unbearable. To add to the misery of this steamy day late in July, flies and mosquitoes swarmed in ever increasing numbers. The recent rain showers filled the hollowed out tree stumps, discarded tires, and anything else that could hold water. This created stagnant pools of water in which the growing mosquito larva thrived to become menacing creatures of misery, much to the dismay of every warm blooded mammal.

The daytime showers caused every field and roadway to become a cloud of haze as the steam rose from the already hot surfaces of the land, much like a drop of water hitting a hot skillet. The rain clouds would move on as quickly as they appeared, causing musty smells of vegetation from the fields and oily rancid odors from the hot pavement on the roads.

Due to the stifling heat, Dewey wasn't wearing a shirt underneath his overalls, nor socks on his feet. He'd developed a deep suntan that was pock marked by welts left behind by what seemed like every kind of hungry crawling or flying insect around that had an appetite for blood. They covered his whole upper body, legs, and ankles. The bite marks were in various stages of healing, from fresh bites, to scabs, to scars. Dewey always had fresh red scratch marks from trying to relieve the constant and ever present itching.

Since school had let out, most of the girls wore shorts with thin cotton shirts or sundresses. The boys usually wore shorts that were made from cutting off the legs of the old pants they'd worn to school or had outgrown their lengths. Many of the shorts had patches sewn on them where the fabric had worn through or became tattered. Much of the time, the boys went without shirts and shoes. Sometimes their feet never felt the inside of shoes until Sunday. Dewey wore only overalls, which held his beloved wooden sword and a pair of boots, so he was especially hot most of the time. Although he had lost a great deal of weight, he was still somewhat heavy, which increased his discomfort from the relentless heat.

Al tried to teach Dewey about tractors and farming before allowing Dewey to disappear into the woods. Early on some mornings, before it became too hot, Al and Dewey would hoe the different rows of vegetables. Less time was spent on this now that many of the vegetables were played out. Although Al no longer had horses or cows, he still maintained the fence along the property line with his neighbors. He believed it not only looked good, but kept the neighbors' cows and horses at bay. He needed to keep others livestock from getting to his crops and destroying his hard earned yield.

Dewey was still interested in play-acting pirates in the loft when not hanging out with the other children, usually after supper and before his bath. No matter how hard Al tried, he couldn't hold Dewey's attention for very long or get him interested in farming. This frustrated

Al because he was trying to prepare Dewey for the possibility of making a living some day. He knew old age was already setting upon himself at a rapid pace and Dewey wasn't too far from the responsibilities of manhood and needed a trade.

"Boy, ya ain't learned ta use that thing between yer ears yet. It ain't jus' for keepin' ya head from collapsin'. Now, let's go over this again." As he had done many times before, Al pointed to each of the tractor implements and repeated, "This here is a harrow. It's used ta break ground. This is a rock rake, for gathering rocks and other objects that are hard and big enough that they need ta be gathered up." He walked down the row of implements and described each one and their uses.

When Al got to the last small lonely-looking implement, he gave a small chuckle and said, "And don't forget, this here is the 'Alabama Tooth.' We call it that because we like ta joke it's like some folks in Alabama, it only has one tooth. But keep it ta ya' self 'n don't ya go sayin' it in front of strangers, 'cause it might offend somebody if they're from Alabama or somethin'. Besides, they say that about us too. It's for bustin' up real hard dirt or makin' a row for buryin' a single line for plumbin'." When Dewey looked at him funny, Al just shook his head and said, "Never mind. Let's go to the barn."

Just as they neared the chicken coop Al spotted a hen's egg in a clump of grass next to the coop. Apparently one of the chickens had laid it there instead of in a nest inside the coop. Al looked up at the sky to see if the sun would get blocked by any clouds soon. Believing it wouldn't he turned to Dewey and said, "Some folks have a notion to say 'it's hot enough to cook an egg' when it's real hot like taday, so lets see if it's true."

After arriving at the barn Al said, "Watch this." He broke the egg open and deposited its contents on the metal top of a crib adjacent to the barn. It had been exposed to the sun's hot rays all morning and would be for some time. "We'll see if it's one of those egg-fryin' days they talk about." Snipe jumped up and put his front paws on the metal top and began to reach for the raw egg with his snout. "Leave it, Boy," Al commanded. Snipe lowered himself back to the ground.

After a few minutes the egg was well on its way to cooking. They could see the egg white slowly turn from clear to white. The yolk seemed more reluctant to cook, so Al broke it so it would spread. They watched for a few more minutes until the egg looked like it was just about done on one side. Then Al flipped it over to cook on the other side. Within minutes Al said, "Looks like it's one of them days don't it, Boy."

Dewey didn't say anything as he took his finger and poked at the almost cooked egg. Only a little of it was still runny. "It sure is hot taday, Granddaddy."

Al replied, "We bes' give it ta Snipe, or he might not want'a be our friend no more. Go ahead 'n give it ta 'im, Boy." With that Dewey scooped up the limp egg and dropped it into Snipe's already open mouth.

Al had worked on something new he invented during the winter. It was a combination of different tools he planned to put together for smoothing the ground after harvest. He used the big tractor to move the largest part of the framework into the barn. He placed it just under the horizontal post that stuck out from the barn's loft, the one Dewey used as his plank for mutinous crew members. The end of the post was already rigged with a large hoist and tackle for lifting heavy objects. Many a time, Al used it to pull engines out of tractors or to hoist objects too heavy to lift otherwise. Dewey only knew it to be his plank for punishing his unruly pirates and sending them to their inevitable doom. He used it often.

"Dewey, help me hook up this tackle ta the frame on this side. That way we can turn over my new 'ground smoother'." With Dewey's help, Al guided the chain and hook through the metal framing. This caused the chain to rattle and clank as the metal struck metal. Snipe decided he didn't want any part of the goings on once the chains started making metallic clanging noises, so he left the barn.

Snipe busied himself just outside the barn in the grassy area chasing after large grasshoppers as they hovered and fluttered their large wings to attract a mate. He'd chase anything that would run from him, except the chickens. Al corrected that behavior immediately upon Snipe's joining the family.

The chain was heavy and didn't move very smoothly through the various tight angles and parts once the tension was placed on it. Working together, they finally got it secured to the pulley's hook.

"Now help me pull down on this pulley chain so we can turn this thing over." With some awkward movements, they were able to lift one side of the contraption to a point of flipping it over. "Now move over here 'n help me flip it over. Be careful 'n jump back if it starts ta come back this way. We don't wanta git stuck under this contraption." After a few missteps they successfully turned it over. "Good job, Boy."

"Ship shape?"

"Yeah, ship shape, Dewey."

Because of the alluring crops, Snipe had daily chances to chase away rabbits, deer or various other animals that had the misfortune of coming within eyesight, earshot, or better still, his powerful sense of smell. He would even take on other dogs. No matter what their size, Snipe never backed down. No longer driven by hunger, he stopped killing things, except the occasional mouse, rat, or armadillo. Al broke Snipe from dragging armadillo carcasses into the yard to show what he'd killed.

Al and Dewey were still inside the barn when suddenly Snipe came running in at full speed with teeth bared while growling. Although caught off guard, Al held his ground as he watched Snipe run directly at him. He barely flinched when Snipe lunged at something near his left foot.

It was only after Snipe snatched up a snake and slung it a few feet away that Al realized what was happening. Al saw it was only a large king snake, which was of no danger to him or anyone else, as long as you weren't a rodent or another snake. Snipe continued to bark and make lunges at the snake until Al came over and calmed him down.

"Good, Boy. Now leave it."

"Snipe save Granddaddy!" Dewey proclaimed as he walked over to look at the snake with his sword at the ready.

"Not really. But he thinks so. It's jus' a king snake. They're good at keepin' the rodent population in check."

Dewey had a puzzled look on his face.

"That means they eat things like rats 'n mice. Unfortunately, they also eat chicken eggs." Al looked down at Snipe and said, "Now, Snipe, ya keep that thing away from my chickens, ya hear."

That seemed to answer Dewey's question and he let his sword drop to his side. "Now, Dewey, don't ya go tryin' ta pick up any snakes, 'cause they might be poisonous."

Staring in wonderment, Dewey nodded his head and gazed at this very large dark snake as it slid along the barn's wall and out through a crack. Snipe watched with rapt attention as it disappeared, then darted outside to follow it.

Al called, "Stay! Leave it alone, Boy!" Snipe quickly reappeared in the barn's doorway once again and came back to Al's side with bouncing steps full of excitement as his tail wagged briskly from side to side.

"Good, Boy." Al was grateful to know that Snipe was there to watch out for him.

Al turned back to the work at hand. "Dewey, ya make sure ta be careful when yer up in the loft. There's a lot of sharp spikes on this thing that could hurt ya. We're goin' ta add a couple of more rollers after I weld spikes on 'em. If ya was ta fall on it, ya could hurt ya' self real bad. Now help me clear the ground around it so nothin' catches fire while I weld."

After they made sure only the dirt was visible around the work area, they put away the rake and broom.

"Now help me set up the tables 'n equipment."

They moved various work benches, two boxes filled with metal spikes, and two large tubes with bearings on each end that would later be connect to the frame. After Al wheeled over the welding equipment, Dewey asked, "Ship shape?"

Al knew that Dewey's attention was about done for the day. With a sigh, he answered, "Ship shape, Dewey."

"Let's go ta the house 'n eat before ya go 'n disappearin' on me." With that, they headed to the house with Snipe close on their heels.

When they were finished cleaning themselves up for lunch, Al said, "Let me make ya an old favorite sandwich of mine. It's called a banana sandwich. Looky here. First ya put mayonnaise on one slice of bread, then peanut butter on the other slice of bread, and then ya slice up a banana ta put in-between 'em. Now ya have one of the best tastin' sandwiches ever invented. Course, it won't be complete without potato chips. There now, we're all set."

Al placed the plate in front of Dewey and watched as he picked it up and inspected it with some trepidation. Dewey's first bite was small, but that was all it took because he then quickly devoured the sandwich. Al knew immediately that he'd started something, so he made Dewey another one. He would make it a point to keep making them for lunch as long as bananas were available at the store.

After lunch, Dewey set off for the tree line across the field. He had only been given an apple for desert. He munched on it as he meandered down the winding trail through the trees and out of sight of the farm.

Dewey stopped at the first creek he came to, took off his boots, and sat down to soak his feet. This was becoming his routine on the way to the hut village. He sat on his favorite rock in the shade and finished most of his apple while he admired the lush scenery nature had provided for him.

He'd learned to sit quietly so birds and animals would come out of hiding. Once he had eaten his fill of the apple, he tossed the remaining fleshy core over to the usual spot. Soon, out came a gray rabbit from the nearby bushes. It began to nibble on the fleshy core. The rabbit had become accustomed to Dewey and made it a routine to be close by at this time of day. The rabbit was fed by Dewey almost daily with treats of carrots, corn, or pieces of fruit. In return, Dewey got to see and admire the rabbit.

"I hope that weren't yer baby rabbit mean ole Bane killed, Mr. Fuzzy." The rabbit didn't acknowledge Dewey as it continued nibbling on the apple core with the occasional lifting of its head to sniff the air for signs of danger. "I don't know why no one would wanta hurt ya babies." Having finished, the rabbit started to hop away when from up above a hawk screeched. The rabbit froze initially, then, sensing the danger had passed, it scurried away.

Dewey arrived to a flurry of words between Todd and Jason who were both eleven years old. They continued ranting and raving about who was the best climber between them. "Oh yeah, I bet I could climb up a tree so fast it'd make a squirrel cry," bragged Todd, jutting his chin out.

Jason pushed Todd out of the swing. Todd recovered but was unable to reclaim the swing because Jason had wrapped his arms and legs tightly to the ropes and seat. Agitated over this turn about, Todd replied, "Well, I'd bet that squirrel'll be cryin' cause ya chewed off one of his legs afore ya started climbin', Sissy."

Dewey watched with interest as the two played out their usual ritual of quarreling. He understood they were the best of friends, as well as foes, over anything and everything. He, like others, became desensitized by the two's constant bickering and fighting.

Bane arrived on the scene and watched the two with a particular interest. Slowly a grin appeared on his face. He decided to have some fun with them. "You sissies ain't nothin' but all talk." This interruption captured their attention.

Upon joining them at the swings, Gabby saw the look in Bane's eyes and said, "Don't listen ta 'im. I know he's up ta somethin'."

Bane's grin quickly turned into a scowl when he shot Gabby a warning look. "Shut ya mouth, before I shut it for ya." He then smiled again as he turned back to Jason and Todd, "You sissies ought'a show us who's the bes' climber. How 'bout a contest?"

Pattie sensed something was amiss when she heard Bane's warning to Gabby, so she decided to stay and see what all the fuss was about. After listening to Bane prod the two boys, she went looking for Crystal and the others to get help. It was too late.

"Alright then, pick out a tree. We'll see for sure then," Jason told Bane.

"Suits me jus' fine," added Todd, while sticking his face close to Jason's, causing their faces to come within inches of each other, their eyes locked in a contest of intimidation.

"Follow me. I got jus' what's needed," Bane said as he turned and began leading them into the woods towards the large oaks down by the creek. Like most trees close to a creek, they were much larger than most others.

"What's goin' on, Billy?" inquired Crystal, as she joined the group heading towards the creek. Having gotten some more materials from her mother, she had reluctantly stopped working on the girls' hut to see what all the fuss was about.

Billy shook his head and explained. "Jason 'n Todd was fightin' over who was the bes' climber 'n Bane done got 'em to agree ta prove it. Bane told 'em that whoever loses has the ugliest momma. So Jason started makin' fun of Todd's momma's eye. Ya know, 'cause one of her eyes is blind and has some sort of white lookin' thingy in it. So then Todd starts makin' fun of Jason's mother 'n her moles, ya know on 'er face 'n neck. Sayin' she has witches warts 'cause black hairs grow out of some of 'em. So now they're mad at each other cause of Bane." Billy looked at her with palms up while shrugging. "I couldn't git 'im ta stop." Because she still didn't understand, he added, "Then Bane dared 'em ta climb ta the top of the tallest tree."

"I don't git why ya couldn't talk some sense into 'em? They listen ta ya most of the time."

"I promise ya, me 'n Gabby couldn't git neither of 'em ta listen." He explained this as they followed the others to an old oak tree down by the creek.

Worried, Crystal ran ahead of the group as they were approaching the tree. She stopped Bane and the others by blocking their path. "What ya won't?" demanded Bane.

Pointing her finger in his face, she said, "You got no right ta make 'em do somethin' so stupid. Why'd ya have ta make fun of their mommas?"

"Mind ya own business. This is men stuff," Bane huffed back at her, while casually pushing her hand aside.

"Todd! Jason! Don't ya do it!" commanded Crystal, only to be ignored as they went around her. Then the two began pushing and shoving one another upon reaching the base of the tree. Crystal's reaction only added to Bane's pleasure, so he smiled as he nudged her aside.

Still hoping to stop the two boys, Crystal and Billy attempted to reason with them. "You're friends 'n don't have ta prove nothin' jus' ta satisfy the likes of him," Crystal said while pointing at Bane.

Bane was gloating as he said, "Hey, I didn't do nothin'. They jus' wanta show who's the bes' climber is all. Why don't ya mind ya own business anyhow? Ya cluck like an old hen every time ya open ya mouth lately."

"Maybe ya think that cause ya got worms in ya head, Bane Taggart," snapped Crystal.

Dewey knew something was wrong, but he didn't know exactly what. He watched as the two boys started reaching for the lowest branches of the oak tree.

Bane asked, "You two sissies ready?"

Neither one spoke, while the others in the gang watched with an uneasy silence once they knew it was inevitable.

"Ready . . . . Go!" Bane shouted.

Todd and Jason immediately took to their respective limb with ease. No sooner than they got up in the tree, the two were fighting over shared paths as they ascended. Halfway up, they fought for control of a limb here and there with almost disastrous results; in their haste, they both came close to falling a couple of times.

Crystal shouted, "You two stop that fightin'! Ya gonna kill each other!"

Bonnie Lou grabbed Gabby by the arm and pleaded, "Gabby, I'm worried. Make 'em stop. They're actin' crazy."

"What can I do? I tried as bes' I could, but they won't listen."

The two could be heard making snide remarks to one another, as well as challenging the other to catch up when one got ahead of the other. When they got closer to the top, Todd began to hesitate after he looked down. Egged on by Jason, he began to climb to the next level when a rotten limb snapped loose and fell away just as he put weight on it. He froze. He was now very high in the tree and further up than he had ever been before. Jason, despite his own growing apprehension, kept climbing with reckless abandonment.

Once Jason climbed as far as he felt it possible, he turned his attention towards Todd and the others. "What happened, SISSY?! Ya scared ta come up here with me? Ya want ya mommy?"

Emboldened, Todd started to move once more, but stopped when he heard Billy shouting, "Todd, ya don't have ta go any higher! Ya went higher then I'd ever go! Come on down! Ya did real good!" When Todd looked down at Billy he was overcome with fright. He now clung to the tree trunk as tightly as he could for fear of falling.

"Go on, Sissy . . . . Keep goin', Scaredy-Cat!" shouted Bane.

"SHUT UP, BANE!" Crystal screamed.

Unfazed by Crystal's outburst, Bane continued to provoke Todd. The others shouted "Don't listen ta Bane!" "Come down before somebody gets hurt." "Y'all don't have ta prove nothin'."

Pattie, who rarely interfered with anyone's doings, had seen enough. She knew Todd was in trouble, so she shouted, "Todd, ya better git down here right this minute or I'm gonna tell ya momma what ya done!"

Jason, satisfied with his victory, started to descend from the top ever so slowly. He became nervous at the realization of just how high he'd climbed. His adrenaline rush dissipated, he began to shake a little as he ever so slowly reached with one foot at a time for the next lower limb. He was holding tightly with his arms and hands until he was sure of his footing.

Once Jason got down to Todd, he realized he couldn't go any further until Todd moved. There wasn't any alternate path to go around Todd. "Git outa the way, Todd! I can't go down till ya move!"

Todd looked at him with terror in his eyes and stuttered, "I'm f-f-fixin' ta move. Hold on."

"Well, what's stoppin' ya?"

Todd looked up at Jason, then back to the ground and then back to Jason once more. He didn't move as he lowered his voice so the others couldn't hear. "I can't move. Ya gotta help me."

Jason, realizing how scared Todd had become, also softened his voice so no one else would hear, "Hey, don't be scared. Ya got up here didn't ya?"

"Yeah," answered Todd, with a quiver in his voice.

"Don't look at the ground no more. Don't think about nothin' but puttin' one foot down at a time. I'll be right behind ya." Todd hesitated a moment and started to move when suddenly a rock bounced off a limb close to them.

"Why don't ya sissies come down? Ya scared or somethin'? Ya want me ta go git ya mommas cause yer a couple of babies that need ya diapers changed?" Bane asked mockingly.

Dewey, now absolutely sure that Bane was being mean again, grabbed Bane's shoulder. "Stop bein' mean, Bane. Ya goin' ta hurt my friends?"

"Get off 'a me, No-Nuts," Bane snorted as he yanked his shoulder free.

Billy and Gabby came around to confront Bane. "Leave 'em be, Bane. It's not fair ta scare 'em anymore 'n they already are."

"Jus' havin' fun's all," Bane replied as he went to pick up another stone.

"Cut it out!" Billy warned.

Bane, realizing he might be pushing it too far, tossed the rock onto the ground and acted like he didn't care. "Geesh, can't anybody have a little fun around here?" Because Dewey was behind him, Bane was unaware that Dewey had pulled his sword out after he observed Bane picking up another rock. Gabby moved over and was about to grab Dewey's arm, when to his relief, Bane tossed the rock onto the ground.

Dewey watched Bane in an almost trance like state with his wooden sword still drawn. Billy and the others shouted words of encouragement until Todd started coming down ever so slowly. Jason kept encouraging him from above.

When the two came within fifteen feet of the ground, Todd's fear dissipated and he regained his confidence. His pride made him want to show out for the others. He became more like himself and began to frolic about and put on a show.

When they got close to the bottom limb, Jason, weary of watching Todd's buffoonery, tried to move past Todd. Because he was caught up in his silly antics, Todd accidentally bumped against Jason. This caused him to stumble. Everyone gasped as they watch Todd's awkward fall to the ground. An audible crack was clearly heard by all.

Todd sat up with a bewildered look. Not sure of his condition, he began to scan himself for injury. He let out a loud yell when he reached out his right arm to brace himself to stand. He grabbed his right arm as he rolled onto the ground. It was broken and a large lump was visible underneath the skin of his forearm.

By that time, Jason and the others were by his side asking, "You alright? We heard somethin' crack."

"I broke my damn arm, no thanks ta **you**, Jackass."

Jason, guilt-ridden, said, "Hey Todd, I'm sorry. I didn't mean ta . . . ."

"It's not ya fault, Jason. He did it ta himself, actin' like a fool 'n such," Crystal interjected. "And he wouldn't a' got hurt 'n the first place if Bane wasn't so damn set on gittin' the two of ya ta act like fools jus' ta amuse hisself." She then bent down and helped Todd sit up.

Crystal looked up from comforting Todd and glared at Bane, who was trying to get a closer look at the damaged arm. She shouted angrily, "I hope yer proud of what ya done! Why don't ya go with 'im 'n explain ta his momma how it happened?! I'm sure his momma'd wanta thank ya real personal-like!"

Bane let out a little grunt as he rose and stepped back, "I didn't do nothin'. Ain't my fault he can't climb trees without fallin'. 'Sides, Jason's the one who knocked 'im down anyway."

Chapter 11 – Broken Sword

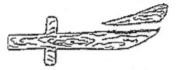

BILLY, Gail, and Jason walked Todd back to the trailer park to tell Todd's mother what'd happened. The rest of the gang watched and worried that their own parents might overreact to Todd's accident and make a big fuss. The group unanimously agreed that what happened to Todd was mostly his own fault, but they still felt sorry for him.

After Todd and the others were out of sight, Bane began making light of the situation, and started making heckling comments: "Poor baby, he broke his arm . . . Did ya see the big baby crying?" and "I guess that proves he's a sissy after all."

"Why don't ya climb up that tree 'n break ya arm 'n see how you feel then, Mister Smart Aleck. Then we'll see if it makes you cry. It's yer fault he went up that tree and now he's hurt, but yer too much of a chicken ta go face his momma." No reply. **"Well?!"** shouted Crystal. Bane ignored her and continued to amuse himself by continuing his callus remarks.

Bane's lack of feelings or empathy for Todd caused the others to become incensed at his behavior. They became emboldened by Bane's lack of reaction to Crystal's open belligerence towards him, so they began to voice their animosity towards him as well. They openly made comments expressing their opinions about how heartless they believed Bane to be and how he was always causing trouble.

Oddly, this had an encouraging affect upon Bane, so he dropped to the ground and mimicked Todd's reaction to breaking his arm. Crystal, flushed with indignation, stood over Bane and pointed down with her index finger at him. "Shut up, Bane Taggart! Shor as there's a hell, yer gonna burn for treatin' people the way ya do!"

Perturbed by her openly confronting him once more in this manner, Bane grabbed Crystal's extended hand, stood up, and leaned in close enough for her to feel the heat of his breath before he said, "I ain't caused nobody ta git hurt! And who the hell are you ta blame me anyhow?! Huh! I git hurt worse 'n than that all the time by my own brother 'n daddy. I ain't never seen nobody 'round here care 'bout that. What ya gotta say about that, huh? **Well say it!**"

Crystal was about to reply when Bane's voice dropped eerily low and full of warning as he went on to say, "I ain't gonna take no more from the likes of you cause I ain't got nothin', I say nothin', ta lose." Bane's body tensed even more as he leaned in even closer towards Crystal, poised to unleash his wrath upon her. Bane's face became almost demonic looking and his eyes revealed eminent danger.

Gabby moved in closer to intercede if needed while the others formed a closer semi-circle around Crystal in a show of unity. Their faces reflected the intensity of the moment. They knew this was one of those volatile points at which things could become horrifically dangerous where Bane was concerned. One could feel static electricity in the very air they were breathing.

Realizing the danger, Crystal held her peace to let the moment pass. The surrounding nature seemed to have realized it as well, because the world around them fell silent. Moments passed as they all stood frozen. Only Dewey didn't seem affected by it, so he asked, "Why everybody so quiet?" Then he looked to the others for an answer. Finally, Bane's expression changed and the world around them returned to normal.

Crystal was so angry that the pain in her hand was blocked out while Bane continued to squeeze it with all his might. She didn't back down as she continued to stare back at Bane without flinching. "Bane Taggart, you're always causin' trouble! Yer as mean as a snake with a thorn up its butt! Why don't ya go off 'n kill somethin'? Ain't that what yer good at anyhow? Oh, I see a bug over there. Don't ya want ta go squash it or somethin'?" she asked mockingly, pointing with her free hand.

"Screw you! Screw all of ya!" Bane retorted.

"I thought that's what ya magazines were for!" As soon as she said it, Crystal knew that she probably shouldn't have and wished she could take it back.

Terror flashed across Bane's face as he let go of Crystal's hand involuntarily and staggered backwards. The jolt of what had just been said openly was his worst nightmare come to life. He felt utterly naked. He was in shock. He became pale as the blood drained from his face and he had to steady himself as his legs became weak. Seconds seemed like minutes as Bane stared at Crystal with his mouth hanging open. Humiliation washed over him like a cold wave.

Bane slowly began to recover and his mind searched beyond the fog so he could attempt to mitigate the damage to his manhood. Betrayal, anguish, and then unadulterated hatred was how Bane felt toward Crystal. No beating could have wounded him as much or as deeply as her words had. Bane was absolutely certain everyone knew what she meant and had known all along because she'd already told on him. He wanted revenge.

Just as Bane took a menacing step towards Crystal with his fists balled tightly, Dewey drew his wooden sword and moved to intercede. Seeing this, Bane abruptly changed course and shoved his way through Gabby and Bonnie Lou. He started for home, but stopped when he got close to the girls' hut. Angrily he then began kicking the wall of the girls' hut until he managed to dislodge one of the large boards and knock it inwards. Immediately he began kicking at yet another board as his anger surged in ever growing waves. Because it didn't give way fast enough, he used his fist as well until it also gave way. It was only after the second board collapsed that he appeared to get some satisfaction and relief.

Crystal called after him. "Big deal, we can fix that!"

It was only then that they saw Jill come into view. She'd been standing on the other side of the girls' hut watching Bane take out his frustration on the hut and waiting for her chance to join the others. While giving him a wide berth, she quickly walked past Bane to the others.

Bane gave Jill only a passing glance as he started to say something, then with a dismissive wave he stormed over to the boy's hut and disappeared inside. He quickly emerged in the doorway with a hammer in one hand and a box of nails in the other. Stopping, he held up the tools for the others to see. "Try doin' it without these, Bitch!" Everybody remained close to one another as they watched Bane leave with their only hammer and the box of nails.

Gabby spoke up first, "At least we still have some nails, 'cause I left some in the other hut." No one responded.

"What Bane do that for?" interrupted Dewey.

"Cause he's sick in the head, Dewey, 'n he can't help but bein' mean. My momma says his folks beat 'im so much it left holes in 'im. 'N the devil likes ta fill holes in a body's soul," answered Bonne Lou. Dewey returned her explanation with a confounded expression.

Once Bane topped the hill and was out of sight, Crystal's expression relaxed.

Jill grabbed at Bonnie Lou's arm to get her attention. "What happened ta poor Todd? All I could git out of Gail is that he fell out of a tree and it was Bane's doin'."

Bonnie Lou began telling Jill every detail as she walked her towards the creek to show her the tree where the accident had occurred. Pattie initially followed, but changed her mind and rejoined Crystal. She thought it was better not to leave Crystal alone.

"Gabby, I guess ya need ta git the nails so we can fix the wall before the critters tear up the place again," said Crystal.

"No problem," he shot back as he went to look for them with Dewey in tow. Soon they were back and showed the jar of nails to the others. "These ain't the best, but they'll do, I reckon."

"Gabby, how are we gonna use 'em without a hammer?" asked Pattie.

"We could find a rock or somethin', I reckon. Come on, Dewey, let's go find a good 'nough rock ta hammer with." He and Dewey headed for the creek, while the girls started moving the broken boards over to one side of the hut.

After a little while, Gabby and Dewey came back with two rocks that looked sturdy enough for hammering nails. It wasn't long before both rocks were broken or chipped to the point of no longer being of any use as hammers. They didn't know until they'd begun their work that other boards had been knocked loose as well. The wall was only halfway repaired.

Dewey stepped forward with his sword and began to pound a nail with it, but only after a few strikes his sword snapped lengthwise with the wood grain. Dewey was left holding two separate pieces that used to be the blade section of his sword. He stared at the two pieces of broken wood with a sad and worried look.

"I'm sorry, Dewey," said Crystal, trying to comfort him.

"Dewey's granddaddy goin' ta be mad," whined Dewey, with a pout on his face. He tried to press the two pieces together again many times without success. With each attempt, the sword's blade immediately fell apart. The handle portion of the sword was still intact, but the blade section attached to it came to a very sharp point at the end.

Gabby said, "Don't worry, Dewey. We can glue it back together soes no one'll ever notice." Gabby walked to the boy's hut to get the glue as he spoke over his shoulder, "I'll be right back." Dewey watched him with a forlorn expression. Crystal tried to reassure him while Gabby was gone.

When Gabby returned he had a plastic bottle of wood glue. "There ain't much left, but there ought ta be enough ta fix it." Gabby took the two pieces from Dewey and squeezed out all the glue he possibly could onto them. It was just enough to give him hope, but not really enough to do the job as well as he'd hoped.

"Now, Dewey, there ain't much glue, so don't go bangin' with it anymore. I'll try 'n git more glue tonight from my daddy in case it comes apart again. Ya can't play with it for a while or it'll come apart again. Ya have ta wait till the glue dries." He took some twine and wrapped it tightly around the broken area of the blade to fasten it into place. The seam where the blade was broken was barely visible because the two pieces fit together perfectly. Dewey beamed as he surveyed the repaired sword.

Together, Gabby and Dewey went seeking out more rocks to hammer with while Crystal and Pattie remained at the hut. When a rock was no longer of any use, they tossed it aside and used others they'd gathered. Bonnie Lou and Jill rejoined them and together they kept at it until the hut was back together once more.

About the time they finished and were in the process of relaxing in the cool shade, Dewey heard his bell ringing in the distance. He tried to slip the sword back into his overall's loop but it wouldn't go in because of the strings. He took off the twine and happily the sword stayed together as he slipped it into his overalls loop and headed for home.

The remainder of that afternoon Bane sat in his trailer and fumed over what Crystal had said in front of the others. While he sat on his hand-me-down bed that'd been worn out long before it was given to him, Bain's embarrassment and anger came back with a vengeance each time the earlier events played over and over in his mind. He had no idea if the others knew what Crystal was truly referring to with her comment about the magazines. He only knew that she had utterly humiliated him.

Because he was hot, Bain tried repeatedly to open the rickety window in his bedroom wider so he could get more air circulation. After giving up trying to force the window to open all the way, he went to the front of the trailer and took one of the only two fans in the house that still worked so he could cool himself.

The trailer was old and didn't have much insulation between the outer layer of aluminum and the interior walls. If it hadn't been for the shade from the trees and hills on both sides of the trailer park, it would have been like living in an oven. It was cold in the winter and hot in the summer. As a result of Joe's bad handiwork, the trailer had patchwork inside and outside. It was the oldest and ugliest trailer in the park now that Ms. Nutt's had burned down.

Later that afternoon, Ricky and JoJo showed up. It wasn't long before they began picking on Bane in their usual manner, telling him what a wimp he was and so forth. They weren't used to seeing him home so early, so they decided to make sport of him. This had become their habit when they were bored, and they were always bored.

Ricky nudged JoJo with his elbow before he spoke to Bane. "What's wrong, Wimp? Ya girlfriend send ya home early? Oh, what's the matter? Did ya have a lover's spat?"

"Least I got one, Army Man," snapped Bane with a sneer. Ricky let it slide this time, as he looked over to survey JoJo's reaction. JoJo diverted his eyes because he didn't want any part of that sore subject, since Ricky was to report to the Army in two days. Ricky gave Bane a stern look that showed that particular subject was closed, or else there would be serious consequences.

Ricky was in good spirits because Joe'd promised to get him and JoJo beers for the next two nights to take their minds off Ricky's imminent departure. Joe was apprehensive about Ricky going, but at the same time he was also proud of him. He'd even gone so far as to brag about his son going into the Army to his co-workers. He'd heard the stories about the cowards who ran off to Canada and such places or changed religions to avoid their duty. To celebrate his son becoming a man, he figured the least he could do was to supply him with lots of beer.

Joe came through the door just after six o'clock with a bag full of groceries and two cases of beer. No sooner did the door start to close behind him than a woman appeared holding another bag of groceries. Never having laid eyes on this person before, the boys were stunned. They sat quietly waiting for an explanation as to who this woman was coming into their home. Joe rarely brought home one of his lady friends. It had been years since the last one.

She wasn't very tall, but she was extremely overweight. Her clothes strained under the stress of her bulging waistline. She had a beehive hair style that was in desperate need of a hairdresser's care and she wore brightly colored makeup. When she gave them a quick timid smile, they could see many of her teeth were being eaten away by blackish cavities at the gum line. Her eyes gave the impression of her having very little self-esteem. Of course this was exactly the type of women that got involved with Joe.

"Boys, I brung Mary Beth home with me soes she can cook us somethin' good for once. Mary Beth, this boy with the nasty looking head of dark hair and the snaggletooth grin is Ricky, my oldest. The fat-ass sittin' beside him is his best friend, or girlfriend, I'm not sure which, is JoJo. The scrawny little thing with the devil in his eyes is Bane."

When she was introduced to each of the boys, Mary Beth wouldn't look at any of them directly. She fidgeted a lot, which the boys noticed immediately.

Right away, Ricky began to smirk when looking at the others like it was some sort of an inside joke. Ricky had met some of his father's girlfriends in the past when he was given the task of picking one up from their job or someplace else from time to time. He had never met or heard of Mary Beth before, but knew what kind of woman she was none the less.

The boys were careful not to make any visual signs of noticing Ricky's mischievous grin. They didn't want to bring down Joe's wrath. Joe always referred to all of his women as "cooking whores." Joe was covered in filth most of the time, so he wasn't exactly a catch himself. His only requirement for women was that they could cook and put up with him showing up at their door unannounced, usually drunk, and looking for a good time.

After a fine supper of cornbread, fried pork chops, and mustard greens, Mary Beth started cleaning the kitchen with the efficiency of an expert. She cleaned it like it hadn't been cleaned in years, or at least none of the boys had ever seen it cleaned this well since Joe'd run off Bane's mother many years earlier. She had a hard time dealing with all the cockroaches that had taken up residence in every nook and cranny.

While she scrubbed for the next couple of hours, Joe, Ricky and JoJo sat around and drank one beer after another while they told stories and bragged about this and that. Bane was given Cokes to drink, some of which he carried and stashed in his room for safekeeping.

At Joe's insistence, Mary Beth reluctantly drank two beers while she worked. He told her it was bad manners not to drink while he and the boys drank. Although she didn't care much for beer and would have preferred a Coke, she was grateful for the cold drink in the hot kitchen as she went about her task of cleaning. Joe, in a very demeaning manner, would blurt out orders about which appliance was to be cleaned next. He did this as a show of authority and for the amusement of himself and the boys.

Joe finished the last beer while Ricky and JoJo sat and watched glassy-eyed. "Hey, boys, watch this." He reclined his chair with his feet stretched out before he gave an exaggerated wink that caused the cigarette in the corner of his mouth to jiggle up and down. "Git yer fat worthless butt in here, Mary Beth. Don't ya want ta git ta know the boys?"

Knowing all too well that she'd already met the boys and spoken with them at the dinner table, Mary Beth replied, "Sure Honey, jus' finishin' the las' bit of this here refrigerator." Her remark seemed to set Joe off, or at least he acted like it did. He'd wanted her to come running like she was his faithful dog.

Angrily, he twisted around in his easy chair and stared at her back with an impatient glare. After mere seconds, he repeated, "Damn it, git ya fat butt in here, **now**! Can't ya see the boys want ta git ta know ya?!"

After a small startled jump, she closed the refrigerator and hurriedly put away the cleaning supplies. She knew all too well not to anger Joe when he had been drinking. She'd been raised by a father just like him.

By this time, Joe had stood up and was walking into the kitchen. He tossed his empty beer bottle in the trash can and announced, "Don't ya ever talk back ta me again, ya hear? Next time, I'll throw ya out on that fat butt of yers."

Mary Beth, after seeing the look in his eyes, got real nervous and her face showed it as she took timid steps towards the den. She let out a tiny squeal when Joe slapped her on the buttocks and shoved her down the hallway towards the back of the trailer.

He stopped on his way behind her and winked back at the boys. "Boys, ya gotta treat them with a firm hand or they'll git the idea they can sass ya. Don't ever let 'em think they can git away with back talkin' or they'll run over ya for sure."

Ricky smiled while holding up his empty beer bottle. JoJo sat looking a little uneasy. Bane stared in disbelief as Joe followed Mary Beth. Soon, they could hear Joe's raised voice and a loud slap coming from the bedroom, quickly followed by a whimper. "Please don't, Joe. I'm sorry!"

"What's the matter, Wimp? Ain't ya never heard of tamin' a woman before?" chided Ricky. "Maybe if ya weren't such a wimp, ya wouldn't need Dad's magazines so much." That remark wouldn't have normally bothered Bane, but today wasn't normal. He was in no mood to broach this particular subject, especially after the events of the day. He jumped up and hurried to his room while trying to block out the snickering coming from Ricky and JoJo.

Bane crawled into his bed while mumbling to himself many unkind things he'd liked to have said to Ricky. Because his lumpy pillow smelled of sweat and musty odors, he tossed it into the corner of his room. He didn't have much use for it anyway. Over the years when the quills of the chicken feathers poked through the cloth and stuck the side of his face, he'd pulled them out. As a result of many years of this plucking of his pillow, there wasn't much of it left and the feathers that remained were thoroughly smashed down. As he lay on his belly, he kept saying over and over to himself that he hoped Ricky would get killed in the Army.

Lying in bed, he could hear his father and Mary Beth. Joe was cussing and she was whimpering. Then everything got quiet after the two finished having sex. Bane laid there thinking about how Crystal humiliated him and he fantasized about doing to her what he had seen and heard his father do to Mary Beth. He whispered, "I'll show her."

The following morning Bane woke up to the smell of bacon cooking. When he entered the kitchen, he was amazed by a wondrous sight. Spread all over the small kitchen table, were lots of his favorite breakfast foods. He'd never seen so much food cooked for breakfast at one time before in their house. Even when his mother lived their, they'd never had such a feast as this for breakfast. Generally, he was lucky if there were eggs or sausage to go along with his oatmeal and toast.

Joe would usually go to the local diner to eat breakfast with his co-workers before work and leave the boys to fend for themselves with the food he brought home once a week. Joe was already eating and had a satisfied grin on his face. "Come 'n eat, Boy. Don't jus' stand there gawkin'. Mary Beth, git the boy a plate. Can't ya see he's hungry?"

Mary Beth said, "Sweetie, sit down 'n eat," in a high-pitched melodic voice as she handed him a plate. She went back to preparing more food and cleaning up as she went along.

Joe leaned over and whispered in Bane's ear, "I'm testin' her out for my next woman. When ya brother leaves for the Army, I figured, what the hell. There'd be enough money 'n room for one more." With a big wad of food in his mouth, he sat back and gave a proud wink.

Bane looked at Mary Beth with his mouth agape in wonderment at what he'd just heard. Joe watched his reaction with satisfaction.

"What's the matter, Sweetie? Ain't ya hungry?" inquired Mary Beth from the kitchen.

Not replying, Bane filled his plate with gusto from the bounty before him. While he sat there gleefully eating the delicious food, he couldn't help thinking, *Hmm, so this is how ya git treated by a woman after ya slap her around a little 'n show 'er who's boss.*

Joe announced, "Your Uncle Elam is comin' over for supper tanight ta have a little talk with Ricky before he leaves tamorrow."

Elam, Joe's brother, rarely went anywhere but to work and back home again, with an occasional trip to the bar once or twice a week. Everybody in the family sort of looked out for Elam because he got a little crazy when he became nervous, which was too often. Story had it that he came home from the Korean War in 1953 "as crazy as a loon." They claimed he saw too many of his buddies die and it left him "shell shocked."

After a failed marriage, that lasted less than a year, Elam had moved back in with his mother and has lived with her ever since. Bane had heard how his uncle drank so much he couldn't hardly remember anything, so no one bothered asking him any questions the morning after he'd had an "all nighter" of beer or liquor.

"So Elam's comin' for supper?" commented Ricky while he sat at the table.

"Ain't that what I jus' said?"

"Well, I hope he don't expect ta git my bed after he passes out. I want ta sleep in it at least one more time before I git shipped off in the mornin'. Damn, look at all this food. Ooh-wee, we goin' ta eat good this mornin'!"

"Don't worry. I'm shore Bane'll give up his, that is if Elam can make it that far after he gits drunk. And while I'm thinkin' on it, don't one of ya slip up 'n call 'im Shell Shock Elam again or I'll beat ya within an inch of ya life. It took me damn near an hour ta git 'im settled down after the las' time ya pulled that prank. It ain't his fault he's got 'the nerves'." The boys exchanged knowing looks. Joe saw them exchange looks so he slammed a warning hand down on the table to get their attention. It worked. They quickly went back to eating.

"Did I ever tell you boys about when Elam first got home from the war 'n how he damn near killed me?"

The boys stopped in mid-chew and looked at their father. They couldn't imagine anyone being mean enough to whoop their ole man. Their father was taller than Elam by three inches and was far stronger. "Yeah, if it weren't for momma, poor ole Elam woulda killed me 'n ended up in jail. Ya know momma's been friends with the Sheriff's folks all her life. Hell, that's what kept my ole man out of jail. Lord knows he deserved ta go ta jail many a time for the things he done. To this day that drunken mean ole dead bastard makes me mad jus' thinkin' about 'im."

Joe finished the remaining food on his plate and lit a cigarette before he continued, "Well, it happened this way. It weren't long after he come home from Korea for daddy's funeral, maybe a week more or less, 'n I come out from behind a tree at night as he was gittin' home from the bar. I was jus' about yer age, Bane. He didn't know I was there, so when I knocked over a trash can sneakin' up on 'im, he dropped ta the ground as fast as lightin'. No sooner than he hit the dirt, he was up again 'n on top of me beatin' my brains out. In what little light there was ta see by, you could tell he wasn't all there. I know he didn't know what he was doin', but it shor was a painful way ta learn a lesson."

"His eyes were as lifeless as Granddaddy Jacob's when we found him dead out in the corn fields. They were wide open but nothin' behind 'em. They jus' seemed ta be seein' without really seein'. Anyway, if it weren't for momma, I'd be dead for sure. She come out of the house a screamin' 'n hollerin' his name while beatin' him with a broom. Seems like it took her forever ta git 'im ta stop beatin' me. That's why my nose is so messed up 'n I have this scar over my eye." Joe pointed to the large scar above his left eye. The boys leaned in to look at it really close. It seemed like they were seeing it for the first time. It was so big it actually made a bald spot through the center of the left brow and traveled from mid-brow almost to his left ear.

"Why'd he beat ya so bad?" asked Bane.

"He didn't know it was me is why. And the next time one of ya little jackasses is thinkin' about makin' 'im 'hit the dirt' again for the fun of it, I'll knock every tooth outa ya head."

They both looked down and sideways at one another. Two years ago, they both conspired to see if it was true that if they threw a firecracker near Uncle Elam, he would jump to the ground. It worked, and it took a week to get over the beating Joe gave the both of them.

"Elam may not 'a come back home with a purple heart, but he still come back messed up jus' the same. I know he's messed up 'n hard ta take sometimes, but he's my brother 'n I don't want ya ta take advantage of 'im. Now finish ya food 'n git out. Me 'n Mary Beth is fixin' ta go shoppin' later, so ya best tell us what kinda beer 'n sodas ya want."

Chapter 12 – What is a Bad Person?

BEFORE leaving the trailer, Bane took two of the freshly cooked biscuits and placed a fried sausage patty in each for later in the day. He placed them in a sack before leaving the kitchen, along with a warm coke. Then he went to his room to retrieve the hammer and nails he'd taken from the others yesterday. While he stood holding the hammer in front of his face he spoke out loud. "If they wont ya back, they're goin' have ta beg first." With a grin he swung the hammer in different directions through the air until he was satisfied. "Yeah, I'll show 'em whose boss."

Bane was feeling good about himself after such a wonderful breakfast. Although he didn't know how long Mary Beth would be staying with them, he sure was looking forward to her cooking for as long as she was around. He paused for just a moment after he stepped out of the trailer and patted his stomach with the side of the hammer. With pride he thought to himself, "*Shor feels good ta be as full as a tick.*" No sooner had he thought it, he realized life wouldn't be the same anymore with a woman around and Ricky gone. Just knowing his half-brother was leaving for the Army the next day–and hopefully never coming back–was just icing on the cake. Also, he was looking forward to his crazy Uncle Elam coming for a visit.

Billy and Gail stopped gathering clothes off the clothes line long enough to watch Bane walking up the trail towards the hut village.

Gail turned to Billy and said, "I don't think I wanta go anywhere taday, Billy." She stopped to glance once more at Bane. "Least ways, not ta the huts."

"Yeah, I don't wanta mess with Bane no-how, myself. Hey, why don't we pass the word along ta the others 'n maybe come up with somethin' besides goin' ta the huts today?"

"I'll go talk ta everybody, okay, Billy?" Before he could reply, Gail had already dropped the basket of clothes she was holding and disappeared around the corner of the trailer.

Billy shook his head and shouted, "Sounds good ta me," as he laughed to himself. At that moment Libby ran past him in pursuit of Gail. Billy, although annoyed by Gail's antics at times, had come to appreciate her gumption. He knew she would always be self-reliant and someone he could count on. Through sheer will, she would become whatever she set her mind to become and heaven help anyone who got in the way. Even more, he felt sorry for whoever she decided to marry because she would always have to be in charge.

After a while Gail showed up with a big smile on her face, fluttering around like she had something exciting to say. Billy knew she wouldn't tell him anything until he asked. Deciding to go along with her, Billy stopped sweeping and leaned on the broom handle before asking, "What's goin' on?" She decided he wasn't in the spirit of the game yet, so she continued to taunt him by jumping around and aggravating him as he resumed sweeping the kitchen floor. "Either ya tell me what it is ya gotta say or leave me be. Momma says we can't go play till I finish sweepin' the kitchen 'n livin' room."

Gail grabbed the broom handle as she whispered loudly, "Gabby's daddy says he could take us all fishing' if our mommas'll let us go. What ya think about that?"

"Well, go ask 'er then, 'n I'll hurry up here," Billy said as he resumed sweeping with renewed vigor.

Gail rushed to the back of the trailer to find their mother and then reappeared almost immediately. "She says we could go if yer finished and we need ta fix ourselves a sack lunch."

It wasn't long before the rest of the gang was gathered around Mr. Grizzles' truck and was loading it with their fishing gear and food their mothers had prepared. Some of the gang brought store bought rods and reels, while others just had long poles with lines, bobs, and hooks attached. Everyone was full of excitement as they piled into the back of the pickup. Unanimously, they assumed that Billy should be the one to hold Libby because he was the biggest. Gabby and Bonnie Lou jumped in front with Gabby's father, John Grizzle.

All morning long, Bane wondered where everyone was. He even went to the top of the hill a couple of times to see if he could spot anyone wandering around the trailer park. Close to lunch time, he resigned himself to being the only one who was going to show up. He settled into the wood swing to drink his coke and eat his sausage biscuits. While he was eating, Dewey appeared at the edge of the compound. Because Libby wasn't there to announce his arrival, Bane didn't hear Dewey approach until he was almost at the swings. Just before he got to the swings, Dewey stopped and picked up something off the ground and placed it in the slot designed for a pencil or pen on the bib of his overalls.

"Well, if it ain't No-Nuts."

Dewey didn't reply to Bane's snarky greeting, but he slowed his pace the rest of the way to where Bane was seated. With apprehension, Dewey stood and looked around while he nervously started twirling the tire swing. Bane could see a large black feather sticking out of one of Dewey's overalls bib pockets. He reached over and snatched it from Dewey's overalls before Dewey had a chance to react.

Dewey clearly didn't like it, but he quickly resigned himself to let Bane keep it as he stepped back away from Bane and stood on the other side of the tire swing. "Where everybody at?"

"How should I know," Bane replied as he took another bite of his sausage biscuit. He then stuck the feather in his hair behind his ear. To add to his smugness, he smacked his lips and said, "Umm! Man, this shor taste good. Anyway, do I look like their mommas? And don't be lookin' at me, 'cause I didn't bring ya no food neither."

Dewey, feeling uneasy, replied, "Dewey don't want no food 'cause I ate 'fore I come."

"Yeah, what'd ya have? Bet it didn't taste as good as this." Bane held up his prized sausage and biscuit as if it was the best thing that ever could be before he took yet another noisy bite. They seemed to taste even better now that he had someone to show them off to and taunt.

"Dewey had peanut butter, mayonnaise, banana sandwich. Granddaddy knows how ta cook real good. They taste better 'n tomato sandwiches."

"Yeah, I remember those. My momma use ta make 'em for me sometimes when I was little." Bane let the hand holding his sausage biscuit rest on his leg as his thoughts wandered for a while. He looked back at Dewey. "You got a momma somewheres?"

"I don' know." Dewey mumbled.

"Ain't ya curious about ya momma? Like if she's still livin' or somethin'?" Dewey just shrugged his shoulders and made up his mind to try and get into the empty tire swing. After much effort, he finally squeezed into the opening.

"Bane gotta momma?" asked Dewey.

"Not no more since my daddy run 'er off. Reckon she got fed up with 'im whooping' 'er all the time. When I was little, I remember 'em fightin' all the time. My daddy claims she's the one that decided ta run off though. Can't say I blame 'er. I'd run away if I had somewheres ta go myself. Guess she didn't wanta be my momma no more 'cause she didn't take me with 'er. Daddy claims she was as crazy as a rabid dog sometimes. Says I have that same look in my eyes she had jus' before she'd tried cuttin' his throat. Wish she'd done it too." He wasn't about to admit he cried for days on end after she disappeared.

"Yeah, my granddaddy say's my momma lit out one day 'n 'll be back when she's ready ta come home." Dewey looked down at the ground and ever so faintly whispered to himself, "She'll come home when she's ready."

Bane finished with his second biscuit and continued swinging beside Dewey for a while.

"My brother is leaving' for the Army tamorrow. He'll probably git killed. Leastways, I hope so." Bane looked out of the corner of his eye to watch for Dewey's reaction to what he'd said. He was a little disappointed when Dewey didn't seem fazed by his outrageous statement.

"What's the Army? My granddaddy's brother was in it."

"That's where they turn ya into a solider 'n they send ya off ta war. Don't ya ever watch John Wayne movies?"

"Ya gonna miss 'im?"

"Nah. He ain't never been nice ta me my whole life. I hope he never comes back." After a short pause, Bane continued, "Can't wait ta make Crystal pay for runnin' 'er mouth yesterday. Bet I make 'er cry 'n that'll learn 'er."

Dewey stopped swinging, looked at Bane and asked, "Why ya so bad?"

This took Bane a little by surprise. He was hoping to rile Dewey up because he knew Dewey was especially fond of Crystal. Since Dewey wasn't going to play his game, he resigned himself to just talking with him and forego the head games. He thought on it a little bit and finally answered, "Jus' seems like the way of it is all." He could see Dewey didn't understand, since he just sat there with a blank expression. "Dewey, it jus' comes like that. Ya know it feels regular ta me is all. Why ya so dumb?"

Ignoring Bane's question, Dewey asked, "Don't ya know no good? Preacher Rakestraw says people know good 'n bad."

For a while, Bane stared at the ground where his feet dangled from the swing before he looked up again. Bane's face gave away how lost and confused he was. "God knows good, but he ain't never thought about givin' none ta me, I spose. Least ways, he ain't never showed it anyway. Wish he'd give some ta me 'n my folks, cause we don't got none."

"I wear a cross cause it shows God loves me. If ya had a cross, maybe ya could be good. Then God would know ya." Dewey beamed with pride as he shoved the cross pendant that was attached to his overalls strap forward to show Bane.

"I don't reckon he'd know me even if I had a cross ta wear."

"God knows everybody. I bet he loves you. My granddaddy says Jesus says so." Just at that moment a dove flew down and landed in front of them just a few feet away. Dewey smiled as he pointed at the dove and said, "See."

Bane sat quietly concentrating for a while as he watched the dove walk around. He seemed to get irritated just before he jumped out of his swing and gave Dewey a puzzled look. Of course this scared away the dove. Bane twirled the black feather between his fingers as he rocked his body from side to side. He stopped, turned to Dewey and extended his hand holding the feather.

"Guess God wanted my family ta be bad. He must'a wanted it that way or he'd fixed it." After Dewey accepted the feather from Bane's extended hand, Bane turned and walked away. Dewey watched Bane walk past the huts for home.

Dewey had touched an area Bane wanted to block out of his mind. Bane felt utterly helpless and knew he had to accept things the way they were to survive his circumstances. Life had become rawer and less joyful the day his mother had left him. He felt the change inside of him once he'd accepted his fate. He put it out of his mind once more as he walked home.

Dewey accepted Bane's explanation as just that. He sat in the now vacant wood swing and quietly watched Bane walk the rest of the way up the hill. Dewey generally accepted things and people exactly the way they were, and believed Bane was telling him the truth. He would no more judge Bane for being mean than he would a bird for flying. Like his granddaddy says, *"A mean dog can't help but want ta bite, but ya can knock the damn thing with a stick for tryin'. Then he quoted the Bible: 'Blessed is the man that walketh not in the counsel of the ungodly, nor standeth in the way of sinners, nor sitteth in the seat of the scornful."*

All alone now, Dewey began swinging. In an almost trance like state, he continued swinging as he felt contentment and joy growing ever stronger in his body's movements and the rhythm of the swing. He basked in the coolness of the wind hitting his sweat as he moved back and forth through the air. For a long time he continued to swing, feeling nothing else but exhilarating joy. This was the first time he'd been alone in the hut village.

After what seemed a long time, he finished swinging and went exploring around the huts. Suddenly he burst into a frenzy of excitement as he brandished his sword and began fighting his imaginary pirates for the prize of being the greatest of them all. "Ya won't git my treasure, you heathens," he shouted. "I'll find yer treasure 'n take it for my bounty. Arrr."

Feeling satisfied he had won the battle, he began looking all around the huts as if he were looking for treasure. Not finding anything he would consider a treasure, he expanded his search to the surrounding woods. He was using his sword to push back thorn bushes when he came across the carcass of the baby rabbit Bane had killed. All that remained was the skin with some bones showing.

While observing the devastation that nature had wrought on it over the weeks, he couldn't help thinking that no matter how hard he tried, he couldn't bring it back to life. He felt sad that he was powerless to help the poor thing. As he stood there feeling helpless, he uttered, "I'll not let Bane hurt nobody no more. I'm sorry, Baby Rabbit."

Just past the corpse, he noticed a small pile of rocks. He pushed further and further into the briar bushes until he reached them. It was difficult, but he managed to reach his hand between the stalks of thorns as they pierced and scratched the skin on his hand and fingers.

Being ever so careful, he moved the rocks one at a time while continuing to get stuck now and then by the thorns. Finally he removed enough of the rocks to uncover a small old metal tool box that was rusting through the faded green paint. The handle held as he picked it up and pulled it into the clearing. "I found the treasure, me mates. Now the treasure be mine," he spoke aloud.

He carried the box over to the huts and sat down in a cool shady place underneath the oak by the swings. With a little effort he managed to open it. Inside were different multi-colored buttons made from fresh water mussels, old brass metal buttons, broken costume jewelry with multiple colored stones, sewing instruments with fading spools of thread, an Indian head penny, the head of a porcelain doll, one small water stained box, and, underneath it all, he found a box with lots of gold coins inside.

Being careful, he opened the water stained box to expose a gold engagement ring with a very tiny diamond setting. In the opening of the doll's head was a rolled up card that a small child must have made. The card had a crayon drawing of a stick figure. The stick figure was topped off with a picture of a woman pasted to be the head. Above it was the word "Mommy," roughly printed in faded orange crayon. The picture was of a round faced, red-headed, and blue eyed woman in her twenties who looked sad.

Once he looked over everything carefully, he placed it all back into the box as close to the way he found it and shut the lid. His excitement having dissipated and his curiosity satisfied, he took it back to where he found it and replaced the rocks. He didn't know why, but he felt kind of sad.

Since there was nothing else to do and no one else to play with, Dewey started back towards the farm. The further away from the huts he traveled the less he thought about the treasure box. When a deer and her doe bounced out of a thicket and exposed themselves in front of him, he froze in his tracks. He watched patiently, trying not to make any noise or movements while they nibbled on some of the lush green underbrush. Once they caught sight of him, no more than twenty yards away, they slowly walked back into the thicket. Dewey stayed where he was until he heard their movements fade farther into the woods.

Reinvigorated in spirit, he walked down to his favorite spot by the creek and sat cooling his feet in the shallow water. He felt bad he didn't have anything to throw to the rabbit this time, since he already fed the rabbit earlier on his way to the huts. After a while he remembered the dog treat for Libby. He threw it to the spot where the rabbit usually came out for its treats.

After a while, the rabbit appeared and sniffed the treat for a long time, trying to decide if this thing was food. Then it took it in its mouth and bounded away to the hiding place in the undergrowth.

Dewey began to feel a little drowsy, so he laid back and daydreamed while looking through the tree limbs at the clouds passing by. He, like most warm blooded creatures of the south, was only reacting to the heat and humidity that occurred during the dog days of summer.

Bane came home to an empty trailer. He figured his father and Mary Beth had already gone shopping for tonight's festivities. On the coffee table he found an almost empty pack of cigarettes and lit one. While he sat relaxing in his father's easy chair with his freshly lit cigarette, he was startled by a loud banging on the front door. Before he could move, his brother Ricky came storming through the door.

"Hey now, what do we have here?" Ricky asked. "Is my little brother the big man of the house now that I'm leavin'? I ain't left yet, ya little wimp. Now git outa dad's chair before I whoop ya. I seen ya through the window takin' one of dad's smokes. Bet he'd bus' ya hide real good if he knew, too. If ya had a hundred dollars in ya pocket, ya still wouldn't be worth nothin'."

This wasn't the first time Ricky had busted him for smoking a cigarette, so he just plain didn't care anymore. Slowly, he got up from the chair and picked up the ash tray. Taking his time, he moved it to the couch and sat down.

"Where's ya girlfriend JoJo?" Bane teased. "Y'all have a lover's quarrel or somethin'?" Ricky, was about to sit in the easy chair, but abruptly charged Bane and began hitting him in the head with his fist.

Bane threw up his hands and arms to protect himself. "Ouch! Ya little turd. You burned me with that damn cigarette."

Ricky went back to the easy chair and plopped down with a loud thud. With a satisfied grin, he watched Bane try to clean up the ashes that'd spilled all over him and the couch.

"I HOPE YA GIT KILLED IN VIETNAM!" Bane shouted as he held up his arms, certain that this would bring on yet another attack. Ricky cocked his head and looked at his brother with a dumbfounded and confused expression. Bane went on "Yeah, I hope they kill ya 'n ya never come back. By the way, Dad said he was replacing ya with that Mary Beth. Unlike you, she's not as worthless as a dead mule 'n she's nice ta me 'n she can cook too!" His voice was shrill and full of hostility.

"Listen, ya little virgin, ya really mean that?"

"Mean what?"

"Ya really hope I git killed like those Army guys we seen on the TV news."

Bane was still angry, but satisfied that he finally told Ricky how he felt. Many a time he'd wished Ricky was dead or gone. He was tired of being beaten and bruised all the time by Ricky. He stuck out his jaw at Ricky, "Yeah. I hope ya die!"

Ricky looked hurt and felt betrayed. He stared at Bane then shook his head. "Damn," was all he said to himself as he shook and dropped his head. After a moment or so he got up and walked back to his room without saying another word to his brother.

Bane didn't regret telling him how he felt, but he was sure he'd better stay out of Ricky's way until he was gone. Before he left the trailer, Bane grabbed the rest of the cigarette pack and a book of matches. He didn't plan on coming back until he knew supper was ready and Uncle Elam had arrived.

Dewey's intuition, more likely his internal stomach clock, must have been accurate, because he figured it was time to start for home. He was almost there when he heard the bell ringing. No sooner had he started crossing the field, than Snipe came running to greet him.

That evening in the den, Dewey asked, "Are we at war? Cause Bane says his brother is goin' in the Army."

This took Al by surprise. He looked at Dewey, "What are ya talking about?"

"Bane says his brother was goin' in the Army 'n they was sendin' 'im ta war."

"Oh, yer talkin' about Vietnam."

"What's Vietnome?"

"That's *Vietnam*, Boy. Well, let me see if I can explain it ta ya soes ya can understand." He thought on it for a while before he started. "Well, Vietnam is a small country in Southeast Asia, somewhere on the other side of the world. It's not all that far from a country named Korea, where I had the misfortune ta stay a while when I was in the Navy. The people there are very poor 'n they have this here war where the north part is fighting the south part, 'cause the north part wants ta take over the south part of the country. One of our late presidents got a notion we'd go help the south part fight the north part."

"Why?"

"He got it in his head that if the north part won, then it would make the world worse off. He may a had good intentions, but he didn't go about it all that good. He got us messed up in the whole fight, 'n now we have a bunch of boys over there gittin' killed. Ya see there are some bad people who are from another country who got the north part ta go 'n kill a bunch a people in the south part. We figured the south part was our friends, so now we're helpin' 'em."

"Are we winnin'?"

"That's hard ta say. I'll try ta explain it ta ya better'n the government explains it so ya can understand. It's kinda like goin' 'n tryin' ta kill a giant ant bed in tall grass with a big stick. The big stick is sorta like our bombs 'n artillery, 'n the ants are only armed with their bites, kinda like little guns 'n knives. When ya hit the giant ant bed with the stick, ya kill a few of the ants, 'n mess up the ant bed real good. But as soon as ya hit the ant bed, all the ants come out ta defend their home. Ya can keep standin' there hittin' the ant nest 'n kill a few at a time, but most all of the ants jus' scatter 'n git away. And ya can be sure they'll be comin' for ya. Sure, ya can kill a bunch of ants, if ya can see 'em, but most of the ants are hidden by the grass 'n sneakin' up on ya real good. That's the ones that start bitin' ya real good when they git a hold of ya."

"Sure ya have the biggest 'n most powerful weapon like the stick, but ya can't kill 'em all before they put a hurtin' on ya. As long as ya stay there tryin' ta kill 'em with ya stick, they're still able ta swarm 'n bite ya because there are too many of 'em 'n ya can't see 'em comin'. Think of the bites as our soldiers gittin' killed or hurt. After ya git bit enough, eventually you'll either git smart enough ta leave or keep standing there 'n gittin' bit till ya git most or all of 'em if ya can last."

Bane, who wandered around the woods and neighborhood after the confrontation with Ricky, came back home once he saw that his father, Mary Beth, and Elam had arrived.

"Hey, how's my little hellion nephew doin'? Ya lookin' jus' like ya ole man when he was yer age. I see ya got the same old sourpuss expression too."

Bane didn't respond as he joined his uncle, father, and brother who were sitting in lawn chairs in the shade of the trailer, just outside the front door. It wasn't long before empty beer bottles started to collect by each chair. "How 'bout a beer, Nephew?"

"No ya don't. That boy's mean enough without adding fuel ta the fire!" Joe exclaimed loudly. "Ya Cokes is in the frig, Boy. Go git ya'self one 'n join us. Supper 'll be ready soon."

When Bane started to enter the trailer, he could hear Elam laughing and saying, "That boy is gonna be jus' like ya."

"That's okay about gittin' the girl's part, but God help us on the rest," replied Joe.

"Why ya wanta deny the boy a cold beer on such a hot day like taday, Joe? I remember ya use ta sneak beer every chance ya got when *you* was his age."

"Ya must'a forgot, it was *you* that use ta be the one ta git me those drinks back then, 'n it weren't beer neither. Back then, it was usually some of daddy's shine."

"Hey, ya'd be right about that. Guess I forgot. Man that was something else back then. Remember all the beatin's he use ta put on us?"

"Yeah, that was somethin'. These boys don't have a clue how ornery their Granddaddy was. I bet he beat the hell out of ole Satan if he got down there 'n no one offered 'im a drink or somethin'."

"Yeah, momma says he couldn't end up in no place else but hell 'cause he was so mean ta her 'n 'er baby boys. Never did git ta say goodbye ta 'im since I was off in that God forsaken war. I'd be dead right now if they hadn't let me come home for the funeral, even though I still ended up gittin' home three days late for it. Jus' glad my time was about done or they'd sent me back. Guess Daddy proved drinkin' 'n drivin' a log truck don't go together." Elam raised his beer to the air, "Here's ta ya Pop! Least ya got me outa that hell hole!"

After Elam guzzled down the rest of his beer in a toast to his father, he turned to the boys with a grin on his face, "How'd ya boys like me to tell ya about the time some Gooks caught me with my pants down while on three day patrol in the bush?" Elam was too loaded with beer to notice their sighs as he went ahead with his story.

Joe gave each of them a look that warned of impending wrath if they showed any more signs of disrespect or interrupted.

Elam slapped Ricky on the shoulder and said, "Ya bes' listen up, Boy. Ya might find ya'self in the same spot some day."

"Well, it starts like this. We'd been out in the bush two days when nature come a callin'. We stopped for a rest in some trees with a lot of undergrowth close by. The lieutenant was tryin' ta git his bearin's while he looked over the map. I couldn't wait another minute, so I tells the ole sarge I needed ta drop a loaf. He says for me ta keep close 'n make sure I use my spade ta keep from leavin' any tell-tell signs. Git it, *tail-tale signs*."

"No sooner 'n I dug a hole 'n dropped my load when I heard a faint sound jus' on the other side of some bush. That was when I froze in place. Ya see those boys' we'z fightin' was as sneaky 'n quiet as a snake slidin' through damp grass. So as quiet as a mouse, I parted the bush 'n what'a ya think I seen. Sure 'nough there was one of those North Korean boys tip-toeing around some trees about thirty yards away from me."

"Of course he probably smelled me, 'cause we stink somethin' bad from those rations they fed us, and boy was it was a doozy too. Eww Wee! I could tell he was tryin' ta git a fix on where I was. I was reachin' for my rifle when I noticed more of 'em right behind 'im. Man I never been so scared in all my days."

"Well let me tell ya, there are times when life throws somethin' at ya that makes ya jus' shut down. Ya can't move a muscle 'n ya head stops thinkin' ta boot. And this was one of them times. It seemed like the world stopped as I squatted there in the bush watchin' them there boys comin' my way. I reckon I'd still be there right now jus' like that if it weren't for my buddies."

Elam's face was contorted as he took a couple of puffs from his cigarette. He opened a fresh cold bottle of beer and downed half of it to calm his nerves. "Yeah, my buddies." He took another swig of his beer. "They must'a seen them boys the same time I did, but didn't let on till them gooks was no more 'n ten yards from me. I hadn't noticed my squad sneakin' up till they let loose on those gooks with everything they had. I was right between both sides with my pants down around my ankles 'n bullets flyin' all around my head."

"They killed them gooks, but I never even got off a shot. I was still frozen in place when my sarge kicked me ta the ground. I can still hear him growlin' at me, 'vacations over Taggart, next time pull up ya pants ya dumb-ass 'n start shootin'. Ta this day I can't take a dump in the woods."

"I'll attest ta that. You've messed me up gittin' many a deer when we go huntin' cause of it," piped Joe as he held up his beer and took a swig.

Elam continued to tell stories all evening until the beer ran out. This time, however, Ricky paid attention.

Chapter 13 – Forlorn Birthday

FOR two days the weatherman on the radio promised that a strong front was approaching Georgia from the west. He promised it would bring cooler temperatures and relief from the rain deficit that had been plaguing Georgia farmers for the past month. Al knew he could predict the weather just as well by flipping a quarter in the air, but he was hoping they were correct and rain would arrive soon. He was pleasantly surprised when heavy rains showered his farm all during the night, watering his crops.

The rain made for a restful sleep because of the soothing noise it made as the rain pelted the metal roof of the house. This event fit in perfectly with Al's annual plans of cleaning and prepping the fireplace for winter. For this he needed the foliage close to the house to be damp.

While cooking breakfast, Al went over the details in his head about all the equipment and materials he'd need for the day's work. Today, July 31st, was his usual target date for this yearly activity. If it hadn't rained, he'd have to wait for a more suitable circumstance, but as it turned out, everything came together perfectly.

Al stopped Dewey. "Stop right there, Boy. Taday we gotta git the fireplace readied for winter, so hurry back with the eggs 'n put 'em in the refrigerator. Then meet me in the den 'n I'll show ya how it's done. Now scurry along 'n don't go wonderin' off this morning." Dewey grabbed the basket from the old oak buffet in the kitchen and quickly disappeared through the screen door. Dewey's exit was followed by a loud bang as the screen door slammed back into place.

Dewey was back in good time, for him, with the morning's collection of eggs. He went into the den to find a large stack of old newspapers piled beside the fireplace under a smelly black log. Al entered the room and knelt in front of the fireplace. Using the fireplace screen as a brace, he began covering the opening with an old dirty sheet.

"Come with me, Dewey." Together they went out back to the shed, where Al handed Dewey an extremely large round brush with a twenty foot long handle. Then they went to the barn and gathered an old wooden ladder that weighed so much that Al had a hard time getting a good grip on it until he found its center of gravity. He was then able to balance it well enough to prevent one end or the other from hitting the ground as he carried it. Together they carried their burdens to the side of the house where the chimney was located.

Al placed the ladder on the ground and walked it up until it stood straight up and fell gently against the roof. Once Al was sure the ladder was securely balanced against the house and in no danger of tilting, he climbed onto the roof. "Hand me the brush." Dewey swung the long handled chimney sweeper, brush end first to Al.

"Good gracious, Dewey, are ya sure yer not really a boneheaded Boatswain's Mate? Turn it around 'n hand it ta me with the handle side first!" Dewey dropped the brush down to the ground and turned it around before attempting to once again hand it to Al. "That's better. Now, git up here 'n let me show ya how ta sweep out the inside of the chimney with this here chimney sweep."

Dewey shimmied up the ladder as best he could, but had reservations just past the halfway point because the ladder began to lean and shake. Dewey soon discovered it was wobbly compared to the ladder in the barn that was securely fastened to framing. Realizing the situation, Al quickly grabbed the top of the ladder to steady it when it started to shift. Dewey was having a difficult time keeping his center of gravity and this caused the ladder to wobble.

"Take ya time, damn-it! Ain't no sense in gittin' hurt. Jus' go slow 'n easy. That's better." Once Dewey slowly stepped onto the tin roof, Al let go of the ladder. Because the winters are light in this part of the state, the roof was not pitched very steep and made for easy footing.

"Lets git ta work. Can't have the house catch fire 'cause of sorriness, now can we? Too many homes is burnt ta a crisp 'cause folks is too lazy ta keep their fireplace clean." Dewey timidly walked across the span of the roof until he stood beside Al at the chimney.

"Dewey wants ta go back down."

"Boy, ya got ta git use ta heights if ya wanta be a good sailor. This is jus' like bein' in a crows nest on a ship. Now don't look down 'n concentrate on the chimney. You'll forget all about how high ya are." Al had to lift Dewey's chin upward towards the chimney's opening because Dewey was still looking down at the ground.

"Try ta remember ta clean out the chimney every year, Boy. When ya burn fire in the winter, ya leave a buildup of gunk on the inside walls. This stuff is made up of residue 'n unburned material that'll cause a chimney ta catch fire if it gits too thick. Plus, ya never know what the critters might 'a left ya over the spring 'n summer." After a minute or so of Al explaining all about the chimney and what they were doing, Dewey seemed more at ease.

Al demonstrated how to take the brush and lower it into the chimney opening before he began scrubbing the inside walls of the chimney. He then handed it to Dewey and monitored him as he continued with the task. Only when Al was certain they had thoroughly brushed out the soot buildup in the chimney did they both climb down off the roof.

They took a large metal bucket and dustpan with them as they went into the den to continue the job. Al gently removed the filthy sheet and folded it upon itself to prevent black dust from scattering all over the floor. "Now, let's very slowly gather the ashes 'n clean up this mess." Using a poker, shovel, and brush they began to clean up the fire dogs and base of the fireplace.

"Go ahead 'n put the fire dogs back in 'n put the creosote log on 'em." Dewey gave Al a questioning look as Al picked up the log with the funny smell. "Dewey, it's made ta burn extra hot ta help burn up the remaining residue in the chimney. Okay, now crinkle up the newspapers 'n stuff 'em in there real tight like. Then we can put the screen back 'n light 'er up." While Dewey loaded up the fireplace with waded up newspapers, Al went outside and charged the water hose and pulled it around to the side of the house where the chimney was located.

After Dewey finished wadding and stuffing all the newspapers, he went outside to look for Al. "What's that for?" asked Dewey after coming around the corner of the house.

"Well, Boy, ya don't wanta start the first fire with all the buildup in the chimney 'less yer ready for it. Now, let's go start the fire 'n we'll come back outside 'n make sure none of the embers that come flyin' out of the chimney catch fire to the yard."

After the fire was roaring and Al was certain there was little danger of it coming into the house, they quickly went outside and watched as the flames could actually be seen shooting out the opening of the chimney. This was followed by newspaper embers floating around in the air, before gently drifting down to the ground on currents of air. This reminded Al of the fireflies they saw almost every night at twilight.

"Try ta remember, Dewey, ta always do this on a mornin' after the rain has wet everythin', 'n be sure ta have a hose ready. Those embers might catch fire ta trees 'n such. Ya always wanta be on the leeward side of the house 'cause of the wind. That means the side of the house where the winds blowin' stuff ta ya. The windward side is the side of the house where the wind's hittin' it. Jus' like ya wanta jump off a sinkin' ship on the windward side, soes the wind will blow the ship away from ya. That way ya won't git sucked down into the ocean by the undertow when the ship goes down. Also, if there's a fuel spill 'n it catches fire, the wind'll push the burning oil away from ya."

Dewey nodded. "And ya swim real hard away from the ship when yer in the water too, huh, Granddaddy?"

"That's right, Boy. Ya remembered what I taught ya."

As the glowing embers fell within Dewey's reach, to his delight, he would swipe at them with his hand and watch them sparkle as they shattered into tiny glowing pieces. Al watched and even joined in on the fun when a large ember came close enough.

After a long while, when Al was certain all was well, he and Dewey put away all the tools and emptied the bucket of ashes on the ground where he would plant next year. He explained to Dewey how the ashes helped change the chemical balance of the soil to make the plants grow better.

"Dewey, we need ta make sure we keep the critters out away from the house, so let's go fetch some lime 'n lye." Together they crawled underneath the house and placed lye in any holes that might house mice or rats in them. Quickly, he covered them up with dirt to kill any creatures that lived in them. Then they placed lime all around the base of each pillar that held the house off the ground. This was to kill insects that might try to seek warmth and shelter in the house during the cold months. After that, they went into the house and gathered up all the old moth balls and replaced them with new ones. Dewey pinched his nose and said, "They smell bad."

"That's kinda the idea. Can't have moths eatin' up the place now can we?"

"Can I go ta my ship now, Granddaddy?"

Al looked at him initially with frustration, then with a sigh said, "Yeah, Boy, but I'll be comin' ta git ya in a little while cause we need ta finish gittin' ready for winter. Git on with ya'self for now."

Dewey quickly pulled out his wooden sword as he scurried down the hallway and out of the back door, almost knocking over the free-standing hat rack that held his and Al's straw hats and rain coats.

Once he arrived at the barn, Dewey fell right into character and loudly proclaimed his arrival to his imaginary crew. "I'm back, me hardy crew! Aye!"

Life filled Dewey with exuberance when he was pretending to be a pirate. He fired his imaginary cannons, looked through his telescope, and made gyrations of swift strong fighting moves in lunges and retreats as he wielded his sword wildly about. This is where Dewey felt free and was most content.

While asleep on the living room couch, Bane was awakened by Mary Beth noisily going about preparing breakfast in the kitchen. Just when as he was stretching and the world around him began to take focus, he was suddenly startled when a glass of cold water was splashed onto his face.

"Thought ya might 'a needed that in case ya was dreamin' of girls, ya horny little sissy." Ricky loomed over him, laughing and making contorted faces to further tease and enrage his younger brother.

Bane jumped up from the couch after his initial shock and realization of what had just occurred. He stopped short though, because Ricky was standing there ready for him to begin swinging. Bane stood at the entrance of the hall with his fists balled tightly by his sides. His hesitation drew a mocking smile from Ricky. Bane glared ever harder at his brother, watching him gloat over his shenanigans.

"Go ta hell!" Bane finally shouted, out of frustration and helplessness.

"Don't ya remember little brother? I'm already headin' that way taday."

Bane relaxed some as he, almost in a whisper, went on to say, "Oh yeah, taday ya go ta boot camp, don't ya? That's even better. I hope ya git the meanest ole sergeant in the whole world. I hope he kicks ya sorry worthless butt all the way ta Vietnam. I'll be thinkin' 'bout ya doin' all them pushups 'n runnin' while I'm back here laughin' at ya sorry butt. Ha!"

Ricky just went on pretending it didn't bother him as he made a show of drinking from the now empty glass. Then he asked Bane, "Want some more? Ya still look mighty thirsty. Ya know ya got ta git as much as possible while yer alive, 'cause I hear they don't got none where *yer* goin' after *you* die."

Bane went on, "Oh yeah, ya better not let 'em catch ya cryin' like ya did the other night, or they might jus' take ya for a girl." Ricky's expression changed from a smirk to embarrassment then to anger, all within a second. "Yeah, I heard ya the other night, so don't go lookin' at me like ya don't know what I'm talkin' 'bout. And las' night I heard Uncle Elam say how they like ta kick the crap outa lazy turds like you!"

"At least it's better 'n that jail cell yer headed for, Sissy Boy." Ricky hesitated as he was about to roundhouse Bane because he caught a glimpse of Joe walking down the hall towards them.

"Have fun, Army Boy," retorted Bane, still unaware of Joe.

For the benefit of Joe, Ricky unfurled his fist and used it to indicate Bane, while he mockingly exclaimed, "Well, look who woke up on the wrong side of the bed this mornin'. Oh yeah, somebody didn't git ta sleep in their bed. Ain't that so, Twerp?"

Mary Beth was watching the two boys while she kept busy preparing breakfast. To break the tension she said, "Boys, I'll have breakfast ready real quick like, so how'd ya like ya eggs cooked?" This got their attention and seemed to distract them, as Mary Beth had intended. Reluctantly they each grumbled their preference.

Suddenly a harsh bass voice behind Bane thundered, "What the hell's wrong with the two of ya?! Ya couldn't a let a body sleep till breakfast was ready?!"

Joe could see Bane's hair was dripping wet once Bane jumped and spun around in surprise. Ricky was still holding the empty glass, so he instantly knew what'd happened. "Boy, ya jus' couldn't let the boy alone for jus' this one day? Jesus!" Joe stepped between them while he forcefully jammed his arms into their chests, causing the two of them to land hard against the wall and furniture as he passed.

"Mary Beth, ya got any coffee ready?" Mary Beth hurriedly poured Joe his coffee and brought it to him as he sat at the kitchen table. "Now, ya boys try 'n git along taday. And don't go waken' up ya poor old uncle. He drank enough beer ta drown ten men las' night. Come ta think of it, he talked as much crap as that many ta boot." Joe, feeling a little too weary to sit at the kitchen table, got up and went to his easy chair, sat down, and lit a cigarette.

While the two boys walked towards the back of the trailer, Bane turned to Ricky, "Let me have the glass. I'll show ya how ta have a little fun."

"Dang, Boy, what ya need a glass for?" inquired Ricky, while standing in front of the bathroom door with Bane.

Bane nodded his head towards the bathroom sink.

"What the hell ya thinkin'?" asked Ricky with a puzzled look.

"Let's make 'im think he peed on hisself. Warm water with some 'a that yellow colored shampoo 'll teach 'im a lesson for comin' over here 'n takin' our beds. And for causin' us not ta git ta go see Grandmamma, 'cause he said we was too much trouble. He'll think he done it on hisself. 'Member how he told us he done it ta his ole buddies in the Army."

"Hell, Boy. Ya don't have ta use nothin' like that. I found a black garden snake yesterday 'n put it in a bucket near the back door. I forgot to use it on ya las' night. Can't let it go ta waste. If ya wanta really make 'im piss on himself, that's probably the trick that'll do it. Remember how afraid he is of snakes? Hell, he might even crap on top a' that.

I don't know how ya gonna stay outa jail after I've gone. 'Stead of protectin' the country from communists, I need ta protect 'em from you."

"Fine! Jus' make sure no one sees me then." Bane quietly snuck out the back door to find a foot long black garden snake in the bucket where Ricky said it would be. He picked it up and carried it inside. Ricky already had some fishing line cut from the night before. He'd had it ready for the gag he'd planned to pull on Bane, but forgot because he'd gotten too drunk.

When they were both satisfied the snake was tied securely and the coast was clear, Bane quietly slipped into his bedroom where he found Uncle Elam fast asleep. While he listened to the gentle snoring for signs of his uncle waking, he fastened the other end of the fishing line to the button just under Uncle Elam's chin. After Bane had gone through the door, Ricky quietly sneaked back to the den.

Ricky motioned to his father and pursed his lips together. Using his index finger, he gave the hush signal while pointed towards the back. Joe, curious, gently walked down the hall to Bane's bedroom door. He pushed the door open just enough to see what was happening and then gently closed it back. After Bane came out of the door, Joe smacked Bane on the back of his head real hard. "Git yer worthless butt ta breakfast. One of these days, I bet ya me or somebody else goin' ta kill ya sorry worthless hide."

With a grin on his face, Joe started banging on the door and shouting, "Git ya'self outa bed. Breakfast is ready." From the other side of the door they all heard Elam wake up and start screaming and cursing. This was intermingled with sounds of things crashing against the walls and furniture being tossed or thrown. The trailer actually shook at times.

Five minutes later Elam came staggering to the table and sat down. "Man, did I ever sleep hard this mornin'. What time is it?"

"Time for ya diaper changin' smells like," Joe replied, as he looked at Elam's wet crotch.

Elam was still shaken up and appeared not to have understood the meaning. Elam lit a cigarette and fumbled with his coffee as best he could with shaky hands. Once he settled down and his eyes were able to focus better, he began to look carefully at the two boys for signs of guilt. It hadn't taken him long to put together what'd happened, it's just he wasn't sure which one of them was the perpetrator. He carefully scrutinized each of them, including Joe, to see if he could tell which one had done this to him. He snatched the remaining fishing line from his shirt, which sent the button it was attached to shooting across the table. Everyone acted normal and didn't give him any undue attention.

Mary Beth didn't know what was going on, but she reacted as discretely as possible to Elam's repugnant smell when she put his plate in front of him. She hurriedly went back into the kitchen to finish her own breakfast before cleaning the dishes.

Unable to ascertain which one was guilty, Elam fidgeted with his breakfast. He was in an ill mood since he hadn't brought a change of clothes and was due at work soon. Elam was on the verge of exploding with rage while listening to Joe, Ricky, and Bane act as if nothing was wrong and conversing about how things would change once Ricky was gone to the Army.

"Which one of ya piss-poor excuses done it?!" he hissed loudly as he stood and towered over the table to glare at the boys seated on the other side. When neither one let on by their reactions, he started to come around the table. Joe quickly put out his hand to stop him.

"Sit down! What's this all about?"

"Ya know damn well what this is about." Elam sat back down and glared at each of the boys in turn. After a few more minutes, he picked up his fork and held it threateningly towards the boys and sputtered, "I swear, I'll rip the eyes outa the one who done this ta me!"

Joe placed a hand on Elam's forearm and forced it down to the table top. "Ya done it ta ya'self by fillin' their heads with all those stories about the practical jokes ya pulled. I told ya ta stop tellin' these heathens all that junk or it'd come back ta haunt ya. If ya got a bone ta pick with somebody, it's ya'self. After ya eat, go take a damn shower 'n put on some of my clothes. Good God, ya stink ta high heaven!"

Elam momentarily looked like he had second thoughts, then just as suddenly his face became soured and hostile. He again started to say something, but only managed a coughing spell. He always woke up and had a coughing fit every morning because of too much smoking and drinking. After the coughing spell passed, he pursed his now purple lips together so tight that they seemed to disappear.

With another burst of anger, Elam jumped up, only to be restrained once more. "Who done it?! I'll beat 'im so hard their children will have broken bones 'n missin' teeth!" Spit began to drool down the corner of his mouth as his breathing became labored.

"Ya boys need ta go about ya business," Joe said, still gripping Elam. Fear kept the boys from moving until Joe growled, "Git!"

Ricky and Bane got up from the table and steered clear of Elam as they left the room. They shrugged their shoulders and rolled their eyes in a show of not knowing what all the fuss was about.

Ricky went to his room and finished gathering the things on a list he was sent from the Induction Recruiter in Atlanta. He was only allowed to take a few meager items. Secretly, he wished he could run and hide somewhere in the hopes everyone would forget about him. His gut churned with anxiety and gripping fear. He stopped to sit on the bed for a while before he could will himself to finish getting ready. His mind raced with morbid thoughts, much like many other young men all across the country who were also facing his same predicament. Eventually he resigned himself to his fate and took one last look at his room and the meager items it possessed. It wasn't much by anyone's standard, but it seemed infinitely better than what lay before him.

Still fearful Uncle Elam would find him out, Bane'd locked the door to the bathroom before he washed up. Coming back out, he checked to make sure the coast was clear before he dashed to his room to change into his clean clothes. He would be traveling to Atlanta with his father and Ricky.

As soon as Bain entered his room, he almost gagged on the smell of cigarettes, beer, and Uncle Elam's horrible body odor. Once he spotted the two pieces of the snake, he all but forgot about the terrible smells. He began to sheepishly grin as a sense of pride welled up inside him at having possibly bested all of the other previous shenanigans he and his family had perpetrated on one another in the past.

Together, Bane and Ricky quietly passed Uncle Elam who was already downing his second beer of the day. Seeing the boys were safely outside, Joe went to shower, shave, and get ready for the trip to Atlanta.

Without speaking, or even looking in Ricky's and Bane's direction, Joe stepped out of the trailer and went to the truck. Ricky and Bane quickly followed suit.

"Ya boys sure know how ta start the day by riling things up. What in tar' nation was ya thinkin'?" They weren't given any time to answer before he went on, "I should 'a let 'im loose on the both of ya. That'd served ya right." No answer.

No one spoke as they drove down the road side by side on the bench seat with Bane in the middle. Being in the middle wasn't so bad because their old pickup had a three speed shifter on the column instead of on the floorboard. This gave each of the slender boys plenty of room. The sun shone directly into their faces as they traveled eastward into the morning sun. Only Joe had a pair of sunglasses to shield his eyes from sun's bright rays. Sweat poured from underneath his armpits in reaction to the humid sweltering heat of the summer morning. The old white beat-up 1959 International pickup truck didn't have air-conditioning, so they had to roll down the windows and twist the doors' small vent windows open completely so the cool wind would blow on them.

Since leaving home, Ricky'd sat looking out the passenger window without seeing anything as morbid thoughts and images ran through his mind. He reflected on the pictures he'd seen in magazines and on television of what Army life was like. Fear continued to grip him and his chest felt tight. Bane, as usual, sat with a blank expression on his face. He didn't want to draw attention to himself. He wasn't sure if he was going to catch it from Joe just yet.

After they were well down Highway 166, closer to Atlanta, Joe began to laugh until it became really hard and loud. "I'll be damned. Bet ya Elam 'n you boys don't forget this day. Even when he's old 'n can't remember his own name 'n wearing diapers, I bet he'll still be mad at the two of ya for that prank ya pulled on 'im. I thought he'd have a heart attack right then 'n there." Bane instantly broke out into a grin. Ricky was grateful for the break from the morbid thoughts, if only temporarily.

Dewey was in the middle of one of his battles when he heard Al call up to him, "Time ta git ta work, Dewey!" When Dewey looked down from the loft, he could see Al was in the process of loading saws, wedges and other such things into a trailer attached to the tractor. Already loaded were two jugs of water, a box with food and two sets of gloves. While Dewey climbed down the ladder, Al watched him with a grin.

"Boy ya goin' ta earn ya supper tanight. Climb in 'n let's git with it."

After a short trip around the plowed fields, Al stopped the tractor at the tree line near the far end of the property and shouted, "Unload all that stuff so I can move the tractor outa the way."

Dewey hopped down and did as he was told. Al moved the tractor well away from the trees and turned it off. "Now let's see if we can make hay while the sun shines. Git a big ole swig of water 'n let's git at it."

After explaining to Dewey that they were collecting firewood for winter, Al demonstrated how to use the ax. He also showed Dewey how and where he wanted the tree hit so it would fall outwards onto the open field. That was where they'd saw the tree into sections. It took some time, but Dewey finally got the hang of it. It wasn't long before Dewey claimed, "I'm hungry."

"We jus' got started, Boy. The only way ta stave off ya hunger is ta be happy in ya work, so git happy. Think about something else while ya swingin' the ax 'n it'll make the work seem less like work." He could almost see the wheels turning in Dewey's head as he watched him process what he'd just been told. "Jus' think about bein' on a ship, Boy. Pretend yer working on ya ship."

Dewey took a long time to work up his rhythm, but he finally fell into it and was making good progress when Al hollered, "Remember what I told ya! TIMBER!" As the tree began to make loud cracking sounds, Dewey quickly moved behind the other trees where Al had prepped him to go once he heard "timber."

Dewey was amazed as he watched the mighty tree fall onto the ground with a dull thud and many cracks as the limbs shattered under the weight. They used a large handsaw with a handle on each end to saw off the large limbs and axes for the smaller ones. Al showed Dewey how to measure and saw the logs into proper lengths to fit the fireplace. It took Al considerably more effort to get Dewey to move in rhythm with him without pinching and binding the long saw as they worked it together. They continued to work diligently the rest of the morning and much of the afternoon on the fallen tree before Al finally said they'd had enough.

They'd loaded all the logs that were trimmed and cut onto the trailer. Al walked alongside the tractor while Dewey drove it slowly to a small wood shed close to the house. After they finished moving all the cut logs, Al showed Dewey how to properly split them using the wedges and sledge hammer. They managed to get only a few of the logs split when Al said, "Boy, we've done enough work for taday. Good job. Now let's clean up for supper." Exhausted, they went inside the house.

There were only four famous places Joe knew about in or near Atlanta; The Varsity restaurant near Georgia Tech University, Stone Mountain Park, The Big Chicken in Marietta, and Kennesaw Mountain State Park where bloody battles took place during the Civil War. Since it was about lunch time when they arrived in Atlanta, Joe decided he would take them to the only one he'd ever been to–The Varsity on North Avenue. He told the boys that they were famous for their burgers, hot dogs, onion rings, and fries.

Joe had only been there a couple of times himself, but he decided it was the only place to eat in Atlanta that the boys would really enjoy. The order takers talked so fast that the boys couldn't understand them, so Joe intervened and gave the food orders for them. Once they got past the greasy shock, they believed they had been given the best burgers ever made by man.

After lunch, Joe figured there was still time to show them around the city before he took Ricky to the Induction Center, so he drove around to let them see all the tall buildings.

Between 10th and 14th streets, they began to see buildings and shop fronts with peace symbols painted in bold bright colors. Outside these same places, you could see men with long hair and beards wearing loud colorful clothing, many of which were tie-dyed. Young girls were dressed in the same garb, and some wore India-type clothing with beautifully designed embroidery. Their jewelry was of peace symbols, marijuana leaves, and large decorative silver pieces with multicolor American and Mexican Indian designs. Some of these "Flower Children" even wore Army jackets as tops that displayed unit patches, rank insignia, and medals they might have worn while serving in the armed forces. Most of these were worn out of protest of the ongoing Vietnam War.

Joe and the boys couldn't seem to contain themselves as they howled with laughter and made peace signs with their hands as they shouted, "Groovy" through the open windows of the truck. They knew about hippies and Flower Children from television and such, but they'd never actually seen them before. Few of the Hippies bothered to look or take notice since they were accustomed to being heckled. A few shot back peace signs with their fingers in a "V" shape and one shot them the bird.

They all had a good laugh about how ridiculous they thought the hippies looked once they'd left the area and were headed for the Induction Center. When they arrived at the parking lot, an apprehensive silence fell over them. Joe parked the truck and turned to Ricky, "You'll do fine, Boy. And jus' remember, if ya git sent ta Vietnam, do whatever it takes ta git home. Like Elam said, over there, there ain't no right or wrong as long as ya git home. And don't git one of those 'too dumb ta duck medals'—that's bullets ya know. Ya don't need ta try 'n git a Purple Heart or nothin'."

Ricky gave a nervous smile as he got out of the truck and grabbed his bag from the truck bed on the passenger side. Bane sneered as he slid over next to the open passenger door, "Do some pushups for me, Army Man." Hearing this, Joe just shook his head as he stepped out of the truck and closed the door.

Ricky looked at Bane hard and long before he said, "Well, at least I won't die a virgin like you, ya little pansy."

"I hope they kill ya sorry butt," Bane sneered back.

With that Ricky stepped closer to the open door and punched Bane hard in the chest with his fist. Bane, who was leaning outwards with one leg extended as he was about to get out, was knocked backwards across the bench seat. His head landed against the driver's door. It took a while before Bane could breathe again.

Joe just looked at the two of them and shook his head. When Bane again started to climb out of the truck, Joe said, "Boy yer a glutton for punishment. There just ain't no good in ya is there? Jus' keep ya butt in the truck and wait for me till I git back."

Bane grunted an acknowledgement and closed the door.

After Joe and Ricky disappeared through the building's main entrance, Bane grabbed a cigarette and a pack of matches off the dash where Joe had left them and lit up. He couldn't help but be glad to be rid of Ricky. He put his feet on the dash and, using his middle finger, flipped off at the door they'd entered while mumbling, "Good riddance."

That evening while Dewey and Al were sitting in the den, Al felt too sore and tired to work on knot tying. Dewey looked like he would fall over from exhaustion as he slowly ate his cookies and drank his milk. Al hardly touched his coffee. He sat back and stared at the pictures of his beloved daughter Jenny and his late wife Mary.

"Dewey, let me talk ta ya about an important word ya need ta know the meaning of, so you'll always know ta do right. The word is 'shame'."

Before continuing, he looked over at Dewey, who was taking a break from his snack before continuing, "Shame is what someone feels when they know, or believe, they've done somethin' wrong. In other words, that's the feelin' deep down inside ya gut that makes ya feel bad for doing somethin' ya know ya ought not ta have done." He pointed to his own stomach.

"It makes ya shy away from the one's you've wronged. Ya don't want ta face the people ya might'a hurt. I believe that's why ya momma hasn't come home yet. I sure wish she would though. I pray for it mos' every night."

"Have ya ever done somethin' bad that caused ya shame?" asked Dewey. Al gave him a quick look and turned back to the pictures.

Al thought on it a while as he pointed his finger. "Yeah, I reckon so. Go over there 'n pick up that pink envelope off the desk."

Dewey walked over to the desk, picked it up, and looked inside to find a drawing of a little girl blowing out candles on a cake. At the top it had words he couldn't read. "Happy Birthday" was outlined in glitter. Al joined him at the desk and picked up a pen and handed it to Dewey. "Try 'n sign it bes' ya can." He opened the card and pointed to where Dewey was to print his name. Dewey scribbled his first name about as well as a five year old.

"Good job." Then Al signed it and added "Jenny" to the top of the inside where it was appropriate. He took the card and stuck it back in the envelope with something he pulled out of his wallet. He then placed it in a desk drawer on top of a stack of similar envelopes. He stood there feeling sad as he gently slid the drawer back into place. Dewey didn't seem curious or seem to care what it was about, and Al never said anything about it being a birthday card for his long lost daughter, Dewey's mother.

"Finish ya cookies 'n let's git some shut eye. Tamorrow'll come mighty early."

Chapter 14 – Tick

"BOY, we need ta finish gittin' the fire wood chopped 'n split for winter, so don't go wanderin' off after breakfast." The only sign Dewey made of hearing Al was a momentary lapse in chewing and a quick glance in his grandfather's direction.

After Dewey finished breakfast, he went to the bathroom to brush his teeth, but soon reappeared saying, "Need more tooth soap." He held up an empty tube of toothpaste for Al to examine. Al took the empty container and looked at it carefully. It was the same tube of toothpaste he'd bought Dewey less than a week ago. It was a new brand of tooth paste that he thought he'd try. It claimed to have a peppermint flavor that would encourage children to brush their teeth more.

"Dewey, I jus' gave this ta ya a couple of days ago. What happened ta all the toothpaste? This should have lasted for weeks. Did ya eat it?"

Smiling, Dewey replied, "It tastes good."

Al just sighed as he dropped the empty tube into the trash can beside the kitchen cabinets. He walked into the bathroom and handed Dewey a new tube of the old-fashion kind of toothpaste that tasted like baking soda, "Here."

"Dewey wants the other kind of tooth soap," Dewey disappointedly replied.

"There ain't no more, Boy. Ya ate it all up like candy." He could see Dewey was discontented, so he added, "Boy, toothpaste ain't candy. It's not for eatin'. From now on we're gonna stick ta the old kind."

Dewey reluctantly took the tube and slowly began to brush his teeth. Al started back to the kitchen, "Don't forget ta collect the chicken eggs before ya go ta the barn ta play. I'll come git ya when it's time to start choppin' wood."

After Al finished cleaning the kitchen, he placed egg sandwiches in the refrigerator for their lunch. He then went to the barn looking for Dewey, with Snipe running ahead and disappearing through the barn's open doors.

Once inside, Al couldn't help but stop and tinker with some of the many metal spikes yet to be welded to the tubes on the leveler. He could feel the effects of old age while lifting the heavy objects for inspection. Old injuries that'd happened in his youth, that he thought were long forgotten, had now come back to haunt him. Because of yesterday's hard labor, his shoulders ached and his hands were sore. The metal parts he picked up seemed to weigh so much more to him today than they did as recently as yesterday.

To give himself a break, he was sorely tempted to forego cutting more wood and work on his new contraption. He quickly put it out of his mind, knowing it was never a good idea to waste good weather for getting outside tasks accomplished. He was relentlessly driven to accomplish every job to the best of his ability, just like when he was in the Navy. Besides, not only was it his routine every year, he felt compelled by something he would not let invade his mind–Jenny's absence from his life.

Al couldn't help hearing Dewey stomping around up in the loft of the barn and speaking to his imaginary crew members. Al caught himself daydreaming as he stood there listening to Dewey. Memories of his boyhood ever so slowly filled his mind and he began to feel a little envious. Unconsciously, as if in reverence to his memories, he took off his straw hat and caressed the brim, taking note not to further damage the places that were beginning to unravel along the rim.

"What ya doin', Granddaddy?" Dewey loudly inquired from the loft.

Al let the memories slide away gently before he put his hat back on. He never raised his eyes, but he raised his voice so he could be heard. "Time ta git at it, Boy."

Just as Al walked out of the barn, in his mind's eye, he could see his wife's expression and hear her voice once more ask, "Why ya cuttin' wood durin' the hottest part of summer for is far beyond me. Be careful of overdoin' it, 'n make sure ya come home for lunch. Lord knows, one of these days I'm gonna find you cooked to a crisp by that sun."

Bane woke up to the sound of multiple voices coming from down the hall and the smell of bacon. Usually, he enjoyed lying in bed for just a little bit when he first woke up, but his curiosity and hunger got the best of him. He quickly dressed and scurried into the bathroom to heed nature's call before going to eat breakfast. Despite the fact that he could hear Uncle Elam's voice, he was feeling good and looking forward to his first meal without Ricky there to taunt him. The feeling quickly vanished as he approached the kitchen table. In his normally assigned seat was none other than Tracer Taggart. He was Uncle Elam's only offspring, whom everyone referred to as Tick.

During one of Uncle Elam's many drunken tales, Bane'd learned that the name Tracer was in reference to a tracer bullet that illuminates its course of movement as it travels through the air that was used in machine gun fire. Uncle Elam had said, "The tracers let you see where yer bullets were going while you was shootin'."

He claimed that his son, Tracer, was proof he'd 'hit his target'. He'd said, "I figured that was as good a name as any I could come up with." The reason he, not so affectionately now called his boy Tick, was because he was obliged to send Tracer's mother money every payday for child support. According to Uncle Elam, "The boy 'n his momma are bleeding me dry."

Like Bane, Tick had wiry blonde hair, blue eyes and was about the same age and size. The difference between the two could be seen quickly though; Tick's left ear was cauliflower'ed and he was walleyed. Whenever the subject came up as to why he looked like he did, Joe insinuated that it had something to do with an accident when Tick was just a toddler, and also the reason Uncle Elam's wife divorced him. He said to never talk about it in front of Uncle Elam, and even threatened to beat Bane and Ricky badly if they ever did.

Tick lived with his mother in LaGrange, which was in the next county to the south. Bane rarely saw him, since he only came to stay with his father for a couple of weeks each year. These were the only two weeks Elam tried to stay somewhat sober.

For as long as Bane could remember, he and Tick had always fought. He couldn't remember why, it just seemed the way of it. He couldn't formulate his feelings, much less explain them, but he actually hated Tick with every fiber of his being. The very sight of him set his insides on fire.

When Bane approached the table, Tick's demeanor immediately changed and he began to carefully size up Bane with his dominant right eye. Bane's face became stoic as he went around and sat in Ricky's usual place at the table. He didn't utter a sound when Mary Beth handed him a plate of scrambled eggs. To this he added bacon, grits and two large lard biscuits. He then tore the two biscuits into halves and reached across the table for the butter while forcefully nudging Tick out of the way.

Elam and Joe stopped talking and watched with rapt attention, waiting for any sign of trouble. They knew that mixing Bane and Tick together was like putting gas on fire. More often than not, when the two were in the same room for more than five minutes, an argument or a fight would ensue.

Finally, Joe broke the silence. "Bane, Tick's goin' ta be keepin' us company for the next few days."

This was met with a quick jerk of Bane's head towards Tick and then to Joe, where he held his gaze for a prolonged moment while he mulled over in his mind the implications of what this meant.

"Ya see Elam got the both of ya a job balin' hay for Mr. Johnson till the job gits done. Mos' likely a week."

Bane dropped his attention back to his plate and began eating with nervous movements as Joe continued. "Ya know my boss said he can't hire ya this year 'cause ya weren't big 'n strong enough yet. So thanks to Elam, the two of ya can at least earn some money instead of jus' wastin' the whole damn summer. Elam has Tick for the next couple' a weeks. So, when ya finished with yer breakfast, the two of ya need ta hightail it over ta Mr. Johnson's place. Mary Beth made the both of ya lunch."

Bane continued to eat without so much as a grunt of acknowledgement while Joe finished explaining. Joe, feeling like he was being ignored, became agitated at Bane's lack of acknowledgement, so he slammed his hand on the table, "Well, don't ya got nothin' ta say?"

With a start Bane looked up at his father, then at Elam and sized up the situation. He could see in their eyes that they were goading him, in the hopes of sparking a fight or get a rise out of him. After looking over at Tick, Bain leaned in with his face to within an inch of Tick's and spoke in a monotone voice, "What's **he** doin' in my chair?" No one made a sound as they watched for a reaction from Tick that never came.

Suddenly Elam burst out laughing while Joe shook his head. They never expected Bane to come up with such a good line. Tick didn't say anything as he watched his father and Joe express their admiration of Bane's comeback. Since he'd already finished breakfast earlier, Tick got up from the table and flopped down on the couch in the living room, which was nothing more than the other side of a large area used for both the dining room and living room.

Bane, feeling good about getting rid of Tick, got up from Ricky's place, quietly moved his plate and glass of milk to its normal spot and sat down while still eating.

Laughing again, even harder, Elam slapped Joe on the shoulder. When he settled down laughing, he said, "Boy, those two beat all, don't they? One's jus' as mean as the other. One of these days they gonna kill each other I bet ya. It's like watchin' two dogs sniffin' 'n sizin' up one another before they commence ta fightin' over a bone. Ya sure we ought'a let 'em stay in the same house, Little Brother?"

No sooner than Elam finished talking, Bane's face turned red and he slammed down his fork. With a scowl on his face, he began cussing up a storm of obscenities as he jumped out of his chair and started wiping something white off the seat of his pants. Somehow, Tick had managed to sneak a pile of grits onto the seat of Bane's chair without anyone being the wiser.

Just as Bane started to go after Tick in the living room, Joe grabbed him and forced him into Ricky's old seat. "Don't git ya dander up, Boy. He didn't make ya move ta that seat in the first place. Ya done it ta ya'self, so let 'er go."

Again, Elam was howling with laughter, only harder, and was holding his big pot belly from the pain it caused him. Joe began to chuckle, as well as Mary Beth, who was standing in the kitchen watching the scene unfolded.

Bane was seething with anger at being duped by Tick, who had yet to say one word or make so much as a peep. Since Bane was all too accustomed to such goings on, he soon was over it and basking in the wonder of all the wonderful food and relishing every bite. The sheer joy of good food quickly put everything else out of his mind, not even Tick's presence or having to go bale hay in the hot sun all day bothered him.

Bane polished off his breakfast in relative peace before cleaning up and getting ready to leave for Mr. Johnson's farm. While in his room, he picked up the pocket knife he'd been given by his father on his twelfth birthday. His father had claimed the reason he didn't give Bane a rifle, as was customary, was because he was sure he'd come home from work one day to find half the county shot dead.

Bane mumbled to himself as he stood there fingering the blade to check for sharpness. Last year, when he and Tick had one of the worst fights of their lives, Bane swore he'd kill him the next time he laid eyes on him. Tick, who sparingly spoke, had retorted, "Tryin' ain't the same as doin'." Bane closed the knife and put it in the front pocket of his trousers before leaving his room.

Joe stopped Bane as he was about to leave the trailer, "Boy, you 'n Tick hang on there. We don't need ya wildcats killin' each other before ole man Johnson gits some work outa ya." Joe had decided to drive the boys to Mr. Johnson's in order to make sure they made it there in one piece.

Upon reaching the entrance to Mr. Johnson's farm, Joe warned, "If one of ya comes home with so much as a scratch, I'm goin' ta take my daddy's old razor strap ta the both of ya. I mean it now. No fightin', or else."

By this time Bane had already gotten out of the truck, slipped his hand into his front pocket in anticipation of a fight, and partially opened the knife with his thumb. That way he could quickly slap it open all the way once he pulled it clear of his pocket to surprise Tick. Slowly he closed the knife and pulled his hand out his pocket while he absorbed the look of "hell on earth" in his father's eyes.

Joe hesitated to leave because he wanted to be reasonably sure it was safe and the two realized the seriousness with which he had spoken before he put the truck in gear and drove away. Although he had misgivings about the situation, he had to get to work. Joe drove away slowly as he looked in the rear view mirror until he could no longer see them, all the while tapping the steering wheel with his right hand between shifting gears.

Todd sat in one of the swings with a large twig pushed deep down inside his arm cast. He was busy pumping it up and down and side to side with vigor.

"What ya doin'?" asked Jason.

"I think I got chiggers eatin' my arm off under this dang blasted thing. It's been itchin' like the dickens for the last day or so." He continued to guide the twig this way and that with little relief. "Daddy said he use ta rub turpentine on his chigger bites, but I can't do it 'cause of this here cast. B'sides, I don't spose it's really chiggers anyhow," complained Todd.

"I don't know 'bout that, but ya sure got 'em all over ya legs. Looky here. My momma put fingernail polish all over mine las' night 'cause I got so many." Jason hiked up the legs of his shorts to show everybody how far up the bites went. He had red spots painted all over his legs. "That ain't the worse of it neither; they got all over my privates too."

With a look of wonderment, Todd asked, "Your momma paint 'em there too?"

"Yeah, but I done scratched all that part off 'cause it felt good itchin' 'em."

Everybody that was gathered around laughed or giggled. Bonnie Lou was the only one who tried to hide her smile behind her hands as she turned away in embarrassment.

"Don't look like Bane's goin' ta be around taday. Seen him 'n Tick ridin' in his daddy's truck leavin' out this mornin'," announced Gabby.

"What's a Tick?" inquired Crystal.

"Well, let me see if I can describe 'im for ya. He's Bain's cousin and one of the ugliest 'n meanest critters God ever put on this earth, I reckon," said Gabby, while he contorted his face and tried to move his eyes into funny abnormally strange movements. Then he put his hands on his head and made imaginary horns with his fingers pointed upwards with a crook in them. Almost everybody else joined in on the mocking of Tick's physical abnormalities and contorted their faces to reflect their personal interpretation of Tick's evil demeanor. They cheered and congratulated each other in turn for capturing Tick's essence, all the while jeering the contorted faces as others made them as if it were Tick himself. Their pent up dislike of Tick was made abundantly clear and caused Crystal to become even more puzzled.

Gabby explained, "He's Bane's cousin, only uglier 'n meaner. I figure he's the worst of the Taggart clan, so stay as far away from 'im as ya can."

"I'll certainly do my bes', if that's the case," replied Crystal.

Billy and Gail, having just arrived, handed out muffins to everyone. With pride, Gail said, "Hope y'all like the muffins I cooked this mornin'." When she extended one to Todd, he just scoffed at it and continued to scratch his arm with the stick.

With indignation Gail scoffed, "Don't ya worry none, Todd Jackson. It ain't got no cooties on it or nothin'."

"Ain't that! It's jus' my arm itches somethin' bad. Ya got somethin' for that?"

"No, but those astronauts goin' ta the moon real soon might bring ya some of that moon dust. I hear they're goin' up there ta see what the moon is made of. My momma says that they might find all kinds of new stuff up there."

"I'd done chewed this thing off by then if it don't stop itchin'."

"Hey, this tastes real good, Gail," said Pattie, as she continued to pinch off one bite at a time.

"Yeah, I added lots of blueberries ta 'em. Momma didn't have ta help me much this time. She said since I learned the difference between sugar 'n salt, I've become a regular Suzie Homemaker."

Billy giggled, then added, "Yeah, I remember when ya made a cake out of salt instead of sugar that one time." With that, Gail gave him an evil glare and tried to snatch his muffin from his hand.

"Don't git miffed at me. I like the way ya cook now. Ain't that what matters?" Gail didn't like being reminded of her first catastrophe with baking. Last year she'd pestered her mother for a week to let her cook the cake for her daddy's birthday. Her mother finally gave in and everybody nearly gagged on her cake, including herself. She had used salt instead of sugar in the icing. She cried so hard they waited until she cooked another one to celebrate his birthday.

Mr. Johnson had never met the two Taggart boys, but he knew of their fathers. The hostility between the boys was soon apparent. He handed each one a new pair of leather gloves as he assigned them jobs. He put Bane in the back of the truck to help stack the bales while the others collected and tossed them up. Tick was assigned to help collect the bales.

It wasn't long before Mr. Johnson realized it would most likely be more beneficial to have Bane collecting the bales off the field too. He thought that maybe he'd take advantage of the competition between Bane and Tick to speed things up. He'd grown weary of listening to Bane heckle Tick. He figured if Bane was too busy working on the ground, maybe he wouldn't have so much energy to run his mouth.

He assigned the two boys to work opposite sides the truck. Mr. Johnson drove the truck while the crew of six loaded it. After Bane was put on the ground, the bales started coming faster and faster as the two boys tried to outdo one another. Some of the men started cheering for one or the other, making bets as to which boy would collect the most bales the fastest.

A couple of times, Bane passed by a bale like it wasn't there. He'd wait until Tick was close by and see if he would come across and get the ones he missed. Sure enough, Tick would rush over and collect them to show he was the better man. Bane was biding his time in anticipation of the right moment. It finally happened. He spotted two scorpions right beside the baling wire where he knew Tick would grab the bale. Tick was close and Bane hoped Tick would take the bait. He passed by the bale like it wasn't there. Sure enough, Tick again came running over to Bane's side of the truck and snatched it up.

"Son of a bitch! Damn!" came a shout from behind him. Bane pretended not to notice as he continued forward to the next bale. He acted like nothing was wrong while waiting for the truck to roll to him. He could see Tick nursing his right wrist. Tick, in his haste, hadn't seen the scorpions. The trick worked just as Bane had hoped it would.

One of the crew members had warned Bane earlier to watch out for scorpions and snakes. Of course with the gloves on, you only needed to thump the scorpions off before you grabbed the bales by the baling wire. Tick, who also had never baled hay before, hadn't heard the warnings, so he wasn't on the lookout for the little critters.

All the other field hands hurried to see what happened to Tick. They saw him swatting at his wrist and shouting in pain. While they looked over Tick's sting, Bane stood watching with a sly grin. One of the men took out a cigarette and broke it apart to get the tobacco out and wet it with his spit. He then put it on the sting and told Tick to hold it there for a few minutes to draw out the fire. Of course it was more than likely an old wives tale, but some believed it actually worked. Most believed it was just something to keep the victim occupied and would make it better through a 'placebo effect'.

Johnny, one of the field hands, said, "Don't worry, Boy. Scorpion stings ain't no worse than a bee sting. You ain't allergic ta bee stings are ya, Son? There now. Jus' hold that tobacco on it for a couple of minutes 'n it'll be fine."

Bane observed the sympathetic attentions given to Tick from a distance and waited for the commotion to subside. Once over, he began making exaggerated gestures of nursing his wrist and kissing it with pouty lips. Tick glared at Bane as he watched him make fun of his misfortune.

Jessie, one of the other field hands who'd warned Bane about the scorpions and had seen what'd happened, walked over to Bane, "Boy, I know what ya done. We don't gots no time for such crap ya mean little turd!" When he walked away, he shoved Bane aside hard, even though Bane wasn't really in his way. Bane had to extend his arms and catch himself before he fell flat on his face.

Bane wasn't accustomed to a grown stranger talking or treating him that way. He stood there stunned and feeling a little indignant. All the same, he still couldn't help but feel pride for what he'd been able to pull on Tick. He'd make it a point to not do anything else today that would draw the ire of the others who were obviously now in Tick's corner.

At lunch time the boys were hot and exhausted. They gulped down tea by the Mason jars full. It sure tasted good with the sandwiches Mary Beth had made them.

By noon, all the overcast clouds had completely cleared, leaving no protection from the sun's fierce rays. When the temperature became extreme, Mr. Johnson, seeing the boys would kill themselves if he didn't do something, stopped the men every so often. He wouldn't let them continue until they'd all filled up on water. Later, when all the grown men went home for supper, Bane and Tick stayed to stack the last truck load of hay into the barn loft.

It was almost dark when they finished stacking the bales to Mr. Johnson's satisfaction. He drove the boys home because of the late hour and in appreciation of their hard work. Joe was waiting on them while he smoked cigarettes and drank beer in the cool shade of the trailer.

Once they arrived home, the two boys rushed inside. Bane sat at the table and devoured his supper, while Tick ate his in the living room with equal enthusiasm.

"I hear ya boys worked mighty hard taday 'cause I went by to see Mr. Johnson while you were busy in the barn. I'm proud of the both of ya, 'n tamorrow I want ya's ta do the same. Tick, yer stayin' in Ricky's old room. Bane, Mary Beth cleaned up that nasty pig sty of a room taday, so don't go messin' it up. Both of ya smell ta high heaven, so shower before ya turn in." Neither one of the boys had any energy or desire to protest. Joe could see they didn't have any fight left in them, so he motioned to Mary Beth. "Lets go sit outside 'n drink our beers while the boys clean up."

Al and Dewey worked hard again all day cutting, chopping, and splitting wood until suppertime. During the hottest part of the afternoon they became fatigued, which resulted in them working at a snail's pace. They were still tired from yesterday. Dewey gulped down well water like he couldn't get enough as the temperature rose to a sweltering ninety-eight degrees with high humidity. By the time they finished, they were both drenched in sweat and had outlines of salt on their overalls from the sweat, front and back.

Al, too tired to spend much energy cooking supper, fried some ham in a skillet to make sandwiches. Dewey didn't seem to care or notice since he was too exhausted to eat much. After Dewey took a bath, Al told him to take his sweaty overalls outside to dry. Standing in the kitchen that evening, Al was only a shadow of himself while he prepared Dewey's evening snack of milk and cookies. He didn't even bother to make himself his usual cup of coffee, using only water for his evening refreshment.

This was the first time he ever remembered feeling so tired at the end of the day. When he finally sat in his chair, his hands uncharacteristically empty, he raised his palms to inspect them for some visible reason that would possibly explain his feeling of weariness. Looking at them, all that was visible to his tired eyes were two thick callused hands with scars from too many cuts from past accidents. Most of the cuts came from working on numerous metal objects over his long years as a mechanic and boiler technician.

How could he possibly measure the worth of his hands? They'd performed, without complaint, thousands upon thousands of hours of hard labor without faltering. After a long period, he finally dropped his hands onto his lap. Out of the corner of his eye, Al noticed Dewey was barely holding up his head. He was watching Al with a forlorn expression, and probably had been for some time. Al couldn't help but wonder if Dewey was seeing what was in his heart and mind, just as the look in Snipe's eyes showed a similar concern.

Al gazed at the both of them carefully before he finally spoke. "Dewey, don't ya worry none." After a short pause and sigh, Al rubbed his hand through what little hair he had remaining and said, "Ya granddaddy is jus' old 'n tired. It happens ta everybody who gits ta be my age." He managed a smile and forced himself to sound upbeat. "Ya jus' be sure ya git ya'self some rest tonight, 'n tamorrow I'll show ya how much vinegar 'n gumption this old man still has left in his bones."

Dewey's expression became more relaxed as an exhausted smile appeared.

Snipe's mood improved as well, because he began to wag his tail and lift his head off the floor. Snipe stood up, stretched his front legs in a bowing motion and yawned. He shook his head, making a flapping sound with his ears that was soon followed by a quick nuzzle to Al's arm. With an almost imperceptible diversion of his eyes towards the door, Snipe signaled that he needed to go outside for one last time to heed nature's call before bedtime.

With a lot of strained soreness and as little groaning as he could manage, for Dewey's sake, Al slowly got out of his chair. He was followed to the back door by his faithful friend, whose claws made a clicking sound with each step against the hardwood floors. Al stood at the back door for only a minute or so before Snipe reappeared. Once Snipe came into the faint light of the porch, Al noticed Snipe had something in his mouth. "What ya got there, Boy?"

Snipe stopped as Al reached down and removed the object from his snout. It was Dewey's brooch. Al went to the kitchen shelf, got Snipe his bedtime dog treat, then stooped down slightly before placing the dog treat in Snipe's mouth. "Good Boy. Looks like Dewey dropped his cross, huh, Boy?" Snipe just went about chewing his treat, not paying attention to Al. "Let's go give it back ta 'im, alright, Boy?"

Al entered Dewey's bedroom door just as Dewey was climbing into bed. "Looks like ya dropped this cross in the yard when ya took ya clothes outside, Boy. Snipe found it 'n brought it in."

Al turned it over to see the place he had soldered it those many years ago before he carried it across the room and placed it on Dewey's Bible. The Bible was sitting on Dewey's chest-of-drawers. It occurred to Al that his dear Mary always kept the cross on her Bible in their room before she'd died, so maybe that's why he'd placed it on Dewey's Bible as well.

"Did I ever tell ya that this here brooch belonged ta ya Grandmamma? I reckon ya mother gave it ta ya when she left ya at the hospital." Al took a moment to pick up the brooch once again.

He stood looking down at the tarnished cross with the badly scuffed fake pearl in the center before he continued. "One day ya Grandmother was gettin' dressed for church. She went ta put this on." He held it up towards Dewey for emphasis. "The fastener on the back'd broken loose. I never knew where ya grandmother got the thing. Anyway, it was the first time she ever went ta church without it. I re-soldered it while she 'n ya momma was at church."

"That evening, after supper, she told me how much it meant ta 'er. Ya see, she said it gave her comfort. She told me as long as she had it, God was watching over her. That was the last time I remember seeing it till ya come home with me."

"It makes me feel that way too, Granddaddy."

"Then promise me you'll try 'n keep up with it better then."

"I promise."

Al placed it back on Dewey's Bible, while ever so faintly whispering, "That was the day she got killed." With a heavy heart, Al switched off the light and pulled the door until it was almost shut, leaving it cracked open so only a sliver of light from the hall shone into Dewey's room.

Chapter 15 – Dewey's Justice

THE following morning while Dewey and Al were stacking the wood they'd just split, their tedium was interrupted by Snipe letting out a sharp yelp. Snipe had been seeking shelter from the morning sun's hot rays in the shade of one of the several neatly stacked piles of firewood. Earlier they'd heard Snipe growling and noticed him making lunges at something hidden in amongst the stacks of wood. They figured he was just after some critter or other and didn't give it another thought as they went about their business. At one point Snipe collapsed and began to make whimpering noises. He was in obvious pain and having trouble with one of his hind legs. Al went to investigate.

After peering around the corner of one of the old stacks of wood, he could see Snipe was in distress, so he rushed over and knelt down beside his faithful companion. Dewey, mildly curious to see what all of the fuss was about, ambled over while still holding his load of wood.

Frozen in place, Al urgently gave Dewey many repeated subtle gestures with his eyes and head to get Dewey to look over his shoulder. Dewey, confounded by his grandfather's strange gestures, stood dumbfounded. He could see Snipe was hurt, and his granddaddy seemed different somehow, but understanding eluded him. A strange sound finally attracted his attention. Dewey leaned over his grandfather to see a very large snake coiled up close to the two of them that was making a funny rattling sound. Finally Al whispered in a choked voice, "Dewey, kill the snake. Kill the snake, Boy!"

"Move, Granddaddy, so I can," Dewey replied in his normal tone with a slight whine.

Discouraged, Al figured that he was likely on his own. Dewey just didn't appear to comprehend the scope of the situation. Slowly letting out a breath of despair, his head fell ever so slightly as he thought what to do next. He carefully turned his attention to more closely observe the snake as he considered his options. He realized he was most definitely within easy striking distance.

In his haste, he'd placed himself in an awkward position to move; he was kneeling on both knees to examine Snipe, who was whimpering and struggling to get at the snake. Al grabbed Snipe and held him in place in the hope of preventing Snipe from provoking yet another strike. To his dismay, the snake again struck Snipe close to one of Al's hands. Al realized he couldn't move fast enough to avoid being bitten himself and Snipe was wiggling and began yelping loudly. With a great deal of effort, Al managed to toss Snipe away from him and the snake. The rattler pulled back, ready to strike once more.

Al turned to once again look at Dewey. With desperation in his voice he whispered, "I can't move, Boy. Ya gotta git at it the bes' ya can." He watched as Dewey peered over both of his shoulders and all around him with a flustered and confused expression. After a long pause and without a word, Dewey suddenly walked away, letting the sticks of wood fall from his hands as he disappeared around the rows of firewood.

Bewildered, Al couldn't comprehend why Dewey had walked away. Disappointed, he slowly turned his head to watch the large snake with its many vibrating rattles crowning the tip of its tail. The snake was obviously old by the number of rattles it had. It was coiled like a powerful tension filled spring ready to explode at the tiniest provocation. Its cold eyes stared at him as it flicked its tongue in and out seeking out the smell of danger, all the while filling the quiet air around them with its eerie warning.

Like the snake, Al would have liked nothing more than to slink away from this tense and dangerous chance meeting. Now adversaries, both became frozen out of fear and danger at this moment in time, while they apprehensively held their precarious positions. Al knew he would have to stay in this position until the snake decided the danger had passed and went on its way.

Sweat poured down Al's face and dripped onto the ground before him and upon his already sweat-soaked shirt. He resolved to wait the situation out and make a conscious effort to relax in the hopes of lulling the snake into believing all was well and the danger had finally passed. He knew the snake was only defending itself out of fear and would have preferred to avoid any contact with Snipe or himself.

BAM! BAM! BAM! Al's trance was suddenly, without warning, interrupted as he witnessed the body of the snake being chopped up by the head of a large ax. The snake split into many fleshy pieces as the sound of the ax struck it and the ground over and over. Al watched in amazement and relief as the ax came down again and again with deadly, forceful blows.

When Al was certain the danger was over, he slowly forced his frozen tight muscles to obey his brain's commands to move. His knees popped loudly while he struggled to stand erect. For the first time since his initial realization of the danger, he took a deep breath to fully expand his lungs and release the tension in his chest. Relief flooded his mind and body as he looked down upon what could have caused his ultimate demise.

Dewey stopped. While still gripping the ax in his hands like a mighty warrior, Dewey proudly proclaimed, "Mean snake is dead. Ship shape, Granddaddy?!" Dewey waited for Al to acknowledge his accomplishment.

"Good job, Boy. Good Job." Al reached over and patted Dewey on the shoulder before he turned to go check on Snipe. Snipe was desperately ill as he lay on the ground lethargic, only able to muster faint whimpering sounds. Al, realizing how badly he was injured, gently scooped him up and cradled him in his arms. With affection, he stood holding his friend and companion feeling regret at not having gone sooner to see what his now dying friend had tried to warn him about.

Helpless and in agonizing pain, Snipe tried to lift his head and focus his eyes on his master, but he was too far gone as the world around him became faded. "There now, Boy. Lets git ya inside." Dewey looked on with pleading sad eyes as Al said, "Dewey, let's git 'im in the house. That snake got 'im pretty good."

Dewey rushed ahead and opened the door for Al and Snipe. Al, already sore from two days of extreme physical labor, struggled. His arms and shoulders began to burn with the strain of carrying such a heavy load. Al hadn't noticed until then, but thunder could be heard as dark clouds loomed overhead. Just before they reached the back door heavy rain began to pour down upon them. This was one of those sudden showers that popped up on hot summer days in Georgia and why people said "If you don't like the weather, wait a little while."

When Al reached the den, he carried Snipe to his favorite spot and gently laid him on the rug at the foot of his chair. He sat down on the floor beside him and carefully began to examine his friend from head to toe. This was the first time Al had touched Snipe, other than to restrain, bathe, or punish him. That's when it occurred to him, that he'd never really patted Snipe out of affection. He now regretted it. Al could see one of Snipes hind legs was swollen and turning black and blue beneath his fur, as well as other areas. The snake had bitten him multiple times, which meant more venom had been injected than his body would be able to handle.

Snipe continued to jerk and whimper as he struggled to breathe. Al, certain his friend was dying, gently began stroking him with affection as he quietly spoke, "Settle down, Boy. It won't be long. Ya was a good shipmate." Al had watched many men die over his long career in the military, yet this time, death had managed to reach deeper inside of him, leaving him with an overwhelming sense of loneliness and dread.

"Snipe takin' a nap cause he feels bad, Granddaddy?"

Al continued to stroke Snipe while rain drops made comforting sounds on the metal roof of the house. "No Boy, he's dyin'. The snake ya killed done bit 'im a bunch of times. God done called 'im home, so lets just sit with 'im a till he's gone." Dewey felt sad at hearing this and went over and sat down in his usual chair in the den. He wanted to help, but felt helpless as he silently watched Al comforting Snipe.

Snipe lay there for an interminable time. He was in agonizing pain as Al tried to soothe him. After the pain appeared to subside and his eyes closed, Snipe had a couple of what appeared to be small seizures. His rapid, shallow breathing began to abate as his body seemed to completely relax. Al, knowing it wouldn't be long now, had his back to Dewey and continued to speak soft soothing words as he stroked his dying friend in his last moments. All too soon, Snipe's breathing stopped and he was gone. Dewey remained still and quiet as he listened to his grandfather speak ever so softly. "Ya was a good mate 'n I wish I could go with ya, but I'm still needed here, Boy."

Al stayed on the floor next to Snipe for a few more moments as hopelessness morphed into deep sadness. Much like at his wife's funeral, the feeling of loneliness drained him of energy. With a new understanding, Al briefly recalled how his father had silently cried when he was younger at the loss of their beloved dog, Skidder. Although it was considered a sign of weakness for a southern man to display emotional grief in public, the men in the south made exceptions for the death of someone's dog. They even openly displayed their condolences to one another in public over the loss of another's dog, where they might not for a family member. Al now understood, as a couple of tears rolled down his cheeks.

Eventually, Al regained his composure and spoke. "This was his rug, so it was a good place for 'im ta go. I'll let 'im keep it. We'll put 'im ta rest outside by the fields so he can keep protectin' the place for us."

Although Snipe arrived on the farm as a stray, Al and Dewey had become very attached to him. He'd become one of the family. Dewey liked Snipe cleaning up all his crumbs when he ate and Al appreciated Snipe keeping his chickens safe from varmints and protecting the crops. He was a busy happy dog and they hated that he had died like that, before his time. They now felt animosity towards the snake. Al was glad Dewey had killed it, and felt a sense of justice had been accomplished in the act.

Gently, Al moved Snipe to the middle of the rug and folded it upon him. Once the rain stopped, together they carried his body to a good place between the fields and the barn where they buried him.

"You two bein' hell-bent on fightin' one another is clear enough, but ya gonna have to wait till we're done tamorrow," shouted Mr. Johnson. He'd worked the boys hard. It was quitting time and the two were out of his sight for only a couple of minutes before he found them close to his truck pushing and shoving each other, all the while shouting obscenities and insults. Today, he was letting them go home in time for supper because all the hay was gathered and stored in the barn or loaded onto trailers for the people who'd bought it.

"I know it was you that put that cow patty in my glove at lunch!" shouted Bane.

Tick just stood looking indifferent. When Bane again started to lunge towards Tick, Mr. Johnson grabbed him by the arm. He spun Bane around so they were facing one another. "You two have been at each others throats all week. I thought the two of ya would be able ta walk home taday, but I spose that's not possible. Git in the truck. No, only one of ya is ridin' in the front this time. The other is gittin' in the back." Tick calmly walked to the truck and sat on the passenger's side while Mr. Johnson continued to hold Bane.

Once Mr. Johnson released Bane, Bane immediately pointed at Tick and shouted, "Your times a comin', ya blood sucker!"

As Mr. Johnson sped down the road, it created turbulence in the back of the truck. This caused the remnants of the hay that they'd collected in the truck bed to create a furious cloud of dust and small stinging missiles that bombarded Bane. Bane pulled his shirt up to cover his face so he could breathe without hay flying into his eyes, mouth, and nose. Out of frustration, he hit the cab with his fist. This caused Tick to look out of the cab's rear window. Tick was grinning when he turned back to face forward once again. Mr. Johnson knew what was happening and felt no shame as he pushed the gas peddle down to the floor to create an even more powerful wind, knowing it would cause Bane even greater discomfort as the hay pelted him more ferociously.

After Mr. Johnson pulled up to the trailer, he stopped Tick from getting out. He bellowed, "You boys need ta settle down. One of ya's gonna get hurt some day. If ya don't act right tamorrow, I'll send the two of ya home!" Then he said "I'm plannin' ta give ya yer pay tamorrow since it's Friday. Do ya think ya can act right till then?"

Tick answered, "Yes sir." Tick waited until Bane was in the trailer before he got out. Then he started for the hill that led to the hut village.

When Tick entered the hut village, he recognized the gang from the previous summer. While he wandered around the huts, Tick glimpsed

Crystal's strawberry blonde hair through the window of the girl's hut. He decided this was something new and went to investigate. He had yet to speak to or be spoken to by the others, as they'd given him a wide berth. When he approached the girls' hut, Pattie ducked inside to warn the others of his presence.

"That Tick's a comin' this way!" Pattie said in a hushed whisper as she moved away from the doorway.

No sooner had Bonnie Lou, Gail and Jill absorbed the bad news, than the curtain door was pushed aside and Tick boldly stepped in. Tick never said so much as a howdy-doody. Except for Crystal, he hadn't even bothered to look at anyone else inside the hut or acknowledge their presence. He was too busy studying Crystal from head to toe and back again.

Crystal felt uneasy and puzzled because she wasn't exactly sure where he was actually looking due to him being walleyed. She was pretty certain he was looking at her though, which made her feel uncomfortable. Tick immediately picked up on her discomfort. He had come to enjoy this reaction by others and use it to his advantage. He also used it to justify his aggression towards everyone whenever he was confronted about his hostility towards others.

"Hello," was all Crystal could muster under the circumstances, while the others stood mutely by. Once Tick stepped closer and she could see him more clearly, she became shocked by his gruesome appearance. Her eyes betrayed her thoughts. She didn't know how to react to this person who acted unnaturally bold, so she began to fidget. All the while her nostrils were being assaulted by the smells of sweat and moldy hay. Eventually, his repugnant smell caused her to wrinkle her nose and take a step backwards.

Seemingly un-phased by Crystal's reaction, Tick continued his intimidating, while not doing or saying anything. As the seconds passed, the moment became more and more awkward and tension mounted. Gail finally broke the silence. "Crystal, this is Tick. Tick, this is Crystal. She moved in jus' after ya visited las' summer."

Gail went on to tell him about how Crystal's father was a mechanic in Carrollton, which trailer she lived in, and other such things. Only now, he began to slowly and menacingly move closer and closer to Crystal. He didn't make any outward signs of acknowledgement that he heard anything Gail was saying as he advanced. He was now almost touching Crystal's face with his own. Gail's voice became nervous and finally faded until she stopped speaking all together. The tension became almost unbearable as the girls looked to one another. Satisfied, Tick looked at the other girls one at a time to get the full effect he was after, intimidation.

Crystal, who was normally unshakable in these situations, decided that she needed some distance between herself and Tick. She pushed her way past him and stepped outside. She was soon followed by the other girls. They all exchanged knowing looks at one another as Pattie leaned in close to Crystal's ear and said, "Now ya know what we meant?"

Crystal whispered back, "Yeah."

When Tick emerged from the hut, the group of girls quickly walked over to join the boys, taking quick glances behind them as they went. Soon, they all gathered around the swings and began softly talking amongst themselves. It was obvious to Tick that he was the object of everyone's conversation. Billy was the only one who didn't seem too terribly worried, as Gabby, Todd, and Jason engaged in intense conversation and agreement with the girls about how much they disliked and distrusted Tick, as well as Bane.

Tick strolled over without saying a word or making a gesture of greeting. Yet he still managed to make it abundantly clear that he wanted the swing Gabby was in by standing over Gabby and staring at him with a look of contempt and forewarning. Reluctantly, Gabby got up from the wood swing and gave it to him. Gabby tried, but failed to be convincing when he acted as if he was finished and wanted to get up anyway. Jason and Todd moved away to give Gabby and Tick plenty of room to swap places.

Billy was the only one to show he was unfazed by Tick's show of dominance as he leaned against the trunk of the tree and watched the others reactions. Tick noticed Billy's lack of concern and sized him up. He decided that Billy was even bigger than last year and, as usual, wouldn't be easily bullied. As time passed, everyone seemed to relax more now that Tick settled into the swing and didn't follow them when they moved away from him.

Within an hour, Bane came down the hill. He had cleaned up and eaten supper before leaving the trailer. Except for Billy, everyone became anxious all over again when Bane approached the group. Bane didn't waste any time going over and standing next to Crystal.

"I see you've already met Cousin Tick. What'd ya think of the filthy blood suckin' insect?" Bane spoke loud and clear as he looked at Tick to drive home the point of his insult.

Nobody said a word as the animosity Bane felt towards Tick began to swell. Tick got out of the swing, acted like nothing was wrong, and stood on the other side of Crystal so close they almost touched.

"What ya think yer doin'?" Bane demanded. Tick didn't reply as he began to touch and caress Crystal's hair with his filthy hand. Crystal stood frozen and mortified. Bane, feeling challenged, became outraged, so he yanked Crystal away from Tick's reach as he positioned himself to block Tick from pursuing her. When Tick attempted to go around Bane, Bane put his right hand in his front pocket and used his left to stop Tick. The two locked eyes as they silently stood toe to toe.

"Jus' lookin' around," Tick replied with a calm, even tone. Crystal winced ever so slightly at hearing Tick speak for the first time since his arrival to the hut village. Even his voice seemed eerie to her.

A dinner bell rang out from over the hill. The whole gang moved in unison as they all headed home. While they were ascending the hill, they began to peer over their shoulders to make sure Tick and Bane weren't following. They could see the two were still where they had left them, still in a tension filled face-off with one another. Everyone spoke quietly amongst themselves as they continued walking home.

"I sure wish Dewey was here right now," said Bonnie Lou.

"Why? Tick'd jus' look for a way ta cause him trouble too. And who knows, Bane might jus' help 'im," chimed Jill. Others acknowledged their agreement with what she'd said.

Gail suddenly grabbed Billy by the arm and stopped him by standing in his way. Everyone stopped and listened as she asked with a stern voice, "Billy, why don't ya ever beat that Bane or Tick. They is always causin' trouble for us 'n yer bigger 'n them. We know ya can, so don't go actin' like ya can't."

Billy looked at his little sister and calmly replied, "Ya gotta let things play out. Ya know, like the whippin' stick daddy keeps on the shelf. He only uses it when there ain't no other choice. It's always there to remind us ta behave, but he don't use it till he feels that there ain't no other way. 'Sides, daddy says ya never start a fight unless ya willin' ta go as far as it takes ya. And with those two, ya never know how far it's liable ta go." Gail crossed her arms and stormed off in a huff.

Tick could tell Bane wasn't going to back down and he was reasonably sure why Bane's hand was in his pocket. Tick had seen Bane pull out his pocket knife several times during the past few days at Mr. Johnson's. Tick'd accomplished what he was after anyway, which was to push Bane to the limits of his tolerance without having to actually fight. He prided himself on pushing others to the edge of their breaking point and stopping. He scowled and dropped his shoulders as he spoke. "The redhead's yer girl, huh?"

"That's right! And I don't wanta see ya sorry face near 'er or touchin' 'er again!"

Sensing the immediate danger had passed Tick just shrugged and began walking towards the hill. He was hungry and decided this was enough information for now. Tick was a true passive-aggressive, in that he liked to hurt or harm others without them knowing it until the deed was done. He liked to use blatant intimidation and manipulation as tools in his arsenal of ways to gain any advantage in his relentless goal of self-amusement at others expense.

Bane, feeling cheated and frustrated, took his pocket knife out and flicked his wrist to snap it open. Then he threw it at the oak tree where it stuck in the trunk at chest level before he once again watched Tick walking away.

Bane checked out all the huts before he disappeared into the boys' hut. Sure no one else was about he pulled out a couple of cigarettes from his socks, along with a book of matches. He lit one as he began to flip through one of his girly magazines.

Later in the evening when Bane returned home, he found Joe, Uncle Elam, and Tick sitting in chairs outside the front door of the trailer enjoying the shade. As usual Joe and Elam had a beer in one hand and a smoke in the other. Tick, who was also smoking, gave a smirk at Bane's approach. Bane made a special effort to not look at Tick while he started for the door of the trailer. He froze when he heard Tick crinkling up some paper and boldly announce, "Shouldn't smoke while ya havin' relations with ya real girlfriend. Ya might accidentally burn her up or somethin'." Tick continued to crinkle the paper to drive the point home.

"Ya daddy got ya a new girlfriend in the mail taday," proclaimed Tick as he reached down and tossed a new edition of a girlie magazine at Bane's feet.

Bane didn't turn around when he heard the thunderous roar of laughter coming from his father and Uncle Elam. They hadn't been told anything beforehand, but easily guessed what Tick meant. Bane began to tremble with anger as he fumbled with the door handle. Frustrated, he spun around to face the group of jeerers and locked eyes with Tick.

His father threw up his hand to stop him. Then he extended an unlit cigarette and said, "Hold on there, Boy. If yer finished with ya business for the night, now's the time ta have a smoke." That brought on a new round of gut busting laughter. This made Elam's last swallow of beer spew out of his mouth and nostrils.

While returning Bane's hostile stare, Tick calmly put out his cigarette, intertwined the fingers of both hands, and rested them in his lap in a show of not being intimidated. Seeing he hadn't yet provoked Bane enough to satisfy his need to humiliate him into action, Tick grinned ever so slightly and blew Bane a kiss.

Bane jumped off the steps and dove at Tick only to be caught in mid-air by Joe. "Hold on there, Boy. That'll be enough for now." Tick hadn't flinched, but now his grin showed he was basking in the accomplishment of thoroughly humiliating Bane.

When Bane entered his room, he could still hear laugher. He pulled out his pocket knife and sat down on his bed. While he thumbed the sharp edge of the blade, an idea started to take shape in his mind. His frown gave way to a smile as he thought more and more about how he'd get even with Tick. It became almost impossible to get to sleep until late in the night just thinking about it over and over again. It was only when he was satisfied that he'd come up with the best plan possible that he was able to close he eyes and find solace in sleep.

After Al and Dewey picked at their lunch of onion sandwiches, made of white bread, mayonnaise, and freshly sliced sweet onions, they went back to the woodshed and inspected the rattlesnake's carcass. With the exception of the rattler, Al used a shovel to pick up all the pieces and sling them into a nearby row of blackberry bushes. He cut the rattler free of the remaining piece of snake and put it in his pocket. Since childhood, it was his habit to collect rattlers of snakes killed on the farm. His father had told him, "Boy, ya always keep a piece of one of the devil's workers ta let the devil know ya ain't afraid to cut his off as well. If ya have enough of 'em, he'd know ya mean business and'll steer clear jus' in case ya jus' might do it too."

"Let's git back ta it, Boy. Watch out that ya don't run across some of his relatives." Al started collecting more of the newly split wood and stacking it on the pile they'd been working on earlier. Dewey, still leery, hesitated somewhat, but eventually followed suit.

It was as hot and humid a day as August could put on them, but Al and Dewey continued to work at a slow and steady pace. A couple of hours later and still too early for preparing supper, Al could see that he and Dewey were depleted of the energy or will to continue. "Go along with ya'self 'n I'll come 'n git ya for supper."

Dewey went into the house and retrieved an apple. He spotted what was left of a cow's hoof that Snipe had been chewing on for the past few days. Al explained that he bought it for Snipe, because dogs really enjoyed chewing on them and it helps kept their teeth clean. Dewey picked it up and put it in his pocket before he went outside. Out of a sense of loyalty and respect, he went to the grave site and placed the cow's hoof on the small mound of red dirt.

Dewey stopped at the doorway of the barn for a moment or two before he made up his mind and headed for the woods. Moving slowly at first, he soon picked up his pace until he arrived at his usual place by the creek. He removed his boots and let his feet soak in the cool water. He only ate half of his apple before he threw the remainder to the spot where the rabbit would normally come to retrieve what was left. He watched and waited, but no rabbit appeared. He sat there feeling sad while he thought about poor Snipe. Eventually, he heard the bell ringing and he went home.

After supper, Dewey and Al took their usual places in the den. Al felt stove-up all over. The pain and stiffness, that had only been in his shoulders and hands the night before, had spread throughout his entire body today. The biscuits from breakfast had become hard and dry by this time, so Al had placed one in his coffee to soak so he could spoon it out of the cup for his evening snack. Dewey was subdued as he sat and ate his cookies and drank his glass of milk.

"I hate that mean ole snake," Dewey suddenly blurted out. Al turned to look at him. He was thinking about something in his past when he was interrupted by Dewey's proclamation.

"Dewey, let me tell ya a story my father told me about a snake. It is the only one I remember that has a snake in it at any rate. I was jus' thinkin' about it."

Al, having already eaten his coffee soaked biscuit, took a couple of sips of coffee and made himself comfortable in his chair before he began. "There was this snake that'd worked hard his whole life tryin' ta make a livin' huntin' down one mouse or rat at a time for food. One day, he come across a hole in the side of an old government warehouse, so he went inside ta investigate. The shelves in the buildin' was empty except for this one smelly block of cheese that'd fallen down behind a shelf. Ta his delight, he found that it had been nibbled on by a mouse. Well, that snake put two 'n two tagether 'n realized this was opportunity knockin'. He figured that if he waited a little while, that there mouse was bound ta come back 'n want some more of this fine smelly cheese."

"The snake sat on that big block of cheese 'n waited patiently till a fat mouse come along. When the mouse started ta eat the cheese, the snake snatched 'im up real quick like." For effect, Al jerked his hand through the air as if he were snatching something.

"Well, the snake finished uncovering that there block of cheese from its cloth wrapper so that it could be smelled by any mice in the neighborhood. Sure enough, along come a tiny mouse. Havin' jus' eaten that fat mouse, the snake wasn't particularly hungry, so he come up with a plan. He figured that he'd take full advantage of the circumstances he found himself in sittin' on that there block of government cheese."

"The snake peered over the edge of the cheese 'n looked down on the tiny mouse, which scared the mouse somethin' terrible. The poor little mouse was so frightened he couldn't move. The snake hissed,

'There ain't no reason ta be afraid of me little mouse. Eat all ya want.' It took a while, but the tiny hungry mouse took a nibble, then another. Seein' he wouldn't be harmed, he began ta eat till he was plumb full. The snake hissed, 'Come back anytime ya want 'n bring ya friends. Ya can plainly see there's plenty for everybody. I'll watch over this here cheese for ya till ya git back.' The tiny mouse, now full, thanked him 'n went outa the hole from which he had come."

"Sure enough, he come back the next day 'n brought a friend. The snake jus' sat there bein' friendly as could be while the two ate. After a couple more days, there was lots of mice eatin' on that block of cheese. Well, that snake figured he'd lured enough ta fill his belly clear ta the brim, so he eat 'em all up." Again, Al made a snatching motion with his hand and smacking noises with his lips.

"What happened then?" Dewey was leaning forward in his chair with his eyes ablaze.

"Well, he stayed there 'n kept doin' it over 'n over till all the cheese was gone is all. Jus' remember, Dewey, politicians are jus' like that snake. They'll take advantage of ya by actin' like they was ya friend by offerin' ya government cheese like it was theirs ta give, but there's a price ta be paid for gittin' hooked on government cheese. There always is. Some folks swear free cheese tastes better'n the stuff they have ta pay for cause it don't have no sweat on it. Those kinda politicians 'll take advantage of ya when ya least expect it. They know how ta buy votes from folks that's too ignorant ta know better." Dewey sat back and let what he heard soak in as Al sipped his coffee with a grin.

"Dewey, that ole snake that killed Snipe taday didn't mean ta do nothin' but protect itself. It was jus' scared 'n struck out at what it thought was a threat ta 'im. But, that don't mean he didn't need killin' though. He'd a bit me for sure if ya hadn't axed him. Nature jus' works that way is all. When some critter or other is around that is hurtin' others, it needs killin'. We do that with people too, ya know. It's called the death penalty. We convict people of murder 'n then take 'em ta jail 'n put 'em down like the wild animals they are. Critters, like some people, are the way they are because they were born that way or made ta be that way is all. Jus' the same, I'm grateful ya killed that snake before it could bite me. Who knows, I might'a jus' been killed myself. I'm proud of ya, Boy."

"We put in a good week's work already, so ya git on ta bed now 'n tamorrow after the chores is done, you can go play." Dewey, who was immersed in thought, immediately perked up at the news that he would be able to go play with his friends the following day.

Chapter 16 – The Counterpoise

DURING breakfast, Joe noticed that Bane was unusually cheerful, even pleasant. "What's got in ya taday, Boy?" asked Joe. Mary Beth and Tick were also interested, so they stopped to listen for Bane's response.

"What' ya mean?"

"Jus' worried is all." Understandably Bane had been moody, sullen, and downright nasty ever since Tick's arrival on Monday, that is, until this morning. Joe couldn't quite put his finger on it, but he knew something was not quite right and it left him feeling unsettled. He decided to let it drop for the moment, but he knew he'd change Bane's mood back to "normal" quickly enough with what he had to say to him next.

"I was plannin' on tellin' ya this evenin', but I changed my mind. I reckon now's as good a time as any. Tick'll be stayin' another night. Tick, I know this is y'all's las' day workin' for old man Johnson and ya Daddy was suppose ta take ya home tanight, but somethin' come up." Joe shrugged. "How's that suit the two of ya?" No reaction.

Joe looked at Tick. "Ya daddy decided he'd go out tanight with some girl he met the other day, so he says he'll see ya after work tamorrow." As usual, Tick didn't indicate any feelings on the matter as he glanced over at Bane, who continued eating breakfast unfazed by the revelation. Joe's eyes narrowed as he watched Bane with growing suspicion, since there was no outburst or objection. He was absolutely certain Bane wouldn't like the idea, especially after Tick thoroughly humiliated him last night.

Joe was just about to confront Bane, but stopped when Bane, fork loaded with eggs, stopped it halfway to his lips. His head was cocked slightly to the left and his eyes were diverted upward as if he were in heavy concentration about something. Bane's smile grew as he nodded his head the way someone does once they've made up their mind. With a satisfied grin, Bane continued eating. Joe's suspicion was confirmed. He knew Bane was definitely up to something extra special and he was intrigued.

"What ya think about it, Bane? Ya cousin stayin' another day."

Bane shrugged. "Why should I care?"

This answer stunned Joe, but the only sign Tick made that indicated that he'd heard it was a flashing glance. Mary Beth's expression showed concern and she placed her hand over her heart before she looked to Joe for reassurance. Joe decided to at least put on a show of acting like he wanted to stop anything that might get out of hand between the two boys.

"You boys listen up. Mary Beth's gonna let me know if anything happens between the two of ya, so ya better not let me come home 'n find out the two of ya had trouble gittin' along." No reply. "YA HEAR ME?" With that Joe slammed his fist down on the table, which gave the two boys a start. They both sat up a bit straighter and looked at him. "WELL?"

Almost in unison they both begrudgingly gave acknowledgement.

While Al was cleaning the kitchen, he automatically turned to put the remaining breakfast scraps into Snipe's bowl. Then it hit him. Snipe would no longer be there to eat it. A knot formed in his stomach, so he turned away with a sigh and scraped them into the trash can instead. He put food in the refrigerator for their lunch.

Once again he looked at Snipe's bowls. The water bowl was still full, but the food bowl was empty. Of course they were just old sauce pans that'd lost their handles long ago, but at the time, he'd decided they were just what was needed for the purpose they'd served. The knot in Al's stomach got a little tighter because he missed Snipe. Snipe's presence had taken the sting out of being alone before Dewey came along and he enjoyed the company. He couldn't bring himself to take the bowls off the floor just yet, so he left them.

Al noticed that Dewey was moving slower and quieter than usual. Dewey didn't come into the kitchen after going to the bathroom with his usual zest and proclaim 'ship shape'. Instead, Dewey retrieved the basket to collect the chicken eggs before taking a dog biscuit off the shelf as he departed the house in silence. With curiosity Al watched Dewey through the kitchen window. He observed Dewey go around the corner of the barn. Dewey, no doubt, was going to visit Snipe's grave. "I'll miss him too," was all Al managed.

Al went to the wood shed to finish straightening up the work area where he'd parked the tractor. Since the tractor hadn't been cranked yet, he decided it was a good time to check the fluid levels and such. Once he'd finished checking the fluid levels, he tried to crank the tractor, but it wouldn't even turn over. He figured the battery was most likely dead, so he pulled his pickup around to it and attached the jumper cables. This quickly brought the tractor roaring to life.

Since the trailer they'd used to carry the wood logs on was still attached, he decided to return it to its normal place in the yard next to the other tractor implements. They wouldn't need it again anytime soon. Afterwards, he then drove the tractor to the barn and parked it beside his work area and tools.

Just as Al shut down the tractor and was about to hook the battery charger cables, he heard a strange crackling noise coming from outside the barn. This unfamiliar noise caused him concern, so he immediately went outside to investigate. When he came around the corner of the barn, he could see Dewey was piling very large heavy rocks on top of Snipe's grave. "What's goin' on here?"

Dewey didn't say anything while he finished placing the last two rocks on the grave. Al could see they were piled in an orderly and well thought out manner. Dewey had gathered rocks from one or more of the many piles on the farm. The rocks had been plowed up in the fields over the years and stacked out of the way into individual piles along the edges of the planting fields. Al admired Dewey's handy work as he went to stand beside his grandson. While Dewey wiped away excess dirt from his hands onto the front of his overalls, he looked at Al and said, "We didn't pray for 'im yet, Granddaddy."

"You're right, Boy. Go ahead," Al took off his straw hat and lowered his head slightly.

Dewey bowed his head and began, "God, take care of Snipe. He was Granddaddy's shipmate. Dewey liked him too. Amen." Dewey then leaned over and placed a dog treat on top of a large white stone, which was obviously the head stone. It was the only quartz rock in the whole bunch. Then Dewey pulled out his wooden sword and saluted Snipe's grave with it as best he knew how. Dewey looked over at Al and said, "Gabby says if ya don't put rocks over the dead, critters'll dig 'em up."

Al placed a hand on Dewey's shoulder. With a subtle crack in his voice, he said, "Ship shape, Dewey." Al felt somewhat better and he hoped Dewey did as well. He decided that he'd just witnessed as fine a funeral as any he had ever attended, and the matter settled properly.

Al and Dewey stayed busy working together until lunch. After lunch, Dewey grabbed another dog treat, along with an apple, just as he was leaving to go play with his friends. Al was pleased to see Dewey was in better spirits and behaving more like himself. It occurred to him that he and Dewey would be alright.

Dewey was in good spirits as he set off down the pathway through the woods. When he arrived at the halfway point, his favorite resting place by the creek, he plopped down and took off his boots. He'd decided not to eat any of the apple and just give the whole thing to his friend, the rabbit. When he tossed it to the other side of the creek it must have landed on a sharp rock, because it burst open as it landed near the briar patch. While he cooled his feet in the creek, the rabbit inquisitively appeared and began eating the apple.

Dewey sat quietly watching the fluffy critter, ever mindful to not make any undue noise or sudden movements which might scare it away. Once the apple was about gone, Dewey felt satisfied he'd done his good deed for the day, so he pulled on his boots and set out for the hut village. He hadn't been there all week because he was too busy working with Al, and he sorely missed the camaraderie of the other children.

Upon arriving at the hut village's perimeter, Libby barked as she rushed over to greet him and nuzzled his leg, expecting to get her usual treat. Dewey took an extra long time petting and playing with her before he gave up the dog treat. Libby was all too willing to let Dewey give her a thorough petting, but in her zest to gobble up the bone, she forgot all about him.

"Hey Dewey, glad ya come back. Git over here 'n give me a push," shouted Todd from a swing. "This dad burned cast gits in the way of buildin' up steam." Dewey joined the group at the swings, and after some more coaxing began pushing Todd.

"Where ya been, Dewey?" inquired Gail.

"Been helpin' chop firewood with Granddaddy."

"Ain't it too early for choppin' wood?" inquired Gail, with a puzzled look.

Gabby joined in, "My daddy says it ain't never too early for gittin' ready for anything. But darn if it ain't too dang hot ta do anythin' like that! Why'd ya chop wood in heat like this, Dewey?"

"Cause Granddaddy told me to."

Crystal, upon hearing Dewey's voice, had come out to greet him. "Hey there, Stranger! Glad our hero captain come back ta see us." This made Dewey light up inside, as expressed by his smile as he walked over to greet her. He missed her most of all, because she was always so nice and treated him with kindness.

"Ya got a busted wing, anyway. Let me swing now!" shouted Jason. Everyone looked to see Todd holding onto the ropes of the swing as best he could with only one good hand while Jason was trying to push and then pull him out of the wood swing.

"I jus' got this shiny new cast, but I'm fixin' ta bust it on yer noggin if ya don't stop," warned Todd.

Frustrated, Jason grabbed Todd around the waist and tried to pull him away from the swing. This caused Todd to let out a loud and long fart. Jason reacted only after his nostrils were assaulted by an overwhelmingly foul odor. Todd smiled as Jason quickly stepped back with a bewildered and disgusted look on his face.

"Damn, Todd, only dead things is supposed ta smell that bad."

Because the air was stale, others soon moved away as they got a whiff.

Jill pointed her finger at Todd and began a rhyme, "Todd, yer a skunk, shame on you. Ya smell so bad that no one loves you. Yer butt is brown, ya farted pooh pooh, now no one wants ta be 'round smelly ole' you."

As everyone laughed at Todd, Gabby asked, "Todd, what'd ya eat ta cause that?"

"My momma cooked pinto beans with a ham bone for supper las' night. Course, I added some hot sauce, raw onions, 'n cracklin corn bread ta the mix. Then I washed it down with buttermilk. Like my daddy says, 'It sure was good, I can truly tell, but shor' ta be hell on the nose and the tail'. Dogs don't mind, but people always do, and gas'll be bad till ya go dodo."

Jason, satisfied the smell had dissipated, moved in again for another try to expel Todd from the swing. Todd, seeing him coming, cocked up his butt cheek and let out another loud fart in response.

Frustrated, Jason backed up again and said, "Ya momma's glasses is so thick she has ta keep her face outa the sun or they'll burn 'er face off of 'er."

"Maybe so, but even with half her face burned off she'd still be better lookin' than yer momma."

Everyone started laughing again, except Dewey, who didn't get it. The two made faces at one another, which indicated the shenanigans were over between them for the time being. As usual their skirmishes ended in a stalemate.

Mr. Johnson, having grown weary of the two boys and their disruptions, decided to take them home early. Once he pulled up to the trailer, he was troubled about leaving the two of them alone, so he followed them to the trailer door. "Anyone here ta see after you boys?" asked Mr. Johnson.

"Yeah, Mary Beth is. She's livin' with us now," replied Bane. To Mr. Johnson's relief, he could see Mary Beth when Bane opened the door. She was sitting at the kitchen table smoking a cigarette.

"You two hold on." Mr. Johnson pulled out two small envelopes from his shirt pocket and handed one to each boy. "There's ya wages for the week. Even with all the crap ya put everybody through, ya still worked hard 'n deserve ta be paid."

"Ya want us back on Monday?" asked Bane as he pulled out more money than he'd ever had in his whole life.

He stood dumbfounded and didn't really listen as Mr. Johnson replied, "No, I think I've seen enough of the two of ya ta keep me for a while."

Bane was almost euphoric as he entered his room, but it wasn't long before he became paranoid. It occurred to him that something could happen to his new found fortune. He no longer had to worry about his brother Ricky and JoJo, but fear still crept into him as he began to figure out how to safeguard his treasure. He worried that Tick might try and steal it from him, so he looked for a place to stash his cash-laden envelope. Not satisfied with anywhere in his room, he decided that the only safe place was in his pocket.

When Bane emerged from his room, he could see that Mary Beth was busy preparing a roast for supper. On the way to the kitchen, when Mary Beth wasn't looking, he took a couple of cigarettes from the pack that was lying on the dining room table. Then he went into the kitchen and opened a bottle of soda to take with him to the hut village.

Walking down the hill towards the huts, Bane could see that Tick was already there. He was standing among a group gathered by the swings. He was standing directly in front of Dewey. He knew Tick had never met or heard of Dewey before, so with a smile he thought, *this is going to be fun.*

At first, Tick didn't realize that Dewey was in any way abnormal. It didn't take much longer than a few moments to figure it out once he spotted the wooden sword, observed the lack of social norms, and Dewey's lack of a normal response to his own unusual appearance. He had seen retarded kids before, but none as big as this one for his age. Tick could spot weakness of any kind in anyone faster than the most highly educated doctor and he prided himself on exploiting it, whatever it was.

Tick took delight over Dewey having a hard time trying to decide which direction he was looking, so he diverted his eyes and shifted his head in jerks to make fun of Dewey's uneasiness. Tick always drew delight and amusement from such encounters with new acquaintances, but rarely, if ever, until this time, let on as he would kept his face void of any hint of what he was really thinking or feeling. He had yet to say anything to Dewey before he reached for Dewey's sword. Dewey immediately pushed him away. Tick didn't let that faze him as he once again invaded Dewey's personal space by getting even closer this time.

Feeling uncomfortable, Dewey turned to walk away. Libby had come over to Dewey and nosed his leg by this time. When Dewey leaned over to stroke her head, Tick kicked her hard in the side. Libby yelped loudly and quickly cowered away. Tick wanted to use this opportunity to try and intimidate Dewey by showing him he was someone to be reckoned with, but most of all, feared.

With the speed Tick could never have imagined, Dewey pulled out his wooden sword and struck him directly in the stomach with such force that he landed on his back several feet away. Tick was lying on the ground gasping for breath as Dewey walked towards him with his sword raised high shouting, "Bad!"

Bane saw the event unfolding as he walked into the compound and ran as fast as he could in anticipation of seeing Dewey finish Tick off.

Just then, Dewey heard Crystal's familiar voice shouting, "DEWEY, STOP!" He froze in place as Crystal and the others came over quickly by his side, where he hovered over Tick's sprawled out body.

Crystal grabbed Dewey's arm that still held the sword high over Tick and slowly, yet gently, pulled it down. She caressed his arm and shoulder as she softly spoke, "Dewey, leave him be. Ya gave 'im what he had comin'." When she was certain Dewey was calmed down, she went on. "Let's go see about poor Libby."

Crystal escorted Dewey away by the arm over to where Libby was cowering, then whispered, "I'm glad ya showed that mean ole' bully." Dewey became more relaxed the further away they got from the crowd that'd gathered around Tick.

"Dewey didn't want 'im ta hurt Libby no more," he said as he looked to Crystal for approval.

"I know," she answered softly.

Tick rarely showed emotion and almost never fear, but surprise, confusion, and fear had overcome him when he'd looked up at Dewey standing over him. What concerned him most of all, was that he was unable to foresee Dewey's violent reaction and the effect thereof.

With the threat gone, Tick felt only agony and pain as he covered his stomach with both arms. Able to catch his breath once again, his breathing returned to normal, but somewhat rapid.

Bane was severely disappointed that Crystal had stopped Dewey. "Next time why don't ya mind ya own business," he shouted after her and Dewey. He stood by the others with a look of satisfaction and amusement.

Bane leaned down, and in a mocking voice said, "Hurts huh? Don't it, ya blood sucking TICK? Come on, give us a cry. Ah, now, give us somethin'. Here let me help ya. Watch how it's done." Bane balled up his fist and began to rub his eye sockets as he pretended to cry in an overly dramatic way. The others became more apprehensive as they focused their attention on Bane's antics, with the occasional nervous glance towards Tick.

Tick couldn't or wouldn't speak as he regained his composure and his anger began to swell. Pure hatred soon replaced the pain as he listened to Bane ranting, but his pain soon returned with a vengeance when he tried to get up from the ground.

Bane went on, "Come on 'n give us a good cry. It's okay."

Ticks face went stone cold blank as he watched Bane walk away laughing. The others knew this look and backed away slowly without so much as a single word spoken. It was apparent that it was time to put distance between Tick and themselves. They all moved in unison and gathered a short distance away. Even Billy didn't want any part of this, and he made sure to keep Gail close.

It wasn't long before Bane's absence was noted. Tick, of course, was the first to realize that Bane was nowhere to be found. Shortly afterwards, to everyone's relief, Tick walked back to the trailer park.

The rest of the afternoon was spent mostly around the swings. The gang talked and speculated as to what'd happened and what was yet to come.

Gabby said "One of 'em is dead for sure now. Remember las' time somethin' like this happened? I thought that was bad. Danged, that was nothin' the way I see it now. Remember, Billy?"

"Yeah, guess it was bound ta happen sooner or later. Ain't nothin' ta do about it but stay clear of 'em as bes' we can."

Pattie grabbed Crystal's arm. "I ain't comin' back here tamorrow unless all y'all are with me." Bonnie Lou, who hadn't left Gabby's side until now, huddled next to Jill, Crystal and Pattie before affirming her agreement.

It took a long time and many thorn pricks to the legs and arms, but Bane finally accomplished what he had set out to do. Needing a rest, he sat down beside the briar bushes along the creek and ate the blackberries that he'd gathered after the last rock was placed. Earlier, he happened upon the trail Dewey took through the woods to go to and fro from home. He'd followed the path of faded orange pieces of string that were tied to trees along the way. Shortly after he sat down to rest, he heard a loud bell ringing. He knew it was the one Dewey's grandfather rang for supper. It wasn't long before he heard and then watched Dewey pass by on the trail, which was on the other side of the creek. Dewey didn't see him because Bane was camouflaged by the briar thicket. Bane lit a cigarette as a reward for his efforts, now that he felt is was safe to do so.

While he puffed away, he seemed to remember something important. "Oh yeah," he spoke out loud as he pulled out the money packet and once again counted the twenty dollar bills. He had sixty dollars! He sat there for a long time daydreaming about what he'd buy with all that money. He stayed there feeling like he didn't have a worry in the world, and eventually smoked the other cigarette.

Bain wasn't in any hurry to go home. Only when the woods became darkened by the shadows of the nearby hills and large trees, did he realize it was supper time. The only reason he was looking forward to going home was to enjoy what he knew would be a good supper. Still, he was filled with reluctance as he crossed the creek and headed back down the trail.

Earlier, Al realized he'd been piddling around most of the afternoon and decided to go into town for a change of scenery. He'd put off going to the store for a couple of days because he wanted to get as much wood cut as possible. When he was about to enter the Piggly Wiggly, he came across an old man dressed in overalls who looked somehow familiar to him. The man was bent over with age and had a slight drag to his left leg. Al realized he was looking at someone older than himself who'd suffered a stroke.

When their eyes met, the old man extended his right hand. A large smile deepened the multiple wrinkles upon his slender jaws. He wore false teeth that were stained by coffee, tobacco and time. He took a moment and turned his head to spit out a large stream of black tobacco juice on the ground before he spoke. "Al, ya look jus' like ya daddy."

Al took his hand and was surprised by the man's firm grip. Al tried in vain to recall who this older man could possibly be and where he knew him from. The old man realized Al's dilemma and let out a little chuckle. "Maybe this'll help," he finally said. "Bonehead, if ya mess with nature, it's only natural for nature ta mess ya up."

Al's mind shot back to a day in his boyhood when he was helping his father and his Uncle James castrate some young bulls. He would never forget how one of the bull's legs broke free and kicked him so hard it broke a bone in his lower left leg. It wasn't a complete fracture. They called it a green stick fracture because the bone had broken lengthwise like a fresh green stick would've. He had to hobble around in a cast for the better part of the spring and some of the summer that year. His Uncle James, ten years his senior, called him Bonehead from that day forward.

Al looked harder now at the old man because it never occurred to him that he might still be alive. So far as he knew, Uncle James had never married and had disappeared during the Great Depression, before World War II broke out. The last time anyone heard from him, he was working as an oil rigger or something. "Uncle James, how ya doin'?"

"Oh, fair ta middlin', I guess. Moved back home after my stoke. Decided I'd come home ta die. Been wanderin' 'round my whole life all over the country doin' this 'n that. Never could hang my hat anywhere for long. One day I decided that this was home 'n I wanted familiar dirt ta cover me. Been stayin' with yer cousin Grace for about two weeks now. She never got married ya know, so she says I could come live with 'er."

The two talked for the better part of an hour as they exchanged their histories and caught up on family and friends. Al could see that Uncle James was becoming weary, so he ended the conversation with, "Ya let me know when yer up ta comin' over for a good meal of fried chicken 'n all the fixin's. I'll come 'n git ya. Tell Grace I send my regards."

"Sounds good ta me. And don't fret none about not seein' ya daughter again. She'll show up when it's needed. I've learned there's always a reason in the way of God's doin's."

It wasn't long before Al heard about Uncle James going in for cancer surgery on his jaw. Rumor has it that when he woke up from the surgery and realized they'd cut out not only part of his jaw, but most of his tongue as well, the shock caused him to have a fatal heart attack right then and there.

When Bane finally showed up for supper, Joe came over to the kitchen table and sat across from him with his sixth beer in hand. Mary Beth had already put a plate of food in front of Bane, who immediately began to eat. While she prepared Joe's plate, she nervously glanced over her shoulder with a concerned look.

"Well, Boy, don't ya got somethin' ya wanta share with yer old man?"

Puzzled, Bane looked up and gazed off into the distance as he concentrated on what this could possibly be about. He could plainly see that Joe already knew something. Had Tick blamed him for what Dewey had done to him? What could he possibly be going on about? He didn't want to make matters worse by denying anything, but he didn't want to admit to anything either.

Joe was becoming impatient. He could see in Bane's face he wasn't sure what he was referring to and that bothered him. "Well, did that cantankerous old penny pincher pay ya or not?"

Bane's brow furrowed as he contemplated his father's motive for asking. "Yes, Sir."

"Well hand it over, Boy." Bane sat there in utter bewilderment as he absorbed the implications while he looked at Joe, then at Mary Beth, who'd just walked up to the table with Joe's supper. With an agitated tone, Joe stuck out his hand and demanded, "Give it ta me. NOW!"

When Bane took the envelope out of his pocket, he hesitated before handing it over. While he held it in both hands and looked down at it with dread, Joe reached over and snatched it from him. Joe quickly opened it up and pulled out the three twenty dollar bills. "Huh. Ain't much, but I didn't expect that ole skinflint ta pay the two of ya much anyway. You sure this is all he give ya?" Joe didn't seem to really care whether Bane answered him as he leaned to one side and pulled out his wallet from his hip pocket.

Horrified, Bane watched as his father opened his wallet and place the three twenty dollar bills into it! Bane sat in stunned silence. It was when Joe began to replace his wallet into his hip pocket that Bane realized that all of his hopes and dreams for that money had just been utterly shattered. His food and everything around him was forgotten and faded into blackness as he became angrier than he'd ever been before with his father. Until now, he always accepted the way things were, but blind fury overcame him as he watched his father begin eating.

Joe had taken only a few bites of food when he heard Bane slam his fist on the table and shout, "THAT'S MY MONEY!" He knocked his father's beer and plate of food out of the way as he leaned over the table and placed both his hands on the spot where Joe's food had just been.

Joe looked up startled and surprised. Then he saw the look in Bane's eyes and the reddish hue on his face. He knew that look as well as he knew he was sitting at his own table in his own trailer. With the speed of a coiled snake, Joe jumped up and struck Bane with his fist square in the mouth with all his might.

Bane didn't even flinch as he saw it coming. He was still leaning forward when he was knocked backwards into his seat with such force that his head struck against the wall immediately behind him. The speed and force from Joe's follow up punches were so strong that the strikes against Bane's face and the back of his head hitting against the wall seemed as one. Bane was stunned and unable to see anything but blackness after the initial white flash dissipated. He could hear Mary Beth let out a terrified scream.

"Don't hit 'im no more Joe! Please Joe, don't hit 'im no more." This was quickly followed by Joe shouting, "Mind ya own business ya fat

BITCH! This is 'tween me 'n my boy." Then there was a shuffling of chairs, a banging sound, and loud slaps just before Mary Beth squealed in pain. Bane didn't know it then, but Mary Beth had tried to get between the two of them.

When Bane began to regain some sense of his surroundings and his vision cleared, he could see Mary Beth slowly getting up from the floor. Joe was leaning over the table looking down at him. Joe grabbed him by the hair before he growled, "Boy, git the hell outa my sight 'fore I kill ya. I won't take no sass from no damn woman, much less some snotty-nosed runt like you. Ya eat my food, sleep in my house, 'n have the gall ta tell me whose money it is!" Joe shook Bane's head as he spoke, but Bane didn't feel anything or care.

By the time Joe finished his yelling, he'd let go of Bane's hair and come around the table before he grabbed Bane by the neck with both hands. With a firm grip on Bane's neck, he lifted Bane into the air and carried him to the hallway before he threw him several feet towards the back. Bane landed like a rag doll with a thud.

Disoriented and semi-conscious, it took a long time before Bane could regain the ability to coordinate his muscles enough to crawl, stand, and then walk. With the help of rubbing his shoulder against the wall, he was able to stumble to the bathroom. His head was clouded with images of what had just happened to him. The pain in his head throbbed as he tried to make sense of it all.

Nausea overtook him when he caught his reflection in the mirror above the bathroom sink, which he held onto tightly to steady himself. His two eye teeth were slightly loose, one broken halfway down, and blood was oozing from multiple small cuts to his upper and lower lips. Above his left eye was another cut that bled down his nose that was also bleeding. His face and head was throbbing with every heart beat. Using one hand to steady himself against the sink, he reached up with the other to discover a large lump on the back of his head.

He quickly fell to his knees and began to vomit into the commode. Even after all the food in his stomach was gone, he continued to feel nauseated. He tried to control the urge to vomit again because it made his head hurt even worse. When he was able to stand up again, he took off his shirt and wet one end of a towel. Slowly he began to clean the blood off his chin and neck when suddenly the bathroom door swung open wide and banged hard against the wall.

"Boy git outa here. All them beers gotta go somewheres."

When Bane didn't move fast enough to suit him, Joe grabbed him by the arm and pushed him out of the way. The bathroom was so small they couldn't help rub against each other while Joe relieved himself. Out of defiance, Bane continued to wipe his chin and neck while Joe did his business. Bane didn't attempt to leave because he was long past caring if Joe hit him again, even if it meant being killed.

When he finished, Joe stood in the doorway and lit a cigarette. He began to shake his head as he said, "Guess ya had ta find out sometime. Every boy does. I remember when I tried ta stand up ta my ole man the first time." Bane looked at his father and turned back to the mirror to survey his cleanup efforts. Joe let out a loud "Woo wee" as he walked back to the living room.

Dewey was subdued all through supper and was especially quiet in word and manner as he sat in the den, so Al asked, "Dewey is something wrong?" No answer. After taking a bite of his cookie, Dewey put it down as if he wasn't interested. Al became worried. "Are ya feelin' sick, Boy?" Dewey just shook his head.

"Tell me what's botherin' ya. If there's one thing I've learned in my life, it's ya need to hash things out, especially if it's somethin' ya feelin' and it makes ya worried. It's usually helpful ta talk ta somebody about it."

Dewey looked at his grandfather for a long time as if he was uncertain if he should tell him what he was thinking. Finally, he said, "I seen somethin' bad walkin' 'round my friends." After a long pause, Dewey frowned and quietly spoke like he didn't want anyone else to overhear him. "It looked like a dark spot sorta. It moved 'round the huts, then in the woods. I didn't like it. When it seen me seein' it, it didn't like it, so it hid in the trees." Al's knuckles were white as he gripped the chairs armrest and the hairs on the back of his neck stood up.

He thought about it for a moment and rationalized it was just a floater in Dewey's eye. Maybe Dewey just didn't understand that if he'd just closed one eye at a time, he'd have seen it was just something in one of them. Al was conflicted with his rational explanation.

"Dewey, can ya still see it?" Dewey shook his head. "Then it was probably somethin' in ya eye. If it was, it probably was jus' somethin' like that." Dewey didn't look relieved like he normally did once his grandfather had explained stuff to him that bothered him.

After a few minutes Al turned back to Dewey and spoke. "Dewey I had a sorta insight or premonition taday about the future of our country after I run inta one of our relatives taday. It's causin' me ta worry. Not so much for my sake, but for you 'n all the folks comin' afterwards." Dewey didn't look all that interested, but Al felt he had to say it out loud to someone, just like he had expected Dewey to confide in him just now.

"Ya may not know it, but every year I have ta pay a bribe ta keep my house. Sure they call it a tax, but that's jus' an official name for bribes 'n such. Although I own this house outright, the government insist it really belongs ta them. They jus' allow me ta keep sayin' I own it as long as I pay 'em for the privilege of sayin' it. They don't even let me have hardly any say in how much I have ta pay 'em either. Miss one year of payin' 'em," Al made a slap with his hands passing one another, "and that's all she wrote. They'd take my house away from me licky-split."

Dewey didn't know what his grandfather was talking about, but he was interested all the same. It was even taking his mind off what was bothering him. He'd begun to eat his cookies once more and sit up straighter. This encouraged Al.

"What's the mos' important thing ta remember about all that is, even if I los' my house, I'm still a free man. Only God has power over me and my life. The Constitution says so. That's why I spent over twenty years in the Navy and helped fight in the two World Wars."

"The reason why jackasses in the government come up with new ways of taxin' ya and make up new agencies, is soes they can grow more powerful. "The Roman Empire fell cause of such tomfoolery. Every time some fool or other comes up with a new scheme for takin' money from taxpayers, all the rest of the polecats in Washington jump in and see how much of it they can git. They usually have the gall to use poor people as their scapegoats, that's how they usually git away with it."

"What makes this system work is the many are usually afraid of the few. That's why bullies git away with so much. And know this, a bully can be someone who waves a cross 'n beats ya up with words like 'don't ya want ta help others'."

"What's a polecat?" asked Dewey.

"Oh, that's a smelly kinda weasel, ya know, a skunk."

"Oh, they'll come at it sideways and call it a tax, but at the rate we're goin' they'll come up with a way ta tax ya for jus' bein' alive in this country. I don't know how they'll do it, but ya can bet some worthless idiot the Devil owns 'll do it. That way, they'll have power over ya that even God himself don't ask for. At least God gives ya freewill. What they're tryin' ta do is replace God with a worship of country. With that comes complete control over folk's lives."

"There's a big chasm between takin' money from folks for havin' stuff 'n demandin' money for jus' breathin'. Once they do that, we ain't free no more, 'n the folks runnin' the government 'll own us then. The person who finally gits elected 'n forces folks ta pay for somethin' jus' cause they're alive, well, his soul is bought 'n paid for by Satan himself. Ta be able ta git away with it, he'll probably be somethin' special by the way he looks or sounds. He'll be popular with the youngsters for sure, since they're naïve. Of course, there's always the ridiculous folks who think they're doin' us a favor by forcin' us inta payin' 'cause they claim it's for the good of everybody. Then they'll use that God forsaken tax man ta force us ta pay it too, or come up with somethin' like Hitler's Gestapo."

"Another thing that gits up my craw, is churches have kept quiet for so long about the right and wrong of politics, that politicians ain't afraid of 'em no more. They don't preach the truth anymore like they ought'a cause they're afraid the tax man will show up and take their money 'n shut 'em down. Hell, many of the churches have turned a blind eye to the crazy perversions some folks are caught up in these days. They claim they don't wanta judge other folks."

"Remember Dewey, if God ain't in a family, it won't usually stay tagether. Same goes for churches 'n countries too. Countries that don't believe in Christianity don't stand a chance anyway. They'll always be at each others throats, 'cause the Devil has a hold of 'em, 'n Satan loves chaos."

"Ya see, Christianity is based on love and the belief in the only true God, but all the others are based on idol worship. You could paint a rock purple and put it on a tree stump, then before ya know it lots of people will start prayin' to it if somebody tells 'em to. It happens 'cause it's human nature to want to believe in something, but they sometimes don't understand God put that in us when he made us so we'll look for 'im. Ya might as well call that purple rock Buddha or Muhammad, because only Jesus was sent by God ta earth. Lord help us if the Muslims ever git a strong foothold in America, 'cause they'll have us livin' in fear. Ya see, their religion is built on fear, hate, and control."

Al could see Dewey was intrigued by his soapbox lecture, but he looked exhausted. Al knew he needed to call it a night, but knew he was prophesying the inevitable course of America. Advances in technology were making the world smaller. Due to the country not being more selective in the types of people it was allowing to enter, he knew America was on a path of moral and spiritual decline.

"Dewey jus' remember, if ya hug a filthy person, you'll git ya'self dirty and ya won't have nobody ta blame but ya'self. You'll know if they're a filthy person by the way they talk 'n do. The reason their tongue will be smooth and slick, is because they jus' drank the blood of the las' person that trusted 'em."

Dewey was on the edge of his seat listening intently to every word Al said at this point. "Granddaddy, I promise ta stop 'em. God says for me to." Al turned and looked carefully at his grandson upon hearing this, but stopped short of replying to this strange declaration. Somehow he had the faintest belief it could be true, but he couldn't imagine how. He dismissed the notion while out of habit he rubbed his chin with his hand.

"Boy, ya need ta git ta bed. Don't forget ta pray."

Chapter 17 – Providence

BANE was awakened by the sound of some of the others in the gang playing outside. He recognized Gail's voice when she shouted, "Billy, ya can't catch me! Ha, I told ya so! Hey, Jill, watch me make Billy . . . ."

Initially upon waking, Bane lay in the bed enjoying the sounds from outside and the aroma of freshly cooked eggs and bacon that'd reached his room from the kitchen, where Mary Beth was cooking. Only moments later as he tried to wet his dry cracked lips with his tongue he felt a stinging pain shoot throughout his lips and face. That's when he was reminded of the awful beating he'd received only last night at the hands of his father.

While concentrating on the muffled voices coming from down the hall, Bane remained very still while he gave himself a through going over to check for the damage that'd been done. All too often he'd had to do this because of the many beatings from his abusive brother or father. The back of his head still had the painful bump that hurt when he touched it, but it seemed to have gone down slightly during the night. He was surprised there weren't signs of a cut or dried blood on it. The initially mild pain in his head increased only when he moved it from side to side. He was able to keep it in check if he didn't move his neck certain ways. He knew this was more than likely bruising of one or more muscles. He confirmed it by touching his right shoulder muscle. This caused a mean, dull pain to shoot up the right side of his neck into the base of his skull.

Ever so carefully, Bane proceeded to touch his face with only the tips of his fingers, starting with the areas that didn't seem to hurt before moving to the places that did. He wanted to categorize the pain as either sharp or dull, and to what degree. Once done, he ever so slowly sat up to see if there was damage to other parts of his body. Satisfied there was none, he quietly left his room and slipped into the bathroom. After he returned to his bed, he realized there were blood stains of various sizes on his mattress and his pitiful-looking pillow.

He flipped his pillow over before laying back down. Although he was hungry, he had no desire to be in close proximity to his father. While he lay there, he recounted the events from the night before, still not sure of certain details. He wanted to compile all the events into an orderly and understandable picture so he could make sense of it all. The last thing he remembered before he fell asleep, was the pain was so excruciating he'd felt disassociated from his body. He literally felt like he was outside of his body, yet somehow still aware of the pain, but yet no longer feeling the pain directly. He'd never done that before.

His father had told him about a time when he'd gotten penned by a truck that'd rolled onto him. He said the pain was so bad that he thought he'd pass out. He talked about how he'd seemed to leave his body because of the pain, but yet he'd felt the pain from a distance. He told Bane that the mind does things like that to protect you so you won't die or something because it was too horrible to take.

Apprehension of what might happen or be said in front of Tick was another driving force that held Bane back from leaving the comfort of his bed. With his tongue, he probed the gap left by the broken tooth, as well as for tender-to-the-touch cuts on the inside of his lips, of which there were many. If he placed too much pressure on them, they opened up and began to sting until he stopped. They would also bleed a little.

He had gone to bed in pain far too many times to let the physical injuries give him much concern. What really bothered him was the audacity and reasoning his father had used in taking the money that he'd worked and sweated so hard for. He felt betrayed, so he laid there conjuring up fantasies of revenge.

Vengeance against his father would have to wait. He needed to once again go over and hash out his plans for today because Tick would be leaving tonight if he failed. That just couldn't happen. The hatred he had for Tick had grown deeper with each day he was near him. He didn't know how, but he was convinced that Tick somehow had something to do with last night. It gave him comfort to have a plan of revenge that would allow him to let loose his full fury on him, once and for all.

Determined he wouldn't emerge from the safety of his room until he heard his father's truck leave, Bane closed his eyes. He was sure that Mary Beth would save him some food. While he lay with closed eyes, he heard a knock at the door just before it opened.

"Boy, ya gonna spend the whole damn day sulking? Believe you me, ya got off easy compared ta what my ole man did ta me when I stood up ta 'im the first time. Anyhow, it ain't like I took all yer money. Now git outa bed 'n clean ya'self up. Breakfast is gittin' cold."

Bane was only half listening out of defiance to his father, but was bewildered at the claim from his father about not taking all of his wages. He sat up as he looked to his father for clarification.

"Look what ya teeth done ta my fist." Joe showed Bane the cuts to his knuckles. "Next time, keep ya mouth shut." Bane looked blankly back at his father.

Joe grunted as he turned and walked back down the hall. Soon Bane heard the truck crank and his father drive away. Through his open bedroom door, he could hear dishes and pans clanging as Mary Beth went about cleaning the kitchen. When he was dressing, it occurred to him just how truly hungry he was. Questions about his father's odd comments about the money would have to wait.

Bane stopped to look at himself in the mirror above his chest of drawers where he could plainly see his lips were swollen and somewhat misshaped. He lifted his tender upper lip to inspect his broken tooth and check the full extent of the damage his father had caused. Looking at his reflection in the mirror, he addressed the angry and bludgeoned boy looking back at him. "I'll show 'em all. I'll show ya what happens when ya mess with me. No more! Never again!"

He'd become more resolute as the anger inside of him burned red hot. With a painful menacing grin, he headed for breakfast still wearing the blood soaked T-shirt from last night in defiance and as a symbol of his resolve.

When he entered the kitchen, Mary Beth let out a startled squeal at the sight of him. Bane couldn't help but get some satisfaction from her reaction. He was a little surprised to find that Tick wasn't anywhere in sight. That was just as well, because he didn't have anything to say to him just yet anyway. Besides, he might give away his newly-born intentions prematurely if Tick'd riled him up with one of his sorry grins of satisfaction. Tick, no doubt, would enjoy seeing Joe's handiwork.

It was apparent Tick had been up and about for a long time. He figured Tick must have eaten breakfast and gone to the hut village already. That suited him just fine, because he'd settle with him soon enough.

"Here, Sweetie, I saved ya some breakfast. When yer finished, I'll take that awful shirt 'n clean it up for ya." Bane gave her little notice as he looked at the busted wall paneling where his head had landed against it repeatedly last night. Checking it first, he sat in his usual place and ate his breakfast slowly due to the pain from his swollen and battered lips.

After Bane finished breakfast, he walked over to the kitchen sink and took out an old grocery bag from underneath it. He then proceeded to place Joe's last five beers inside it along with a pack of cigarettes from a carton sitting atop the refrigerator. When Mary Beth started to protest, he gave her a look that stopped her cold. "I paid for 'em, didn't I?" She returned his angry look with a concerned expression. For just the slightest moment, Bane looked at her with admiration.

"He's gonna be sore when he gits home, Sweetie. Ya sure ya wanta rile 'im so soon, ya know, on account of las' night?" Mary Beth half-heartedly protested. Bane just grinned as he turned and went to his room carrying the bag of goodies. For just a moment he flirted with the idea of changing his shirt, but decided to keep it on. He made sure he had his pocket knife with him.

Bane stopped just before he went out of the trailer door and looked around. He got a strange feeling of déjà vu. He shook the feeling and departed for the hut village. On his way to the hut village he noticed none of the gang were anywhere to be seen. He also noticed the position of the sun on the trailers. It was only then he realized just how late he must have slept. He couldn't understand why his father had stayed home so late. He knew his father had rarely done that before and was going to be late for work. It hit him that just maybe his father stayed home to make sure he was okay, but he quickly dismissed the thought.

The children arrived at the huts as one group, just as they'd planned, only to find Tick was already there. He was perched in the wooden swing smoking a cigarette. Simultaneously, their eyes met in quick glances at one another in the unspoken fashion found in a tight knit group. They could read in each other's expressions that it was okay as long as they stayed together.

Tick watched their approach with a sense of satisfaction and awareness of what they were feeling and why they'd hesitated. He was, after all, quite content to intimidate people because it served his purpose. He learned early in life to make others afraid of him, or they would, as he'd learned in the past, make fun of his deformities. He still was the butt of many jokes and cruel taunts by others bigger than himself at school and home, but he was determined to control every aspect possible in his life.

To no one in particular, the children made excuses for needing to always be with their pals in all their activities. When Tick became bored, he'd occasionally tag along to have something to do or to satisfy his curiosity. Once Bane arrived, much to Crystal's discomfort, Tick decided to stand close to her and make it appear as if they were being intimate with one another.

When Bane got closer, even Tick's eyes revealed a momentary bit of surprise at Bane's appearance. Everyone present expressed surprise and disgust. "Whew." "Good Lord." "What in tarnation?" "Goodness gracious."

In unison, they recoiled from Tick. Many, if not all, thought that this was the result of his doings. Crystal, thinking the same as the others, quickly moved away from Tick with revulsion, but he followed her and continued to stay close. When Tick realized the others were thinking he'd beaten Bane, he scanned the group and said, "His daddy done it." This had a calming effect.

Crystal leaned towards Tick and whispered, "Why would he do such a thing?" Tick just shrugged. He relished the memory of last night when he recalled the events of his time spent with his Uncle Joe, before Bane had gotten home. He'd sat down near Uncle Joe, who was drinking beer and chain smoking in his easy chair, before he'd taken out his pay envelope. He'd made a show of counting his money aloud.

"What ya got there, Boy?" asked Joe.

"Oh, Mr. Johnson says we was through for the week 'n paid us."

"How much ya got there?"

"Sixty-five dollars." Tick didn't lie, he just didn't tell Uncle Joe he'd already had five dollars his mother had given him before he came to stay with his father, Elam.

Even more, as he looked a Bane's injuries, he relished the scene as it played out again in his mind of his Uncle Joe taking Bane's money and the tragedy that followed.

Bane continued to focus on Crystal and his arrogant cousin, Tick, while walking to the boys hut to unload his bag of beer and cigarettes. Consumed by jealousy and anger, he almost hurled the bag into the corner of the hut until he remembered the glass beer bottles. Instead he kicked one of the boxes that served as a seat. It landed hard against the back wall of the hut with a loud bang. Anyone in close proximity of the boys' hut quickly moved away. This display of anger kept the others, who had gotten comfortable, from straying too far out of sight. Even Billy became edgy.

From the hut's window and the occasional stroll outside, Bane kept an eye on Crystal and Tick. His dander would again rise when he thought they were getting too friendly. He was absolutely convinced they were talking about him. Like everyone else, occasionally they glanced in his direction and whispered amongst themselves. Bane, blinded by his jealousy, misinterpreted the many attempts by Crystal to shed herself of Tick's company.

When Bane didn't emerge from the hut for a prolonged spell, the others figured it was okay for the time being. Soon they were milling about amongst themselves as they enjoyed the swings, went down to the creek in search of critters, or just sat around and talked. No one seemed immune to the stifling heat as the temperature rose to a balmy ninety-five degrees.

Bane sat in the hut sulking and smoked a few cigarettes while he drank the first of the beers for his lunch. This seemed to soothe him for a while. He decided he'd go out when the time was right.

After more than an hour, he finally decided it was time, since he knew everyone'd gone home to eat lunch. Before he left the hut, he hid the last three beers and pocketed the remaining pack of cigarettes.

Bane was taken aback when he discovered that Tick was still there. Tick was on the wooden swing. He was rocking it back and forth on his toes and heels, just enough to make the swing move without his feet leaving the ground. Tick stared back at Bane while Bane strolled over to him at the swings.

"Looks like Joe got sore at ya. Wonder why?" Tick wore a menacing grin that always appeared when he'd accomplished some cruel act on another and he was getting the benefit of seeing his handiwork first hand.

"What's it ta ya?" Bane scowled back.

"Jus' noticed is all." Tick replied back in an innocent and flippant manner.

"Well keep it ta ya'self."

Neither spoke for a long time. Bane had taken refuge in his own thoughts while he swung in the tire swing and thought about his plans for Tick. Tick noted the quiet between them and decided to leave well enough alone.

Bane could hear the gang coming back from lunch. They were talking loudly as they crested the hill. Libby darted away from the group while barking vigorously at a squirrel, chasing it up a tree.

"I don't want'a see ya talkin' ta my girlfriend no more, ya hear me?" Bane demanded in a threatening tone, which Tick didn't acknowledge as he watched the others approach.

The compound was filled once again with children playing and laughing. Jason and Todd were going at one another again over who was the best at this or that while they roused about.

It didn't take too long before Tick made it a point to once again get close to Crystal. This fact wasn't lost on Bane. Tick even went so far as to place one of his hands on her shoulders in a half hug while he whispered in her ear, "I think ya boyfriend's mad at me."

"He ain't no boyfriend of mine," she mumbled with scorn, as she jerked away. Tick was glad she didn't say it loud enough for anyone else to hear, because he was trying to provoke Bane. He then looked at Bane and gave him one of his rare full-toothed smiles.

Angered by this scene, Bane began to relieve his frustrations by picking on anyone close by. Billy was the only one who didn't back down so easily. Billy diffused the situation before he walked away.

"Bane, no one wants to fight ya, so give it a res'. We'll stay outa ya way if that's what ya after."

When the opportunity presented itself, Bane cornered Crystal. "I don't want ya around that blood sucking Tick no more."

Caught off guard, Crystal replied, "What?!"

"I said I don't want ya talkin' ta Tick no more! Yer mine!" That made it clear enough what he meant. He was boldly proclaiming that Crystal was his property.

Crystal was infuriated at the insinuation that Bane felt he could tell her what to do and with whom to do it. She didn't want to be anywhere near Tick, but she was indignant at Bane's bold audacity to tell her what to do.

"I'll talk ta whoever I wanta talk to 'n do what I want'a. 'N who do *you* think ya are telling me what ta do?!" By this time Crystal was pointing and shaking her finger at Bane's face. Everyone, including Tick, had stopped to listen intently when Bane first raised his voice to Crystal.

Tick accomplished what he had set out to do, which was get under Bane's skin and make him jealous. He remembered how Uncle Joe had bragged about Bane having the pretty little redhead as a girlfriend during one of their recent chats. Tick already noticed how Bane looked at Crystal yesterday, but he wanted to be sure Bane would be jealous and angry before he pretended like he was sweet on her today.

The tension was broken when Libby announced the arrival of Dewey. Dewey would have been there sooner, but he'd sat by the creek longer than usual. He'd waited a long time before he lost hope of seeing the rabbit come out and eat the other half of the apple he'd thrown across the creek. Eventually, he gave up on seeing his long-eared friend and continued to the hut village.

"Hey, Captain Dewey's here!" shouted Pattie.

Bane was seething with anger as Crystal stormed away to join the others greeting Dewey. Everyone seemed to have found the excuse they needed to break the tension. Crystal plainly wanted to put some distance between herself and Bane.

Dewey was delighted that everyone made such a fuss over his arrival. He quickly petted Libby and gave her the dog treat before he hurried over to meet the others.

Tick, of course, wasn't pleased that Dewey had returned, so he hung back at the swings and unconsciously covered his stomach with his hands. Bane of course, could have cared less about Dewey, with the exception of watching him hurt Tick yesterday, so he walked over and stood at the entrance of the boys' hut. Both boys watched as everyone made a fuss over Dewey's arrival.

Dewey, and the group surrounding him, migrated towards the swings where Tick remained. When they approached, Crystal announced, "Dewey has somethin' he wants ta say."

Looking at the ground, Dewey softly spoke. "Dewey didn't mean ta hurt ya so bad."

With that, Crystal, who was holding Dewey's arm with one hand and stroking it with her other, smiled and said, "Dewey jus' don't like it when somebody hurts other folks. If it makes ya feel any better, he'd do the same ta anyone who was hurtin' you."

Silently, Tick stood looking on contemptuously at Dewey and the others.

While this was going on, Bane went into the boys' hut and then emerged with two spears. He walked over and split the crowd by pushing through the middle. He stopped once he stood directly in front of Tick. He then took the spear that belonged to Billy, which had the best blade as a spear head, and thrust it in front of Tick. "I'm challenging ya ta a contest. If ya not too chicken ta hunt." Tick didn't say anything as he took the spear. Bane became antsy waiting on some sort of response.

Crystal broke in, "What's this all about, Bane Taggart?" Bane didn't respond to her, continuing to stare at Tick.

"You," replied Tick as he returned Bane's gaze.

"WELL?!" shouted Bane.

"Suit ya'self," replied Tick.

"Whoever comes back with the biggest animal on their spear is the winner. If ya win, she's all yers. If I win, ya keep ya scummy self away from 'er." With that, Bane trotted off into the woods down the trail from which Dewey had just emerged. It wasn't long before Tick followed Bane.

Crystal decried, "I don't give a damn about either one of ya Taggarts. 'N I'll be damned if I let either one of ya near me again!"

Everyone stood transfixed by the situation until Gabby broke the silence. "This I gotta see. Bet ya one of 'em don't come back. Ya see the look in their eyes?"

"That ain't funny," said Crystal in an admonishing tone. With that, Gabby grinned and started for the woods. "Gabby, git ya'self back here this instant." At hearing this, Gabby stopped in his tracks and looked at Crystal.

Bonnie Lou walked over to Gabby, and with imploring eyes, spoke. "Gabby, ya gotta stay 'n let 'em be. There ain't no reason ta git caught up in the devil's work. 'Sides, ya gotta stay 'n protect us." With that, Gabby resigned himself to forget about following them.

"Shor wish Tick hadn't come here this year, but maybe it won't amount ta nothin'. Jus' wish Bane hadn't given 'im my spear's all," complained Billy.

"I think they are both jus' piss 'n wind, myself," proclaimed Gail. With that Billy turned and looked at her with admonishment. "Well, it's true. They're both jus' a lot of hot air."

Now that Bane and Tick were gone, the cloud of anxiety lifted and the children became care free in their activities. Dewey, Billy and Gabby went to the creek to hunt salamanders and crayfish, while the girls went to their hut to gossip and make necklaces out of old buttons. They had mason jars filled with old buttons of many colors, shapes and sizes. Jason and Todd went back to fighting over the best swing without the threat of Tick taking over.

Jill spoke first after the girls entered their hut, "I don't mind boys fightin' over me, but I shor' wouldn't like the idea of the devil and his ugly cousin doin' it."

"Yeah, I couldn't imagine the likes of those two hell-bound jackasses comin' after me," Patty said as she gathered her string of buttons from the chair where she'd been working earlier.

"Well, I don't give a damn what they think they're about, but I'll be certain ta set 'em straight real quick like, that's for sure," said Crystal.

"Ta tell ya the truth, I think Satan himself has a better chance of gittin' in ta heaven than either one of those two," interjected Jill.

Tick, who'd never actually been hunting before, decided to follow Bane. He made it a point to be as quiet as possible while he pursued

Bane through the woods. It didn't take him long to realize that he was actually following a well-worn path. Occasionally, he spotted one of the orange strings hanging from a tree or bush. He also noticed that the lower limbs of trees were broken off, allowing him to walk easily through the woods. He could easily hear Bane ahead of him, but couldn't see him because the trail went up and down small hills, across ravines, and wound through the occasional thick stand of trees or underbrush. He was ever vigilant to anticipate an ambush. He suspected Bane had more in mind than just hunting for animals.

While waiting for Tick to catch up, Bane rechecked the old butcher knife attached to his spear to make sure it was securely fastened, and tested the sharpness by lightly gliding his finger across the edge. The edge had a large chip out of it and this caused him to ever so lightly prick his finger.

Bane continued to make a point of being noisy as he once again traversed the path towards Dewey's place. He didn't want Tick to become discouraged or lose his way. He'd rightly anticipated that Tick would shadow him, if for no other reason than he knew Tick didn't know the woods very well and he'd probably want to steal his catch. To his satisfaction, everything was working just as he'd planned. Soon, the trap would be set.

Bane's shirt was saturated with sweat when he finally arrived at the spot where he planned to ambush Tick. The spot he'd chosen was only a small clearing just across the creek where he'd prepared his trap yesterday and then watched Dewey pass by on his way home.

He crossed to the other side of the creek and stood in the clearing, surrounded mostly by briar bushes which would conceal his position until the last moment. Although his mouth was as dry as cotton and his heart raced with expectation, he successfully fought off the urge to reach over and snack on the juicy ripe blackberries within reach.

Thirty, possibly forty yards away, he heard sounds of his prey, Tick, approaching. His heart began to pound hard with blood lust. His heart beat so loud in his ears he actually became worried momentarily that Tick would hear it and it would give away his position. He could no longer hear Tick's approach because of the pounding in his head. He knew this was the perfect place for an ambush.

With dilated pupils, he eagerly watched for Tick to appear. He kept shifting his position in anticipation, when suddenly he slipped on something that nearly made him fall. He looked down in astonishment to find he had stepped on a partially eaten apple?! **Where had that come from?!!**

Bane was temporarily distracted, and unbeknownst to him, Tick had arrived in the clearing on the trail. Tick stopped cold in his tracks once he spotted Bane looking down at something on the other side of the creek.

Seeing Bane's spear held above his head at the ready, Tick quickly understood his predicament. He wasn't surprised that Bane was capable of such a diabolical scheme, so he anxiously readied his spear over his shoulder in anticipation of a possible attack. He hesitated only long enough to step away from the foliage behind him so he could throw his spear without it becoming entangled.

Bane, satisfied with knowing what made him slip, kicked away the partial apple and turned his attention back to the trail. With shocking revelation Bane realized that Tick had not only arrived, but was ready to strike! Bane, caught off guard, fumbled with the spear as he hastily reared back in readiness to throw it at his adversary.

Tick let loose with his spear, knowing he only had one chance. Tick's depth perception was off because of his eye condition, so the spear went high just as Bane'd bent forward from the follow-through after releasing his own spear.

Bane'd got off his throw only a mere fraction after Tick did. It pierced Tick just below his left nipple. The only thing that stopped it from going any deeper was the wood shaft that held the knife blade securely in place. Tick was knocked backwards by the blow into a small dogwood tree directly behind him. This caused him to twist as he fell to the ground.

Bane, feeling adrenaline coursing through his body, excitedly ran over to Tick's now crumpled body lying on the ground and shouted **"AH HAH! I showed ya, ya sorry blood suckin' insect!"**

With satisfaction Bane leaned down and turned Tick over onto his back using the spear as a lever. Tick looked up with shocked disbelief and fear as he was being rolled onto his back. Bane grabbed the spear with both hands and pushed down on it as if Tick were a mere bug being skewered at the end of a needle. This shoved the blade deeper into Tick's flesh only as much as his rib cage would allow.

Banes' face was ghoulishly distorted from the beating he'd received the night before, and now it was contorted into an even more demonic grimace as the wounds in his lips and on his face began to ooze fresh blood mixed with drool. As Bane looked down with hate filled eyes at his impaled nemesis, he felt justified in killing this antagonistic monster.

No longer would Tick frustrate and confound him ever again. All the pent up anger he felt, not only at Tick, but his father, brother, and all the authority figures in his life, was being channeled into this act of causing as much pain as he could bring to bear. He felt exhilaration at having finally achieved ultimate control, if only for this moment. Oh, how glorious this moment at achieving total ecstasy at seeing one of his tormentors writhing in pain and knowing they were doomed!

Tick looked up into Bane's face and knew he was dying. The pain all but dissipated and his breathing became ever more labored. Gasping for air, he coughed up blood. He gave one of his evil grins as if to say 'you didn't win, and now I've got you'. He wanted Bane tortured by the fact that he hadn't truly gotten him, knowing it was all he had left to give. Tick's expression of satisfaction was starting to rob Bane of the thrill of his newly won victory and vengeance.

"What ya grinnin' about?! I got ya this time!" His voice must have given away his growing feeling of uncertainty. In response, Tick reached up with both hands and grabbed the handle of the spear as more blood began to spurt out of his mouth when he coughed and struggled ever harder for air. To torture Bane all the more, he struggled to grin after each choking breath. Tick felt his life force beginning to wane, but he kept looking at Bane with an expression of mockery that only he could deliver.

Bane became further enraged and began to twist and turn the spear handle in the hope of inflicting as much pain as he possibly could, desperate to bring back his feeling of triumph over Tick. He shouted over and over, **"I SHOWED YOU! I SHOWED YOU!"**

Tick's hands relaxed and fell away just as his body became limp and his eyes dilated when all life departed his body. He was dead.

Bane, unaware of the futility of his attempts to inflict more pain on the now dead corpse, strived to derive more pain until the blade broke free of the spear with a loud snap at the point where the blade had been chipped.

The spell Bane was under finally broke and he staggered back, drained of energy. He stood looking down at the lifeless body of his cousin while using the spear handle to steady himself.

Exhausted, Bane staggered back across the creek after dropping the spear handle. He plopped down on the ground where he'd sat hidden the evening before. With shaking hands he wrestled the pack of cigarettes out of his right sock. He'd folded the upper part of his sock to secure it in place. After fumbling with it, as well as dropping his matchbook twice, he finally lit a cigarette and began to smoke. Only after he stopped shaking and settled down did he remember Tick's envelope full of money. He was sure it had to be on Tick's body somewhere.

He went back to Tick's body and searched for the envelope Mr. Johnson had given him. It didn't take long before he held it in his hands and shook it in front of Tick's open lifeless eyes. "It's mine now. Guess ya won't have this for spendin' in hell, now will ya?" Then he pushed the envelope against Tick's face in hostility.

Satisfied that he'd received the ultimate trophy, Tick's money, Bane returned to his spot across the creek and sat down before he began counting the cash inside. When he realized there was sixty-five dollars, not sixty like he'd received, he recounted it two more times to be sure he'd counted it correctly. At first, Bane thought maybe Mr. Johnson had made a mistake. Then he dismissed that idea.

He recalled how some of the men were nicer to Tick because he had a messed up eye and ear, but he knew Mr. Johnson was just as frustrated with Tick as he was with him. He couldn't for the life of him figure out why there was more money than he was given, unless Mr. Johnson did like Tick better than him. He became enraged when he supposed that Tick'd been paid more than him.

Bane became indignant and decided that this was just one more reason why he should feel justified in killing Tick. He looked over at Tick's body across the creek and shouted, "IT'S MINE NOW, YA BLOOD SUCKER!"

After a few more minutes, it hit him. *Maybe, just maybe, that's what his ole man meant about not getting it all!* He shook his head in the hope of knocking loose the thought that somehow Tick had gotten him one last time and he just now was finding out. He was too drained to think about it. He'd have to forget about it for now. There were too many other things to think about.

Two more cigarettes later, Bane began to think about the rest of his plan. He realized he needed to get back to the hut village, but first there was the need to retrieve the carcass of the rabbit he killed yesterday afternoon for his alibi. It didn't take long to remove the rocks that he'd placed over the dead animal so scavengers couldn't steal it during the night.

He became disgusted when he realized maggots were inside of the mouth of the carcass. He took the rabbit's body out of the old pillow case he'd used to store it in and carried the dead rabbit to the creek to wash it.

Knowing his spear was broken, he started to panic. His head was in a fog as to what to do now that it was no longer any good for skewing the rabbit's body. Then he remembered the other spear. It didn't take him long to find it and skewer the rabbit's carcass. He carried it across the creek and laid it beside Tick's body.

Bane once again looked to the briars as the best hiding place to hide a body. When he grabbed Tick's hands, he found that dragging his limp body was too difficult. He attempted to use the fireman's carry and place Tick on his shoulders, but after a couple of attempts, he realized it was too difficult for him, especially with the remainder of the knife still protruding out of Tick's chest. He never expected dead weight to be so heavy.

He finally settled on picking up Tick's body by hugging him under the armpits. Tick's feet dragged along the ground and the creek bottom as Bane moved the corpse over to the thorn bushes. He placed a few dead limbs on top of the body, along with some rocks. He wished he'd thought to bring a shovel, but it was too late. He quickly surveyed his handiwork before he crossed over the creek to retrieve the spear holding the dead rabbit. Seeing the broken spear lying on the trail, he picked it up and tossed it over by Tick's body before he walked back to the hut village.

Bane felt confident that he had gotten away with his plan so far and put on a victorious smile once he entered the hut village. "That blood sucker got back yet? I bet he don't have anything as big as this." Bane held the rabbit's carcass in the air.

Everyone had rushed over to see what Bane had killed. When they got close enough to inspect it, Gabby said, "That's been dead a long time. The body's already stiff."

Bane pushed him down and shouted, "I jus' killed it, ya LITTLE RUNT!"

"Why ya have my spear?" asked Billy. "I thought Tick had mine."

Bane screwed up his lips and looked around, trying to come up with an explanation. Unable to quickly think of a good one, he mindlessly blurted, "What ya talkin' about; this is my spear. Don't ya recognize it?"

Billy, Gabby, Jason and Todd exchanged glances, but didn't dare say anything else about it. They sensed it was in their best interest to keep quiet for the moment.

Gail asked, "Where'd all that blood all over ya come from? It's a lot more'n ya had before ya left. I don't even see none on the rabbit."

Bane looked down and realized that there was fresh blood all over his shirt and trousers. He took a longer time than he intended to come up with an answer as he wiped at the somewhat fresh blood. "Guess I got all the blood on me when I killed the rabbit. Yeah, that's it. It was still alive when I picked it up. It must'a got it on me then."

"Why ain't there none on the rabbit then?"

"Oh, I washed it in the creek. I reckon I jus' forgot ta wash myself."

This seemed to be as good an explanation as any to the others, except Gabby. Gabby decided to not let on that he didn't believe him. Gabby kept his distance for now but waited for his chance to prove otherwise.

"Well, has Tick come back with anything yet?" inquired Bane as he made a show of looking around.

"No, he must still be lookin'," replied Jason.

Dewey was becoming more and more upset at seeing the dead rabbit. Crystal, who was standing beside him, sensed his uneasiness. "Come on, Dewey. He can't help bein' mean." She led him over to the girls' hut. Libby followed.

It didn't take long before Dewey announced, "Dewey needs ta go home."

Crystal could see he was really upset about the rabbit. She patted him on the back and said, "It's okay, I'll see ya tamorrow." A few people shouted 'good bye' to Dewey as he headed for home.

Chapter 18 – Helix

BANE continued holding the spear up with the impaled rabbit's body while sneering at Dewey's back. "Good riddance, Retard!" Dewey didn't show any sign of hearing Bane as he continued walking towards the tree line. Eventually Dewey disappeared into the forest and the lingering sounds of his retreat could no longer be heard.

With prideful zeal, Bane waved the dead carcass about, jutting it into the faces of the others so they couldn't help but get a closer look at his kill. Once satisfied that everyone had gotten a good enough look, he went to an open area and shoved the butt end of the spear into a soft part of the ground. It took several tries before it would stand on its own.

Turning to the others, he triumphantly announced "If that bloodsucker ever gits back, he'll see it for sure."

Bane walked over to the boys' hut and disappeared through the doorway while the others talked among themselves, giving their opinions or just making comments about the events of the day. "How disgusting!" "Did ya see all that blood?" "Wonder what Tick comes back with?"

Gabby whispered into Bonnie Lou's ear, "Somethin's bad wrong. I'm gonna go see for myself. Be back in a little while." With that, he trotted down to the same trail Dewey had taken. Once across the earthen dam that crossed the creek, he veered off in a different direction in the hope of figuring out where Bane and Tick might have gone. He followed the same path he and the others had taken when they'd gone hunting for deer a while back. He decided it was as good a place as any to begin his search, because he figured Bane would lure Tick back to the same spot where Bane had killed the baby rabbit. If the mother rabbit was still living there, she would make for easy prey.

Crystal said, "Guess I'll go work some more on my necklace. I shor' don't won't nothin' ta do with all this killin'." Bonnie Lou followed her.

Jill turned to Pattie. "I'm goin' home. Bane's got somethin' up his craw 'n I don't wanta be around when it comes out," Pattie agreed and they both started for home.

"Yeah, ain't no sense hangin' 'round no more with Bane actin' all crazy like. Bound ta be more trouble when Tick gits back and I don't want no part of it," complained Todd as he gestured towards the boys' hut.

"Yeah, yer probably right. Sides, it's almost time for supper any ole way," replied Jason. Together they joined Jill and Pattie on their trek home.

Gail grabbed Billy by the arm while she watched the others walking away. "I don't think we ought'a be here when that other good-for-nothin' heathen gits back." Billy couldn't recall his sister being this skittish before. He couldn't help feeling it was his responsibility to take her home if she felt uncomfortable.

"If ya scared, Sis, I'll take ya home," replied Billy.

"I ain't scared. I jus' don't want no more of it is all. We ought'a skedaddle before Tick comes back."

"Yeah, yer probably right. But we ought'a let Crystal 'n Bonnie Lou know we're leavin'. Once they know we're all goin' back home, she 'n Bonnie Lou 'll probably come too." Together they followed the others.

Billy and Gail stopped at the girls' hut. Gail poked her head in the doorway "Me 'n Billy is fixin' ta go home. Y'all really ought'a come with us. Everybody else is leavin'."

Crystal jutted her chin out defiantly as she exclaimed, "I'm sick 'n tired of the likes of them Taggarts thinkin' everybody else ought'a run away every time they take a notion ta act like fools. We got jus' as much right ta be here as the likes of them." Bonnie Lou didn't say anything, but she didn't indicate she wanted to leave either.

Gail looked at the two of them apprehensively for a prolonged pause, as if trying to decide something, before she looked behind her at Billy. Then she turned back to her two friends and shrugged. "Well okay, we'll see ya tamorrow."

No sooner had Gail let the doorway close back, than Bonnie Lou began to look worried. She looked out over the grounds of the hut village through the window. "Ya reckon we ought'a leave too? Looks like everybody else has gone! Even Gabby took off inta the woods."

With defiance and resolution in her voice, Crystal replied, "I ain't finished with my necklace yet, and besides, my momma said her 'n Daddy was goin' out ta eat before they started for home tanight. Anyway, don't ya wanta wait on Gabby ta git back?"

"That why yer momma always drives ya daddy ta work on Saturday?"

"Yeah, I guess . . . sometimes, but mostly she drives 'im ta work on Saturday so when she picks 'im up from work in the evenin' they can go do the shoppin'. Ya see, Daddy gits paid on Saturdays. Besides, I ain't gonna let no Taggart tell me what ta do no more. No sir. I ain't afraid of Bane, nor that mean ole' cousin of his no more."

Dewey's heart felt heavy as he walked home. He stopped at his usual place by the creek. Like other times before, he decided that since he hadn't heard the bell ring yet, and he wasn't especially hungry, he'd just pull off his boots and sit or wade in the creek until he heard the tolling of the bell. He had hopes of getting to see the rabbit. He sat down beside the creek and pulled off his boots. He was still upset at Bane for killing that poor rabbit and it showed on his face. He looked over to the spot where his friend, the rabbit, usually appeared.

"Dewey sure hope it weren't you he got."

Dewey remembered the apple he'd thrown earlier, so he looked over at the spot where it had landed to see if the rabbit had come out and eaten any of it. He couldn't tell if the apple had been nibbled on or not, but he knew it wasn't where it had been. *Maybe the rabbit started eating it 'n got scared away.* He sat quietly, hoping the rabbit would come back so he could watch it eat.

After a while he noticed something was different about the small clearing. He couldn't quite put his finger on it, so he got up and waded across the creek for a closer inspection. Just as he stepped onto the other side, he noticed a stick jutting out of the briar bushes. He moved in for a closer look. That was when he realized it looked like one of the spears the other boys had played with. Once he was within reach, he gazed down to see if it had anything on the other end, all the while hoping not to see a rabbit or something.

Dewey became unsettled as he thought that maybe he'd find his rabbit friend injured or dead. He pulled out his wooden sword so he could use it to move the dense briar bushes aside and see what lay behind them. He was on edge as he listened to the all too familiar sound of flies buzzing behind the thicket.

It took a couple of seconds for his eyes to adjust to the shadows and darkness as he leaned further into the opening in an attempt to get a better look at what might be hidden there. Finding loose branches and limbs obscuring his view, he reached in and moved them aside to reveal none other than Tick's body! Tick's face was staring blankly back at him with dull lifeless eyes set in a ghastly pale face, mouth agape.

"AAAAAAH!" Dewey screamed loudly as he swung his sword and struck the spear and limbs that were on top of the body. Loud cracking noises filled the air with every strike. Moments passed while he absorbed the truth of what he'd seen. "Ohhh! Dewey, gotta tell somebody. Dewey, gotta tell somebody," he repeated over and over to himself while in shock as he walked in circles in the small clearing.

Without thinking, he bolted across the creek and started back down the trail to the hut village. He'd left in such a fog that he'd forgotten to get his boots and put them back on. For a long time he didn't realize he hadn't anything to protect his feet. Eventually though, after stepping on several rocks and roots, his feet began to hurt. At one point he stumbled and fell. His single-minded determination compelled him to quickly get up and keep going.

Bane was in the boys' hut watching as the others went home. He could hear Crystal and Bonnie Lou talking in the other hut. After being confronted about not having the correct spear and the stiffness of his kill, he'd begun to smoke cigarettes. Once he brought his nerves under control, he began to drink another beer on an empty stomach. Enjoying the effects, he continued to drink until he'd finished the second one. He was halfway through the last beer when he decided to go outside and make sure none of the others had come back to the huts. He wanted to be certain it was just the three of them.

He hadn't seen Bonnie Lou leave the girls' hut when she went to answer nature's call. The entrance to the girls' hut was hidden from his view. The brush also obscured the trail she'd taken. As usual, the girls used the area on their side of the village, while the boys went to the other side closest to where their hut was located.

Bane, with the remainder of the last beer in hand, circled around and was caught off guard by Bonnie Lou when she emerged from the shrubs on her way back. She'd surprised him as much as he'd surprised her. Not a word was spoken as he stood between her and the girls' hut. Feeling emboldened, he stood defiantly facing her with his feet spread far apart. He lifted the bottle to his lips and finished off the third beer, all the while glaring at her menacingly between swigs.

Horrified by the thought that he was going to attack her, she'd become frozen in place and was too scared to speak. He was standing only ten feet in front of her, but because he was so much bigger, it seemed closer. His eyes were glassy and he had a grimace on his face as he ever so slowly stepped closer towards her. After tossing the empty bottle aside, Bane raised his fist in a threatening manner and made a gesture of silence with the forefinger over his swollen lips. He whispered, "Git or I'll beat ya good, Piss Ant." Terrified, and without so much as a peep, she took off running for the trailer park.

Bane began to gloat as he watched the frightened young girl scurry up the steep hill. Satisfied she would no longer be a distraction, Bane turned and swaggered to the entrance of the girls' hut. He flung back the curtain doorway so roughly that it partially tore off its fastenings.

Startled, Crystal looked up from her necklace work. "**What'd ya do that for?! Now we gotta fix it back!**" Bane crossed the short distance and grabbed her by the hair before he yanked her out of the chair and onto her feet.

"HEY! Let go 'a me! Yer hurtin' me, BANE TAGGART!" The necklace she'd been working on fell to the ground and the loose buttons scattered all about the floor of the hut. She could smell the beer and cigarettes on his breath as he put his face within an inch of hers. Sensing danger, she tried in vain to push him away and free her hair from his grasp. "**LET GO OF ME!**"

"Ain't nobody here but me 'n you, Bitch! It's time ya learned not ta backtalk me no more!" With his free hand he tore at her shirt until he partially exposed her breasts. She struggled to cover herself with the hanging pieces from the torn shirt, all the while trying to wiggle free of his grasp. When she realized he was reaching for her shorts, with desperation she grabbed him with one hand and with the other she hit him in the face, scratching him with her fingernails. Stunned, he stopped momentarily, but soon renewed his efforts with even greater excitability and force, adrenalin coursing through his veins.

She began to scream when he started after her again with renewed vigor. Even more sexually aroused, he was intensely determined to overpower and subdue her. With glee he punched her hard in the face, which to his amazement, added to his pleasure and made him all the more excited. "Damn it, I'll show ya how a woman ought'a be treated!"

He then threw her on the ground and straddled her body with his legs, pinning her down. He struck her a few more times until all she could do was whimper.

Just as he'd finished completely ripping open the front of her shirt, fully exposing her breasts, Bane heard something behind him. He turned his head to find Dewey looming in the doorway. "BAD BANE!" Bane jumped up quickly as he desperately tried to pull his knife from his pocket, but his knife fell from his hands while he fumbled to open it.

Seeing Crystal's bludgeoned face, Dewey shouted even louder. **"BAD, BANE!"** He'd already brandished his wooden sword, but was now thrusting it with all his might into Bane's abdomen while he grabbed Bane's neck so he couldn't get away. A faint crack could be heard as the blade of the wooden sword split into two pieces where it had once been repaired. The smaller piece fell away while the remaining piece of wood, with its sharp jagged edge, pierced deeply into Bane's abdomen. It ripped Bane's intestines as the remaining splintered wood impaled him. Blood immediately spilled out of the gaping wound when Dewey withdrew the sword.

Gasping, Bane fell to the ground next to Crystal. He put both of his hands across the blood-filled wound as he drew his knees up in searing agony. He was bleeding profusely, all the while the sound of Crystal's whimpering cries filled the air. He looked up to see Dewey towering over him. The sweat dripping from Dewey's face fell onto him and his wound.

Bane groaned, "I'll kill ya, RETARD!" Unable to staunch the tide of the bleeding, the crimson pool around him grew bigger. Bane was growing cold and starting to shiver. His voice trembled weakly when he tried to say, "I'll show ya who's boss."

Dewey could see Crystal was having trouble getting off the ground, so he helped her into a chair before he once again stood vigilant over Bane's body in case he tried something else.

Crystal grabbed Dewey's hand to let Dewey know everything was okay. She was mortified by the sight of Bane and unable to speak. With her hands she tried to comfort Dewey with gestures. Together they watched as Bane's body began to relax and his breathing became weak. To their confusion and amazement, they heard Bane plead, "Dewey, give me the cross. Please, Dewey, give me the cross."

They both leaned in closer to make sure they understood what he was saying. With a shaky hand Bane reached for Dewey's overall strap and pleaded once more. "Dewey, give me the cross so God 'll know me." Crystal looked at Bane, then at Dewey in bewilderment. Why would he make such a request? Bane's strength drained even further and his hand fell away.

Dewey dropped his sword before he slowly reached with both of his hands and unclipped the cross from his overalls strap. He placed it in Bane's hand, which Bane immediately clutched to his chest. Bane's eyes went lifeless and he no longer moved. Bane exhaled his final breath and a faint death rattle ensued.

From the doorway came an almost inaudible voice, "Dewey? Crystal?" Together they turned to find Gabby in the doorway, leaning down in an effort to get a better look at the body on the floor. He was holding Dewey's boots. Coming from outside, Gabby's eyes hadn't fully dilated enough to get a very good look at the body lying on the floor.

"What happened?!" asked Gabby imploringly. He was in awe as he looked upon Crystal's naked upper body, with Dewey standing over Bane. He could see Dewey's broken and blood stained sword lying beside Bane's body.

"Dewey sorry. He didn't mean to." Dewey looked down at Gabby's feet when he spoke. Gabby turned momentarily when he heard several voices coming from the top of the hill. Billy, Jason, and the others were talking loudly as their group made their quick descent. Gabby turned back to Dewey and extended the hand holding Dewey's boots while he stared at Bane's disemboweled corpse. Dewey picked up his sword and slowly slid it back into his overalls loop before reaching for his boots.

After Bane'd frightened Bonnie Lou, she'd run to the trailer park to find Billy and the others. She let them know that Crystal was by herself and Bane was acting drunk and crazy. When enough of them were gathered together, they all rushed to see if Crystal was alright and to bring her home. They'd heard shouts just before they began to ascend the hill from the trailer park. They'd come running as fast as they could. Gabby and Dewey walked outside of the girls' hut upon their arrival.

"Where's Crystal?" demanded Bonnie Lou. Gabby diverted his eyes to the open doorway. The curtain that had served as a door was lying on the ground in a heap.

When Gail, Bonnie Lou and Pattie entered the hut, they all started screaming. Pattie began shaking and waving her hands with her fingers spread far apart, as if trying to sling something wicked and painful off them. Jason and Billy pushed their way into the cramped space to see what was wrong, only to stumble out of the hut in shock.

The girls pushed everybody out of their way as they pulled Crystal out of the hut with them. Bonnie Lou had torn down one of the window curtains and was holding it around Crystal to cover her upper body. The girls supported most of Crystal's weight as they embraced her.

No one spoke for what seemed like an eternity when Gail blurted out, "What happened?!" Gabby looked to Dewey, who was silently staring at the ground. Soon everyone was bombarding Dewey and Gabby with questions in the hope that they could shed some light on the situation.

Billy shushed everyone. Then with a gentle voice he asked, "Dewey, what happened?"

"Dewey wanted ta help," he said it so soft he could barely be heard.

"Leave 'im alone," demanded Gabby. "You can see for ya'self what Bane was doin', can't ya?" He looked at Crystal who was being supported by the others. Silently she looked at Dewey while tears streamed down her bruised and bloodied face. Everyone was horrified by what they knew had occurred. Crystal was bleeding from her nostrils and upper lip. Her tattered shirt could be seen hanging from underneath the curtain that now covered her upper body.

In the distance a bell could be heard ringing. Dewey knew it was his granddaddy. He started for home as everyone watched in stunned disbelief.

"Where's he goin'?" someone said. "Ain't somebody gonna stop 'im?" said another.

"Leave 'im be. We know where he lives. Besides, he didn't do nothin' wrong," demanded Gabby.

"Let's git goin' so we can git Crystal home 'n call the Sheriff," exclaimed Billy. They all agreed and started up the hill. It was a slow trip because they had to encourage Crystal the whole time to keep moving. Traumatized, she could hardly move her legs or hold herself upright.

Joe and Elam were settled into their chairs just outside of the trailer with a beer in one hand and a cigarette in the other. Joe asked, "How'd ya meet that girl ya took out las' night?"

"Oh, the other day I went ta the store for momma and bought a big ole pack of pork chops. When I got ta the parking lot I accidentally dropped it on the ground. Well, this big ole fat thing with drool comin' outa 'er mouth looked like she'd gnaw off 'er lips while she stared at them there chops on the ground. Soon 'er fat sister was doin' the same, so I just picked out the one with the mos' teeth and asked her out." Together they laughed.

"By the way, did Tick ever spend that fiver his momma give 'em? I plan on makin' 'em pay for stayin' here with ya. I figure he made enough workin' for Mr. Johnson so that he won't miss it none."

With a funny look Joe looked at Elam while he recalled the events of the previous night. He thought about this revelation concerning the five extra dollars. Then he came to the conclusion that he'd been duped by Tick. *No harm,* he thought.

Joe didn't say anything for a while as he mulled it over in his mind. Finally he said, "I reckon those two 'll show up when they git hungry." He turned to the trailer door and shouted, "Git that food cooked! Ya got two starvin' men out here!"

Joe again turned to Elam, "Where'd ya git those steaks anyway?" When Elam had arrived, he'd brought a large bag of steaks along with a case of beer.

"I found a deer that'd been hit by somebody on the side of the road las' night. I figured, why let it go to waste. So I stayed up most the night 'n slaughtered it in the shed. Boy was I tired at work taday."

"I should'a known you was too cheap ta git some real steaks," replied Joe.

"Waste not, want not, 'n free meat tastes just as good as the stuff ya pay for. 'Sides, you was raised on rabbit, possum, deer, 'n whatever mystery meat daddy found on the side of the road anyway. So don't ya go gittin' uppity on me now," answered Elam. "Hey, look at that bunch of kids comin' down the hill. That red-head must be Bane's girlfriend, huh? I reckon Bane'll be along soon for sure now." Joe didn't reply as he sat watching the group descend the hill.

"I wouldn't be surprised if one of 'em comes back dead. Ya can't let those two alone for too long 'fore they git in a fuss or a fight. How'd ya keep 'em from killin' one another anyhow?" asked Elam.

"It took some doin' that's for sure. I figured I had ta make 'em more scared of me than ta try somethin." Elam saluted Joe with his beer before he took another swig. Joe grunted at the acknowledgement.

After a few minutes of silence, Joe bellowed "I'm fixin' ta go in there 'n bus' Mary Beth's fat butt if she don't bring us some food!"

"Maybe the boys 'll show up soon. Sure ya don't wanta keep Tick till he has ta go back home?"

"Nah, he's yer problem, Big Brother. Besides, the way Bane acted yesterday, I think he's got it in his head ta do somethin' he's gonna regret. Ya gonna love how he looks taday though, if he ever gits his sourpuss face home. Las' night he tried ta show his butt by standin' up ta his ole man. I don't reckon he'll try that again anytime soon. But I gotta bone ta pick with 'im for taken my beers after I left for work this mornin'." Elam laughed hard at hearing that.

"Hey, ya hear sirens? Wonder what that's all about?"

Word quickly spread throughout the trailer park about what'd happened. Half the residents were gathered at the house near the entrance of the trailer park where Gabby lived. Still, in all of the excitement, no one actually had the nerve or desire to go tell Joe and Elam. Gabby explained to everyone what he'd discovered at the creek where he found Dewey's boots. He explained how he'd heard Dewey shout while he was looking for signs of Tick. It didn't take too long before most of the Sheriff's Department arrived at Gabby's home.

It took some doing, but the sheriff was finally able to get most of the story once he talked to Gabby. Crystal was still in shock and couldn't speak yet, so the Sheriff sent her to the hospital in an ambulance to be checked out. Because her parents weren't home yet, Gail's and Billy's mother went with her. The sheriff sent a couple of deputies to go round up Joe and Elam so they could identify the bodies once they were located.

Unaware as to what all the fuss was about, Joe and Elam grudgingly followed the deputies to the hut village. No matter how much they tried, they couldn't get the deputies to tell them what all the fuss was about, so they figured their two boys had gotten into some of their usual mischief. No one dared to look directly at Joe or Elam, so they hung back and whispered among themselves. Most of the residents from the trailer park were present before Joe was sent inside the girls' hut.

The Sheriff explained to Joe his son was in there and he let him go inside to see for himself. When Joe came back out, he went crazy, so he had to be restrained. He'd begun to cuss and threaten all of the children. Elam tried to help calm Joe down until the Sheriff told him his son was also dead somewhere in the woods.

No one would tell Joe and Elam who was responsible for the deaths of their sons or how it'd happened. This further enraged the two. Before long, the Sheriff placed the two under arrest for their own good. He then had Gabby show them where the other body could be found.

When they arrived at Tick's body, Gabby explained, "I heard a shout from over there 'n come running. When I arrived, I found Dewey's boots over here 'n then I found Tick on the other side of the creek in the bushes." He pointed to where he had come from and where he found the boots. "I don't think Dewey done it 'cause Bane come back with Billy's spear." Billy confirmed the story while Gabby explained all the details.

"So let me git this straight. Y'all are tellin' me Dewey probably found this body? Then went back to the huts and killed the other boy." Gabby and Billy nodded their heads in agreement.

It was getting dark when Crystal's parents arrived home. They realized that most of the trailer park residents were hanging around Mr. Grizzle's house and there were several police cars there as well! It wasn't long before they heard what'd happened and soon they were on their way to the hospital in Carrollton to find out about Crystal's condition.

It took several hours before all of the children were thoroughly interviewed and the Sheriff was satisfied. Also, the coroner gave him more information about what was found, such as the empty beer bottles, the broken piece of the wooden sword, the envelope with sixty-five dollars inside of it on Bane's body, and many other clues how the two died and how the events possibly unfolded.

Once the Sheriff arrived back at the courthouse, he interviewed Joe and Elam. He was now certain that Bane had killed Tick and Dewey had killed Bane. Joe explained that only Tick could have had any money because he'd gotten Bane's. With all the facts coming together, the Sheriff issued a warrant for Dewey's arrest so they could detain and interview him.

Once Dewey arrived home, he went straight to the barn loft. This was the one place he felt truly safe. No matter what the world threw at him, it was here he'd created his own world where he was in control as the captain of his destiny. When Dewey hadn't shown up in the normal amount of time since the bell had been rung, Al went back outside and rang it once again, but harder. He was unaware that Dewey was already home.

Dewey heard his grandfather ringing the bell just outside the barn, but remained hidden in the loft. He sat thinking things over until Al finally found him.

"Boy, ya had me worried somethin' happened ta ya. Now git ya'self down here 'n clean up for supper." Dewey wouldn't come down no matter how forceful or gently Al spoke to him over the next fifteen minutes. Al was tired and hungry from working hard all afternoon welding spikes onto the rollers of his leveler in the barn. He figured Dewey had come home while he was in the kitchen preparing supper and that's why he didn't know Dewey was home.

"Well, if ya git hungry, ya welcome ta join me for supper." Al went to the house thinking Dewey would come in and eat when he was ready. He figured the boy must have met with some sort of disappointment that day and just needed some time alone to work it out.

When Dewey didn't come in for supper, he became concerned and went to check on Dewey every hour or so. He tried to encourage Dewey to talk to him and come down, but he didn't feel as if he should go up and physically confront his grandson.

"Dewey, come down! Ya need ta eat 'n git some shuteye, Boy. We don't have ta talk about whatevers botherin' ya tonight. Whatever it is, it can rest till mornin' if that's what it takes." Dewey remained unmoved.

It wasn't long after the sun had set that Al was once again trying to talk Dewey into coming down. Then he heard sirens outside. Al went out to meet two deputies in the driveway. They had come to pick up Dewey and take him back to the courthouse for questioning.

"What's this all about, Deputy?" Al demanded of the one who wore sergeant stripes.

"Sir, I can only tell ya he's wanted for questioning in the death of a boy named Bane Taggart. We have a warrant for his arrest." He presented Al with the warrant. Al's greatest fear was now realized as he stood dumbfounded and silent until the deputy brought his attention back to the matter at hand. "Sir, ya have to tell us where he is."

"He's a good boy. Ya must realize he's slow and all. I hope ya have more luck than I've had gittin' 'im ta come down outa the loft." Al turned and led them to the barn where the lights were shining dimly inside.

When they entered, they could see Dewey was standing on the end of the beam that jutted out from the loft's floor towards the barn's center. For a moment Dewey had trouble keeping his balance as he stood on the rigging that fastened the hoist to the beam. Once he regained his footing, he stood erect and looked on as the trio walked over and stared up with trepidation. Dewey had donned his fireman's helmet, whistle, and drawn his sword. They could see that the wooden sword was broken and bloodstained since Dewey was standing underneath and within a few feet of one of the two light fixtures overhead.

Due to the serious nature of the deputy's visit, Al firmly demanded, "Dewey come down from there before ya fall 'n hurt ya'self. These fellas need ta talk to ya."

"Dewey has ta walk the plank. He killed Bane."

The deputy, in an attempt to try and calm Dewey, spoke in a friendly tone. "Son, we jus' wanta talk about what happened. That's all. Come on down 'n lets git with the Sheriff 'n hash this out."

"Dewey jus' wanted ta help. He didn't mean ta kill Bane." He quietly spoke these words as he looked down on the waves of steel rollers with welded spikes just twelve feet below him.

With tears gently flowing down his cheeks, Dewey thought back to the episode when the rattlesnake killed Snipe and remembered his grandfather's words. He recalled how his grandfather had said, "Dewey, that ole snake that killed Snipe taday didn't mean ta do nothin' but protect itself. It was jus' scared 'n struck out at what it thought was a threat to 'im. But, that don't mean he didn't need killin' though . . . Nature jus' works that way is all. When some critter or other is around that is hurtin' others, it needs killin'. We do that with people too, ya know. It's called the death penalty. We convict people of murder 'n then take 'em ta jail 'n put 'em down like the wild animals they are. Critters, like some people, are the way they are because they were born that way or made ta be that way is all . . ."

Dewey began to blubber hard as he lifted his hands to his face, dropping the blood stained sword onto the leveler below, where it proceeded to bounce onto the floor. Grief stricken, he looked imploringly at Al, and with broken words between sobs, pleadingly said, "Granddaddy . . . Dewey, jus' . . . tried ta help . . . Dewey sorry . . . . I wont hurt nobody no more . . . promise! I know I have ta pay!" All the while Dewey spoke, Al and the deputies pleaded with him to come down.

Gabby heard Dewey crying and the men talking just as he stepped into the barn. He looked up at Dewey standing on the end of the beam. He watched Al and the two deputies, who had their backs to him, try desperately to coax Dewey down. Dewey soon spotted Gabby. As soon as their eyes locked, Dewey stopped crying.

Dewey stood up straight as he spoke clearly. "Dewey is the captain. He killed Bane. Dewey must walk the plank." The junior deputy ran over to the ladder and began to climb up to the loft when it was clear what Dewey's intentions were.

Al and the sergeant watched, while for just a few seconds, Dewey's demeanor changed to one of determination as he looked off into the distance. They were unaware of Gabby's presence and didn't know Dewey was actually looking at his young friend.

With their eyes still locked, Dewey watched Gabby take a pensive step forward while holding up the cross brooch in his hand. With quiet resolution, Dewey stepped off the end of the beam.

"**DEWEY!**" shouted Al as he thrust out his hands, as if to catch him. There was a loud **clang** as Dewey's body landed face down on the sharp spikes of the leveler. The junior deputy came back down quickly and joined Al and his sergeant beside the leveler. Dewey's body lay unmoving in the prone position on the rollers.

Al swiftly moved over to see how badly Dewey was hurt. Without question, he knew that Dewey was severely injured, knowing all too well the sharp spikes would have pierced deeply into his grandson's torso. Fearful of causing further injury, and with shaking hands, he ever so gently touched Dewey's body with his fingertips as anguish overcame him.

Al, with the help of the deputies, lifted Dewey's body off as gently as they were capable of doing under the circumstances. It was extremely difficult because of Dewey's size and because the spikes snared his now limp body.

Dewey was bleeding profusely when they laid his limp body on the ground. Deep puncture wounds could be seen bleeding from his head, neck, torso, and limbs. While he lay on the ground and his life prepared to leave his body, he gave a weak smile as Gabby stepped between the men and placed the cross brooch, still bloody from Bane's grasp, upon Dewey's chest and moved one of Dewey's hands to cover it. During all the distress, no one had noticed the young man until he'd given Dewey the brooch. The men watched in quiet reverence while Gabby performed this last act of kindness. Dewey closed his eyes as if falling asleep and died.

Speaking in a comforting tone, Gabby softly said, "Ship shape, Dewey," just before he stood and walked out of the barn and into the night. With tears in his eyes, Gabby walked away silently as the nearly full moon in a cloudless sky shone down on him, casting enough light to see by as he walked to the tree line across the fields and disappeared into the shadow of the trees.

Chapter 19 – Leeway Corrected by Legacy

UPON reaching the edge of the field, just before entering the forest, hidden by the shadows cast by the moon, Gabby hesitated. He turned to look back at the barn where his friend lay dead. Due to the low rolling hills, he could only make out the upper half of the barns' structure in the moonlight. There was a faint glow emanating out of the loft's outside doors where Dewey liked to play pirates. A sort of quiet sadness filled his heart at the thought of poor Dewey believing what'd happened to Bane was anything but Bane's own fault.

While he looked on with dampened eyes, Gabby witnessed a strange cloud of light coming from the loft that bent skyward and then hovered above the barn's roof as a single form. It began to undulate as if slowly dancing, all the while moving all about the roof line, then once circling below the roof of the barn.

Gabby wiped his eyes, thinking it was only an illusion from the tears, but found that the strange eerie misty cloud of light remained the same. Gabby smiled at the thought that this was possibly Dewey, his friend, playing one last time before he went to heaven. After a minute or so, the light that danced above the barn began to contract and go back inside the barn. Gabby stood in wonderment as he once again could only see a faint glow of light shining out of the loft's opening.

Comforted by what he'd seen, Gabby was now glad he'd been there when Dewey fell to his death. In a strange, unexplainable way, when they'd locked eyes just before Dewey plunged to his death, he'd felt a supernatural connection of understanding with his friend. That connection of kinship still remained in his heart, giving him a sense of peace at knowing Dewey could only do what was right, even if it didn't make sense to everyone else. Yes, he understood why Dewey felt compelled to step off the hoisting beam in the barn onto the waiting spikes below, but what now? He knew Dewey didn't see it as suicide, but rather an act of honor and contrition for the part he'd played in Bane's death. He lamented that if he'd only had a chance to talk to Dewey, maybe he could've helped him understand that what he'd done to Bane was justified.

With determined resolve, Gabby's pace was quick and sure footed as he entered the forest, but soon he had to slow down due to the darkness and unseen obstacles. Gabby began to feel an ever growing numbness as his feet pounded the uneven earth beneath him on the dark trail. He tried to make the best use of the moon and starlight to help him find his way safely down the trail back to his home, yet ever mindful of the two places he would have to pass. He felt no remorse at his own gladness that the two Taggarts had died that day. He actually felt a sense of gratitude for the providential act of nature's or God's hand in their destruction.

Gabby reconciled that Bane and Tick had gotten what they deserved by and through their evil intentions and wicked acts. Their misdeeds, not only on one another, but on everyone they came in proximity to, still stained the moral fabric of those left behind. Bane's brutal betrayal of poor Crystal lent him to whatever horrible death that could be thrust upon him. That much was easily acceptable; however, the price of their evil deeds was Dewey's death. It was because Dewey was so good and honorable, that Gabby was sure his friend's actions could never be judged as anything other than noble.

At times, Gabby had to rely more on instinct than what he could actually see as he made his way down the pathway. The overhead foliage obscured most of the light from the starry sky, all the while coolness nipped at Gabby's sweaty and damp short-sleeved shirt. At twilight he'd run all the way from the trailer park to Al's farm in a rush to be by his friend's side and to tell Dewey's grandfather what'd happened.

Frustrated by darkness and unseen hazards as he made his way down the path, he became vulnerable to his emotions, which came like a flood. He strongly felt the urge to release a torrent of emotion, but something inside of him prohibited the use of tears to cleanse his body of the anguish he felt. He stopped and leaned against a tree to steady himself. Gabby's soul was in turmoil with itself as he languished over the events of this horrific day and the images he would carry with him forever.

He became angry and began to mumble unclean thoughts as he reclaimed his power over himself. Soon his emotional well seemed empty and he didn't have anything else to draw on. He felt weary and tried to make his mind go blank as he began to walk once more. There was nothing else to do but to keep moving.

Upon reaching the spot on the trail where Tick'd been killed, the hairs on the back of his neck stood up. Although there was a large opening in the foliage overhead, it seemed as if light itself had been banished from entering this place. He could see the almost full moon and stars shining brightly up above, but their light wouldn't or couldn't illuminate the earth around him. He slowly felt his way along the path beside the creek, opposite the small clearing where Tick's body had been discovered.

Gabby froze when he heard a low throaty growl of some animal approaching from the clearing across the creek. It sounded every bit as much like the slow low growls he'd heard on television or in the movies of mountain loins, tigers, or other large cats made as a warning to other creatures. He feared that some large predator cat may have been lured by the scent of Tick's blood in the bushes.

Trembling with fear, Gabby tried to stand as still as possible while he attempted to control his breathing so as not to be discovered. When the low throaty rumble of the creature came within a few yards, he quietly fell back against a tree in an attempt to conceal himself.

His mind raced with alternatives to escape and he desperately wanted to run, but he knew if he moved or tried to flee, the unseen creature would easily overtake him and pounce. Instead, he slumped down against the tree until he could feel the ground around him in hopes of finding a large rock, a fallen tree limb, or anything else that might be used as a weapon. Finding nothing, and out of desperation, he reached into his pocket for his small pocketknife. He fumbled with it at first, but finally was able to retrieve it and get it opened.

Intensely he watched and listened for any movement of the predator. It was then, out of the corner of his eye, that he saw what appeared to be the faint glow of light coming quickly down the trail. He felt a glimmer of hope as it got closer, believing that someone had followed him from Al's farm. The light was getting closer, but he couldn't detect any sound like a person would make while walking through the woods. When the light was close, Gabby became disappointed because it appeared to be no more than a dense puff of fog that reflected the moon's rays.

Although Gabby had yet to see it, the large cat could be heard stepping onto the loose rocks on the side of the creek's banks, followed by the faint splashing as it waded into the shallow waters. Knowing it was within mere feet, Gabby became too afraid to breathe as he listened to the panting of this still yet unseen creature of the night.

Suddenly, a large flash of light rushed past Gabby, which was immediately followed by violent growls that permeated the night. Something inside the glowing misty cloud was attacking the unseen predator. Intense and furious tones came one after the other as the cat fought and raged with desperate growls mixed with high pitched noises of desperation. Something the white cloud was doing to it was causing it tremendous pain. The yet to be seen cat desperately tried to fight off its attacker. Only seconds had passed before the violence peaked, and the animal and the ghost-like illumination retreated deep into the woods and faded.

Feeling the danger had passed, Gabby slumped down to the ground into a sitting position with his back still against the tree. He gulped down air in deep waves as his chest heaved. He attempted to calm his nerves with the knowledge that whatever it was had fled, defeated by the light. His mouth was bone dry and he felt too weak to move as his heart could be heard beating in his ears. Eventually he crawled on hands and knees to the creek's edge and gulped down water with his cupped hands.

Once his heartbeat slowed enough for him to think, he retrieved his knife and stood only to discover his legs were shaky. It was then that he realized that the utter and complete darkness had dissipated. He came to the conclusion that the cat may or may not have been real. He never saw it even though it was so close, yet he knew he'd heard it as it had approached. What about the supernatural darkness? Had it all been an illusion? What about the illuminated misty cloud? Could it have been the same one he saw floating above the barn? His mind raced and he became confused and overwhelmed by it all. He decided to just accept it.

With sudden clarity, Gabby was sure it had to be his friend and that he had once again come to the rescue. Gabby shouted triumphantly into the night sky as he raised his arms and hands skyward. "DEWEY! SHIP SHAPE, DEWEY!" Oh, how he believed with all his heart that it had been the spirit of Dewey who had come to save him from the evil creature that was or was not real. Perhaps it was an aberration of something evil or perhaps it was actually real. He didn't care, because he believed he'd been saved by Dewey.

Relieved and reinvigorated at the thought that Dewey was still watching over him, he smiled with delight as he put his knife back into his pocket and continued down the trail towards the hut village.

By the time Gabby arrived back at the hut village, he'd vowed to not ever let himself become vulnerable or feel utterly helpless again. He walked silently by the remaining deputy who was assisting the coroner finish with her work at the girls' hut.

The deputy took notice of Gabby. "Son, ya need ta git on home now. Ya parents is probably worried about ya." Gabby gave a quick nod of his head as the deputy aimed his flashlight upon his face. Gabby wasn't interested in hanging around anyway, so he continued on without replying.

Gabby picked up his pace as he ascended the hill from the hut village. Although he was tired, he wanted to put distance between himself and the two people working in the girl's hut. It wasn't long before he crested the hill. From there he could see the ambulance and fire trucks were gone. Only the deputy's patrol car and the coroner's van remained in the trailer park.

He could sense that something had changed in the atmosphere of The Robin's Nest trailer park. The quiet was almost palpable. Then it dawned on him, most of the trailer's lights were either turned off or people had their curtains drawn tight. Only the sounds of fans and air conditioners could be heard permeating the quiet.

This suited Gabby just fine, because it reflected his own mood. He wanted to be left alone. He somehow knew he had changed and was transformed into a different person than when he'd last entered the woods. It was a feeling he couldn't explain to himself, much less anyone else, but he could feel it deep down inside. He felt almost like he'd shed his skin.

Although he felt completely exhausted, he drew from a new source of strength and determination that he'd never experienced before. For a moment, he stopped and scrunched his face in bafflement as he tried in vain to search for this new found source within himself, only to be left wanting. Unable to discern what it was exactly, he sought the solace of home.

When Gabby walked into his house, he found his father, John, sitting in the living room watching him as if he were examining him, or perhaps looking for something. Berta, Gabby's mother, stood in the kitchen and looked on with concern for a moment before she said, "Honey, we were worried about ya." She stepped closer and attempted to hug him. Gabby abruptly turned and stepped away in rejection of her attempt to comfort her only child.

"Dewey's dead. He killed himself." Mortified, Berta clutched her hands to her chest and John took a deep breath and sighed as he dropped his head for a moment. When John looked back up at his son, his eyes betrayed his sense of pity that soon gave way to an expression of understanding of what his son must be feeling over the loss of his friend.

John remained silent due to the wisdom he'd acquired over his long life. He knew his son had seen and experienced life at its worst on this tragic day, but he also appreciated how this was a milestone in his boy's life. He regretted what his son was going through, but he knew that one day Gabby had to see the raw reality of what God and nature would bring. He just wished it had been further down the road. Gabby was still so young he thought.

"Don't ya jus' sit there. Say somethin', John," demanded Berta as she waved a dish towel in his direction and then at Gabby. After watching his mother take on so, Gabby waited for his father's response with a blank expression.

"Boy, all of us is eventually consumed. It's nature's way. I'm sorry it cost ya a friend." With that said, Gabby looked away. He stood there for only a few seconds before he dropped his head ever so slightly and nodded before he walked down the hall. When Berta began to follow Gabby, John shouted, "Leave it! The las' thing he wants is to be coddled!"

Gabby cleaned up and lay in bed before he realized he'd missed supper. The pangs of hunger he'd felt hours ago were gone. He sighed and decided against leaving his room. He didn't want to be subjected to seeing that look in his mother's face again, at least not for a while. Instead he lay on his bed and reflected on the day's events. After a long time of mulling it over and reliving the anger it brought, he had an epiphany: *'Anger is a tool, just like a screwdriver or hammer. If used correctly, it could be used to accomplish something besides letting it eat away at me.'*

Gabby reminisced on how his anger had eaten away at him when he was unable to express his frustration and the sense of helplessness while being picked on or being wronged. He resolved to no longer let that sense of futility have its way with him ever again. Instead he would use it to his advantage. While he contemplated on this thought over and over, he felt a sense of calm just before he fell into a deep exhaustive sleep.

Time and time again in his dreams, he witnessed Dewey's expression of determination and remembered his almost spiritual connection with Dewey, just before he intentionally fell to his death. Then he heard the clanging of metal. Only now in his dreams, it was himself and not Dewey that fell onto the spikes. It didn't hurt, but he could sense, as well as feel the spikes going into his body while a sensation of calm and lightness overtook him. He could smell the barn, feel the men grab and lift his body from the spikes, and hear the men speak as they hovered over him. The last sensation he would feel, was how the cross felt as he gripped it in his hand just before he was jolted awake once more.

With each episode of the dream revisited and as the sweat trickled down his neck, Gabby would again fall asleep and relive the dream once more.

The ambulance arrived soon after Dewey had fallen to his death. The ambulance crew and the two deputies exchanged information for their respective reports and exchanged gossip on all the tragic events of the day. Out of respect for Al, who sat silently at his workbench in the corner of the barn, they spoke in hushed tones. It took over an hour for the coroner to arrive to pronounce Dewey dead.

After the coroner was finished taking pictures, measurements, and statements, the ambulance crew enclosed Dewey's body into a body bag and departed. When the ambulance drove away from the barn, one of the deputies approached Al and removed his hat before speaking. "Mr. Hewin, again let me say I'm sorry about ya grandson. Do ya have anyone who could come 'n be with ya?" Al shook his head.

"I was told that ya need ta come down to the courthouse 'n fill out some paperwork. Jus' ask for Detective Jackson. He'll help ya with everything 'n have ya grandson's body taken ta wherever ya want. Are ya sure ya don't need us ta contact anybody for ya?"

"I'll go see yer Detective Jackson," replied Al. It was a struggle for Al to get up from the stool. He took one last look before he switched off the lights in the barn. The deputies walked slowly along beside him until they got closer to the house.

Thinking better of it, and seeing the weariness of this aged man, the deputy turned to Al. "Mr. Hewin, I'd be much obliged ta take ya down there myself. I'll have someone drive ya home as soon as yer business is done, if that's alright. I can see how tired ya are. Ain't nobody who's gone through what you have should be drivin' anyway." That suited Al, because he hadn't driven at night for a long time. He'd stop driving after dark because of his deteriorating vision and growing cataracts, so he just nodded in agreement.

It only took twenty minutes to arrive at the courthouse. The normal one-person operation of the night shift at the Sheriff's Office was now bustling with activity. Nearly all of the sheriff's office staff had been called in to help with all the interviews and to fill out paperwork. Al was escorted and seated at Detective Jackson's desk. Al was questioned for a good hour or more. Eventually, Detective Jackson was confident all the paperwork was complete. Wearily Al signed where he was shown before he was told, "Sheriff Latham 'll probably want to speak with you. I'll go see if he's ready."

After almost an hour or so of waiting, Detective Jackson, seeing how exhausted and weary Al had become, decided he'd been through enough for the time being. "Mr. Hewin, why don't we send ya on home 'n someone will git with ya in the mornin'."

On Al's way out, a reporter tried to waylay him. The deputy who was assigned to take Al home, quickly blocked the reporter. Much to the reporter's dismay, he was detained by Detective Jackson and another officer until Al was safely away.

Al arrived home in the wee hours of the morning. He was completely and utterly exhausted. He decided he was in much need of a cup of coffee. He felt the need to try and sort it all out before he would consider going to bed. While at the courthouse, he'd heard snips and pieces of what had or may not have happened. It was certain there were two other boys dead besides Dewey. He still didn't know how or the why it'd happened. He just knew that Dewey had probably killed one of the boys. No one seemed willing to tell him much. He also witnessed one of the dead boy's fathers being tackled and restrained when he become belligerent and tried to fight with the officers.

Al was feeling so weak that he couldn't stand up straight. He had to struggle to make it into the house and the kitchen where he brewed a pot of coffee. He suddenly yearned for a cigarette, but knew there weren't any in the house, so he dismissed the thought. After he prepared his cup of coffee, he went into the den and sat down in his chair. He glanced over at the chair Dewey normally occupied and wished Dewey was in it eating his snack and drinking his milk.

In an effort to seek some solace in the meaning of it all, he picked up his Bible and opened it where he had left off: The Book of Job, Chapter Thirty One:

1. *I made a covenant with mine eyes; why then should I think upon a maid?*

2. *For what portion of God is there from above? And what inheritance of the Almighty from on high?*

3. *Is not destruction to the wicked? And a strange punishment to the workers of iniquity (sin)?*
4. *Doth not he see my ways, and count all my steps?*
5. *If I have walked with vanity, or if my foot hath hasted to deceit:*
6. *Let me be weighed in an even balance, that God may know mine integrity.*

Al laid the Bible in his lap as he thought how appropriate the verses were, because he knew that Dewey was an innocent boy. Surely his motives for his actions had always been for good. He was consoled by the idea and certain that Dewey was in heaven.

As Al sat in wonderment of what he had just read, he let his eyes rest on the framed newspaper article about Dewey saving the baby from the burning trailer. Even in all his anguish, Al still hadn't shed a single tear. He laid back his head against the chair as he closed his eyes to pray, seeking comfort the only way he knew how.

Al woke up to the sound of someone knocking loudly on the back door. At first he was confused and unaware of how he had come to be awakened in his chair. When the fog started to lift from his brain, he began to recall the events of last night. It soon became apparent that sleeping in his chair was not conducive to his well-being. His neck, back, and hips screamed in agony while he struggled to get up. Glancing at his pocket watch and seeing it was almost ten in the morning, Al realized he had gotten only a few hours sleep. He couldn't even remember falling asleep.

Al was aware it was taking him a long time to get to the door. He wasn't even sure whether the person knocking would still be there by the time he made it. He went through the kitchen onto the screened back porch and opened the screen door just enough to speak with his visitors. He wasn't surprised they'd come to the back door, because it was customary for folks to use the back door when they came to visit someone's home in this part of the country.

Sheriff Robert Latham was waiting patiently with a young female deputy by his side. "Mr. Hewin, I'm sorry about ya grandson and apologize for not having the time ta stop 'n speak with ya las' night at the courthouse. We have a lot ta talk about that I'm sure will give ya some comfort, if nothing else."

Al gazed at the two through tired eyes as they stood patiently waiting for an invitation to come in. Reluctantly he stepped aside and pushed open the screen door enough for them to enter. Al, in a tired voice, said, "Let me put on a pot of coffee." Sheriff Latham and his deputy followed Al into the kitchen. "Make ya'self at home. Coffee 'll be ready in a couple of minutes." Al gestured for them to sit at the kitchen table.

Even though Al slept through breakfast, he didn't feel the least bit hungry. It was as if life itself and all the joy of God's wonders had departed. Every movement seemed to take an enormous effort.

The Sheriff and his deputy sat quietly as they watched this old man move slowly about the kitchen. Al poured out the old coffee he'd made upon his arrival back home and prepared a fresh pot. Al stood and stared at the pot as it slowly heated up and the coffee began to percolate. At one point Al looked down at the place where Snipe's bowls used to be. Loneliness seemed to saturate him like a cold rain that went all the way down to his bones.

When the coffee was ready, he poured each of his two 'guests' a cup before he poured one for himself. He sat down across from the two and pushed a sugar bowl towards them. "Don't mean ta keep ya waitin', it's jus' it's been a hard night 'n I'm feelin' plum tuckered out."

Sheriff Latham replied, "We understand. We jus' thought ya might ought'a know what happened now that we have all the facts. Only got couple 'a hours sleep myself. This is gonna take a little while."

"Ain't got nowhere ta be, so let it out," replied Al.

"First, ya need ta know that Dewey saved a girl from bein' hurt or possibly killed yesterday." Al's eyes lit up at this unexpected bit of news.

"Dewey apparently stumbled upon a dead boy named Tracer Taggart. Apparently he got so scared he left his boots beside a creek in his hurry ta go tell somebody . . . . From what I understand, the two Taggart boys were cousins and didn't git along . . . . Well, then Dewey come upon a girl who was bein' beaten by this other boy tryin' ta rape 'er. He must'a broke his sword somehow, because we found part of it on the floor in the hut where he killed this boy, Bane."

"Anyway, he stabbed Bane Taggart in an attempt ta stop 'im from . . . . The girl was only able to tell us what happened to her a short while ago because she was in shock 'n had ta be sedated by the doctors las' night. Once she was able ta tell us what'd happened . . . . Looks as if she's gonna be alright. She only has . . . ." Al, although disturbed by the horrible acts of yesterday, was pleased at what he heard about Dewey. It was as if the good news about Dewey's part in all that'd happened was feeding him life. By the time the Sheriff was finished, Al was overcome with pride at knowing his grandson had acted with valor.

"All the other witnesses corroborated these facts. Dewey left the scene before we could talk ta 'im. At the time we didn't really understand his involvement, so we had ta issue a warrant for 'im so we could bring him in for questioning. We initially thought he'd killed both boys. We know better now. He ended up bein' a hero again and basically innocent of any wrongdoin'. I'm sorry it ended the way it did. Ya know the rest." The sheriff dropped his head as a sign of respect and acknowledgement of Dewey's tragic demise.

"I know it ain't much, but jus' thought ya should know his name's been cleared." Once the Sheriff finished, he sat back in his chair. He was glad he could be the one to tell Al.

He'd met Al at the courthouse. He'd told Al how proud everyone was of Dewey for saving Mrs. Carolyn's baby. He also remembered Dewey's name because he helped stop Little Jay from hurting the smaller children. "I'm truly sorry it came ta this. I jus' wish he hadn't died las' night. It's a terrible tragedy."

Al began to understand how Dewey's simple understanding of life lead him to believe he needed to be punished and walk the plank. He just wished Dewey was around so he could tell him how proud he was of him. He understood that Dewey was simple minded, so in his grandson's pureness of heart, he was unable to see the different shades of things the way others could.

"I guess we'll let ya git some rest, Mr. Hewin." With that the two stood up.

"Thanks for comin' 'n tellin' me." Al shook Sheriff Latham's hand as he and his deputy walked out the back door.

As soon as Crystal arrived home from the hospital, word quickly spread and the whole gang showed up to tell her everything they could about what'd happened. When she learned that Dewey had gone home and committed suicide, Crystal cried so hard that no one could console her for a long time. Some of the other girls cried along with her.

After the other children eventually left, Crystal told her mother and step-father everything about Dewey and how he was such a wonderful person. Her mother held her in her arms as she told them everything. She looked up in her mother's eyes and said, "Momma, it was almost like he was a guardian angel ta me 'n the others. I'm gonna miss him bad, momma." With this, her mother broke down and cried violently, to the confusion of Crystal and her step-father, JJ. For a long time, Crystal and her mother held each other for comfort as tears rolled down their faces.

After a meager meal, because they weren't very hungry, Crystal's mother told her, "Tamorrow we're goin' ta go see Dewey's granddaddy." They stayed up most of the night talking and occasionally crying.

The next day, when Al arrived home from making arrangements for Dewey's funeral, he saw a beautiful young girl standing beside the barn looking at his tractor. Once he got out of the truck, she slowly walked over to him. He could see her beautiful long strawberry blonde hair, blue-green eyes, and the fresh bruises and cuts on her nose and mouth. She gave him a big smile. He figured this must be the girl he'd heard about.

"Hello, Young Lady." Al seemed to remember something. He pointed at her and gave a small smile as he asked, "Aren't you the young lady who stood beside me at the courthouse awhile back when Dewey was rewarded for savin' that baby?"

"Yes sir," replied Crystal. She smiled even bigger because she was flattered that he'd remembered her.

"Are ya by ya'self?" He knew she wasn't because he could see a strange car parked beside the house.

"No sir. My momma's in the kitchen." She pointed to the screen door that led to the kitchen. He was surprised momentarily at this bit of news. Of course no one locked their doors in those days, but only people you were very were familiar with would ever take such bold liberties.

Al walked to the back door followed closely by Crystal. As he entered the kitchen, his eyes adjusted just enough to make out the face of a woman about thirty something. "Hello, Daddy."

Bewildered and taken aback, Al looked closely at this beautiful young woman and then recognized her as his long lost daughter, Jenny. Stunned, he stood frozen as he stared transfixed at the face of this beautiful young woman. Al had to grab the back of one of the kitchen chairs to steady himself. After a few moments, Jenny, with pensiveness and uncertainty, closed the distance between them and hugged Al. Al still held onto the chair as he used his other arm to timidly hug her back. He looked off into the distance, as if looking for something, then grabbed her with both arms and squeezed her tightly.

Crystal watched their reactions to one another in amazement and with tearful pride. Her mother had explained everything to her into the wee hours of the morning.

At the funeral, it seemed that half the county showed up. All of Dewey's friends attended along with their parents. Preacher Rakestraw gave a wonderful sermon on how blessed they were to have had Dewey in their lives and how much he would be missed. He recounted how Dewey saved a baby from a burning home and brought light into the lives around him.

While they stood to pray, Al was flanked by Crystal hugging his left arm and Jenny holding his right. It was then he knew what his Uncle James meant when he said, "And don't worry about not seein' yer daughter again. She'll show up when it's needed. I've learned there's always a reason in the way of it."

When the prayer was over, Al whispered, "Thank ya, Dewey. Ya was a good mate 'n grandson."